Zero Sum

(Dr. Steven Cross Series #1)

Book One ~ Kotov Syndrome
Book Two ~ Focal Point
Book Three ~ Checkmate

Russell Blake

First Edition

ISBN: 978-1480279476

Published by

Reprobatio Limited

INTRODUCTION

The Zero Sum trilogy is a serial trilogy that chronicles the saga of one man's struggle against a corrupt Wall Street predator. The story is fiction. The following facts are not. A comprehensive list of all documented examples of the intersection of Wall Street and organized crime, clandestine government agencies, hostile rogue nations, and Jihadists/terrorist financiers would require hundreds of pages. It is beyond the scope of this novel to catalog the extensive labyrinth of criminality that is the reality of the modern market system, however the facts are available to anyone interested in researching them.

In 2009, Bernard Madoff was convicted for operating the largest Ponzi scheme in history. A former co-chairman of the NASD and a Wall Street icon, his fraudulent activities cost his investors over fifty billion dollars. Among those who claimed to have been defrauded were several Russian Oligarchs, who were invested in Madoff's scheme via an Austrian brokerage whose owner subsequently went missing. In reality, none of the Russians lost any money; they actually made billions from their participation. The list of connected criminal entities who participated in Madoff's fraudulent activities is too lengthy for inclusion in this introduction.

During the 2008 financial meltdown, shares of major banks like Lehman Brothers and Bear Stearns were sold in massive quantities (many multiples of typical trading volume) via a few small brokerage houses during the week leading up to their collapses. During Congressional testimony, the heads of those banks stated point blank that the massive naked short selling (where sell orders are placed, but no shares exist to settle the trades) of the banks' stocks was an obvious manipulation effort largely responsible for their stock price collapse. To date, the SEC has never investigated these trades, nor has anyone ever been prosecuted for them, in spite of the fact that it was the collapse of those two banks that took the global market system to the brink of financial catastrophe.

A.B. 'Buzzy' Krongard became head of the CIA after departing Deutsche Bank-Nicholas Brown in 1998, where he ran the private client group which handles the accounts of many high net worth offshore clients. He was also Vice Chairman of the Board for Bankers Trust, and resigned from that position at the same time. Bankers Trust subsequently pleaded guilty to having created a slush fund and misappropriating unclaimed client funds to prop up their underperforming divisions. It is not unusual for this type of slush fund to be used for transactions where complete anonymity of the client is required.

Several funds, including Lancer, Anthony Elgindy's, and those of Mark Valentine have been investigated by the Department of Justice, which revealed they have ties to organized crime figures, Middle Eastern arms money, and corrupt government officials. In the Lancer case, $650 million was lost via a scheme wherein the fund invested in largely worthless penny stock associated with a known organized crime figure. Where the money went from there is unknown. The Lancer directors were never prosecuted. In the Mark Valentine case — Operation Bermuda Short — one of the main perpetrators fled the country after ostensibly receiving a warning of his impending prosecution. The list of La Cosa Nostra, Russian Mafiya and terrorist financiers connected to Valentine is so lengthy as to require a non-fiction book of its own.

Refco, a brokerage house that was shut down in a huge IPO scandal involving hundreds of millions of hidden debt (believed to have been largely embezzled by CEO, Bennett), was involved in negotiations with the SEC to determine the amount of fines to be paid in the aforementioned Operation Bermuda Short case when the accounting scandal came to light. Some of the largest creditors and customers of Refco were a Russian fund and a major Austrian bank; to be later embroiled in a massive fraud case emanating from the Refco blowup. Hedge funds were used to conceal Refco debt from the company's auditors — in a series of sham transactions — and there are multi-billion dollar transactions that appear to be large-scale money laundering. The SEC allowed Refco to go public even though the top managers were involved in this prior stock manipulation scheme, and sanctioned for it. No explanation for this remarkable decision has ever been offered by the Commission.

The rest of this trilogy is intended as a work of fiction. Any similarity between the characters depicted in this work and real persons, living or dead, is coincidental.

Book One ~ Kotov Syndrome

This chess phenomenon, first described by Alexander Kotov, occurs when a player does not find a good plan after considerable consideration of a position. The player, under time pressure, suddenly decides to make a move – usually a terrible one which was inadequately analyzed.

PROLOGUE

Outside the parking garage the temperature had dipped below freezing, and the rumble of traffic had long since faded as the city shut down for the evening. Even the smallest sounds reverberated through the stark expanse, cascading in a diminishing ripple of echoes. A fluorescent light flickered overhead, occasionally sputtering a warning of imminent demise – resulting in an uneasy illumination of the ominously darkened space.

A grey American-built sedan with government plates punctuated the late-night silence as it pulled down the ramp onto the lowest level and parked in a far corner, cutting its lights and engine. Inside the vehicle, the driver sat motionless, scanning the car's surroundings. One hand silently toyed with a worn key fob, an unconscious habit, mechanical in its regularity.

After several minutes, footsteps disrupted the equilibrium as a figure approached the vehicle from the far end of the garage. The passenger door opened and the new arrival sat down, passing a CD-ROM to the driver. The passenger's grey eyes darted to the rearview mirror, peering into the dim light of the garage…searching.

"This is the outfit we need help with. We have nine months," the passenger said in a low voice, seasoned with years of cigarette abuse.

The driver nodded and waited for more. His passenger smelled of alcohol, garlic and dried sweat.

"We appreciate the hand. I…I know it's a hell of a favor, but your guy said he could make this happen, so…"

Satisfied there was nothing more of value the visitor could impart, the driver leaned towards him…slowly…invading the passenger's space to whisper in his ear.

"I'll get it to him. This meeting never took place."

CHAPTER 1

Rick brushed past the Marine guard, offering an imperceptible nod of greeting, and entered the familiar confines of the large foyer that led to his office. Another day of non-stop action, people moving urgently down the heavily carpeted hallways, earnest looks and murmured dialog the rule.

His secretary handed him a sheaf of papers as he passed her desk. Mandy had been with him in one role or another since his days at the law firm, and when he'd accepted his current position she'd been part of the deal. She organized his life and kept his days running smoothly; no small feat, considering the number of hours he spent working on behalf of his master. Rick made a slitting gesture with his thumb across his neck, and she smiled at him as she continued her telephone discussion. She knew it meant he didn't want to be disturbed by anyone, either in person or by phone. It was the beginning of another brutal week and he had his hands as full as usual. He settled back behind his neatly organized desk and considered the trees out on the expansive, snow-covered lawn.

What a month.

Every possible nightmare scenario had come hurtling down the pike at them; from a new terrorist threat emanating from the Mexican border to a bio-hazard scare in Boston, then the discovery of E. coli in the San Antonio water supply. And the month was only half over. He loved the adrenaline rush of the job, but four years of it had put a lot of miles on the chassis.

Another late night yesterday, and he'd had more than his usual glass or two of wine with Stewart as they'd discussed the Beltway's intrigue and power plays. The whole point of the evening had been to request some deniable assistance – and the mission had been accomplished; he'd asked Stewart to help out with a delicate matter, and Stewart had agreed.

But his head felt a little thick today, which was no way to operate in this environment.

The red com light on his phone blinked, and the synthesized ringer issued forth its annoying chirp. He stabbed the speaker button.

"I don't want to be disturbed, remember?"

"*He* needs to see you. Now." Mandy didn't need to say anything else.

"Any idea what to bring, what he wants to talk about?"

"He didn't say. Just asked to see you 'soonest' as he put it."

Rick sighed. "I'm there. Thanks. Sorry if I'm snappy."

He didn't wait for a response, punched the button again, got up and pulled on his suit jacket. Grey, conservative cut, nothing fancy. Muted tie over a starched white dress shirt, fine quality, but not too fine. Discreet, nondescript. He cracked his neck, heard a pop, and pushed his shoulders back as he walked through his office door and back to the main hallway. He smiled at the older woman who was the gatekeeper. She waved him into the large office, books lining one wall halfway up to the high ceiling.

"Ah, there you are, Rick." The man sitting in his shirtsleeves looked up as he came into the room, took off his reading glasses and fixed the younger man with a penetrating gaze. A look passed which spoke of power, and a disposition accustomed to being accommodated. It was unmistakable.

"Good morning, Mr. Vice President."

అం

Sweat trickled down Steven's face, and the ocean breeze did little to mitigate the increasing heat from the rising sun. The usual parade of crazies was absent in the early hours of the morning. Later, the nonstop rollerblading bikini models and faux gangbanger/surf punks on elaborately configured bicycle choppers would clog the boardwalk and the running path, but for now it was the province of the athletically inclined, the pet owners out for some pre-breakfast relief, the odd can collector and metal-detecting hopeful scavenging for the previous day's residual treasures.

The Newport Beach maintenance squad noisily raked the sand as he ran. The group of modified tractors ensured that every new day was orderly and clean on the long beige stretch, and that no cigarette butt or soda bottle was left to sully the main attraction for the town's summer revenue. A placid ocean offered up the odd ripple to the ever-optimistic surfers awaiting the perfect curl a few dozen yards offshore.

Mornings like this were the norm for the privileged few who resided in the twenty-foot wide homes squeezed along the beachfront. At three million dollars and up for a sheetrock dwelling only slightly wider than a trailer, the inhabitants had endorsed their love of the setting with their wallets, and had a vested interest in keeping the locale picture-perfect.

This was his favorite time; when his mind could wander over whatever thoughts bubbled into his consciousness, accompanied by only the rhythmic pounding of his soles on the spotless pavement and the occasional cry of a seabird. To any observer, Steven would appear to be a lean late-thirties male with nondescript features – other than a crooked nose from an ancient fracture and a small scar under his right cheek – with carelessly cut light-brown hair and a somewhat vacant expression of puzzled concentration on his not-quite-movie-star-handsome face. His muscle tone was unusually well defined from years of martial arts practice. He looked fit, tanned, easy-going and friendly.

The run was part of his morning routine. He got up at 5:30 and gulped down a cup of scalding black coffee, threw some dog food into a bowl, pulled on sweats and an old T-shirt and followed the strand for two and a half miles to the second pier, and then back again.

Same routine every weekday, without fail, for the last five years. His Belgian shepherd, Avalon, loped alongside him, easily keeping pace and more than familiar with the circuit. The green bungalow with the porcelain panda sitting in the window meant only one more mile to go. He was in the home stretch now. From here it was a cakewalk.

Breathe in, exhale slowly, shake out incipient cramp in shoulder, brush sweat out of eyes.

Almost there now. Almost there.

Put on a final burst of speed, feel the familiar burn in his quadriceps and calves, and then hop over the low gate that separated the patio from the thoroughfare.

Back in the house, he had enough time to rinse off, towel dry his hair and then sit down at his computer and log on to see the pre-market activity and scan the news. Any passers-by seeing him hunched in front of his dual screens at the oceanfront picture window would have probably thought he was a securities analyst or portfolio manager or financial planner, chained by vocation to his monitor in the wee hours.

Nothing could have been further from the truth.

Steven had retired several years earlier, having sold his software engineering company, pocketed some 'fuck you' money and happily declared himself out of the business world for good. At thirty-nine he'd been one of the luckier entrepreneurs to emerge from the subsequent economic carnage; many of his friends had lost everything and were struggling to start over. And finding that in the current environment, doing it all over again was harder than it had ever been.

He couldn't bitch.

The plan had been to devote some time to mastering his martial arts hobby, and perhaps open a dojo to occupy a few hours whenever he ran out of ways to amuse himself. But events had conspired against him. Plans had changed. Bad investments in real estate had eaten almost half his capital, which left him far short of where he needed to be for permanent retirement. So he spent the better part of 6:15 a.m. through 1:00 p.m. staring at rows of numbers on ever-changing computer screens, interrupted only by fits of frenzied typing and the occasional phone call.

"Damn it. They're doing it again," Steven muttered to himself. "The stock's up again on no news – it's like the market's completely ignoring reality."

"Honey, what's up now?" a sleepy female voice called from upstairs.

"Nothing. I'm just watching junk being sold like it was platinum, and losing money each tick up."

"Don't get too worked up," she said. "I'm going back to sleep. Wake me up around eight, and don't forget to turn off the coffee machine or it'll boil down."

Steven focused on the screens. On the right were three windows with tables of numbers blinking and changing constantly. On the left was the familiar format of the Internet message boards. Overlaid were several open browser windows with websites partially displayed.

All the windows and screens had the same symbol on them.

APDT. Allied Pharmaceutical Development.

Not exactly a household name; a Milwaukee-based conglomerate that specialized in early stage biotechnology development – one of thousands of entities that made up the landscape of publicly traded companies in the U.S. markets.

And Steven's current object of fascination and frustration.

☞☜

Across the continent, the same symbol was displayed on another set of computer screens twenty-four stories above Wall Street, in a lavishly appointed office with a panoramic view of the New York skyline.

"Take it up another few bucks, and then let's dump it and take out the stop losses." The voice belonged to a man in his late fifties hunched over a speakerphone, his grey, curly hair framing an artificially tanned, heavily-lined face. "Knock out at least twenty percent and run it into the ground before we start covering…"

Nicholas Griffen was also not a household name, and yet he'd achieved a certain notoriety on Wall Street – an infamous trader, investment banker and financier who specialized in biotech. He managed a $1+ billion domestic venture fund that invested exclusively in early to mid-stage biotechnology stocks, and also operated an offshore fund based in the Caribbean.

Griffen's technique was to make money promoting companies, and then create volatility, swinging the stocks up and down by related-party trading and passing out insider tips – profiting from both the increases and decreases in price. He'd be long on a company, holding options and shares whose value increased significantly when the hype started on the stock, and then when his network of media cronies and pet analysts created a frenzy of buying and speculation resulting in triple or quadruple-digit percentage gains, he'd contrive a media event that would tunnel the company's share price. Of course he'd have sold all his long positions at or near the top, and gone short to profit again from the fall – and once he'd panicked the market, he'd reap even larger gains on the trip down.

Shorting stocks involved borrowing shares from a broker and then selling them, in the expectation of being able to buy them back and return them to the broker later, when the price was lower. It was a bet on a price decline, where the value of the short sale increased as the price of the stock fell.

Griffen had long ago discovered that the economics of manipulation and destruction, of pumping prices up artificially then driving prices down, were far better than those of trying to choose winning companies and buying their shares, waiting for the world to discover their merits. It was much easier to create a mania over a company's massive price increases and hugely profitable potential, and then panic the crowd by screaming fire in the crowded theater, profiting from the ensuing chaos via short selling. In the ensuing panic, investors sold first, and asked questions later. And the more pronounced the fall, the more panicked they became.

Griffen's group was expert at using his network of media sources to create a bubble in a stock by hyping a company with marginal or no real technology or value, and then using a deluge of unlimited selling to panic the market, thereby destroying the company's share price. The term for it was pump and dump – it was illegal, but the regulators rarely if ever enforced the rules, so what the hell. Only an idiot would drive fifty-five if there were no cops around. And Griffen was no idiot.

He knew from experience the market was a zero sum game – and for him to make a fortune, investors on the other side of the bet had to lose. That's just how it worked. Zero sum.

The trick was to ensure you were on the winning side.

The second line rang.

"Griffen – what?" he barked at the box.

"They're nixing any more shorting until we deliver the slug from last week on Allied. Said this afternoon's a non-starter; the regulators are in today and they're looking over shoulders," advised the calm, unemotional voice.

"Is there any room to wiggle?" Griffen inquired.

"Not now. Maybe tomorrow, once the shop's back to normal. At the moment everyone's on their best behavior."

Griffen sighed. "All right. Puts a crimp in our move today – but them's the breaks. Let's talk tonight..."

He punched the other line back into active status. "Change of plans. Start covering the shorts. Pick up a few thousand, sell off a few hundred from the Pac Ex, walk the ask down and then see if anyone bites. Rinse and repeat. Get us whole for the day."

"No *problemo*, boss."

Terminating the call, he watched as the stock price slowly fell, went back up a few cents, swooned again, went up again. He considered his performance that of a virtuoso musician, and he delighted in being the stock-gaming equivalent of a maestro...in a long tradition of master manipulators who'd worked on Wall Street for the last hundred years.

This was his province, his world. He was in his element with the ticks on the screen, representing tens of millions of dollars to be made or lost.

Griffen was one of a rare group of financial movers and shakers who were largely above any regulatory or law enforcement probes – small token fish were occasionally nabbed, but the real money jockeys were untouchable. On the contrary, he received preferential treatment from the SEC, which came in handy when he needed help with a particularly troublesome stock. There was nothing like a trading halt or an investigation to crater a company, at least long enough for him to make a few bucks.

He was sharp, smooth, refined, and completely amoral. And most importantly, he was rich.

ત∞ન્હ

Emil spoke into the specially configured phone in a soft, emotionless voice. The phone's encryption technology ensured prying or eavesdropping ears would decipher nothing but a screeching data stream, using Department of Defense-level scrambling.

"It really is perfect. Given our level of financial commitment to the opposition party, we could easily get them twice as much as they need this year."

Emil Weingard worked within a rarified division of the government's clandestine machine, responsible for making things happen in deniable ways. Officially he was in the Information Operations Center/Analysis Group, but his real role was much more important than that. He was a fixer, and had gained notoriety at West Point by writing his thesis on a highly autonomous strategy for running covert missions, coupled with some intriguing alternative mechanisms for funding them. He was recruited shortly thereafter.

His job was to procure large amounts of cash for delicate projects that were essential to national security – projects that Congress wouldn't necessarily approve of. He currently had two active deals, one of which involved the continued support of an anti-establishment dissident group in Iran, and another which involved untraceable support for a splinter faction in the German government.

Emil fancied himself a secret agent of sorts, but deep in his heart he knew he was a banker. The irony that he'd conceptualized a self-sufficient team approach to clandestine operations and had wound up being the bean counter wasn't lost on him, but he was pragmatic. After the disastrous revelations of Iran Contra, the more sensitive agencies couldn't afford any embarrassments and the only way to compartmentalize and seal off the risk was by using a tightly limited approach to the problem. Emil had come up with his team's funding sources, which later became the standard for most of the other teams. How many others, he didn't know – and 'Need to know' was still the guiding principle.

Right now he was on the phone with his man in Istanbul, who interfaced with the Iranian contact every few months. Another payment into a numbered account in Austria was required at the end of the quarter, and the man in Turkey wanted to ensure they were game-on.

They were.

They always were when Emil was running the money.

CHAPTER 2

Griffen pored over the pile of computer printouts stacked a foot thick on his scarred mahogany desk; a relic from the 1920s rumored to have been the infamous short seller Jesse Livermore's, that he'd acquired for twenty thousand dollars when he'd opened his offices. Its battered presence was a constant reminder of the history of Wall Street, and the brutality of the market's whims. Fortunes had been made and lost in hours during frenzies, and Griffen, more than most, understood that you had to be driving the frenzies in order to come out on the winning side. To do so meant rigorous determination, exhaustive research, and most importantly, the ability to control what information made it into the marketplace, as well as the timing of its dissemination. He who controlled the printing presses controlled destiny, and Griffen bought ink by the barrel. He created reality, and his associates in the media parroted his spin without question. That's the way the markets had worked since the stock exchange was built, and he'd merely refined a time-honored tradition and applied it to his own specialized segment.

Griffen absorbed the row of figures, mentally digesting the balance sheet and preparing a rationalization that would paint black as white, and make a loser into a winner. It would take some massaging to prepare a story where the endless bleeding of cash in this company's history could be sold to the rubes as having built a foundation for limitless success in the near future, but if anyone could make it happen, Griffen could. He was a master of putting lipstick on pigs, and convincing hapless investors that this time was indeed completely different.

In the only clear corner of the scarred table-top a forgotten cigar smoldered in a heavy onyx ashtray. The office, even though well-ventilated, had a perennial odor of leather, cigar smoke, and agitation. It was the smell of the market – the smell of money.

He kept long hours, driven by a love of the action involved in fiddling the system. There was never enough time to accomplish everything, never moments where he could let down his guard – and the challenge of staying on top kept him energized and motivated.

Griffen had triumphed in a world where only the most cunning and nimble survived. He'd amassed a fortune building manias and then collapsing them.

Unlike many traditional venture capital funds, his investment group was nothing more than a large pool of cash which traded however he felt appropriate. A big attraction of his fund was that nobody asked where all the money came from; there were no annoying disclosures to make, no boxes to check, no forms to complete. Even in a world of Patriot Acts, reduced rights, and financial transparency, Griffen enjoyed complete secrecy in most of his affairs. That had always been the lure for him – as a young man, he'd seen a lot of possibility in Wall Street's selective lack of regulation. He remembered it like it was yesterday.

A Yale graduate, he'd paid his dues by spending eight years as an analyst, and then later as a trader with one of the big brokerages, hating every second of it while building a network of contacts. In the late seventies he quit and launched his eponymous fund, partnering with a childhood friend from New Jersey.

Griffen had pitched several Italian union pension funds and waste management groups on a neat way to invest the deluge of cash pouring in from the surge in demand for their services; as well as from the expansion of cocaine and heroin trafficking on the eastern seaboard. The groups had been receptive to creating a veneer of respectability, and were enthusiastic in their response to his proposition; their money got laundered via his venture capital and stock trading activities and they saw a good return on the newly sanitized loot. It was a win for all involved.

With those early investors he'd found his first serious money, and from that point things accelerated as the newly respectable investors told their friends about their smart new investment advisor. Griffen soon had a runaway success, and was oversubscribed from his first formal funding raise. In time, legitimate clients were attracted by his spectacular results; and over the years, the Street forgot the hints of his questionable beginnings.

Building on his initial relationships, Griffen became a 'go to' guy for shady figures wanting an in on Wall Street biotechnology action. His door always open to the fringe players and the dirty money – a specialty that rewarded him handsomely. His unique customer mix and their powerful contacts shielded him from intrusion by the authorities, enabling him to refine his pump and dump game to a fine art.

Create a bubble, then pop it, and only *he* knew when it would collapse. It was simple, effective, and highly lucrative, albeit illegal and unethical. Then again, all great fortunes had great crimes at their root, and Griffen was simply using the same techniques the stock manipulators of the Roaring Twenties had used to build dynastic wealth. Just as icons like Joe Kennedy had created manias in worthless companies, then once the public was enraptured with their shares, kicked the chair out from under them and made millions as the stocks plummeted, so too did Griffen. Human nature hadn't changed much in a few generations, and the same techniques worked, again and again. Only an idiot obeyed the laws, especially when the regulators were asleep at the wheel and virtually never enforced them. He was comfortable that he was a criminal – actually reveled in the knowledge, truth be told. All the wealthiest of the Wall Street mob were gangsters at heart, in spite of the tripe the industry's PR machine put out day after day. It was just far more lucrative to carry a cell phone and a calculator than a machine gun, these days. Everyone at the top knew how the game was played. Big gains required big balls, and often meant crossing lines that lesser mortals were barred from even considering breaching. That was the game, and he was very, very good at it.

At the same time, he was on the invitation list for the Governor's dinners and Mayor's functions; rubbing shoulders with celebrities – a fixture in the New York social scene. His investors were highly appreciative of his continued performance and discretion, and always ensured he wanted for nothing. The best looking call girls, pharmaceutical grade cocaine, two hundred dollar scotch. If Griffen could imagine it, he got it; there were literally no limits for the man with the golden touch.

༜

Steven watched in fascination as the screen normalized, and trading that had been erratic and plunging slowed to a crawl.

"Unbelievable. It's like they flicked a light switch," he muttered to himself.

He moved to the other screen and brought up a window. The message boards had also slowed to nothing. When the stock was being pummeled the boards had been saturated with hundreds of posts advising shareholders to sell, that somebody knew something, that institutions were bailing, that the stock was going to zero. Psychological warfare – all par for the course. Organized teams hit the boards, attempting to sow the seeds of panic and confusion.

Then, just as suddenly as the selling normalized, the panicked posts were gone.

The rest of the day's trading wore on, slow, plodding, predictable. Once Griffen's related accounts stopped trading back and forth to create artificial volume, the stock action was stagnant. The close was a non-event, down a few pennies. The polar opposite of the chaotic frenzy of the earlier part of the day, and further evidence to Steven of the omnipotence the manipulators wielded.

CHAPTER 3

"Wonder how they're going to enjoy having their bullshit exposed?" Steven muttered.

Avalon looked up from the floor, evaluating whether there was a promise of a treat in the statement. Finding none, he resumed his well practiced canine repose, uninterested in whatever drama was unfolding with his master.

Trading had concluded hours earlier, and the stock chat forums Steven monitored had largely gone silent, other than to rail at the obvious manipulations of the stock and the conspicuous absence of any regulatory intervention. After wolfing down lunch, Steven had returned to his workstation and spent the rest of the afternoon typing furiously on his keyboard, putting the final touches on the website he'd been working on for the last month.

He was able to use off-the-shelf modules for it, and had designed it to be easy to read, informative, and balanced, eschewing hyperbole and hysterical language in favor of an almost academic tone. He figured that in order for it to have maximum impact and be taken seriously, it had to avoid any whiff of being kooky-sounding or angry, favoring instead a dry, factual approach. Studying the layout of the home page he tweaked a few small items, resizing some of the margins and image files to be more visually appealing and easy to read. Satisfied with the way the fields lined up, he clicked 'save' and decided to call it a day. He looked at his watch, then reached his arms over his head and stretched, finally finished with the huge project he'd taken on.

Steven padded over to an overstuffed chair in the corner of his den and sat down, assuming a familiar position – hands clasped in his lap, eyes closed, head slightly bowed. His breathing subsided to a few intakes per minute, shallow breaths, hardly discernible. His blood pressure dropped, heart rate slowed, awareness of his surrounding receded until he was in a psychic vacuum absent any thought or mental activity beyond simply being.

Meditation had been an important part of his martial arts discipline for eighteen years. The experience inevitably left him feeling cleansed and focused, and he found it helped every aspect of his performance. Synapses were better aligned, reflexes improved, responses more immediate.

He stayed in a meditative state for twenty minutes, until some distant part of him signaled a return to awareness. His vital signs gradually increased, breathing became deeper, and after several moments he opened his eyes, revitalized and refreshed.

The first few moments were always dreamlike, almost the same as walking out of a quiet museum or a church after mass; the senses re-calibrating to motions and sounds and near- constant stimuli.

Rising from his tranquil spot in the corner, he ambled over to the sliding glass doors and considered the view. It was dusk, and the sun was beginning its spectacular descent into the glittering sea.

Avalon lollopped over to greet him, hopeful for an outing. They walked onto the patio, taking in the non-stop passage of tourists and locals skating and rolling and pedaling past his vantage point. He noticed Gilbert, the resident homeless guy who invariably shuffled along this very route every evening, engrossed in discourse with invisible companions who assisted him with his inspection of the garbage cans lining the path.

Steven went inside and rummaged through the refrigerator for last night's leftovers and searched in his pockets for a few small bills. He knew Gilbert would never beat whatever afflicted him, but to Steven's way of thinking, it didn't matter. Sometimes you win...

He hopped over the gate and greeted Gilbert by the little bench on the strand, as was his custom. They talked a while, and Steven handed him what he had to offer, which was always gratefully accepted. Avalon, adept at following Steven over the gate, looked up at him hopefully, tongue lolling happily out of his mouth.

"Don't worry, boy. There's still some chicken left for you."

They returned to their little patio to watch the show. Catalina Island shimmered in the distance and remote oil platforms jockeyed with tankers in the shipping lanes for preeminent position for the evening's sunset performance.

He registered the garage door opening and closing, and soon felt hands on his shoulders.

"You're a lucky bastard, my friend." Jennifer had already changed out of her work outfit – khakis and black blouse – and into sweat pants and a tank top.

"Rather be lucky than smart." They'd been dating for a couple of years, a comfortable relationship that had developed a rhythm that satisfied their needs.

Jennifer considered his profile before looking over to the desk with the pile of research and notepads inside the house. She knew about his web project. "Aren't you worried about waving a cape in front of the bull?"

"These dirt-bags are selling junk to widows and orphans, wiping out life savings, and ruining the market," he said as he leaned back and closed his eyes. "I'm just leveling the playing field. No big deal."

"When are you planning to put it online?" she asked.

"Why not tonight?"

"I don't know, Steven. I've had a bad feeling about this since you started with it." She pulled away and was quiet for a moment. "Where do you want to go to dinner?" she finally asked, moving the dialog to neutral ground.

Steven pulled at his chin. "Hmm...let's go down the strand and do Italian. A little chicken Marsala never hurt. Yum yum yum. A little wine, a little song..."

"Sure. I'll throw on some shoes and grab a sweater." She stared at the top of his head for a minute, the ocean breeze tickling her face as she thought about saying something more, then she sighed, and turned to go back into the house.

The website had been structured as an expose of the junk science and questionable nature of the technology Allied was touting and the suspicious trading patterns the stock routinely enjoyed. Steven had conceived the site after finding sites targeting the shady dealings of large Wall Street banks, like GoldmanSachs666.com. If a site like that could expose the underhanded actions of Wall Street's icons, he figured he could create one on a smaller scale and illuminate the crookery in play with Allied and the Griffen gang. If the misdeeds were memorialized in one place, his theory was it would be easier for anyone investigating to spot the manipulative patterns in the trading, as well as the obvious chicanery that was the network's standard operating procedure.

His new website detailed the questionable nature of the science the company claimed to be developing and pointed out that many of the company's proponents were a network of physicians, scientists and stock promoters who'd been active in other, ultimately worthless shams that had cost investors everything. It also pored over public filings and exposed the ownership of the company's stock, highlighting the massive role Griffen played.

All in all, it presented a compelling argument that trading in Allied was anything but fair and honest, and went into significant detail to link the players in the nefarious pump and dump scam.

Damaging stuff to be sure, but a hair shy of proof. *Oh well, nothing was perfect.* The time had come to put the site up and fire a salvo across the opposition's bow.

When they got back from dinner he uploaded the site files to an internet service provider in Texas. He'd deliberately chosen a company in a different state so anyone interested in silencing the site would be looking in the wrong places. He'd registered the domain name using the address of a now-defunct Irish pub in New Orleans, and created a blind account for e-mail contact. It all added up to making the site's creator invisible and impossible to trace.

www.AlliedExposed.com went live at 12:04 a.m..

He knew it would likely take a while until it propagated and was available for viewing everywhere, but figured that within six to eight hours most areas of the country would be able to view it. Before going to bed, Steven typed a post on one of the most popular internet message boards, inviting readers to the website. With any luck some exposure would get the regulators and the mainstream public interested in the doubtful technology and trading chicanery, resulting in some badly needed enforcement of the anti-manipulation rules. Steven just hoped it would go viral after his fellow message board denizens spread the word around. He'd done all he could at this point by collecting the data and highlighting the abuses; it was in the public domain now, and would take on a life of its own – or die – based on forces outside of his control.

Steven powered down his system and scratched his head, realizing for the first time how late it was. But the deed was now done, and he felt like a weight had been lifted from his shoulders. It was a job well done, and could actually have an impact on the ultimate outcome of the pump and dump scheme. He supposed he'd know soon enough.

Exhausted, he padded up the stairs and began his bedtime ritual of tooth brushing and giving Avalon the final treats of the day, and after studying his bloodshot eyes in the mirror and registering how much time he'd been in front of the computer, barely made it to the bed before he started snoring.

CHAPTER 4

Griffen was thoroughly livid. He wasn't accustomed to being challenged, and certainly wasn't used to being publicly mocked and put on display. His livelihood and success depended on obscurity, on being able to operate in the shadows without prying eyes disturbing his plans. He knew how to play the media game. He understood exactly how effective propaganda could be, and didn't like it directed at him.

The last thing he needed was some website documenting the blow by blow of his promotion of Allied, and exposing his network. He, more than anyone, grasped the power of information control; and he realized there was a potential disaster in the making the second he heard about the site. There was way more at stake than just the one company's fortunes. His funds enjoyed invisibility from regulators by virtue of the unseen hand of one of his investors, and publicity and exposure invited the kind of attention he didn't need. The website posed a massive threat to his entire operation and was an obvious disaster in the making. This had to get stopped cold, or he'd be incurring significant risks he couldn't afford. And with those risks could come ugly consequences.

His staff knew from harsh experience he was best avoided at times like this, opting to give his desk a wide berth as he screamed down the phone.

"Goddamn mother fucker!" Griffen hollered. "Can't you sue this shithead, get an injunction or something? He's calling me a fucking criminal and saying the company's voodoo. You're my attorney. Do something!"

"It's not that straightforward," Vesper told him. "He's clever. He never actually says you're breaking the law or acting criminally; he just documents your holdings, shows your connection to the media outlets who've been supportive, lists other companies the positive analysts hyped in the past, and then hypothesizes that your massive stake in the company makes you extremely interested in the stock skyrocketing at all costs. It's all opinion." Glen Vesper knew the law cold. "He's suggesting that if you were engaging in a scheme to pump and then dump Allied's value, that would be criminal, but he doesn't come out and say you're breaking the law. That's a critical legal distinction."

"So what's your suggestion?"

"Just don't say anything at all," Vesper advised. "Ignore it. The flip side of the site is that it doesn't prove anything. It's all conjecture. I'd regard it as a conspiracy kook's hobby and pretend it doesn't exist. If you go after him with an injunction you'll only increase the exposure and publicity; if we could even *get* an injunction in the first place."

"So I let the cocksucker call me a liar and a thief in front of the whole planet and just smile and ask him if he'd like to fuck me in the ass when he's done?" Griffen asked. "That's the best you can do?"

"Nicholas, we don't even know who's behind this – it could be anybody. At this stage we know nothing about them…or their motives." He paused, collected his thoughts, sighed. "I pulled the registration info on the site and it places it in New Orleans, owned by a guy named Stanley Jorgenson with a Hotmail account; probably a dead end. That's all we have. I'm looking into the address and the ID, but it smells fake. For now, just let it go. That's my advice."

"Thanks for absolutely fucking nothing," Griffen hissed, frothing with seething indignation. He slammed down the handset. Lawyers. Bloodsucking parasites.

Still, Glen had a point.

～◈◈～

Steven spent the whole morning at the computer, monitoring the trading action, the stock not doing much. Eventually the increasingly strident growling of his stomach tore him away from it to make a sandwich, which he wolfed down in just a few minutes. Following his hurried lunch, he switched to polishing his new site, trying to improve the user interface and make it more presentable. Why did everything usually take longer than it should, with nothing ever as easy as it initially looked? Websites were apparently no different.

After a full day of staring at screens he decided he needed to depart cyber-reality and work the tension out of his system. He drove to the dojo where he practiced his skills, and donned his white gee. Steven was an eighth degree black belt in Karate, a gold sash adept in Wing Chun Kung Fu, and at master level in Jeet Kune Do.

He began with Karate, always, starting with the *Geri Waza* and *Uchi Waza* form, then through the *Tsuki*, *Uke* and *Hiji*. Switching disciplines, he practiced the various nerve strikes and hand forms for Kung Fu, and finally wound down with stretching and isometric exercises.

His fascination with the disciplines stemmed from watching Bruce Lee films when he was ten years old, and from the first days when he began learning the initial stances and kicks he'd been mesmerized by the sense of self-possession they instilled. His interest had continued unabated throughout his adult life and he'd now evolved to the point where the requirement to practice the forms was more out of homage to the skills than from necessity.

That lifelong involvement in martial arts, along with four years in the military, had instilled a quiet confidence and self-reliance in him, even if it had also made him a loner. Perhaps that solitary streak explained why he'd never gotten married and settled down – had a family – it always seemed like stuff of the future, but right now he wasn't in a big hurry to get to that future. He was comfortable with things as they stood.

Back at the house, he rinsed off and checked his e-mail. His new mailbox had thirty-eight messages congratulating him on the new site. Jennifer was spending the night at her place, while Avalon was chasing rabbits in his sleep in the den, so Steven was free to begin slogging through his inbox.

Once done, he logged into what he thought of as his 'paranoia group', an invitation-only collection of cyber friends with 'unusual' interests in fringe topics and esoteric conspiracy theories. He'd been invited to join years ago, when his company had developed software for a longtime friend who structured privacy solutions for clients concerned with cyber-snooping. Steven had always been interested in clandestine and off-the-beaten-path knowledge, probably a kickback from his military days, or perhaps just a function of his somewhat conspiratorial personality – so the invitation had been readily accepted. When Steven's friend had moved to Ireland, he'd remained in 'The Group', as it was called by its participants, and Steven was still an active poster.

If you could sit through the sometimes contentious sparring over the best mechanism for creating a Trojan horse to invade a server, or the ongoing debate over the level of Big Brother's encroachment into everyone's privacy, he found the repartee and information exchanged was often riveting. Everyone was anonymous in the group, and used aliases. Steven's was 'Bowman'.

He hadn't shared with The Group that he'd created the site yet. All the participants would have strong opinions on everything from the font style to the background color. He figured he'd work out any bugs before letting the gang have at it.

Still, he couldn't resist a tickler post:

[Fellas, this is Bowman. I've got a little surprise for you. I'm a webmaster now - been working on a hobby site that's live and kicking.]

Immediately several responses came back.

[What's the URL?]

[Since when do you know how to work anything more than a mouse?]

[What program did you use to write it?]

[Is it porn?]

Ahh, you could always rely on the lads to be inquisitive.

[Sorry gang, not porn, though if it was I'm sure you'd know how to route it through Kabul. Just a little project that will be ready for your shredding in a day or two.]

A few seconds, and the predictable:

[If it's not porn, I'm not interested.]

[Just what the world needs, another site hosted by a sad geek who wants to whine about how misunderstood he is.]

[You mean he ripped off your site?]

And so on. Fun banter, but these guys were some of the sharpest he'd ever encountered.

After spending a few hours catching up on the latest scuttlebutt he decided to log off, scarf down a sandwich, read a little and tuck in early. He was beat from weeks of focused activity developing the site, and needed some rest.

One last look confirmed the site had already gotten 2,861 hits; my, but word spread quickly on the web.

CHAPTER 5

Steven had never registered the slightest interest in stocks or financial markets until he'd sold his company. Once retired he'd gone stir crazy, so as a pastime had indulged a lifelong fascination with fine timepieces by collecting high value watches; favoring Patek Philippes and Rolexes. That had gotten old quickly and he'd switched his focus to cryptography, which still engaged him as an ongoing fascination; he'd gone so far as to acquire a few medieval parchments encrypted with the popular ciphers of the time and had begun building a modest collection. But that didn't pay well so he began dabbling in the market as an avocation — a fun way to make a few bucks and follow trends in industries that interested him. It started out more as a hobby than the borderline obsession it had evolved into over the last year.

He'd lucked out and inked his company's sale when a competitor had wanted to consolidate, and his cut of the proceeds had come to a little over five million bucks. Thanks to his attorney, Stan Caldwell, he'd been able to structure the deal so that virtually no tax was paid, leaving him set for the rest of his life. Timing was everything; one year later, he'd have been lucky to get the value of the furniture.

Steven would have been set for life if he hadn't subsequently gambled $2 million on a friend's 'can't miss' real estate play — which crashed and burned in the ensuing economic crisis and had consumed the entire bankroll. After that experience, his investment philosophy became all about minimizing losses while positioning for outsized gains, and thus he gravitated to biotech — with a lot of research carried out before any real money got invested. He'd gotten more involved over the last eighteen months as his comfort with the market grew, and had begun actively trading his holdings; making a decent chunk of change by playing the dips. He was hooked…but only enough to keep him occupied during his days.

So far so good.

And then he discovered Allied.

Steven's former partner and technical half of the setup, Jason Mallory, now ran a consulting firm specializing in designing computer networks; when he'd gotten back from Milwaukee last year he'd been talking about his new client, Allied. He'd built a scalable network for them capable of growing ten-fold over the next five years; which Jason had been highly skeptical they'd ever need, given his assessment of the operations and the cynicism of the employees.

Steven did a slug of due diligence on the company and discovered several things he found surprising. First, Allied was mainly involved in vaccine development, which was not the typical small company play – it was usually the big boys who were involved in that sort of thing. Second, the internet message boards on Allied were abuzz with rumors about Griffen Ventures, which had apparently been instrumental in funding the last investment round and taking the company public. Griffen was one of the more controversial investors one could have because many of his past 'triumphs' ultimately blew up – to the detriment of most smaller stockholders. And one of the board regulars had discovered Griffen was a sponsor of several online business sites that had been writing puff pieces on Allied since February; about the time daily volume of the stock had quadrupled, and the price had gone parabolic for no apparent reason.

It looked to Steven like a classic stock manipulation from the 1920s; he couldn't believe it still happened in this day and age, but if he was right it could mean huge returns – and then some. Manipulation was usually a short-term game to create volatility and control the price. It could be effective for a while, but fundamentals and performance ultimately carried the day. A savvy investor could ride the upside wave with the big boys and make a killing – and if it came out the company was a dud, and that investor was short, he could be set for life.

Jason's insights told him the market had gotten it badly wrong so far, and that Allied had the stink of rat all over it.

Peter Valentine was one of Steven's longtime friends. Originally his father's buddy, he'd become Steven's mentor when Steven's dad had passed away 28 years earlier. They'd developed a lifelong bond and Steven duly respected Peter's perspective and opinions.

Years of working for the FBI had left Peter with a substantial network of contacts, and when he cashed in his chips and retired he became a part-time private investigator to supplement his pension. As a concession to retirement he moved to a place where the weather was warm and he could fish every day: Sarasota, Florida. Peter was an amazingly resourceful guy, and his wife, Penny, was among the nicest and most patient women Steven had ever met.

Steven had phoned on a weekend, figuring he'd be able to get them at home. The phone had rung and Penny had picked up. Her distinctive, chirpy voice never failed to raise his spirits.

"Why, hello, Steven. To what do we owe the honor of this call, mister rich guy?"

This was Penny's customary greeting – never failed. They'd dubbed him 'rich guy' ever since he'd sold his company. In their universe it was unheard of to retire in your late thirties.

"I was trying to make an obscene phone call and hit speed dial by mistake. How's everything at geriatric country safari?" Steven asked.

"Oh, pretty wild. We had a shopping cart get away from a neighbor last Saturday at the market, and it almost hit a car door. You probably got it on the satellite news."

"Yeah, I heard about that. I hope you're all okay, I was going to call..."

"You want Peter? I'll get him. He's out wrestling a crocodile or something. Hang on a sec."

He heard her yelling in the distance, a door slamming.

"Hey, Steve." Peter was the only person who called him Steve.

"Hey, Peter. How goes the war?"

"Bloodied but not bowed, my friend. What's up on *your* coast?" Peter asked him. "How's the beach bunny action? Still with Nadine?"

"Uh, no, actually I've been seeing a girl named Jennifer for a couple of years." (Peter knew this full well, but liked to make mischief with Nadine; a spectacular brunette Peter had sworn he'd leave his wife for had he been twenty years younger). "Peter, I need a favor, professionally-speaking."

"All right, Steve, what's up?"

Steven had laid out the whole Allied story for Peter, giving him a breakdown of Griffen's involvement, backed up with a summary of the trading irregularities. Peter had listened carefully, stopping occasionally to write down a name or ask about spelling. At the end of the discussion they'd agreed Peter would look into Griffen and Steven would e-mail him all the info he'd accumulated.

Steven took his time before investing in Allied, preferring caution over being foolhardy. All his inquiries confirmed his negative impression, and experience with other biotech bombs had taught him the stock could easily fall ninety or more percent within eighteen months; it was perfectly positioned to drop off a cliff if the science turned out to be bogus. If he was right, it was a once-in-a-lifetime opportunity.

He decided to get involved. Big-time.

Over the course of the next few weeks he violated every investing rule he knew and went short seven hundred thousand dollars worth of stock. In his view, the collapse wasn't a matter of if, but rather a matter of when.

The problem was that short positions required he pay to borrow the stock he'd sold short, and if the stock kept going up he could get badly hurt – if not wiped out – so once he'd established his position, he'd taken to following the stock minute by minute, real time, every day.

The trading chicanery and implausibly glowing press kept coming and hardly a week went by where some pundit didn't opine that the company was on the brink of greatness, or at least of being acquired at a substantial premium. So even as the company sucked money and generated nothing of apparent value the positive rhetoric was undiminished, and there were days where it rose five percent for no reason. It was disheartening, although he could see why many shareholders got sucked into the feeding frenzy. He remembered vividly one man from the message boards who claimed to have made millions from his position. It was heady stuff. Steven couldn't believe a company with such obvious question marks surrounding its investors and technology could rate such optimistic coverage in the modern, supposedly safe markets, and his anger at the manipulation mounted even as his determination strengthened.

One morning, after watching in frustration as the price jumped for the fifth straight day on little or no volume, he had an epiphany. The idea was so simple.

Griffen had his captive media buddies to inflate the Allied bubble. Why not create a website that laid out the case for manipulation, and which skeptically evaluated the company's supposed innovations and scientific 'breakthroughs'?

It seemed straightforward. Just a matter of creating a few pages — finding a place to host it — and uploading it. A snap.

What could be easier?

CHAPTER 6

Another morning, and Nicholas Griffen was furious again. He'd gotten calls from several of his investors who'd seen the new site and wanted to know if his involvement in Allied, and the precariousness of the technology, were true.

One in particular had indicated that any publicity could endanger their 'special' relationship, and Griffen was no idiot. He understood the stakes involved, and further understood that while he was an important part of that particular investor's strategy, he could rapidly lose value as his machinations were exposed. And he didn't ever want to have his currency devalued with that player.

The problem was, word spread faster than the speed of sound nowadays as a result of the internet, and that was hurting him. His first stage pumping of Allied had worked like a charm, luring the dumb money speculators in droves. But he still had a long way to go before they'd hit his target of a market top for the stock, and he was long in a massive way. Now, with this new website, he recognized he had a problem brewing; the longer the speculations about manipulation and the doubts about the technology were out there, the greater the likelihood a predatory player would come in and take the other side of the bet, which could be a killer given the current size of his position. The last thing he needed was a few big short funds to sense blood in the water and go to work tunneling the stock.

He couldn't afford that because he'd over-invested on the way up without bothering to hedge his bets, meaning the Allied shares and options were now a considerable chunk of his fund's position; and given that he'd continued buying for months to keep upward momentum going, he was very, very pregnant with the stock.

Trading was about to begin for the day, and he planned to temporarily dump the stock into the toilet, hopefully causing some panic selling so he could make some short term profits from a slug of short positions and put options he'd bought – both of which were time sensitive, but could make a lot of dough if the stock lost twenty percent during the day and he covered, then took the other side of the trade and the stock magically recovered.

This was a fairly routine exercise for his group, and was just another in the myriad ways an inventive and enterprising fellow could eke out profits in a relatively flat market. Unexplainable and unexpected radical stock moves were exceptional profit-making exercises if you were in control of when and how the dips and rises happened. That was one of Griffen's specialties, and he was about to make some easy gains from what he referred to as the moron money, which would sell at the low and then buy back in at or near the high. If he could control the emotions of how the small retail investors traded, he could play them like a violin. And today was the day for another of his concertos.

Griffen punched in the digits for his attorney.

"Glen, any movement on the matter we discussed yesterday?"

"I'm working on it. Let's get together for lunch, someplace quiet. The club?"

Griffen frowned. "Today's kind of busy, can't we do this over the phone?"

"I'm hungry. Let's make it around one o'clock. I'll have some news."

Griffen paused, calculated. "One o'clock. Sounds great."

That was a good sign. It meant Glen had some information he wasn't comfortable sharing over the phone. Perhaps things were improving after all.

∽∾

Steven finished his morning run and was at the computer by 6:20 a.m.. The markets were jittery and rumors were floating on the message boards about insiders wanting to sell ahead of bad news.

Allied opened on time and the trading was muted, with sixty thousand shares trading hands and the price up twenty cents in the first forty-five minutes.

Then it all crumbled.

The boards lit up with negative chatter, the volume spiked, and the price started fluctuating wildly. The carnage hit at 10:30 EST as the stock went into freefall for six minutes.

Breaking through $34, it fell quickly through the $33s, and then into the $32s. It just kept dropping and dropping.

There was nothing on the wire service; no news or reason for any of it. Steven sensed opportunity and decided he'd call the bluff – he'd witnessed enough of these attacks to know a head fake when he saw one. If this was a short term manipulation he could throw his day trading budget at buying shares and call options – which increased in value if the stock went up – and use the profits from the swing to offset most of this month's losses on his Allied short position. It definitely wasn't for the faint of heart, but he'd been watching the trading for enough time to have a pretty fair idea of the game that was being played.

He started buying shares and calls at $32.10 and kept reloading his three thousand-share buy order every time it was hit. After accumulating eighteen thousand shares and five hundred near-term expiration call options, a bid jumped in above his, and then another bid jumped in above that one. Pretty soon steady buying was coming in and the price climbed above $33.00.

He watched as other buyers came into the market and the price stabilized. As the day progressed it became obvious a wall of buy orders sat at $34, allowing him to sell his day's shares and options towards the close, making a tidy profit from just a few hours of understanding the nature of the beast.

Not a bad Friday; he was up six percent on the session's buys, which had bought him breathing room on his underwater short position. It hadn't gotten him whole by any means, but it was better than sitting idly by watching the price swings and doing nothing.

The trading day done, he spent the rest of the day preparing for his flight to the East Coast for an impromptu weekend trip he'd thrown together. Jennifer was staying in California; she detested flying and wasn't a big fan of New York. She'd agreed to stop by and take Avalon for walks and keep him in kibble, so he couldn't complain. He kind of didn't blame her; New York in the summer could be brutally muggy, and Jennifer wasn't much of a big city girl, so the population density and crowds inevitably made her claustrophobic. There was a part of him that was secretly glad she was staying at home. For what he wanted to do, it would be better if he flew solo on this one.

Griffen entered the hushed foyer and was greeted by a vested attendant. Cherry wood paneled the walls and oil paintings of long-forgotten dignitaries scowled down at the heavy green velvet furnishings, setting a somber tone. Very old school, old money, cigars and cognac-feeling establishment. He was known at the Manhattan Polo Club, and was shown to one of the private dining rooms by the *maitre d'*; a serious British gentleman who'd held the coveted position for decades.

Glen Vesper was already seated, a glass of Chardonnay half consumed, looking appropriately lawyerly. Glen was thin to the point of resembling a praying mantis, and had looked sixty-something for the fifteen years Griffen had known him. During that time, he'd seen Glen smile twice. It wasn't a pretty sight.

"Sorry I'm late. We're getting creamed in the market today." Griffen ordered a glass of Shiraz from the waiter, who disappeared soundlessly.

Glen nodded. "I took the liberty of ordering two poached salmons. They should be here in a few minutes. I've some good news. We have some info on your mysterious admirer." Glen paused to sip his wine. "First, we think it's a civilian, not a pro. The site address was bogus, the Hotmail account a dead end; the name a fake. But we know who their service provider is, and we know they were careful. We hacked into the server and scanned the pay statements before the security software shut us down. A year's worth of service was paid for via postal money order. No name other than the fake one, so dead-end there."

"Why do you think it's a civilian, then? Seems pretty sophisticated to me," said Griffen.

"A pro wouldn't have used a domestic server, for starters. And they would have used an anonymous registration service rather than filing false information. And most importantly, they wouldn't have used a registration service that demanded payment with a credit card, which is how the registration service selected does it. You can't fake a credit card. It was their only slip-up, and one we would have ordinarily missed."

Griffen smiled. "Ahhhh. I get it. You work upstream through the registrar. Have you got a name?"

Glen shook his head. "Not yet. The registrar's in Germany, and we've got one of our correspondents over there working that angle. It'll be a few days but we should be able to get it. May cost a few bucks. I figured you'd have no objections."

"Gotta spend money to make money," Griffen conceded.

"Precisely. We also contacted our person at the message board service and were able to secure an IP address for the poster who's the site creator, but unfortunately it's a cable company IP, so there's an additional level of diligence required to get individual account info. That probably isn't possible, but we're working it as well. So far Germany looks best."

"What can we do once we know who this is? Can we get the site shut down? Can we sue him for libel?"

Glen looked at the ceiling. "I'm going to say this very carefully. In my opinion, there's little to be gained by suing the person responsible for this inconvenience; I don't see it as being worthwhile or ultimately successful." Glen returned his gaze to Griffen. "As an officer of the court, I can't condone you taking matters into your own hands or doing anything rash. Can I presume you won't do anything untoward if we discover the creator's identity?"

"Of course not. You have my complete assurance..."

Glen held back a smile. "I anticipated your response and instructed the German firm to contact you if they're productive in their endeavors. How's the Shiraz?"

Griffen considered the wine. "Beautiful finish. I think we understand each other, Glen."

After lunch, Griffen returned to his office to find that a two million dollar profit-making session had turned into a net one million dollar loss on Allied.

They'd tried some more runs at the stock later in the session but once the momentum was broken on the day's swings they'd been forced to liquidate their remaining trading shares at a loss. Not a good day. As he closed his office for the evening, Griffen had one thought at the forefront of his attention.

The site was screwing up his ability to make money and needed to get taken off the air, and quickly.

CHAPTER 7

Steven had come to New York after discovering that Griffen was going to speak at a fund-raising dinner for the Vice President. On Saturday afternoon, Steven stepped out of the cab he'd taken from JFK airport and checked into his hotel at 51st and Lexington. After getting situated in his room, he went down to the business center, got online, and broke the Allied site address to his Group. He was roundly chided for the amateurish job on the interface, not to mention the technical glitches and formatting flaws. Several of the gang found typos and grammatical errors, and one hacked his computer while he was online and momentarily superimposed a baboon flashing his bulbous bottom on one of the pages. The boys were having fun with it, as Steven had expected they would.

One of the more cynical regulars suggested that he could get a photo of Griffen for the site, as he lived in New York and 'knew some people'. Steven responded that it would be a hoot.

The site was now up to 4,700 hits, so people were visiting it. The message board dissemination campaign had been more effective than he could have hoped for. Word was spreading, the collusion gathering more exposure, the boards full of talk of filing SEC complaints referencing Allied's suspicious trading – and apparently some money guys were coming into the stock on the short side. Whether any of this related to the website was anyone's guess. But still, it was positive.

Finished with the internet, Steven returned to his room and donned a light summer suit for the dinner. He'd shelled out two thousand dollars to sit at Griffen's table because it appealed to him to sit within twenty feet of his adversary without Griffen ever knowing who he was. He wanted to get a feeling for the man – up close and personal – look his enemy in the eyes and take his measure; and he'd flown a long way to do just that…

Steven enjoyed the caress of the balmy, blustery evening as he walked the few blocks to the event. He admired the baroque interior of the overblown hotel lobby before making his way to the large banquet room. At the door, security went over him with a portable metal detector before allowing him to enter the room and pick up his reservation. Griffen was scheduled to deliver a speech about the importance of free enterprise in the market system, which Steven supposed could loosely be translated as 'why no one should ever regulate me'. He was genuinely interested in seeing the great man make his presentation.

Seated at a large round table, along with twenty or so other well-to-do men and women, he chatted with the older fellow on his right, who worked in real estate in Connecticut. Steven had decided to pose as the owner of a software company from Washington, in town for the week, and having taken the seat in place of a friend who'd become ill at the last minute. Nobody seemed particularly interested in discussing his background, which was just as well.

Griffen entered at precisely seven o'clock, the start time for the function, shaking hands and greeting people all the way to his table. He seemed to know many of the attendees, which wasn't surprising since he and one of the Fed governors were the event's main draws. It reminded Steven of a celebrity high-fiving audience members at a concert. Griffen was clearly a star.

The filet turned out to be outstanding, the wine pretty good, and the speeches self-importantly tedious and predictable. Griffen's seat was on the far side of the table so the opportunity to interact was limited and Steven felt disappointed his target was out of reach for discourse. After the entree, as he'd listened to Griffen's self-righteous presentation about the importance of keeping the markets as unregulated as possible, he'd grown increasingly angry at the man – and the situation before him.

Some of his anger could be attributed to the wine, which reduced his tolerance for bullshit in general, but the biggest irritant was the knowledge that this weasel enjoyed a position of prominence and prestige even as he cheated Joe Sixpack out of his retirement money. He thought about the shareholders who'd lost their life savings on Griffen's pump and dumps, and had to bite his cheek to sit still.

Steven's mood had upgraded to belligerent by the end of Griffen's speech, and built up a full head of steam while he'd watched his hard-nosed target pontificate on free markets from his bully pulpit – even as he orchestrated a criminal conspiracy.

After the coffee was served, a gentleman in a tuxedo circulated with a humidor. Steven watched Griffen select a cigar. He did the same, and followed Griffen out to the veranda which was designated as a smoking area.

Steven waited until Griffen finished lighting his cigar before approaching him to ask for a light. Griffen obliged.

"That was quite a presentation," Steven said.

"Thanks." Griffen was obviously not interested in chitchat with some peon. Steven forged ahead anyway, figuring this would be his only opportunity to annoy the man in person.

"I especially enjoyed the part where you defended the actions of big money pools as being helpful in maintaining necessary liquidity in the market," Steven recalled innocently. "It made pumping and short selling seem almost like doing the Lord's work."

Griffen regarded Steven, appraising him carefully.

"Look, everyone on Wall Street cheerleads for the stocks they're pushing and bashes those they're betting against. The whole street talks its book, and the media sings along with them. That's the way things have worked since shares started trading. You don't like the game, too bad. It has nothing to do with the players." Griffen tapped his ashes on the railing.

Steven nodded. "That's probably true. Still, if you happen to be able to read tomorrow's headlines today, that would mean making huge money was as easy as knowing which reporters to call, right?"

"That's an oversimplification," Griffen said. "Eventually in any market, all facts will be known. That's the whole idea of the system. I tend to believe that the system works pretty well, and that the last thing anyone needs is a bunch of regulation in a market that's working just fine." He held up a manicured finger. "Everyone whines when they're on the wrong side of the trade, and wants government to step in and get them out of their bad bets. I say, too bad. The market isn't about coddling losers."

Steven considered the logic. "Hmmm. Perhaps. But in your case, where you hold sway over a lot of media outlets, I could see where the temptation to pump the prospects of loser companies you'd gotten into for pennies would be pretty strong, then once the moron money was following along and believing your line of BS, taking the opposite side of the trade and crushing them would be child's play. Seems to me like that's a recurring pattern in companies you've discovered – probably just coincidence, right?" Steven smiled. "Anything for a buck, and all's fair, right?"

Griffen's face flushed with anger. "Everyone's got an opinion. One man's treasure is another man's junk. Nobody holds a gun to anyone's head to invest in anything." He stopped and narrowed his eyes. "I didn't catch your name," Griffen said.

"I didn't mention it. Just thought I'd share an idea with you; you're more vulnerable than you think. I know what you're trying to do with Allied, and it's not going to work. I wanted to tell you that you've overstepped this time. You've bitten off a big piece – bigger than you can imagine." Steven stubbed out his cigar in the ashtray and turned to walk away.

Griffen grabbed his arm. "Just who in the hell do you think you're–" he started.

Steven pinched Griffen's wrist at the nerve meridian, causing him to yelp and release his grip on Steven's arm and clutch the spot from where the pain emanated.

"It's rude to get grabby with people you just met." Steven smiled again. "Consider this fair warning. You're nothing but a thug, and you're not going to get away with your little game on Allied." Steven glared at Griffen, who had a scowl on his face from the surprise of being accosted – and the discomfort of being so easily swept physically aside.

Steven looked him up and down. "Have a nice night. I'm sure the rest of your cockroach buddies are waiting for your next line of horseshit. You don't want to disappoint them, leave them waiting." With that, Steven turned and walked back into the banquet hall, made his way to the exit, and then out onto the street.

Griffen was suitably annoyed by the incident, and his wrist hurt like a bitch, but he was unfazed by some idiot's threats. He'd made a lot of enemies over the years and was accustomed to his adversaries vowing to bring him to justice. It never amounted to anything. Talk's cheap.

This was undoubtedly some disgruntled investor who'd taken the wrong side of the Allied bet and was losing his ass. Boo hoo. Everyone wanted to blame someone else for their bad investment decisions, and Griffen was always a highly visible target for their ire.

As the pain diminished, he rationalized that if you weren't pissing people off and making enemies, then you probably weren't doing anything worth talking about.

The Police Commissioner came out onto the balcony with a cigar and greeted Griffen like his long-lost brother. They toasted with hundred-dollar-a-glass cognac, and the incident was forgotten.

For the most part.

CHAPTER 8

Sunday morning, still at the hotel in NY, Steven checked in with the Group and was delighted to find a picture of Griffen walking out to pick up his morning paper. That was hysterical, especially since he'd been standing across from him in a business suit just twelve hours earlier. The photographer explained he'd tracked down Griffen's home address in Connecticut. His buddy had snapped some shots that very morning using a telephoto lens. Nice to know the great man went to the bathroom the same as everyone else.

Somehow the sight of his adversary in a robe, with his hair matted to one side, clutching his paper, made the battle seem winnable. He uploaded it to the site, and linked it to the message boards, under the heading, 'Wall Street Wizard Plots Next Master Move'.

Funny, funny stuff. Maybe Griffen would feel a little more vulnerable after seeing the photo. He hoped so. The prick's arrogance was palpable, and it was high time somebody took him down a few notches.

Steven packed his bags and checked out of his room early, and made it to the airport with plenty of time to spare. He was scheduled to arrive back in California by two o'clock, leaving much of the afternoon available for relaxation. He considered an early evening cruise on his sailboat with Jennifer to watch the sunset, and calculated that he had plenty of time; the trip hadn't been such a big disruption after all.

The flight across the country was smooth – the traffic from the airport home predictably terrible.

In the late afternoon, Peter called from Florida, catching Steven on the way out the door to the boat. His news on Allied was largely negative – the management team was sketchy; there had been virtually no external audits of the technology or their financials, and it had many of the earmarks of a classic stock promotion scheme lacking any real underlying fundamental value. It had all the telltale signs of a company with something big to hide. His news on Griffen was not as encouraging.

"Steve, these are bad guys. Even by Wall Street standards, they stink. There's rumors of them being mobbed up, and they seem to have unusual connections in a lot of regulatory areas. My contacts at the SEC went dark when Griffen's name surfaced, other than to disclose he'd developed a reputation as a very savvy player. The NY attorney general won't comment except to point out that securities regulation is the province of the SEC. There's nothing in the FBI computers on him, although they had a jacket on his former partner. That was closed, but they're digging it out for me."

"I didn't even know he had a partner. Why was it closed?" Steven asked.

"That's standard operating procedure when the subject is deceased."

"Deceased? When did he die?"

"About three years ago. It was in the organized crime file section. It'll take a few days to pull it out of the archives."

"I really appreciate the input, Peter."

"I don't know the full scope of what these jokers are up to, but I can tell you that in my day at the Bureau this would have been more than enough to get a full-scale investigation going. But it doesn't look like anyone wants to know anything about it, which is just strange, is all I can say." Peter paused. "Be careful, Steve. I don't like the way this is shaping up, and if my gut's right this may be something you should walk away from. I hope you aren't doing anything to piss them off."

"It's a little late for that."

"Watch your back. I'll check in when I have something more solid."

Steven picked up Jennifer at her condo and they made their way down the coast to the boat; a 34 foot Catalina berthed in Dana Point. It was his one foolish indulgence, which he'd acquired the second year his company had been profitable. When he was working ten hour days, he needed some reminders of what he was slaving away for, and the boat had proved a powerful symbol of freedom and success. The upkeep on it was a small fortune, but there were some idiocies that one just had to participate in, no matter what the cost.

Once past the breakwater a moderate offshore breeze kept the summer doldrums from requiring the little engine be run, which made for a quiet and peaceful afternoon on the water. They both enjoyed the sensation of being pushed through the waves by the usually mellow wind and tried to get out as often as possible, which wasn't easy given their schedules. They tacked out a few miles, then up towards Newport before pointing the bow back south and heading for home.

After the cruise they enjoyed a wonderful dinner at Jennifer's favorite place in Laguna Beach, and rounded off the day by weaving tipsily back to Steven's house, replete and at peace with the world.

～⚶～

"Un-fucking-believable." Griffen was lost for any other words. That didn't happen often.

"I figured you'd want to see it firsthand," Glen said.

"I want this prick. I don't care what it takes. He's totally fucking with the wrong guy. Who does he think he is?"

"I didn't hear that. Any of it."

Griffen was sitting in the study of his expansive home, staring at the flat screen monitor on his ornately crafted desktop. There was his picture, from that very morning, hair askew, face puffy, windblown, disheveled. It wasn't the most flattering shot. Glen stood next to him as they considered the image, arms folded over his chest, the golfing hat and sunglasses on his sepulcher-like features creating the impression of an animatronic vision of death on holiday.

"This is way over the line. Fucking unbelievable. I spent half of yesterday, a Saturday for chrissakes, fielding calls from investors wanting to know if I'm in trouble on Allied. And now I have my fucking privacy blown apart by some anonymous shit-rat? How did he find out where I live? Is he trying to threaten me? Is he trying to say I can find you but you can't find me? I want this asshole." Griffen trembled with rage at this invasion into his life.

"Germany should have some feedback soon." Glen paused, reading the caption underneath the photo. He carefully considered his next words. "I think he's trying to be funny."

"I'm laughing inside. I want him."

"I'll show myself out," Glen said. "Enjoy your weekend."

Griffen listened to Glen's footsteps retreating and the sound of the front door closing.

He leaned back in his chair. From the doorway of the study the smell of jasmine floated into his space. A strikingly beautiful Eurasian girl, half

French, half Thai, about twenty years old, entered. She was slim and looked much taller than her five foot three frame suggested. She wore a red silk gentleman's smoking jacket and five-inch heels, and nothing else. He quickly closed the offending web window, pulled out a vial from his center drawer, dumping a little powder onto an antique mirror he kept in the same drawer. He drew it into his nostril in one powerful pull, using a jade tube with an elaborately carved dragon motif on its side. Viagra and cocaine cocktail.

"What's wrong, don't you want to spend any more time with me today? Isn't there something I can do to make you feel better? Let me help you relax…" She came around the desk, and lowered herself to her knees in front of him.

He slapped her. Hard. It was so sudden, so brutal, it took her completely by surprise. She looked up at him and winced through forming tears.

"I told you not to talk unless I tell you to. Now shut up and suck."

Late that night Griffen's phone rang. Groggily, he fumbled through the dark to reach it, stubbing a finger in the process and swearing as he lifted the handset to his ear.

"Hello?" he croaked into the receiver.

"Mr. Griffen? This is Gunther Peck, an associate of Mr. Vesper's in Germany. I hope I'm not calling too late, but Mr. Vesper indicated I was to call as soon as I had any information available. Do you have a pen? I have the name from the credit card used in the registration. There is no address information but a post office box, yes?"

"Just a second. Let me turn on the light and get this."

≈∽

In the hour after dawn, the grey Town Car made its way through the Washington suburb of Georgetown to a small coffee house that opened at 5 a.m.. It double-parked outside until a young man in a sweater vest and skater shorts exited the building and jumped in. Upon closer inspection the young man was in his thirties and looked less like a student than a yuppie who watched too much MTV.

He handed the driver a key-sized flash drive. "Here's the data we have so far. It would be most helpful if site creator was kept occupied – his interest shifted to other areas. We have reason to believe the site's an impediment, and he's beginning to have a negative impact with his activities. We'd appreciate if he was kept busy for the duration." The speaker was nondescript, calm, but with a note of steel to his voice.

"I'll see what we can do. This becomes complicated if it goes much further. We have to be careful of domestic operations. We can hassle him, but not much more. But I'm thinking if we do it right, we can tie him up for months." The driver never looked over at the passenger.

"Any help will be welcomed," said Emil. He shouldered the door open, stepped out onto the curb and was gone in seconds.

CHAPTER 9

Griffen sat in a small deli on the upper West Side, deep in discussion with a giant of a man squeezed into the booth across from him as Manhattan's Monday morning rush hour crawled past outside. The big man spoke in a hearty voice as he sipped his espresso from a cup that resembled a shot glass in his massive hand.

"Tell me what you need and I will see that it is taken care of. We've had a good working relationship, and I am very happy with your management of our assets." Sergei Rajeslsky spoke deliberately and could have been thanking Nicholas for buying lunch.

Griffen nodded. "I appreciate your understanding of my difficulty. I have some insight now into who's causing me the discomfort. It would be helpful if any solution was handled discreetly." Griffen watched Sergei's face for any reaction. As a successful import/export broker, his wealth qualified him as an important investor in Griffen Ventures, not to mention that as the head of the Red Mafiya in the U.S. he commanded significant unorthodox resources.

"I am always happy to solve a problem for a friend. Think no more about this. It will be attended to… is the correct word, expeditiously?" Sergei had a better command of the language than many English professors, but still liked to play the Russian bear on occasion. It was a habit that he'd developed to cause adversaries to underestimate him; not a mistake they typically got to make twice.

Griffen had some initial trepidation about approaching him, as there was always an inequity to the quid pro quo, but he needed the website issue to go away before it really got out of hand.

Who could have predicted the site would call the science into serious question, and also map out the links of some of his network of media cronies and investors? There really was no precedent for the website thing. He was definitely not accustomed to seeing most of his proprietary pump and dump strategy laid out in black and white.

That was too close for comfort.

Now he was taking financial hits, and if the price began tumbling...it could be terminal. If he started unloading shares to get out of his long position, the price would collapse and take his fund with him – there wouldn't be enough patsies to sell to, much less to go short and make money on the downswing. He really needed at least two more months or so of upward trajectory, then a couple of months to sell around the top and establish his short. The website was causing the bubble to lose air far too soon – it took a lot of time and trading volume to unwind as massive a stake as he'd accumulated. The timing right now couldn't have been worse.

He was already in enough financial trouble. Several other unlucky bets along with the Allied play had turned the $1 billion in his domestic and foreign funds he'd started the year with into about $800 million as of today, meaning he needed some short term volatility successes, as well as a short sale home run to get back to even before he had to do his year-end investor report. That left about six months to pull it out of the bag.

He needed this debunking site closed down yesterday, and the noise to fade so he could get on with business as he was used to conducting it. Griffen needed a level playing field with investors taking a skeptical view of Allied like he needed a hole in his head. Desperate times called for desperate measures, and Sergei was the court of final appeals.

Only he would be settling out of court...

Griffen sipped the dregs of his tepid coffee and looked up at Sergei. "I knew I could count on you."

Sergei smiled back. A cozy breakfast on a busy day in the big city. Neither one's eyes had a trace of friendliness residing in them. Bills would come due eventually, and the piper always had to be paid. Griffen didn't want to guess what this go-around would cost.

CHAPTER 10

Steven groaned as the alarm went off at 5:30 a.m.. He pawed at the clock to silence it and then reluctantly rolled out of bed, almost falling over Avalon, who'd decided to sleep at his bedside; uncharacteristic for him. Maybe he was feeling under the weather. They both padded downstairs into the kitchen, where Steven downed his coffee as Avalon munched his dog food; their usual preparation for the morning run.

They loped easily down the strand in tandem; two lone figures covering a lot of ground in a relatively short time, surprising the occasional gull with their approach as they made their way to the pier and back. The weather was ideal for it, and by the time they were rounding the home stretch Steven felt invigorated. When they returned to the house, Steven noticed his answering machine was blinking.

Strange. He didn't get a lot of calls, much less at six a.m.. He punched the play button and turned the volume up.

"Mr. Archer, this is Kevin at Lone Star Web Associates. Please call us ASAP; we have an issue. It's urgent." Steven replayed the message, grabbing a pencil to jot down the number. Satisfied he had gotten the digits correct, he deleted the message.

He dialed the number.

The same voice answered. "Lone Star, this is Kevin."

"Hi, Kevin, it's Steven Archer. I got your message. What's up?"

"Uh, Mr. Archer, we've never had anything like this happen before, but apparently the server was hacked sometime last night, and your website was corrupted. The files are unreadable." The voice sounded hesitant.

"That's not the end of the world, I've got it on my hard drive; I'll upload it in a few minutes."

Kevin cleared his throat. "That's not really what's disturbing to us. We have a pretty bulletproof firewall, and it's virtually impossible to breach it. In the past, attempts have been shut down within seconds. This was different. We're still going over the logs and trying to figure it out, but it appears that this was extremely sophisticated, unlike anything we've ever seen."

"What are you trying to say?"

"There's a chance some user data was compromised. We have you listed as Stanley Jorgenson and your payment listed via money order; but the servers clock the IP's coming in, and yours could conceivably have been logged on a site upload. I don't see how an intruder could have gotten to it, but it's a risk that's there nonetheless."

"I understand, Kevin. Thanks for the heads up. My IP is one of a group from my cable company, so anyone who wanted the IP identity would have to subpoena the user data to get anything. That would take months, according to my lawyer, and it wouldn't be a given. So I think we're good. I'll get online and reload the site this morning." He paused. "You don't have my phone number in the system, do you?"

"No, not in that section of the files, anyway. Your number is in a blank field in our contacts log files, with no associated site or name."

Well, that was something, anyway. Didn't seem much had been compromised.

"All right. I'll upload in the next few minutes," Steven advised.

"I'm really sorry about this. We've never had one of these breaches succeed. It's an anomaly, and we're contacting the firewall software manufacturer to see if they know how it could have happened."

"Keep me posted if you figure it out. I'll be online in five."

Well, he had to expect there'd be some sort of attempt to hack the site. It was always a calculated risk, hence all the precautions surrounding his identity. Still, it was unnerving to have the possible become the actual. But if they kept trying to hack it, he would just keep uploading it. Two could play that game.

Steven took the stairs three at a time, diving in and out of the shower in record speed, and pulling on a threadbare sweatshirt on the way to his desk downstairs. He logged onto his system, and began the morning ritual of opening the streamer windows – and then his system crashed.

He rebooted, and waited patiently for Windows to restart all the files. Halfway through the process, the system crashed again. An error message declared 'damaged sectors or files'. He'd been meaning to get a new computer for the last six months, and today of all days his hard disk had decided to give up the ghost. One more try, but no go. Damn.

Fortunately, he'd backed up his data to CD-ROM, so he grabbed his laptop from upstairs and hooked up the monitors and peripherals. He copied all the data to his hard disk, and then logged in and reloaded the site. The whole annoying process had taken almost an hour, and the market had been open for most of that time, so his next step was to load the quote systems and see what the damage was. Amazingly, they were down eight cents, on light volume. That was a relief.

Finished, he went back upstairs to check on Jennifer, who'd left a note for him when he was out running that she'd called in sick and was asleep. She'd started feeling out of it Sunday night and was pretty miserable by Monday morning.

He got her some water and gently woke her. No fever, just a little achy. She insisted she'd be fine and wanted to stay and just hang out and watch TV. No problem. Provided the market kept stable today, and he wanted to go out and run some errands anyway.

He checked on the stock one more time. Still up eighty-four cents, low volume. No fireworks. On the way out the door, the phone rang. Steven snagged it. "Hello."

Silence on the line.

"Helloooo…"

Faint clicking and more silence. He hung up. After a few moments, *ring ring…*

"Hello?" More clicking, line buzz.

Odd…still, with cell service you occasionally got dead spots where you could hear the other person but they couldn't hear you. It happened sometimes when the caller was driving. The wonders of a digital world. If it was important, they'd call back. They always did.

Steven hopped into his car, a convertible mid-eighties Porsche he'd owned for eons. It still ran like a charm, looked good, and was indestructible. The Germans definitely knew a thing or two about building a car, and his 911 was the proof. He dropped the top and pulled out of the garage, narrowly avoiding taking out a skateboarder who rolled behind him as he backed out. The kid glared at him like he was the biggest asshole on the planet. Have a nice day, and welcome to Newport Beach.

He buzzed up the peninsula, enjoying the sharp acceleration from the powerful, throaty engine, and dropped off his dry cleaning, hit the coffee shop, and stopped in at the grocery to pick up some odds and ends. Next up, he went by the tackle shop to collect a reel he'd left for maintenance. Of course it wasn't quite ready yet - a perennial problem with the tackle repair guys, but they assured him it would be in just a few minutes, which turned into forty five.

The whole exercise took half the day – mainly due to the summer beach traffic clogging the streets with the usual chaotic abandon. Throngs of bikini-clad nymphettes orbited PCH like satellites, checking out their male counterparts, who were displaying every variety of tattoo and piercing and nonchalant muscle-flexing conceivable. It was a state of barely-controlled pandemonium that occurred every summer; part of the price one paid for living in paradise.

Steven arrived back at the house to find Jennifer languishing in the living room, watching the parade of humanity go by on the boardwalk.

"How's the head?" he asked, moving the grocery bags into the kitchen.

"Getting better. I went back to sleep after you left, then the guys from the Gas Company woke me up, and I've been down here ever since." She sounded better, if a little groggy.

"What guys from the Gas Company?"

"They knocked on the door, needed to check the kitchen and garage with their sniffer. It was routine. They said they were doing all the houses around here today."

The hair on the back of his neck prickled. "What exactly did they do? Where did they go?"

"Why? I just told you, they sniffed around in the kitchen and the garage. What's wrong?"

"Were you with them both at all times? How long were they here?" He tried to sound light.

"Well, I let them in, and walked them back to the garage. One of them spent some time by the water heater looking around the pilot light, and the other one went into the kitchen and sniffed around the stove. Oh, and he went upstairs for a minute to check the heater in the attic. They said everything looked fine... What? Why are you looking at me like that?"

"So the one in the house was alone some of the time?"

"Well, now that you mention it, I guess he was for a minute or two. Steven, you're scaring me. Why are you asking all these questions? What's wrong?"

Steven sighed. "Probably nothing. It's just that the website was hacked last night, and my system crashed this morning, and I guess I'm a little rattled."

"You didn't say anything about any of that. They were very polite, had the little blue jumpsuits – I didn't even think twice about it."

"No worries. How long ago was that?"

"About forty-five minutes... Steven, should I be worried?"

"Nah. I'm just a little wound up right now. Damn...I'll be right back, I forgot something in the car."

He hurried into the garage and looked around. Everything seemed fine, nothing out of place. Still, his stomach had a knot in it, little butterflies singing the 'something's not quite right' song. He pushed the garage door opener and went out onto the street. Looked in both directions. No Gas Company trucks. Didn't mean anything, but didn't mean that everything was okay, either. He lowered the door and went back in.

"Did you find it?" Jennifer called from the couch.

"What? Oh, I just left the top down. I wanted to put it up so it wouldn't wrinkle. I'm going to go hit the head."

He ran upstairs, checked on his watches. None missing. He'd held onto a few high-end Rolexes and Pateks from his collecting days to wear occasionally on dressy occasions. The Gas Company ninjas had apparently passed them by.

Maybe he was just being paranoid.

He snagged the phone as he went into the bathroom. Dialed information.

"Newport Beach, the Gas Company." He selected the 'put me through automatically' option, before entering a call tree from hell. "If you'd like to be put on indefinite hold, press one. If you'd like to report your house blew up, press two." After a few symphonies of music-on-hold he got a real, live person, who grilled him for his account number, which he didn't know, then took him through the fifth degree to establish that he wasn't an identity thief. Once he was verified as genuine, he asked about testing at his address.

That led to another five minutes on hold because the customer service rep didn't know – such knowledge required a supervisor. When the supervisor came on the line Steven repeated his question, but the best she could do was take his details and commit to calling back with more information later – the crew schedules weren't accessible from the telephone service center. Steven gave her his information and hung up.

He returned downstairs and got on the computer. Allied had closed down almost a dollar, an unexpected and happy development. The message boards were relatively quiet. He logged onto his 'Group' forum and posted a greeting. A message immediately popped up.

[Dude, the site's awesome, but man, if I were that Griffen prick I'd be pissed – Pogo]

He bantered a bit, before telling the Group about his ISP getting hacked. One of the more heavyweight guys, who sometimes intimated a deeper knowledge of a broad range of topics, some not strictly legal, posted

[That's a pretty alarming breach on the firewall. I just pinged it and it's bulletproof at first glance. If they were able to not only breach but also access security areas, that's heavy talent. You better be careful. Gordo]

He spent some more time debating strategies to safeguard his privacy, but had been set on edge by Gordo's post and the open Gas Company issue, so he logged off sooner than he normally would have. He heard Jennifer in the kitchen and went to see how she was doing.

Jennifer was looking better, though she knew him well enough to know something was bugging him, and she called him on it. "What's your deal, Steven?" she asked him. "You're here, but you're not."

He considered telling her about the warning from the Group and his unease over the Gas Company visit, but thought better of it. Nothing had happened that warranted any concern other than a half-expected hacking attempt a thousand miles away – and he was dealing with that.

"I just have a lot going on at the moment. I'm gonna go upstairs and meditate; that should bring me back to earth." He looked out at the beach and cocked his head. "Honey, it's really beautiful out. Let's put the top down and run down to Corona Del Mar for dinner. Martinis are on me."

"Deal."

CHAPTER 11

Steven's meditation was troubled. Instead of a sense of descending to progressively lower and lower levels of awareness, or rather of increasing the level of tranquility and peacefulness at each stage, it was punctuated by random leaping thoughts and a vague sense of unease.

It was far from relaxing. When he came to full awareness, he remained distinctly anxious. He'd come to trust his instincts, and they were insisting that something disturbing was on the horizon – and drawing ever closer.

Jennifer went upstairs when he came down. He'd changed into a linen shirt and loose linen trousers with a pair of huaraches, sort of the dressed-down version of white guy on vacation. He filled Avalon's water bowl, cleared the remaining items off the counter – and vowed to stay away from the computer. While he was waiting for Jennifer to freshen up and return, the phone rang. He picked up.

"Mr. Archer?"

"Yes."

"It's Monica Sweeney at the Gas Company. Sorry to take so long to get back to you."

"No problem. Any news?"

"I'm still checking, but I haven't noticed any activity in your area for today. It's quite possible a crew was there, but I don't see it on my printouts. We aren't perfect, though, so this isn't the last word..."

"Well, that's not very reassuring," he said, "considering there were two guys in my house earlier claiming to be your employees."

"Did they show ID when they arrived?"

"You kn...I...I don't know, I wasn't here. My girlfriend was."

"Always ask to see identification before admitting anyone into your house."

"Thanks, I'll remember that," Steven said patiently.

"And like I said, there could be a crew out there, it's just not on my system. Sorry I can't be more help."

"Well, thanks for checking."

"You're welcome. Have a nice evening, and thank you for calling the Gas Company."

Well, that hadn't left him any the wiser, but given nothing had been touched, though, the best bet was the obvious; it was a routine check, and he was just a teensy bit on edge from the drama surrounding the website and the message boards.

His ruminations were pleasantly interrupted by Jennifer's descent down the stairs. She was stunning, wearing a simple white summer dress that accentuated her deeply tanned skin and mane of blonde hair; the scent of tropical flowers and coconut accompanied her into the room.

"Wow. Someone could get lucky tonight if she wanted. You fully recovered?"

Jennifer smiled. "Better by the minute. What does a girl have to do to get a decent Cosmopolitan in this town?"

"Hop into the beach-mobile. Your chariot awaits." He grabbed his keys and cell phone, and escorted her to the garage, opening her door for her and holding it as she got into the Porsche. The engine turned over with a meaty roar, the top went smoothly down, and soon they were cruising down Pacific Coast Highway with the warm summer breeze in their hair.

Monday night at the restaurant was relatively quiet, and in spite of the popularity of the area at that time of year there wasn't much of a crowd. Jennifer ordered her Cosmo, and he a Malbec. They were seated in a booth overlooking the kitchen, and enjoyed watching the crew frantically turning out the orders and preparing the food, rushing about in a controlled and well-choreographed pandemonium. They made small talk – she complaining about her job, he about property taxes being raised on the boat. They deliberately stayed away from any discussion of Allied. Jennifer had made it clear she didn't enjoy that topic, and at this point, Steven sort of agreed with Jennifer that Allied had gotten enough of his attention for a while.

It was a pleasant enough dinner, although a tension played between them that was only somewhat eased by the alcohol. That had been a recurring theme for the last few weeks, but Steven didn't know what to do about it. She'd just turn distant on him, with no explanation.

Their relationship worked because they both wanted the same things, or at least they had until recently, since Jennifer's younger sister gave birth to a daughter. Ever since, Jennifer had been probing his sentiment about families and marriage, but that wasn't on his radar at the moment. The nesting noises kept coming up, and he knew he needed to discuss things with her, but it was bad timing right now, what with all his focus being on the market and the site. He just wanted to get past this period and have a more normalized life, and then he'd be in a better position to consider things with her. He figured they'd work things out with time. Just not right now.

The beach traffic was dying down as they returned to the house, and the frantic throngs of revelers along the sidewalks had dispersed, leaving the area temporarily tranquil. Steven pulled into the garage and shut off the engine, returning the top to its closed position. He kissed Jennifer softly, but she pulled away from his embrace. The romance had evidently been put on hold for the evening. Such was life – he'd long ago given up on trying to predict feminine behavior. They entered the house, she following him, and she almost ran headfirst into his shoulder blades.

He'd stopped abruptly in the hallway leading into the living room.

"Steven, what the hell are you..." and then she saw what had frozen him in his tracks.

He turned, his hand over her mouth, and whispered in her ear. "Back out to the car. Now."

They moved quickly back into the garage, and he raised the door and started the engine. He pulled out, so he could see his front door and garage while parked diagonally, and dialed 911. Jennifer opened the car door and quietly vomited her dinner into the street, then sat sobbing quietly beside him.

"Newport Beach Police, Emergency," the voice on the line declared.

"I need police at 811 Boardwalk on the Peninsula immediately. My name is Steven Archer, I live there, and I'm reporting a break-in and a killing." Steven's voice was steady, with only the slightest quaver to it.

"Sir, I'm dispatching two cars at once. What is your location and telephone number, and can you please describe what's happened? You're being recorded."

"I'm parked outside the house in a blue Porsche. I don't know if the intruders are still inside, or whether they're armed or not, but I do know they've killed my dog and left him in the middle of the living room. I'll stay on the line until someone gets here." He choked down some rising bile, caught his breath. "You should hurry."

CHAPTER 12

The crime scene van arrived twenty minutes after the first squad car. According to the police, there was no sign of a forced entry; and the house appeared undisturbed, other than the butchered corpse of Avalon lying in a rust-colored pool of blood on the living room carpet and the heavy metallic smell of expended bodily fluids sullying the air.

Avalon's head had been severed and placed on the small coffee table in the living room, positioned so it would appear to be waiting for and watching anyone entering from the garage. The effect was chilling, and the cruelty and sickness of it resonated in the room even after the technicians had removed the remains.

The police were sympathetic to the situation, but given that the alarm hadn't been activated and nothing had been stolen, the actual teeth for a serious investigation weren't there. Everyone was horrified by the viciousness of the crime, but at the end of the day it was a B&E and cruelty to animals charge – not exactly murder one.

Jennifer was deeply shaken, and after the police took her statement she adjourned upstairs and left them to Steven.

"Do you have any idea who might have done this? An angry ex or disgruntled employee? Has anyone threatened you?" Sergeant Matthews was courteous and efficient, but clearly not the sharpest.

"No. It's the first time anything like this has ever happened to me. I don't know anyone who would do something like this." Steven considered telling him about the website, but decided against it. What would the theory be? Steven wanted to point the finger at Griffen, but even in *his* head it sounded pretty stupid that a multi-millionaire Wall Street icon would be butchering pets at a beach rental as retribution for speculating that one of his companies was junk. That, and he didn't want to go on record as being the creator of the site. What would be the point of going down that road?

He did mention the Gas Company visit, and the sergeant noted it, however, even as he uttered the words he realized how idiotic his concerns sounded.

"Okay then," the sergeant ventured. "You mentioned you had a software company, correct? Did you ever do anything business-wise that might have come back to haunt you?"

Getting colder, colder.

"No. I just don't understand why anyone would do this," Steven said. "I mean, what kind of sadistic rat fuck would cut a dog's head off? And such a good dog, not a mean-spirited bone in his body."

"I know, it's a weird one, but it's not the first weird one around here during the season. Look, there are a lot of oddballs in town, street people, crazies, kids high on all kinds of wild shit. Summer brings them out of the woodwork. It's possible one of them got in somehow, or that it was some kind of really fucked-up skinhead initiation, or a dare or something." Poor Sergeant Matthews, eyes glazing over even as he said it.

Steven was becoming annoyed with all the holes in the idiotic theory the cop was trying to force the situation into fitting. "There's no sign of a struggle, and no blood anywhere but where he was hacked up."

"Good points." The officer walked towards the door, Steven following. "Let me offer some advice. Change your locks, set your alarm, and be watchful for any odd characters loitering around. The majority of destructive or vandalism crimes don't make a lot of sense, and most of the time we get nothing like all the facts. This one is probably no exception. It's one of the frustrations we all have when something bad happens. There are no resources to do a full-scale multi-day investigation on something like this. I know that isn't comforting, but this week we'll probably have fifty vandalisms, double that many DUIs, a whole busload of B&Es, fights, assaults, two or three rape charges per night, stabbings, hit-and-runs…you get the picture."

Put like that, Newport Beach sounded like Beirut.

"Officer, I understand what you're saying, but–"

"It's Sergeant, Mr. Archer. Here's my card. We've dusted the entryways for prints, we've checked for signs of forced entry, we've shot the crime scene, we've talked to your neighbors. There isn't a lot more we can do. Most of the time these things are either someone you know, or a crazy. You don't know anyone who would do this, so that leaves crazy. If anything comes up or you see anything suspicious, or if something occurs to you you've left out, then call me."

Time to get out and handle real crime. Dog butchering vs. drunken bar fight. Tough call.

Steven could appreciate this was going nowhere fast. It's not like they could call in satellite footage of the area and isolate who entered between the hours of six and eight-thirty.

"He was such a gentle dog. You should have seen him. A teddy bear." Steven was choking up. God damn whoever did this.

"Call Doug at 24/7 Locks in Costa Mesa. He's in the book. He'll fix you up and won't charge an arm and a leg. Try to get some sleep." He took a few steps towards the door. "I have a chocolate lab. I'd want to kill the son of a bitch if it happened to me. It's not that I don't care, it's just I can't do anything. I'm really sorry. Honest to God." He seemed sincere, and Steven recognized he was right. There was nothing more to be done.

"Thanks for spending the time, Sergeant. I'll call if anything else comes up."

"I'll have a car drive by every hour or so tonight just to keep an eye out. It's a little slow – you're lucky it isn't Saturday night."

᷾᷾᷾

Peter was having a hell of a time figuring out why most of the Griffen data was inaccessible to him. He'd been doing the PI thing long enough and knew enough people on the inside of various law enforcement agencies to usually get all the info he needed within a few hours. Not this time. He was running into a lot of brick walls. And that set off his alarms.

This smelled different, and dangerous. He kept hitting roadblocks, dead ends, sanitized reports, stonewalling. He'd never encountered anything like it before, outside of the top-secret, clandestine world of international espionage. But this was a money manager, not the undercover station chief in Uzbekistan, so why all the subterfuge?

Peter was developing a nagging sense of something far larger than what appeared on the surface. An iceberg of shady dealings, of carefully crafted secrecy, of influence and access far beyond what he'd expected. And that worried him. Why had Steven taken on something this dangerous? Why invite a street fight with unknown adversaries? Who needed this kind of grief?

But that was Steven for you. Ever since a boy, he'd been stubborn as a mule. Peter could still remember times when they'd butted heads, Steve no more than twelve or so, with that look of determination in his fierce little eyes; a look that said, 'Talk all you want, I'm still going to do it my way'. That had been one of the primary reasons he'd steered Steven into martial arts. The combination of discipline and physical demand was perfect for his temperament and offered positive ways to channel and develop his energy. If he didn't figure out a way to get it under rein, that quality could easily have gone down a more destructive path. Steven liked to play by his own rules, and that could turn criminal if he wasn't guided correctly.

Peter got up and walked over to the coffee maker, pouring another cup into the oversized mug that was his perpetual companion when he was working. His eyes absently roved over the plaques, the awards lining the walls of his study, a tribute to his skill and professional dedication. He'd been good at his job, and responsible for a lot of twisted examples of humanity getting locked up. He paced a little, then slid back into the worn high-back chair that had been one of his few luxuries when he set up his home office.

Peter had always wanted a son, but fickle chromosomes had conspired against him. That had been a regret for years, but he'd mellowed with time and eventually made peace with his lot in life. He was successful at a career he enjoyed, with enough money to do anything he felt like, within reason. He had a wonderful marriage, their union blessed with two beautiful daughters, now long out of the house and through college, making their own ways in the world. There were no complaints.

Steven represented the son he would have wanted and Peter reveled in his every success. Over the years he'd developed from a gangly, slightly rebellious kid into a strong, confident alpha male, capable of anything he set his mind to. He couldn't have been prouder, although he'd never said the words out loud to Steven. He didn't have to. They knew each other too well.

So it wasn't a comforting thought that Steven's conflict had put him at odds with a group that all preliminary signals flagged as dangerous. Peter knew Steven would never back down, and further, that he hated crooks. He'd gotten into trouble in school a few times for confronting bullies, always defending less capable classmates; it was in his hardwiring. This had all the elements that would make for a cage fight for Steven. Powerful interests screwing little guys, abusing the system, breaking the rules.

He needed to quickly get to the bottom of whatever was going on, so he could understand the malevolence he was sensing, and persuade Steven to stand down if this was an un-winnable battle. Peter had been around long enough to understand life wasn't fair, and it didn't surprise him that bad guys did bad things all the time and got away with it. He was all for moral outrage, but it was foolish to take on an enemy who had you outgunned.

He hoped against hope that wasn't the case here. It seemed like Steven was already in deep water, and as smart and resourceful as he was, he wasn't bulletproof.

Peter leaned back in his chair, stared at his computer screen, then made a few notes on the ever-present yellow legal pad on his desk. Old habits died hard, and he'd never gotten used to substituting his pads for a computer file; he did his best work writing longhand. There was something cathartic about the flow of ink upon paper. And you couldn't doodle on a word document...

He jotted down several names and numbers and picked up the phone. Time was wasting. It was late, but he knew a lot of home numbers and had collected a lot of favors over the years. He hammered out the first set of digits – and resigned himself to a late one.

❧❧

The house took on a hanging emptiness once the police left. Steven called the locksmith the cop had recommended, to be told that two hundred dollars would get the locks changed. Jennifer came down the stairs and perched uneasily on the couch furthest away from the blanket covering the bloodstain.

"I know how much you loved him. I loved him, too." She had tears streaming down her face; her body language turned inwards, defensive, borderline shock setting in.

"He was such a good dog." Steven choked up, he didn't know what else to say.

"Why? Why would anyone do this?" she asked.

Steven debated telling her about his concerns, then thought better of it. There was no evidence the break-in was anything but a nutcase on a meth binge. He had his doubts, but after the last few hours tonight wasn't the time to start the sharing-fest.

"It doesn't make any sense, honey. Listen, I called a locksmith, he'll be here in a few minutes. I'm going to get the locks changed and set the alarm." She needed to see he was doing something to safeguard them. Against what or whom…well, that was a more difficult question. "The cop felt this was some crazy, or a drug-induced crank gone wrong. I don't know what to think." He looked over at the blanket.

She narrowed her eyes at him. "I'm not stupid, and I know you well enough to know you're worried. You were agitated over the Gas Company visit, and now this happens. Have you done anything that would make you a target? Could it be something to do with your website?"

Jennifer was smart, and sensed his unease. He didn't know what to tell her. It all sounded so far-fetched, and he'd been so painstaking…

"I've been extremely careful. Am I concerned? Yes. Do I think it's really possible? No. These guys aren't psychic. The site's tied to a dummy e-mail account using a phony name. I use an alias on the boards. No one knows who I am. If they're looking for somebody, they're looking for some guy named Stanley living in New Orleans and working in a bar. I don't want to get all paranoid and see boogie-men everywhere. There's no chance at all they could trace me." It was all true, but it sounded hollow to him.

"I don't know, Steven. I hear you, but I have to tell you I never liked what you were doing – it just seems like you're asking for trouble. I hope you're right."

"Jen, I appreciate the sentiment, but tonight's really not the night. We've both been through a lot, I'm beat, and nothing I say's going to make any of this better. So can we just agree you don't like me doing the site, and leave it at that for now?" It came out sounding terse, which isn't how Steven intended it, but it was too late.

She pouted. "Sure. You know best, right? I'm going to go to bed, Steven. I agree we've both been through a lot, and this conversation isn't helping."

"Jen…" Too late. She was already on her way up the stairs, fear easily replaced by anger. He should have expected it, but what was done was done. He'd deal with it tomorrow.

Doug showed up a few minutes later, and true to his word, had the locks changed in twenty minutes flat, and was gone in twenty-five. Once he'd departed and the house was at least superficially safe again, Steven took the time to log on and check his e-mail. A quick scan showed eighteen messages; most of them suggestions from the Group for additional security, mirroring, etc. for the site. He realized as he read he was fading in and out; exhausted, but still jittery from adrenaline.

When he got up to the bedroom, Jennifer was asleep, out cold. He envied her. Steven went back downstairs and set the alarm, checked all the locks again, and finally gave in and took a sleeping pill. It did little good. Eventually he drifted into an uneasy slumber. Bad things were happening was the last thought he had before he went under.

CHAPTER 13

The next day was surrealistic for Steven, in no small part due to the residual effects of the pill. He felt like someone had thrown a wet blanket on his senses. He barely made it through his morning run, as much from a lack of will as from exhaustion; this was the first time he'd ever done it without Avalon by his side. He found himself choking up with emotion as he passed places where he and Avalon had paused while Steven ritualistically tightened his shoelaces, and several times he had to wipe away tears. The whole episode seemed like a bad dream, and a part of him kept hoping he would wake up at any moment, and Avalon would be lying in the floor, gazing at him expectantly. It seemed impossible that his constant companion of years was suddenly and permanently gone forever. And yet he was.

Back at the house, Steven halfheartedly checked in on the stock and the boards; volume was low, and there was little action today. He put off dealing with the cleanup issues presented by Avalon's untimely demise, unwilling to confront the gory reminder of that reality, and instead went upstairs to wake Jennifer. He stood over her in the soft morning light and watched as she slept, her face untroubled and looking all of eighteen years old. She really had been put through the wringer in the last twelve hours. He debated letting her sleep, but then remembered she had a job and couldn't just fan all her obligations due to a late night.

Steven slipped into bed next to her, kissed her.

She jerked awake, opened one eye and peered at him. "God, Steven, you scared me. What time is it?"

"About 7:45."

"I'm going to call in sick again and help you deal with the house. I feel like shit. How about you?" She opened both eyes and appraised him.

"I've had better days. The run was hard. You don't have to stay home, you know. I can deal with things."

"I'll be useless today in an office. Let me catch another hour or so, and I'll be up and around. Try not to piss anyone off while I'm asleep." She apparently wasn't going to let up on him.

"All right. I'm gonna go get some bagels." He pulled on a baseball cap and grabbed his sunglasses off the dresser. As he made his way down the stairs, he was again confronted by the area still covered by the blanket. Sickened, he grabbed his keys, wallet and cell phone and climbed into the car.

Steven considered the events of the previous day as he drove. The break-in was hugely disturbing, the hacking only mildly troubling, the Gas Company visit ultimately noise. He thought about taking the website down, but rebelled at the thought. He'd be damned if he'd intimidate himself by jumping to conclusions and throw in the towel when he'd just started; Steven had absolutely zero logical reason in the cold light of day to believe Avalon's murder was related. It would serve no purpose to get overly suspicious and assume everything that happened was caused by Griffen's invisible hand.

Even if he was inclined to take it down, which he wasn't, would that change anything? Griffen's problem was that the information was now out there. That damage was done. You couldn't stuff the toothpaste back into the tube.

And there was the ultimate issue, namely that Steven was plain old stubborn. He had a strong sense of right and wrong, and didn't like being controlled or told what to do by anyone.

He'd started his own company for the same reason. Building his business before successfully selling it reinforced his conviction in his own abilities. Losing money by depending on others taught him to only depend on himself. Self-sufficient and confident by nature, backing down wasn't in his makeup.

He pulled up to the bagel place and got a couple of still-hot cinnamon raisins, and then stopped to fuel up. That sucked the last of his cash, so he hit the ATM at his bank to pull out a few hundred bucks. He inserted his card, punched in the PIN, and after a few seconds a screen he'd never seen before flashed at him: Access Denied. That was weird.

His card ejected, so he re-inserted it and re-entered the PIN, figuring he must have flubbed it the first go around. Access Denied. The bank was just opening, so he went in, the only customer, and approached the teller. Her nametag said Linda, and she looked sleepier than a narcoleptic. He explained what had happened and handed her his ATM card, asking if she'd look into the problem and help him withdraw $300.

"Sure, mister, uh, Archer. Let me swipe the card and I'll see what's going on."

Nice girl, helpful. So far, so good.

"Uh, that's strange. Let me go to another screen." She typed in more data. Punched at things. Clicked things. Swiped the card again. "Uh, just a second. I, uh, need to get a manager."

Great. Where had he heard this before?

A few minutes went by. A rather rotund woman approached him while his original teller hovered in the background.

"Mr. Archer, I'm sorry for the confusion. I'm afraid we can't help you with any withdrawals at this time." She stared at him. He stared back. Her porcine face was shiny with perspiration, no doubt caused by the effort of moving across the floor to meet him.

"Come again?"

"I'm afraid we can't help you with any withdrawals today."

"I don't understand. I have over a hundred fifty thousand in my account. I want three hundred dollars. What's to help?" He felt his anger rising, but also the anxiety was creeping into his stomach again.

"Sir, we value your patronage, but at this time we are unable to allow any withdrawals from your account. Perhaps you should speak with Ted, the manager?"

Like a robot. A fleshy, sweating robot.

"You have my money," Steven began, arms now folded, "which I gave to you for safekeeping, and now you're telling me, the owner of the money, that I can't have it? Am I hearing this correctly?" His blood pressure rose, bit by bit. "You're damned right I want to talk to Ted. He was more than happy to help me when I was opening accounts and referring friends." Enough of this horseshit. Time to get into someone's face who would do something about the situation.

"One moment, please." She departed to the rear office area, returning a minute later.

"Ted will see you now."

Great, sounded like a doctor's visit. He'd see me now. You bet your ass he'd see me now. They proceeded to Ted's hallowed office.

"Steven, I'm so sorry for this. Sit down. I don't know what's going on, but I'll get to the bottom of it." Ted exuded bankish conviviality. "Let's see now, here's the account, blanket hold placed, see file notation A(6), hmmmmmmm, A(6), A(6)…oh…hmmmmm…I see…" Ted looked decidedly paler than he had two minutes earlier. He was also uneasily avoiding Steven's gaze.

"So what's the problem?"

"Steven, I can't really say anything due to banking regulations, but because you're such a high value customer, let me ask; are you in any kind of dispute with, say, the IRS?" Ted inquired. "Maybe being investigated for something, no doubt all a big mix-up?"

"I have absolutely no idea what you're talking about. I called the cops because my dog was killed last night, but that's it. What's going on? What are you trying to tell me?" Now the blossom of anxiety was turning into a full-fledged incipient panic attack. Breathe in, breathe out. Breathe in…

Ted pinched the bridge of his nose. "I'm so sorry to hear about your dog. No, according to my screen, your account has been frozen by a law enforcement agency. I can't go into more detail. Shouldn't have even said that. Didn't…if you take my meaning." Ted was not having a good start to his day. That made two of them.

"That's impossible. It's a mistake." What the hell was going on here?

"It's not the bank. It's actually out of our hands. I'd suggest if you have an attorney, you get in contact and have him talk to our headquarters to see about clearing this up. I'm really sorry we can't do more." Ted was ready to conclude the meeting.

Steven walked out of the branch in the fog of a daze. Account frozen? A hundred and fifty grand inaccessible? He looked in his wallet. Three one-dollar bills. Fucking just great. The bagel had completely lost its appeal now. His mouth tasted like tin.

He got into his car and called Stan Caldwell, his attorney and asset protection specialist…and also his very good friend. Stan listened intently to his story, then suggested they get together in half an hour in San Clemente. Stan made his living in part by being ultra-paranoid about privacy concerns and didn't like cell phones.

Steven was in turmoil as he drove down PCH. Why would his account be frozen by a government agency? Didn't the IRS have to file something, some sort of notice, if that was it? Besides, he didn't owe anything, wasn't being audited. Could it be identity theft? That had been a big topic with the Group a few months back. Could someone have used his ID to do something illegal, forcing him to jump through hoops to clear it up? What a pain in the ass.

At least he had a full tank.

Cash wasn't an immediate concern, as he still had about seven thousand dollars left from what he'd won in Vegas at the last bachelor party. But not having access to a little over a hundred and fifty Gs was an issue, that was for sure. He wondered if they'd also frozen his credit cards. And who *they* were. And why. Which brought him right back to the beginning again...

Stan Caldwell was a very smart man. Quiet. Looked nothing like an attorney, more like a successful real estate developer. Heavyset, usually smiling, relaxed, did a lot of listening and spoke rarely. He had many high net worth clients for whom he'd structured asset protection solutions. Discretion was his mantra. His specialty was creating transactions for company sales so they wound up being tax-free events, which is how Steven and he had met. They'd been friends ever since.

Steven told him about the account, and he jotted down the information, asking a question now and then. Stan assured him he would get to the bottom of it quickly. Steven then told him about the events of the last thirty-six hours or so; Avalon, the ISP, Griffen, the website. Again, Stan asked pointed questions, clarifying a point here, requesting more information there.

Stan quickly decided that Steven was playing with very hot water, and cautioned him that not all factions of society played nice.

"Steven, if you hit a snake on the head over and over, eventually it *will* try to bite you. Law of the jungle. Seems to me you've made a hobby out of hitting this particular snake pretty hard, and pretty regularly."

"Griffen's a liar and a thief, and he's robbing little old ladies. All I did was create a website and shine a light on his latest scam. There's nothing illegal about creating websites, last time I checked – besides which, it's too late; the damage is done." Steven didn't need any more statements of the obvious.

Stan framed his fingers together and looked through them at Steven.

"A colleague of mine used to go on safari, in Africa, years ago. He had a saying: If you're going to go elephant hunting, bring an elephant gun and be willing to use it. Otherwise you have no business elephant hunting. Steven, my point is you've been elephant hunting. If you have even half of this right, he's been doing this for years, successfully, and is well connected. Your current situation may or may not have anything to do with him, but it isn't lost on me you've had a lot of strange things happen since you started with this..."

"Stan, I'm not saying you're wrong, or that I wouldn't change anything if I could. But I can't. So what do I do?"

Stan considered the question for a long time. "I'm not sure you have the means to get a gun big enough to bring this particular beast down. Let me think on this. I'll take care of the bank first thing." They shook hands and agreed to talk soon. Stan looked at Steven again.

"At least your life's not boring, I'll give you that. And sorry about Avalon. I liked him."

As Steven pulled onto the freeway to return home, his phone rang. He looked at the caller ID and saw it was Jennifer. He picked up.

"Hi there. All rested?" Steven asked.

"Where are you?" Alarm...no, make that borderline panic in her voice.

"What's going on? What's wrong?"

"You need to come home now. I don't think I can deal with this anymore, Steven."

"Deal with what? I'm twenty minutes away. Tell me what happened." He hated when people said things like 'there's a problem' and then refused to elaborate. This was very unlike Jennifer.

"When you get here. I have to go." She hung up. Christ, she'd hung up on him. She'd never hung up on him. He stepped on it. He figured he could be there in fifteen minutes if he worked it.

He made it in twelve.

He rushed through the door from the garage and found Jennifer sitting in the living room. The blanket was gone, but a dark stain remained on the beige carpet. Her arms were crossed as she gripped her shoulders. She looked scared. He'd never seen her like this before.

"What's going on, honey?" He approached her, but she pulled away.

"Two men came to the front door this morning, at around ten-thirty. They wanted to speak to you. I told them I didn't know where you were, which was the truth – you were just supposed to go get bagels. You were supposed to be here with me..." She started sobbing.

"Oh, Jennifer, I'm sorry. I had some emergencies come up I had to deal with." He tried to hug her, but she pulled away. Shock? "I picked up the bagels, then stopped to get some cash from the ATM. Turns out my account is frozen; some law enforcement agency froze it, no explanation. So who were the men?" Steven asked.

"They were from Homeland Security, and yes, I made them show me their badges," Jennifer sobbed. "They wouldn't discuss why they needed to talk to you. They just asked a bunch of questions." She was still crying, scared, and angry. He should have been there. She'd been dealing with the mess, cleaning up dog blood, and now this.

Whatever *this* was.

Homeland Security? Wasn't that the terrorist people?

"Honey, I have no idea what this is about. I swear," Steven protested. At least that much was true.

"They wanted to know where you were, when you were coming back, if you had an office around here. I told them you were out, maybe for the whole day." She was staring at him.

"I haven't done anything wrong. This is crazy," Steven exclaimed.

"They wanted to come in, and I told them no, someone had broken in and killed your dog last night, and you didn't want anyone in the house without you being here. They didn't seem to know about that. One of them left a card and asked you to call as soon as you could. It's on the counter." Jennifer pointed at the kitchen.

"I don't get it." *What was happening here?*

"Don't you? DON'T YOU?" Jennifer finally lost it, screaming at him now. "Steven, your dog's dead, they've frozen your money, and now they're coming for you." She beat upon his chest with her fists. "What don't you get? Your little game with the goddamn stock has turned into a nightmare and you've endangered everything we've got, everything we had. Avalon's dead and they're after you. WHAT...DON'T...YOU...GET?" She'd expended her energy, and he held her shaking wrists as she collapsed back onto the sofa.

She looked up at him. Composing herself a little. Then suddenly calm. "You thought you were so damned smart, and now Homeland Security's at your door. This isn't a game, Steven. It's real life. Real consequences. You lost Avalon, for real. You could lose everything."

Jennifer looked away, then back at him, directly at him, with an intensity born of betrayal and anger. "And you've lost me, Steven. I didn't sign up for any of this."

So there it was. He was to blame for everything, and she wanted no part of it.

And she was right.

"Jennifer, I haven't done anything wrong. Don't you see? There's no law against creating a website. This is lunacy. There's gotta be some other explanation." Even to him, that sounded empty. Lame even. The only new variable in his life the last few days was the website. They must have tracked him, even though he'd been extremely thorough; or so he'd thought. And they wanted him off the air enough to pull out all the stops.

"Well, you're going to have to figure it out without me around, Steven. I love you, but I didn't agree to risk everything for some stupid stock, and this isn't the life I want. Maybe I'll feel differently later, but right now, you're living in some kind of nightmare, and I'm scared, and I want out."

She was beautiful even as she hated him.

"You're not the man I met. You spend more time on that stupid computer than you do with me, and now it's gotten you into big-time trouble." Her voice cracked raw, hoarse from the strain and emotion. "I don't want this life. I want our old life back. But it's gone, and it's all because of you and that fucking company. I can't take this, Steven; I don't want to be involved in whatever you've exposed us to. It isn't fair."

She'd pretty much nailed it. He'd impacted her right to happiness by taking poorly calculated risks without accurately understanding how much was being put on the line. And now he was in crisis mode, and Steven in crisis mode wasn't a good partner or mate. She wanted security, stability, not chaos and danger and change. Hard to argue that.

He'd sensed a confrontation coming for a while, the dissatisfaction building, the resentment over his time involvement in the market becoming a simmering issue. Just as with the kids and family thing, he'd hoped to deal with it at some vague point in the future, hoping it could wait. But it hadn't, and the last two days had tipped the already teetering balance.

"Maybe we should take a break while I figure this out," was the best he could manage. It sounded shallow, but the reality was he had bigger problems right now. Internally he was churning, trying to figure out the next step, and Jennifer's dissatisfactions weren't at the top of the list – even if they were justifiable.

Her being right wouldn't fix things, and he needed to focus on fixing this quick-smart.

"Yeah, Steven, you do that…figure it all out." She got up and stalked across the room, kicking the rag she'd been using to scrub the rug as she went. She stomped upstairs and he heard drawers closing, closets being slammed.

She flounced back down a few minutes later with two suitcases and her purse.

"I hope you come out of this okay," she conceded as she opened the door.

He went over and kissed her lightly on the cheek, and held her tightly for what seemed like could be the last time. Tears welled dangerously in her eyes, but she looked resolved.

"Take care of yourself," she said.

And then she was gone.

CHAPTER 14

Steven felt disoriented. The day's events had already overloaded his system, and it was only mid-afternoon. He had to take some time and calm down, to think. Everything seemed like it was coming apart at once, and it took every ounce of control he had to keep from panicking. He went into the kitchen and picked up the Homeland Security card, looked at it, put it into his pocket. He absently stared at the stain on the carpeting – the lingering evidence of the reality of Avalon's death, and realized he was spacing out. Snap out of it and think, a voice in his head commanded. Focus. He couldn't help himself if he zoned out. He needed a plan of action.

He sat down at the computer that had gotten him into all the current trouble and logged into his Group. Described the morning's events.

A few minutes later a post popped up from one of the gang:

[Consider your physical location and your lodging compromised. Stow all your CCs, don't use them. Use only cash. Leave now with any high value items that can be converted into $. Pull your hard drive, take the CPU and discard elsewhere, take laptop and any CDs. Create a new Hotmail account from a remote location, use alias for info, log on here and give us the address. I'll set up a new private chat room. Leave soonest, time probably critical. G-luck. Spyder]

Wow. The lads were taking this seriously. Then another post came up:

[Do it. Now. Gordo]

He'd been involved with them long enough to recognize when they were right. He also realized he hadn't been thinking clearly, had already spent too much time as a sitting duck. He powered down, disconnected the computer and took it out to the car. Back inside, he grabbed the laptop and his CD-ROMs, then went upstairs and packed a small duffel with a few days' clothes, the seven grand in hundred dollar bills from Vegas, and his three most valuable watches; a yellow gold Patek Philippe 3970, a platinum Patek 3940, and a platinum men's Rolex President. Everything fit in the bag, along with some socks and underwear, and a rudimentary shaving kit. He looked at his watch. Seven minutes since he'd disconnected.

He stuffed his gear into the front seat of the car, started the engine and raised the garage door. No black helicopters circling. He backed out, again nearly taking out the same skateboarder who offered the same *watch what you're doing, asshole* look, then pulled down the street.

So far, nothing suspicious.

No sedans with men on headsets, no sirens, no SWAT truck.

He realized he had no idea where he was going or what he should really do next. He called Stan, but got his voice-mail.

"Stan, it's Steven, there's been a situation at the house. Some gentlemen had been by looking for me, gentlemen I think you'd be better at talking to. I'm on my cell. Please call as soon as you get this." That started the ball rolling on the lawyer front. There was little Stan couldn't deal with. Short of being caught with a body in the trunk, Stan would know how to respond.

He drove around for a while, paying special attention to ensure he wasn't being followed. As far as he could tell, he had no tail. He ran a couple of yellow lights at the last possible second, confirmed no one made it through after him, and then gunned it around a series of corners into the back bay side streets. From there he made his way to a frontage road, and then onto the freeway and out to Irvine.

He didn't want to be anywhere near Newport Beach until he knew what the hell was going on. Irvine was big enough so he'd be invisible for the time being. He felt a little sheepish, wondering if he was over-reacting, but then considered the Group's response. They weren't hotheads or alarmists yet they seemed pretty agitated by the day's events. Best to trust that collective judgment, especially when he was in uncharted territory.

Once he'd gotten into the heart of the town he pulled off the freeway and spotted an office supply superstore that featured web access. He parked in the back and threw his computer into a dumpster. In the superstore he rented twenty dollars of computer time from a spike-haired kid with an attitude and halitosis. Steven was the only one in the computer section.

He logged on. Went to Hotmail, created a new ID, confirmed it was set up, then logged onto the Group site and posted his new e-mail: [ArcherX@Hotmail.com]. Logged out, went back to Hotmail and saw a message had arrived. It contained a chat-room address he committed to memory before deleting the message and signing out. He logged into the new chat-room address and found yet another chat-room address with the instruction to go to the new one.

The Group loved their cloak-and-dagger stuff.

He did as advised, and logged into that final address. Posted a message:

[It's Bowman. I'm on]

Instantly a message responded:

[Give me a second, I'm destroying the other chat room - Spyder]

Thirty seconds went by, and then,

[Are you clean?]

Steven advised them he was in a public computer area and hadn't been followed.

A different poster, Pogo, popped in:

[Lose your cell phone – they can trace them – do it now and come back in a few minutes. Destroy the phone. Pogo]

What? How was he supposed to communicate? Shit. What about his address book?

[Is that really necessary?]

Immediate feedback:

[Do it]

What a pain in the ass. He logged off, went out to the car, and drove a block away to another parking lot. Wrote down the ten or so numbers he didn't know by heart. He got out, put the phone under his back tire, and reversed over it, and then pulled forward again for good measure. He looked at the flattened lump of plastic and metal and wondered whether he'd finally lost his mind.

Avalon's dead, you've got no access to your cash, and Homeland wants to chat.

Maybe these precautions were prudent. He did the same thing with the hard drive he'd removed before tossing his desktop system to eliminate any chance of data ever being recovered. Mission accomplished. He drove back to the store and logged on.

[It's done, crushed it, now what?]

Spyder responded:

[You didn't really think we were serious…did you?]

Steven fired back,

[Ratfuck]

To which Spyder replied:

[Just kidding. You need to be ultra careful. Cells can be tracked. When you're done here, get a calling card with 2000 minutes, pay cash. Use that for all calls. Go buy a disposable cell phone with a time card in it, and use that to call the 800 number on the calling card. Never use the ArcherX account again. That was a one-time deal. Spyder]

Steven appreciated the instant access to such unusual expertise, and took it seriously. Phone card, disposable cell, got it.

Another post popped up:

[It's Gordo. Did some checking, and Griffen's Barbados fund is only a PO box. It's actually registered and domiciled in Anguilla. Unusual.]

He wasn't sure what to make of that. These guys had amazing access, though. He remembered his friend had told him there were some 'ex-spooks' in the Group. Gordo looked good for one of them. Spyder too.

Another post:

[My buddy on the trading desk at one of the big brokers says a lot of the trades that came in over the last few attacks were done via Canadian brokers and haven't cleared yet. Stinks. Pogo]

This went on for half an hour or so.

Spyder introduced the topic of IP addresses:

[Every time you post on Yahoo or anywhere else they tag your IP. That may be how they tracked you. Use an IP mask when accessing e-mail or posting or uploading to the Web. Here's the best site – www.Be-invisible.com – use it from now on]

Seemed like a prudent plan. God he'd been sloppy; of course, an IP mask was ideal, he should have been using one all the time. Dumb. Wouldn't happen again.

He smiled at the irony that a cyber-contact thousands of miles away could help him remain anonymous five miles from home. No wonder governments hated the web.

When he advised them he was signing off, Pogo popped in and recommended he use the WiFi areas in Starbucks whenever possible; it was convenient and anonymous. And Pogo owned Starbucks stock. Ha-ha.

Steven purchased a calling card, then went over to the mall cell phone store and bought a prepaid cell phone with 250 minutes of time; forty bucks for the phone, and twenty cents a minute for the airtime card. The kid behind the counter activated the phone in the name of John Smith. No one seemed at all interested in having him sign anything.

He went outside and called Stan, who answered on the first ring.

"Steven. I tried calling earlier and your number just rings. What's the problem?"

"Cell phone's on the blink. Just bought a temporary one. Convenient… Stan, we need to talk." That was the understatement of the year.

"I see. Yes, they are convenient, aren't they…?" Stan answered cautiously

"I had some folks stop in from Homeland Security while we were meeting this morning. They left a card. Wanted to talk to me in the worst way. I haven't called yet. Been occupied," Steven explained.

"In light of this morning's problem with your bank, I think perhaps I should field that call for you, or rather an associate of mine who's also an attorney specializing in criminal matters should field it." Stan was quick on his feet. Attorney client privilege twice removed, creating an honest ability for the attorney in question to say he had no idea where Steven was, or even what he looked like. "I'll sign a retainer agreement with him on your behalf. I still have one of your powers of attorney around here somewhere."

"Any movement on the bank issue?" Steven asked.

"The Justice department froze it, most likely at the request of Homeland Security. It can be unfrozen in time, I'm sure, given you aren't guilty of anything and aren't involved with anything Homeland Security has purview over. But for now we have a problem with that."

"I'll touch base with you tomorrow with the Homeland Security phone number. I want to take care of a few things today."

"It's your call, Steven. The sooner the better, in my opinion. We need to get this cleared up."

His next call was to Peter Valentine.

"Peter, it's Steven. What's the word?"

"Some funky stuff down in the islands. Did you know Griffen's partner died in the Caribbean?"

"Let me guess. Anguilla?" Steven asked.

"What, are you psychic? Do you already know all this?"

"No." Steven went on to explain about the Barbados fund actually originating in Anguilla. "It was an educated guess, is all."

"Well, it's pretty weird. I can't get much out of the locals. It was billed as an accident. I called down there and talked to the folks running the paper, and they vaguely remembered some kind of boating thing, but couldn't do much for me. There's no microfiche, and the file has been misplaced, so nothing to reference." Peter sounded annoyed at the Island inefficiency.

"And when I called the police there to ask about it, no one had anything to say; it felt like I was getting stonewalled. I'll keep digging, though. Something's definitely up."

"I gotta say this, even though you already know it. Be careful," Steven warned.

"I'm not completely defenseless, Steven. Appreciate the concern, but you'd do well to follow your own advice. I'm not the one giving them the middle finger with a Fuck Allied website. And I do have experience with bad guys..."

"Sorry, Dad. Hey, I have to run, but I'll call in a day or two. E-mail if anything comes up. My cell's broken."

"Sure. I'll do that. You be careful too. I mean it," Peter said.

Steven went to the nearest Starbucks to give the wireless network a try. He's never used it, as he typically did all his online work from home.

He sat in a corner in a surprisingly comfortable overstuffed chair and updated his website real-time, creating a page devoted to the information he'd uncovered. He started with the fact that the Barbados fund was Barbados in PO box form only, with the trading likely going through Canada in order to circumvent U.S. rules. He closed the page with the tidbit that Griffen's ex-partner had died in Anguilla several years earlier under a shroud of mystery, which was also the true home of the fund. He saved the page and uploaded it, even as his mind returned to his present, real-world problems.

It had been a long day. Now he needed to contend with the open question of where it was safe to stay while he waited for Stan to deal with the Government wonks. The boat made the most sense. It was in a gated, locked marina, and he could move it at will. There was a lot to be said for a home that could be in international waters in a few hours' time.

He ate in Mission Viejo, and considered his situation. He'd been relieved of most of his worldly attachments in little more than thirty-six hours. Avalon, gone. Jennifer also gone, barring a miracle.

That got him thinking.

Did he really dislike the idea of them parting ways that much? It wasn't as though he'd clung to her, begging her not to go, swearing it was all going to be different. In fact, he was strangely ambivalent about the end of the almost-two-year relationship.

Perhaps it had been more convenient than impassioned lately. She'd seemed almost too ready to call things quits, as if it had been on her mind for a while. He couldn't say he blamed her. He was a lousy pick for a nesting partner at present, and circumstances hadn't improved his odds for papa of the year.

In the end, whatever was meant to be would be. That had been his philosophy for years, strengthened by his meditation and his martial arts involvement. There was a definite pattern to the way energy flowed, and events were simply singularities of energy; snapshots, if you will, of a greater energy.

The same awareness that enabled him to catch a rod thrown his way while blindfolded or block an unseen but intuited strike from behind was nothing more than a harnessing of that same energy. The Chinese called it Chi, and other philosophies called it many other names: Holy Spirit, cosmic consciousness, super string theory; all explanations for the same inter-connected fabric of underlying energy.

Still, it helped if you were not just aware but also proactive, so Steven solidified tomorrow's plan of action in his mind, paid the bill, and drove down to Dana Point Marina, where 'Serendipity' floated in peaceful solitude.

CHAPTER 15

The next morning Steven awoke to the gentle rocking of the incoming tide. He slipped his running gear on and went above-board to survey the marina, which was silent except for the faint creaking of dock lines and the low drone of a small dinghy approaching the bait dock at the mouth of the harbor. After carefully closing the main hatch, he hopped onto the dock and made his way up to terra firma to begin his daily run.

Dana Point Marina was surrounded by a verdant, park-like setting, deserted in the early morning except for the odd gull nosing around for scraps of edible litter and the ubiquitous, strutting pigeons congregating for their daily social. Steven's footfalls marked time and distance through the park and up the hill to the main drag, where he noted the French bakery was open for business, as usual.

For fifteen minutes, his run took him south along the streets paralleling Pacific Coast Highway, then he circled back around to finish the route with a morning cup of coffee. He realized this was the first weekday morning in months he hadn't been watching the market open, and that realization produced both a sense of anxiety at having missed the open, tempered by a feeling of calm acceptance at not being agitated with concern over the daily price movements. Conflicting forces at work.

He returned to the dock area and climbed back onto the boat. The decks were slick with beady condensation so he had to be cautious as he balanced on the sideboard, admiring the other vessels bobbing in the water. Some of the larger boats sold for over three million bucks and cost fifteen percent of their purchase price to maintain and operate every year. The boating thing wasn't a poor man's game, that was for sure, and other than a heroin habit or a jet, or both, he couldn't think of a more impractical way to burn money. Still, mornings like this on the water made it almost worth it.

Steven went below and rinsed off in the onboard shower, which was an intimate-sized affair, to put it charitably. Finished, he called Stan, who was also an early riser.

"Stan. How's it going? You up for breakfast?" Steven inquired.

"Have you ever known an attorney to turn down a free meal?" Stan joked.

"I figured I knew how to get your attention. Let's hook up in your neck of the woods, maybe Carlsbad – someplace by the water. How about that place we met last year?" Steven asked.

"Perfect. Give me an hour."

It was a date.

He tidied up the interior of the boat and packed his duffel. After making the bed, he began packing his laptop, but was interrupted by the sound of footsteps on the dock – and approaching the boat. He froze at the unmistakable sounds of someone climbing aboard and moving about on deck. Steven scanned the cabin for anything he could use as a weapon. There was nothing obvious.

Shit.

Although he was adept at close quarter combat, if the intruder carried a gun the odds of his walking away from this diminished if absent a weapon.

Footsteps creaked overhead. He slowed his breathing, reduced his heart rate, and felt his focus narrow to just the immediate area around him, time slowing as he prepared to engage. Strange, he didn't sense danger or any kind of tension, which he always had when he'd been in combat, and in competitive fighting. Still, the adrenaline heightened his awareness and he moved soundlessly to the rear side of the small companionway immediately aft of the entryway stairs.

Someone fumbled with the latch. He readied himself to deliver a rapid series of brutal strikes.

The hatch opened. Light flooded in.

"Mr. Archer? You onboard? Anyone here?" It was Todd, his boat washer.

Steven felt like a complete idiot. Time resumed its normal flow and he drew a series of slow, deep breaths and relaxed his upper body, which had tensed in anticipation of conflict.

"Yeah, Todd, it's me. I thought I'd spend a night aboard, get some sea salt in my hair. I didn't realize you'd be down here today."

"Well, it was such a nice morning I figured I'd get her out of the way, then maybe see if I can hook one of those big yellowtail running out by the jetty. Hope you don't mind… I can always come back if it's a problem," Todd said.

"No, I was just getting out of here. But you might want to try the fishing now, and rinse her off afterwards. She'll still be here later today," Steven suggested.

Todd was a great maintenance worker, conscientious and skilled. Didn't charge an arm and a leg, either. He lived on a boat on the other side of the marina and did odd jobs and cleaning to supplement his lifestyle. Not a bad existence for a bachelor. Simple. Easy.

"Give me a second, and she's all yours." Still burning off adrenaline, Steven hastily grabbed the duffel, mounted the stairs and disembarked.

"Have a good one, Todd." Steven waved goodbye.

"Okay, then. Later."

Traffic going south crawled agonizingly slowly. The I-5 freeway had fallen victim to the perennial California budget crisis and the surface was as bad as any he'd ever driven on in Baja. All that was missing was a burro and the odd roadside shrine.

Carlsbad was a sleepy little bedroom community by the sea roughly half an hour north of San Diego, and Stan had lived there for years, apparently enjoying the slow pace and relaxed lifestyle.

Stan was waiting for him on the patio of the restaurant when he pulled up. They exchanged pleasantries while considering the menu, and both ordered coffee and waffles. Once the waitress had left, Steven described the events of the last eighteen hours in more detail. Stan considered the situation.

"I haven't made any progress with the bank – they referred me to Justice, who in turn referred me to Homeland Security, who said they can't discuss ongoing investigations." Stan looked disgusted.

"The runaround."

"Yes, that would be the technical term. Ever since 9/11 there's been a stretching of governmental power; all, of course, in the interest of keeping us safe. A few years ago no one could have unilaterally frozen your bank account. Not so today. I'll get through it, but I hope you don't need that money anytime soon. Where's their card?" Stan was not the type to forget details, and wanted the Homeland Security agent's card.

"Here you go," Steven said. "See if you can find out what they want."

"I'll have my friend call them today." Stan looked at him over his spectacles. "Now, I have to ask: have you been involved in anything that would have our terrorist hunters after you?"

Steven shook his head. "Stan, honest to God, I don't have the faintest idea what any of this is about. The only thing I'm involved in is the Allied website, which has nothing to do with anything but a Wall Street lizard and a loser biotech company. I told you all about it."

"It doesn't make any sense that a financial guy would be able to wag the dog and get the full might of the Federal Government to come down on you; things just don't work that way. So that's unlikely. Let's suspend any speculation until we know more."

Steven nodded. "I agree. Now I have a request for you. I need an ATM card that can also work as a credit card, drawn on some neutral corporation's account, so I have access to cash," he explained.

Stan considered the request. "Such a thing can be done. It'll probably take a week, maybe less. In the old days, it would have been twenty-four hours."

"I appreciate your flexibility, Stan. That'll help me out a lot. I don't want to be on the radar. And one more request. I need a new blackberry." Being able to log on from the boat would be invaluable if he was forced to be mobile for a while.

"Easy enough."

They sipped their coffee and munched their waffles. He told Stan he and Jennifer had decided to take a break. Stan said he understood, sometimes that was best, it would all work out if it was meant to be. Blah blah, platitude, blah.

Stan paid the check, and they made their way back to the car park.

Stan wound down his window before driving off. "I'll let you know what happens with the call and the card and the PDA. Consider the latter two done." Stan looked hard at him again. "You call me. I don't want to have any way of getting in touch with you, so I can respond to any questions about knowledge of your whereabouts honestly," Stan told him. "I don't foresee a problem, but better safe..."

Steven's next stop was a nearby hotel to use the business center. He paid $10 for fifteen minutes, doing a double take at the price. He asked what the fee would have been if he was checked in as a guest.

"Let me look it up. Hmm. Hmmm. Oh, here it is: $10."

They really said fuck you with style in Carlsbad.

"Things are kind of expensive in Carlsbad," Steven remarked with a blank expression.

"Try La Costa. It's $20."

He moved to an available computer and logged on. The stock was up thirty cents from the open. He checked his S_Jordan e-mails, to discover dozens of complaint e-mails from the boards advising that the site was down.

Huh. He tried the site. Nothing. Just a screen that said cannot locate site.

Dammit. Another hacking attack? Maybe the server was down? The first e-mail was at 4 a.m. California time. He tried the Lone Star homepage. That was down too. So it was probably a server or connection issue, not a site-specific takedown.

The only message in his normal e-mail was from Jennifer. Short and to the point.

[Hi. Will drop off the bags and keys today. Hope you got some rest. J]

No response necessary that he could think of.

He checked in with the Group, and asked if they could figure out why his site was down. They pinged it, got nothing. Probably a power outage or a truck plowed into a pole.

Steven signed off, his $10 about up, and asked the young lady at the guest desk if there was an Internet café or computer superstore anywhere close by. She gave him directions up the street.

With the valet charge the whole episode cost him $16 for fifteen minutes. He wasn't sure he could afford much more Carlsbad.

Steven drove to the office supply chain store and got back online. He spent the rest of the afternoon researching the SEC's regulations for offshore investment funds, and surfing the boards to catch up on any news. There was a lot of commentary on the sections Steven had uploaded before the site went dark. He'd really stirred up a hornet's nest.

Checking his inbox, he saw Spyder had sent him an article. Steven's arm hair stood on end as he read. The author was a name he didn't recognize, but the content was alarming. One part of his psyche told him it sounded like conspiracy junk, while another part of him got a sinking feeling in the pit of his stomach.

The article centered around the stock action in the airlines and insurance companies immediately preceding the terrorist attacks on the World Trade Center, and documented the brokerage firm that placed most of the winning trades that went through the roof when the value of the stocks fell off a cliff after the terrorist strike – a firm run by a fellow who later became the head of the CIA.

The implications of the article were staggering. Were the connections between Washington and Wall Street such that there could be collusion at that level? It seemed impossible, but then again, so did much he'd seen lately. He'd always wondered why the government turned a blind eye to Wall Street's obvious malfeasance, and in fact actively aided it in robbing the country. He considered the 2008 financial crisis, and the massive bailouts so many had received. And still, to the present day, taxpayer dollars were being siphoned from the real world economy and funneled into Wall Street's coffers. This connection made the inexplicable suddenly make sense. On the one hand, the government prattled on about how banks needed to increase lending to stimulate a recovery, and then on the other the Federal Reserve began paying interest on overnight deposits from banks, for the first time in history. What bank in its right mind would risk lending money if it could get a return risk free? Sure enough, the amount banks were hoarding at the Fed went through the roof once that policy was in place. Who benefited there?

A lot of things fell into place if one viewed things through a cynical lens. Glorified trading houses that were cynically referred to as investment banks were given access to the Fed overnight window when they were made 'banks' during the crisis, and now could borrow virtually unlimited amounts of cash from the Federal Reserve at near zero interest, and then turn around and buy T-Bills from the government that paid them a three percent or so yield. The difference between a quarter percent borrowing cost and three percent might not sound like a lot to most folks, but if you did it with, say, a trillion dollars, suddenly you were talking real money, even by Wall Street standards.

And then there was the question of why so much obvious fraud had been perpetrated during the financial crisis, and yet nobody had gone to jail.

Steven had recently seen an article that discussed a hedge fund manager who had made three billion dollars in one year betting against mortgage securities he had a hand in selecting to be sold as AAA to unsuspecting investors. There was plenty of fist shaking and rancor, but in the end, nobody had cuffs on, and it looked as though nobody ever would.

Spyder's wry commentary interjection was short and to the point:

[Ya think the reason there's no appetite to clamp down on the bad guys is because they're running money through some of them, and in bed with some of the others? Ugly world we live in, huh? Watch your ass, Bowman. Spyder]

Spyder then went on to underscore that the same sort of thing was taking place as in the 1920s, when powerful interests would front-run the trading and make fortunes by short selling companies into the ground – witness the massive put options (which increase in value as a stock price goes down) traded right before the 'unexpected' crash of Bear Stearns in 2008, and the government's odd reluctance to investigate that obvious smoking gun. Parties they could easily identify had taken massive bets that Bear would collapse before it did, creating a self-fulfilling prophecy as tens of millions of shares that couldn't have possibly existed were sold into the system, collapsing the share price. Day after day the trading showed incredible volumes of sell orders seemingly designed to do nothing but take the firm's stock price into the toilet, creating the very crisis that would make the bearish bet pay off in a colossal way. The cost to borrow for Bear became huge as the stock price fell and the cost of credit default swaps on its debt went through the roof, guaranteeing it would run into a situation where it couldn't meet its daily demands for ever increasing collateral, ensuring it would fail. And yet nobody seemed interested in who had done it. The media played ball and the whole episode was quickly forgotten, even as new outrages surfaced daily.

The more he read, the more corrupt it appeared to be.

Steven called it a day at 3:00, his head whirling from information overload and the ramifications of all the data Spyder had supplied. He approached the counter and paid for his time, and after concluding that he didn't have anything else he needed to do, began the drive back to the boat. When he dialed the Lone Star number from his disposable cell, it just rang.

No answer.

It took him almost two hours to make it to San Clemente, and by that time he'd talked himself down. He had immediate problems to deal with, in the real world, and didn't currently have bandwidth for CIA conspiracy theories or a world where the government actively aided and abetted criminal syndicates in raiding the U.S. economy. A big rig had blown a tire, and most of I-5 North was a parking lot past Oceanside, making any further driving a nightmare for at least another hour.

Steven pulled over and hit a restaurant for an early dinner, figuring he could wait out the snarl of immobilized vehicles. He really wished he'd brought his laptop, instead of forgetting it on the boat – that PDA was going to be worth its weight in gold to him. After eating, he stopped by at an Internet cafe to check in with the Group. One of them immediately posted:

[Check your mailbox. Trouble?!]

His fingers flew across the keys as he typed in the address of his e-mail account. He went to his S_Jordan box, where a blind re-mailer had sent him a message with an attachment. He opened the attachment, and it was an article from that day's Austin newspaper describing a massive fire at the strip mall that housed, among other things, Lone Star.

Steven's gut tightened again.

This just couldn't be a coincidence or conspiracy nonsense. Whoever was after him was clearly serious, and ruthless. But part of it made no sense – Homeland Security and the Justice Department didn't go around burning buildings to shut down websites. If they had grounds to shut it down, which they didn't, they'd just get an injunction and seize the server.

In spite of his recent run-in with Homeland, maybe it was exactly what it appeared to be – an accidental fire. They did happen all the time. The whole world didn't revolve around his website.

Here he was again; wavering in a never-never land between feeling sheepish and paranoid – imagining assailants behind every tree, and reconciling all the coincidences before taking prudent precautions.

Accident or not, from a practical standpoint, he now had no site and no server. Finding another ISP wouldn't be that big a deal – he could sign one up over the web in minutes. The problem was the only copy of his site was on the boat. At least he'd backed it up on the laptop.

He sent a post to the Group:

[Weird coincidences, huh?] and got an immediate response:

[Check six. There are no coincidences. I'll be on late if you need anything. Gordo]

He signed off and left the café to go and retrieve the laptop, fatigued from the stress of it all. He felt like he'd been starved of sleep for weeks.

CHAPTER 16

As Steven crested the hill to the marina he saw emergency vehicles everywhere and a plume of black smoke rising from the inky water. He couldn't get his car anywhere near the entry because the lot was glutted with fire trucks. He drove to the next lot over and parked as close as he could get to his area, then hurried to his dock's gate, only to find it closed off with yellow crime scene tape and a police barricade. He approached one of the park security men standing around the barricade. "Wow. What a mess. What happened here?"

"Some guy's boat blew up. Took out half the dock."

"You're kidding! Which boat? What caused it?" Steven asked.

"Don't know. Sailboat, down at the end of A dock." He pointed nonchalantly in the direction where Serendipity was berthed. "A bunch of other boats were damaged, too. They think it was a fuel leak – filled the bilge with fumes."

Inside, Steven was thinking, God, no, say it isn't Serendipity. It had to be an accident – somebody else's boat, not mine, not mine, not mine.

"The divers are pulling up debris and looking through what's left of the hull right now. Doesn't help that visibility's down to nothing with all the oil in the water." The kid seemed as interested as Steven was – probably the biggest thing that had happened since he'd started working for a living. "The owner was on board. They found some parts of him. Pretty gross."

Steven felt like he'd been hit in the face with a hammer. He squinted as he peered down the dock, and it looked a lot like his slip was now gone.

He needed to know. Had to get by the kid. Stay calm. Think.

"My buddy sent me down to check on his boat. He saw the smoke over the hill and called the marina. Can I take a quick look? Check on the lines, make sure it's secure?"

"No one's supposed to go down there. It's a crime scene right now. Give me the slip number and I'll have someone on the dock check." At least the guard was willing to try.

Steven's slip was A-32. He didn't hesitate. "A-20."

The security guard spoke into his walky-talky. "Guy wants to make sure his boat's okay. Slip A-20. Can someone look at it? Over." The radio crackled for a minute.

Then through the static came the fateful words Steven dreaded hearing. "It's fine. Boat that blew was A-32. Over."

Steven smiled at the guy and croaked out a weak 'thank you'.

His head spun and his heart trip-hammered from the sudden jolt of adrenalin as he walked away, registering there were plenty of other spectators perusing the dreadful scene.

He started processing automatically. Todd was dead – it had to be him. So this wasn't all in his head. Someone blew up the boat. Someone set the web building on fire. Someone was willing to kill to stop him, to silence him and keep the website off the air.

And they could still be here. Watching.

He needed to blend in. Couldn't draw attention to himself. He walked in the opposite direction from his car, and stopped to ask a couple walking their dog what had happened, doing a slow scan of the parking lot as he listened to them.

There was nothing overtly suspicious, but it was hard to tell.

He listened as they recounted the same basic story the guard had told, then thanked them and continued walking along the perimeter of the marina. A man with binoculars was studying the aftermath of the carnage; could be innocent, but maybe not. There was no way of knowing whether this was an interested vulture or a deadly predator.

Steven kept moving past him, quickly glancing at his watch – for all appearances a man on his way home for dinner. He made it to the main access street for the marina parking lots and walked slowly up the hill to the town, never looking back.

His laptop was now either melted at the bottom of the harbor or in the hands of whoever blew up the boat.

There could be no doubt it wasn't an accident. Diesel fuel hardly ever caught fire, and was incapable of generating huge explosions like the one that had taken out the dock. They'd probably rigged it that afternoon, with some sort of trigger set to go off when he opened the hatch. Poor Todd had probably taken his suggestion to wash the boat later; in retrospect, likely a fatal recommendation. Or they could have been watching the boat to ensure the job got done right, by triggering the explosion remotely. Watched for a male in his late thirties going onto the boat, and then pushed a button. Simple, no mistakes. Kaboom. Problem over.

The laptop was the least of his worries. If they knew his boat, then they knew his car – which meant they had to have the license plates. Then again, if they believed him to be dead, they wouldn't be looking for it other than to confirm it was in the vicinity. That was a small advantage he might be able to use.

He needed to get his duffel out sooner rather than later.

Steven walked into town and found a little cafe where he could kill some time as he thought through a strategy for retrieving his bag from the car. He ordered a cup and a croissant, and determinedly waited for the sun to set. The forensic team would undoubtedly figure out it wasn't him on the boat, but that could take days, or even weeks. As long as he didn't post anything on the boards, or call anyone who couldn't be trusted, he was safe, for now. But what to do about his conviction that the boat explosion had been deliberate? He couldn't go to the police; they'd just turn him over to Homeland Security, which would be much like being stuck in a gulag. He'd read about HS detainees held without access to their attorneys for years. No thanks.

Steven felt the anxiety over the hopelessness of his predicament threatening to overwhelm him, and fought down the urge to panic. He needed to stay clear-headed if he was going to come out of this alive. But the transition from being a comfortable retired investor ensconced in a familiar, controlled environment to being a fugitive on the run was jarring. He knew he'd need every internal resource he could summon to make it, so he couldn't afford to waste time grappling with the emotional shock of recent events. That would come later. For now, he needed to think tactically and take simple, achievable steps that would keep him breathing.

The klaxon scream of sirens wailed in the distance; obviously the commotion at the harbor wasn't over by any means. Steven nursed his cup of coffee and got a second one, for all appearances savoring life without a care in the world. Gradually, the frequency of the emergency vehicles racing to the scene slowed and then stopped, and as evening arrived and the sun slowly sank into the ocean a sense of tranquility returned.

Once it was dark, Steven walked cautiously down the bike trail into the harbor park – the back way. The cops were still at the scene, and they now had large spotlights mounted on stands shining into the water. He looked around the lot his car was in, and saw no one. Plenty of other cars there. Good. Cover.

Steven sat by a tree across from the lot for ten minutes, watching for any movement or any signs of surveillance. Nothing. Eventually satisfied that the area was likely safe, he got up, walked across to the lot, kept going past his car, and entered the restroom at the far end of the lot.

He quickly scanned the confined area, moving from stall to stall as though deciding which to use. Satisfied he was alone, he moved to the sink and ran some water through his hair, then considered his reflection.

Steven, you're in the eye of a shit-storm, he concluded. *No room for mistakes.*

He listened for sounds around the building. Nothing. Just radio chatter from the docks, and the whine of a winch motor.

Okay. Showtime. He moved out of the building, seemingly preoccupied with getting the last of the moisture off his hands with a paper towel. Tossing it into a trash can, he did one last visual sweep of the lot. Still empty. He allowed some time for his eyes to re-adjust before walking towards the Porsche.

There was a sudden flurry of motion by his legs.

He jumped back. A cat tore by in hot pursuit of an errant pigeon.

Adrenaline coursed through his already on-edge system, and his heartbeat pounded in his ears as he focused on controlling his breathing and staying calm. He kept walking, reached his car, opened the door. No light overhead, as it was an older convertible. Thank the Germans for small favors.

He reached behind the passenger seat and grabbed the duffel. So far, so good. He pulled the phone charger out of the lighter socket and pocketed it. Quickly checking the interior of the car, he didn't see anything else that he'd miss or might need.

Done.

Steven looked around. All quiet. He got out of the car, softly closed the door, and locked it with his key. He walked away with carefully measured steps, heart still racing, feeling like he'd just succeeded in doing a prison break; Steve McQueen in *The Great Escape*, sans motorcycle.

The evening blew a soft, cool breeze but his shirt was soaked with sweat. He edged back to the bike path, scanning the lot a last time to confirm nobody was watching. It appeared that no one had noticed or cared about his stealthy parking lot mission, and for the moment, at least, he was safe. He hefted the duffel and confirmed it was zipped tightly shut, and put the shoulder strap over his shoulder, pulling it tight against his torso.

And then Steven began to run.

He ran hard, and he didn't stop for a long time.

CHAPTER 17

A techno jazz beat swirled softly in the background as Griffen absently watched the two girls pleasure each other. He idly fondled a breast as the brunette slowly drew him in and out of her pouting mouth, moaning as her young friend set her tingling with her tongue while probing deeper with the humming vibrator. Tanya and Sophie, both from Guadeloupe, with charming French accents, and here in the big city with a burning ambition to break into theater. Tanya was a singer, and he forgot exactly what Sophie's claim to fame was, other than a shaved mons. It didn't really matter. They had a double-trouble thing they marketed to gentlemen of discriminating tastes, and Griffen was currently enjoying the proficiency of their performance.

Neither could be more than eighteen years old. All the better. Tanya, the brunette, shifted and shuddered, her pace becoming more urgent as Sophie expertly brought her nearer and nearer to climax.

His cell rang. The distinct ring he'd programmed for Sergei. Great timing, Sergei. He disengaged from the delicious tangle of appendages and reached over to grab the phone.

"Your problems are over. Have a nice night." Sergei's voice rang flat and unemotional. He hung up.

Griffen considered the words. He smiled, and tossed the phone onto the floor.

Sighing, he ran his eyes over the two hard-bodied island girls in his bed, the empty champagne bottles, the mirror with the dusting of powder.

"Now, where were we…?"

Steven slowed to a steady jog after the first half hour of running, realizing he was somewhere in the hills of Mission Viejo – a staid suburbia, where lawns were trimmed with regularity by hard working gardeners as soccer moms delivered their charges to private schools in tinted-windowed Range Rovers. The evening breezed cool, for summer, with the traffic thinning out as the dinner rush wound down.

He approached one of the never-ending strip malls and rested on the bench in front of a fruit smoothie place that was still doing reasonable business. He bought a faux pina colada concoction, found a seat outside, and watched the high school girls come and go for their evening libations, chatting about boys, music and the other mundane stuff of youth. Everyone so concerned over their small dramas and challenges, convinced their life was unique and special. A wave of sadness washed over him as thoughts of Avalon intruded into his psyche unbidden, and he fought the overwhelming despair that came with them, recognizing that an emotional breakdown wouldn't solve anything. He could grieve for his canine friend later. For now, he needed to stay focused and determined.

The calories and the run had helped clear his head, although he was still at a loss as to what to do next. He had no place to sleep, no plans, no computer, and couldn't show his driver's license anywhere – which would be a requirement at any hotel. And the credit cards were obviously unusable. The government had unknown powers of surveillance, and he wasn't going to put them to the test. He'd overestimated his ability to remain anonymous once already, and he'd learned his lesson; a lesson that had presumably cost Todd his life, Lone Star their livelihood, Avalon his head, and him at least a hundred and fifty grand, his relationship, and potentially his life.

He retrieved his newly acquired cell from the bag, and dialed Stan using the calling card.

"Stan, it's me. Don't say anything. Today got much worse since we talked. I got back to the boat, and it had exploded and killed my boat-cleaning guy. It wasn't an accident. And the place hosting the website burned to the ground this morning; supposedly an electrical fire, but I'll bet it's arson. People are dying, Stan." Steven paused, waited for a response.

"Are you on a secure line? In a safe place?" Stan always approached things methodically.

"On a disposable cell, via a calling card."

"Hang up and call me from a pay phone."

"Done."

He walked over to a public telephone on the far side of the strip mall, called his card's 800 number, then dialed Stan.

"Stan, I'm on a pay phone."

"What's going on? Homeland doesn't blow up boats and commit murder." As always, Stan had hit the ground running, already piecing together the incongruities.

"I thought about that. I don't know what to expect or believe anymore," Steven said. "But I do know a friend is dead because someone thought he was me."

"Presumably. We don't know that for sure. But let's assume you're right. What are you thinking?"

"I need somewhere I can be anonymous now that I'm dead," Steven said. "Someplace low profile to use as a base, where I'm not endangering anyone if I'm found. Any suggestions?"

"I'd offer to have you stay here, but that seems imprudent to say the least. I'll go rent a room and pay in advance for a week at the Best Western down the street. I'll leave the key somewhere you can find it. Call me when you get into town."

Regardless of the apparent danger, Stan sounded like he was game to help, for which Steven was hugely grateful. Steven had hardly doubted it, but it was still good to hear that Stan would go to bat for him. The stakes had gone up considerably since morning, and he hadn't been completely certain he could count on Stan's continued good humor.

Steven had another, bigger request, and he needed to make it sooner rather than later.

"Stan, I also need a foreign passport, preferably in a different name."

The line went quiet; he could almost hear Stan thinking.

"Well," Stan finally said, "there's no law against an American citizen having dual citizenship, so no problem there. The issue is one of time, expense, and logistics. Let me nose around and see what's available. A formal name change could take a while; that might be a problem…and I don't think you want to wait the eight to twelve weeks a front door program from Dominica or such would take – nor the scrutiny through Interpol. I'll put out some feelers and have more info tomorrow, although that could be a sticking point. Since 9-11 many doors for second citizenship programs have closed. But not to worry, where there's a will and cash, there's always a way." He paused. "Anything else?"

"No...but, Stan...thanks for going to the mat for me."

"Call me when you get here."

"I don't have a car," Steven explained. "It's in the lot with the boat. I figured it was best to leave it there – another dead-end."

"Take a cab to the Denny's off the freeway in San Juan Capistrano, then switch to a different taxi company and catch it at one of the bars a few blocks away in town – then take it to the Sandbar cafe in Carlsbad. It's just at the bottom of the hill from the motel. Are you good on cash?" Stan asked.

"For now. I'll be there in a few hours."

Steven hung up. He was lucky to have Stan. As an asset protection attorney, Stan was well versed in second citizenship programs, offshore banking, and a myriad of other specialized topics. There weren't many people he could ask to procure a new passport or citizenship on a rush basis and expect results. Stan would come through for him, no matter what it took. It might be difficult, or expensive, or both, but he would find a way. That was sort of what he did; made things happen.

He called a cab company, to be told there'd be a car there in fifteen minutes. He was on his way. Strange how he'd gone from inhabiting a comfortable house, owning a boat, a car, possessions of all shapes and sizes, to a man with a duffel bag and a cell phone. He felt uneasy, but unusually free. Maybe the whole 'passport, credit card and travel bag' lifestyle had merit. If the world's most powerful government and parties unknown weren't trying to find and kill him it would almost be an enlightening adventure.

He crossed the street and waited for his cab.

It took the best part of an hour to reach San Juan Capistrano, where he dutifully called another cab company and waited for the taxi's arrival in front of a biker bar a block from the restaurant. The crowd inside was loud and rowdy, and he could hear a chorus of male shouting and cursing over the din of a jukebox cranking out southern rock tunes. It was amazing to him that in the quintessential epicenter of prosperous suburbia a roadhouse straight out of central casting could flourish. It just showed you that you never knew what you were missing, just moments from where you'd spent much of your life. After ten minutes of watching poorly muffled Harleys pulling into the bar's lot, he saw car headlights approaching from the freeway, and the second cab pulled to the curb. Steven got into the car and gave the address of the cafe in Carlsbad. Tonight really was the driver's lucky night; it was at least an easy forty-dollar fare.

They drove south in mutual silence. The driver spent most of the drive on his cell phone, speaking in a foreign tongue with someone he alternated being frustrated, angry, and delighted with. Probably a wife or girlfriend, Steven though; being on the night shift had to be pretty lonely and boring. When they reached the cafe, Steven paid the driver in cash. Once on the sidewalk, he dialed Stan's number.

"Stan. I'm here."

"The key's in a red planter a couple of feet away from your room. Number 202. It's not the Ritz, but it's large enough so you won't be noticed if you keep a low profile. I threw a six pack of soda and some granola bars in the room in case you want a snack."

Steven smiled to himself; Stan loved granola bars, and assumed everyone else did as well. "Thanks again, Stan. I'll call tomorrow."

Steven kept alert as he sauntered up to the motel and located the colorful planter and key. He did a quick scan of the doors, and quickly found his room. Once inside, he flopped on the bed and thought for several minutes about the day's events and the items needing attention tomorrow. His body was still pulsing with nervous energy from his flight from the boat, so he decided to put it to use by compiling a to-do list. He fumbled in the bedside end-table until he found a pen and a few sheets of hotel stationary, which he carried over to the small teak desk. As he sat staring blankly at the sheets of paper, wondering where to even start, the reality of his predicament threatened to overwhelm him with a sense of helpless despair. *Yeah, it's a bitch, Steven, but you don't have the luxury of falling apart, do you, so better get busy,* his inner voice commanded. It was true. The time for regret or recriminations was past. He'd have to be proactive, and throwing a pity party wasn't on the agenda. His brain focused on the task at hand, and he began making notes.

He needed to get a laptop and a car, convert watches into cash, let Peter know what had happened, get into contact with the Group and give them a heads up, and figure out how to get the site back up and a server set in place without alerting his adversaries that he was alive. And buy some clothes.

That made for a full agenda.

Steven checked his watch; one in the morning. Too late to call Peter, or do any of the rest of it. Still restless, he counted his cash. Sixty-five hundred dollars. Figure a grand, worst case, for the laptop by the time he was done, and two grand or thereabouts for a beater car. Five hundred for miscellaneous BS. That left him a few grand. Pretty thin.

He needed to sell at least one of the watches in the next few days. The Patek 3970 was probably worth a hundred thousand, which meant he could probably get eighty thousand from a dealer, but that was a hard piece to move quickly. The 3940 was worth half that, and the platinum Rolex would bring twenty on a fire sale. That gave him a lot of firepower in terms of value. He decided to sell the 3940, as that way he could carry maximum cash value on his wrist with the 3970, and have an easy-to-sell piece with the Rolex if he ran into another bind; portability would be critical if he was going to stay mobile.

He didn't know how long it would take to get the ATM card, but he wanted to have options, and cash bought options. Steven was okay wearing the 3970, as it looked like an 'old man watch' according to Jennifer, and didn't shout big money to the average person. It was just a yellow metal watch on a strap, low profile, discreet. He didn't need attention at the moment.

Any. At all.

Feeling slightly better about his future, he collapsed onto the mattress and was out cold within three minutes.

CHAPTER 18

Steven was awakened by the roar of a leaf blower a few yards from his window. Momentarily disoriented, he looked around, trying to get his bearings. Then he remembered. The motel. Todd dead. On the lam.

He lay back. So it wasn't just a bad dream. That would have been too easy.

He went into the bathroom to rinse himself back to life, then threw on a new shirt and yesterday's pants. No time for a run today. It was already 8 a.m.. He'd grab breakfast at the restaurant down the hill and take a walk into town. There'd inevitably be an area where cars were parked with *For Sale* signs on them, and this close to the border he'd likely encounter quite a few inexpensive clunkers; the trick would be to find one that ran well enough so he didn't wind up broken down on the freeway, chatting with the Highway Patrol – that would be compromising, to say the least.

While unpacking his clothes and putting them into the drawers he found several of his CD-ROMs. A bit of luck – finally. He'd backed up the website on them recently, so it was still uploadable; he'd totally forgotten about stuffing them into the duffel in his rush out the door.

His spirits rose. Not a bad start to the day. He stuck the wad of hundred dollar bills into his front pocket, checking that it didn't make a noticeable bulge.

Snagging his list from last night, he grabbed his cell phone and room key and headed for the restaurant at the bottom of the hill. He dialed Peter's number as he made his way down the drive. An unknown voice answered the phone. He hung up, redialed the number. Same voice picked up.

"Hello," said the voice, older female, probably seventies.

"Hello, I'm trying to reach the Valentine residence."

"This is it. May I help you?"

"Um, yes, I'm trying to reach Peter. Is he there?" Steven asked. Strange. Maybe a neighbor was watching the house while they were off on an impromptu vacation?

"Who's calling?"

Now this was a problem. Maybe nothing, but he was getting that feeling in his stomach again.

"Tell him *Rich Guy* is on the phone."

"One moment, please."

Several minutes went by, making him increasingly uneasy. What the hell was going on here?

Then Penny's voice came on the line. "Oh God, Steven. He's dead, Steven, Peter's dead…" Her voice broke in anguish as she spoke the awful words. Her sobs of sorrow twisted Steven's gut.

"Penny, stop. What happened?" *No. This can't be real. It has to be a nightmare.* He bit his tongue, tasted blood with the numbed-out pain. God, it was really happening…

Penny's voice cut him deep a she sobbed out the anguished account. "He…last night…went out to meet somebody…didn't say who…I got a call two hours later…a car hit him…hit-and-run…someone saw a dark SUV. Oh God, Steven, he's dead…"

"I'm so sorry, Penny." Words were completely inadequate at moments like this. Inside, his devastation swelled, threatening to become an all-encompassing primal scream. Peter dead. Impossible. It wasn't supposed to be like this.

"I'm so, so sorry. Is there anything I can do?" His words echoed stark and empty in his reeling mind. *Is there anything that I, dead-guy-running-from-the-law-and-who-knows-what-else, can do for you, who have just lost your lifelong mate and are no doubt in shock, not to mention also facing an empty future of loneliness?* Do the questions get any more insipid?

"No. I know he loved you. He would have done anything for you." She choked up again.

He closed his eyes. "And I loved him. And you, Penny." He struggled for more words, but none would come.

"I need to go now, Steven. I'm not doing so great. I'll call and let you know when the service will be."

Shit. He had to tell her. He struggled momentarily with alternative explanations, but realized that only the truth would excuse him for missing the funeral – even though the truth would likely burden her more.

He swallowed his grief. "Penny, I know you've been through a lot, but you need to listen to me. I can't come for the service. I'm in trouble with some bad guys who are making my life complicated. It's not good, and I don't know when I'll be able to get out there next."

"...I don't understand...trouble? What kind of trouble? Are you all right?"

The worry in her voice increased his remorse.

"Penny, it's hard to talk about. You've known me forever. You have to trust me on this. If anyone asks, you haven't talked to me. Not for weeks. And if anyone calls you or comes to see you, no matter what they say, you haven't heard from me. Even if you hear stories about me being dead. I'm not, but you have to play along. I wish I could say more, and I wish I didn't have to do this now, with Peter..."

"Peter told me you were involved in something that might be dangerous. He seemed agitated the last week. I know he was worried about you, even though he tried to pretend nothing was wrong. Steven, how bad is it?" Even in her grief, Penny wasn't stupid. You couldn't be married to Peter forty-plus years and not hear the stories.

"It's bad. Very bad. Bad enough so I can't come out to see you. Bad enough so you haven't heard from me. I'll call you in the next few days and tell you what I can, once I know more. But you have to do this for me. Promise me. Please?" Steven implored.

"Oh God, Steven. I...all right, if you say so. But be careful. I can't lose any more men in my life. I know Peter had times when he couldn't talk about what was going on with his work, so I'm used to that. But I don't like it." She paused. "When will you call again?"

"Soon as I can, Penny. I love you."

"I love you, too. Be careful. I'll pray for you."

The woman who answered the call came back on the line. "She's having a really rough time right now. I'm staying with her for the next day or so. I'm Nora, I live next door. And you are...?"

"Steve...Steve Radcliff. One of Peter's friends from New York. I'm sorry to hear about the accident. He was too young." Steven disconnected.

He was standing in the middle of the sloping driveway between the motel and the restaurant, staring at his phone like it had bitten him.

A horn honked behind him, making him jump. A pickup truck was trying to exit the motel. Steven stepped to the side and got a glare from a burly guy wearing a confederate cap; no doubt one of his new neighbors.

As he sat at a booth in the almost empty restaurant his mind raced. Peter had been run down, his life ended in a few seconds as steel intersected with flesh in a no-contest exchange, which meant from a pragmatic standpoint, any help or info from Peter's sources within the FBI or at the other agencies he'd had clout with were effectively terminated. So now he was left with only his cyber connections and Stan for support and any investigative requirements.

His thoughts were interrupted by the waitress, who not unexpectedly wanted to take his order. He nodded yes to coffee and asked her for a few more moments. After the news about Peter, his appetite had deserted him.

Steven's mind went back to times during his youth Peter had been there to steer him the right way. He remembered his dad's death, unexpected and mercifully quick. Peter by the side of the hospital bed with Steven's mom and Penny, Steven sitting in the corner of the room, not completely comprehending what was happening. The day before, his father had been walking around, laughing, joking with him; then suddenly he'd been through emergency surgery and was a pale shell, the doctor cautioning that he'd lost a lot of blood before they'd gotten the aneurysm, and that his outlook was poor.

Peter had been there the entire time, and had acted as an anchor for the family after his dad succumbed to the trauma.

Peter took him to the first dojo he'd ever seen, encouraging his interest in martial arts and introducing him to his first teacher, Sensei Fujiko-San. It was Peter who provided the impetus to keep working at his skills when his motivation lagged or he became discouraged. Peter always in attendance during competitions or sparring bouts.

All through his developing years, Peter was there. High school graduation. Moving into his first apartment. Advising him to join the Marines, see the world, develop some character. Loaning him money when things got unexpectedly tight.

At his mother's funeral four years ago.

Peter had even helped get him his first job in the computer industry through one of his contacts. That choice for a career path came at a time when Steven was floating directionless, killing time in college with no real objective after four years in the service, two of which were spent in ugly situations during Desert Storm.

After returning to the States he hadn't been too concerned about things like the future, or much of anything but the here and now, martial arts, girls, and the obligatory college courses to appease his mom. That had changed as he'd gotten older, and Steven had even gone on to get a doctoral degree in math from UC Irvine while building his company, but during Steven's formative years Peter had acted as his moral barometer.

What had he unintentionally done? What forces had he put into motion, and what chance did he stand of success against a group of unknown antagonists willing to kill on a moment's notice?

Peter had been one of his closest friends, who'd died under mysterious circumstances, mere hours after his boat had burned to the waterline – leaving another innocent soul dead. Steven's little interlude to stimulate an otherwise orderly existence had turned deadly, and now he found himself running for his life, with those around him dropping like flies. Peter had committed to help him, and after a life of successfully cheating the grim reaper, suddenly he was gone.

Just like that.

A hit-and-run. He wanted desperately to believe it wasn't connected. Peter was just a fringe player in this, doing peripheral nosing around into some arcane financial matters. That wasn't something people would run you down for.

Was it?

His head swam with the terrible implications, which if true, meant everyone he'd been in contact with could be in danger – they were all potential targets.

Oh God. How had this spun out of control so quickly? Who else was vulnerable? What other slip-ups had he made? Would anyone tracking him relax now the boat was history, assuming he'd been dealt with? But that was a temporary fix. They'd figure it out. And then they'd come for him. This time, they'd make sure the job got done right.

He didn't even know who 'they' were, or what 'they' looked like.

A busboy dropped a plate on the other side of the restaurant, jarring him out of his fugue state. *Think, Steven. You need to snap out of it and begin processing, taking action.* The pity party would have to wait. The sick feeling in his stomach and the recriminations needed to go on hold.

Scanning the restaurant, he saw none of the customers were aware of or gave a shit about his personal drama. They were engrossed in their own struggles. He wasn't in their movies.

That was strangely reassuring. At least for now, he was invisible, if not bulletproof.

All right.

Plan.

Take the offense.

So, what was the priority for the day? He needed a car and a laptop. Without a car he couldn't get up to Los Angeles, which is where he'd have to go to sell the watch; Beverly Hills was the ideal place for that kind of transaction, and he knew a shop on Rodeo Drive that trafficked in Pateks and would have the reserves to buy it on the spot – he'd purchased from them before, and had a good enough relationship to request cash without raising any eyebrows.

And then there was his overall appearance.

Perhaps it was time for a comprehensive makeover.

He thought about the options. Probably a buzz cut or at least really short, some hair dye, and a goatee or a mustache. And maybe some glasses. He hadn't shaved for two days, so had a good running start on the facial hair thing. He extracted his list from the previous night and scribbled. It was turning into quite a project template.

When the waitress returned with the check, Steven asked if there was anywhere in town people parked cars they wanted to sell. Sure enough, she knew of a spot on Pacific Coast Highway.

He cut through the side streets that led to PCH. On the right hand side, about a quarter mile past the intersection, stood a row of destitute vehicles parked along the road with various For Sale and *Se Vende* signs in their windows. He perused the frozen procession of tired transportation, looking for something suitable – he finally settled on a little Mazda pick-up truck; a 1989 extra cab in pretty good condition; five-speed with A/C, and 'only 111,000 miles, rebuilt clutch at 70,000'. The tires looked relatively new, nothing leaking. Asking $1800. He called the number in the dirt streaked window.

"Yeah, this is Tony."

"Hey, Tony, I'm looking at your Mazda truck, and wanted to get some more info on it. How does it run? Are you the original owner?"

"Oh, the truck. Uh, yeah, I'm the original owner. Runs like a charm. No problems with it, just tuned it up a few months ago, always changed the oil every three thousand miles." Tony sounded quite proud of the truck's condition.

"Well, it's what I'm looking for. Would you take sixteen hundred for it, right now?"

"Make it seventeen hundred and you got a deal. I can be there in ten minutes with the keys and the pink slip. You got the money on you?"

Tony was hot to trot. That was good.

"I'll go get it. Meet you at the truck in ten minutes." Problem solved. And under budget too.

Tony showed up two minutes early, a soiled Harley Davidson T-shirt and shorts struggling to contain his stocky frame. Like Steven, he hadn't troubled himself with shaving recently. He offered a folder with receipts that was surprisingly organized given his appearance.

On their test drive the little truck did run well and Tony boasted that it got over twenty miles per gallon on the freeway and didn't burn any oil – the only thing tougher was a Sherman tank.

Steven asked all the requisite questions and agreed to buy it when they returned to the parking spot. Tony methodically counted the hundred dollar bills and signed over the pink slip, and pumped Steven's hand enthusiastically, assuring him that he'd never find a more dependable or trustworthy conveyance in his life, and that he'd made a great choice. Steven believed him. He asked Tony to step on the brakes so he could confirm the lights worked, as well as hit the turn signals. All was well, so he wouldn't have to worry about being stopped by the police for inoperative safety lights or some other avoidable issue. Steven noted the truck still had a registration sticker good through November, so he wouldn't be getting pulled over for expired registration, either. The little Mazda was the perfect vehicle for Steven's situation, and he was grateful he'd solved his vehicle problem so easily. It wasn't the Porsche, but then again, nobody was trying to blow it up, either, so on balance he could live with it.

The entire transaction, start to finish, had taken forty-six minutes, according to his Patek. He pulled into a gas station, filled up his tank to the brim and drove to a mall he knew of in Oceanside. The stores were just opening. He went into a computer place and spent some time considering his technology options. Eventually he realized that all the features and speed were roughly equivalent at the price point he wanted, so he made a selection and walked out with a laptop tweny minutes later. Twice as fast as his old one, weighing only five pounds, $800 – laptop bag another $49.

Steven declined the extended warranty.

Next up, he found a modest clothing outlet, where he picked up a couple pairs of pants, several pairs of socks and some casual shoes and sandals. He expected that he'd be living out of a suitcase for some time, and not always have access to laundry facilities, so selected apparel that was darker in color so it wouldn't show dirt easily. He wasn't planning on going spelunking or hacking his way through the jungle, but you never knew.

Steven felt a sense of achievement, even though all he'd really done is shop. But he'd managed to shorten his to do list and get a car, in a fraction of the time he'd believed it would take.

Mission accomplished, all by 11 a.m..

A Starbucks appeared on his right as he drove away from the mall. He pulled the Mazda into a parking space, then took a few minutes to unpack the computer and become familiar with it. Satisfied, he went in, got a cup of coffee, and plugged in the laptop charger.

First, he checked his S_Jordan Hotmail box, which was at capacity due to complaints and warnings about the site being down. Next, he checked his personal e-mail account. He went through the messages methodically, and came to one from Peter, dated yesterday late afternoon, Florida time. The hair on his arms bristled as he opened it:

[*Making some progress on a number of fronts. A friend of mine with the Canadian SIS has been working on a case with the Canadian stock exchange people involving a Toronto brokerage suspected of being a conduit for terrorist money. They have a whistle blower who's still working there. One of the clients is Nicholas Griffen, but only his personal account. My contact said he could do some digging if it was important. I told him I'd appreciate any help he could offer. His name is Cliff Tomlin, e-mail ctln@gc.ca.*

I also have some disturbing info about Griffen's ex-partner – my source indicates he thinks his death wasn't an accident. He was mobbed up. This is all very preliminary; I need to read the file in detail – I got a copy today but no time yet. I'm supposed to find out more this evening from a promising lead. Peter]

The blood drained from his face. He closed his eyes and spent a few minutes clearing his head, detaching from the immediacy of the situation. Opening his eyes, he considered the message again.

So there it was; confirmation Peter's death had not been an accident. That made three lives Steven's carelessness had claimed. Peter had been an extremely careful man, and there was no way he'd compromised his security from his end; he was far too savvy and professional for that. So how? How had they known Peter was involved?

Steven's laptop. Of course. They must have gotten it when they were rigging the boat with explosives. A given really, when he thought about it – but for his stupid rationalizing, he could have warned Peter about the implications; he should have warned him, immediately.

The e-mails he'd sent to Peter asking him to dig into Griffen had probably been automatically archived in his laptop's e-mail log. He'd never thought to check, much less delete them.

Which meant all Steven's contacts listed on the old laptop were blown, and in mortal peril. He did a mental checklist of anyone else he'd contacted via e-mail about Griffen when using the laptop; Peter had been the only one. Had he sent anything to Stan? No, thank God. He'd only contacted Stan the day of the bank problems, and never via e-mail. Anyone else? No. Had he saved his passwords or any other account data on disk? No, he'd followed good security on that, at least – even a fool knew that laptops were frequently stolen. Nothing prejudicial.

Just the e-mail exchange that killed the closest person in the world to him.

One small slip and people died.

Steven realized he had more questions than answers. He saved Peter's message and went numbly through the rest. What the...there was another message from Peter. With an attachment. From 5:30 p.m. Florida time. Had to be within an hour of when Peter had left his house, never to return. He opened it.

[*Steven, got a copy of the original article from the paper in Anguilla on the partner's death. It was in the file I'm starting to go through. Copy attached. Also got name of barrister in Anguilla from my contact who used to set up international corporations. Says this guy can get any info from the Government or banking records for the right price; no doubt extremely expensive. Very connected. I spoke with him, seems like a reasonable sort, told him you may be contacting him. His info is below. I'm off to dig more dirt.*
Peter

Alfred Reese, LLB, LEC. PO Box 99141, The Valley , Anguilla, British West Indies.]

There was also a phone number, which he jotted down. Steven opened the attachment.

[*The Anguillan Times. April 26, 2008. A visiting tourist was killed yesterday morning when the speedboat he was piloting exploded, having struck 60 Yards Reef outside Island Harbour Bay at about 10am. The 32-foot Scarab caught fire, and there was a tremendous explosion shortly thereafter. Mr. James Cavierti was in Anguilla on holiday from New York City, USA. He was a respected financial figure and partner in a prestigious New York venture capital firm. He is survived by his wife, Patricia.*]

So Griffen's partner went up in a puff of smoke and salt water in an Anguillan boating accident. No hint of foul play. Then again, hadn't another boat just gone up in flames, taking someone with it?

The article didn't offer a lot of additional information, but it did raise some questions. Whose boat was it? How long had Cavierti been on the island? Who else accompanied him? Was his wife with him on the trip? What was he doing on Anguilla? He made mental notes. Peter had felt the Anguillan connection was important enough to get in touch with an attorney there and vet him. Steven had to be missing something.

As he thought through his next move, he felt the disequilibrium of the last hour being replaced by a cold and calculating clarity. The senseless, vicious slaughter would not go un-avenged. Any doubt or confusion had slowly been replaced by an even colder fury. He'd be damned if Peter's life would be sacrificed without him exacting retribution, and he silently honored his friend with the promise that whatever happened, he would get the people responsible for his death and extract a terrible price.

Steven had long ago rejected violence as a way of life, and had committed to being a creator, rather than a predator. But at the end of the day, when the barbarian hordes showed up at your door and kicked it down, dragging your loved ones from the safety of the shelter you'd built, and then murdered them without hesitation, the time for philosophical niceties was over. You were either a victim or a hunter at that point, and Steven decided that he wasn't going to be anyone's victim. He'd already lost too much, and now it was up to him to take the initiative and hunt the hunters. There were scores to settle, and in the end, he was going to make those who had taken everything from him rue the day they'd decided to take him on. Everything carried a price in life, and others had given their lives because of a battle that, in the end, was Steven's fight. And he never backed away from a fight.

Peter was dead, and he couldn't bring him back, but what he could do was go after those who imagined themselves insulated from retribution, and make them pay – with interest added…

Book Two ~ Focal Point

A chess term which describes the square upon which a player focuses an attack, e.g. by repeatedly attacking that square or sacrificing a piece there.

CHAPTER 1

The area where Emil worked was nondescript; standard government-issue desks with a minimum of personal touches. Everyone in the compound gathered there strictly for work, and knickknacks and decorations were not encouraged. Emil's office measured the industry-standard eight by ten, with a computer monitor and various accessories occupying a good third of his desktop.

He was online, reading with interest the news about the fire in Texas. Something was afoot apart from the steps he'd initiated, and he didn't like that. Emil knew the ins and outs of how the government worked, and razing buildings to stop a website didn't jive; there was another hostile element in the mix, and that surely complicated things. There was a danger inherent when amateurs were involved in any kind of fieldwork – they could leave tracks; footprints that could lead back to embarrassing places.

Emil considered his next step. He could start running interference in the fire investigation, but didn't really know what he was trying to cover up, which made that tricky. It was hard to be effective when an unknown quantity was on the game board.

He inwardly cursed whoever was making the moves outside of his direct control, and calculated the options.

Rubbing his face, he picked up his telephone and dialed a New York number. He stopped halfway through, stared at the handset momentarily, and gently replaced it in the cradle.

He needed more information. There was nothing to do but patiently sit in the background and wait for more to develop before taking any additional steps.

Emil was lousy where restraint was involved, but had become proficient at forcing himself to wait for his adversary to make a move. Now it was a waiting game. He just hoped whoever was responsible for the fire was competent. He hated amateur night, and that's what he was sensing in the Texas conflagration. Sloppy, gratuitous destruction; using a shotgun to kill a fly. He unconsciously shook his head, and returned to more pressing issues.

❧❦

Steven logged onto his new, confidential chat room for the Group, and posted a message:

[I'm baaack – it's Bowman here, guys]

Soon thereafter another post came in.

[Your site's been down for almost 48 hours. What's wrong, Bowman? – Spyder]

Steven explained about the damage to Lone Star likely being deliberate, and then shared the whole story with the Group. Boat destroyed, Avalon gone, Todd and Peter dead, Homeland Security in the mix. The reaction from the Group was supportive, but cautious.

[I can set up a server in Costa Rica, paid via money order, and move the site every two weeks. Consider it done. I actually have the last version downloaded. Figured there might be trouble. I'll get it up in 12 hours. Check six. Gordo]

[You need to stay dead. I'll post on the boards that 'we' have taken over the site maintenance as concerned shareholders. I know how to stay hidden via anonymous proxy servers bouncing all over the planet. That should drive them nuts. Pogo]

Pogo was the resident computer geek who knew all there was to know about anything related to technology or the web.

[You need to lay low, Bowman. Stay under the tripwires. HS has resources you aren't aware of. They can track cell phones to within three yards. If you're going to stay in-country, I can get you a cell phone that doesn't have the clipper chip in it, from Asia, but they're pricey. For now, stick to the disposables and change yours every couple week, even if you're using a calling card, and even if you aren't in the US. Avoid US airports and don't use any ID or credit cards. Cash is king. And stay away from familiar areas. The last thing you need is to be tagged at your favorite bar. Spyder]

[I'll set up a mirroring system in Latvia for the site, so it's not obvious Costa Rica is the new home. Send me the password and the code for the domain and I'll move the pointers to Latvia. Bounce it to Costa Rica. Pogo]

The Group was certainly up for this, Steven realized; actually seemed to be enjoying themselves. That figured. A legitimate, real intrigue was just what they'd been hoping for. He knew he was fortunate to have access to them, and that they collectively represented a powerful force to contend with. Maybe he had a better than running chance after all.

[Remember to use the IP mask at all times. Proxy servers are your friend. Change the IPs hourly and use offshore addresses. I'll e-mail you a utility that will do it automatically. Pogo]

Steven acknowledged their input and thanked them for helping. He signed off as Bowman and closed the computer, leaving it charging while he sipped another cup of coffee.

He thought about what to do next, but came up blank. He wasn't processing particularly well, so he decided to go back to the motel.

Steven parked down the hill and walked up to the room with his bags. The news of Peter's death threatened to overwhelm him with despondency – he felt immobilized, impotent, frozen. He didn't really want to do anything but go to sleep and make it all go away, but he realized that wouldn't do any good; he had to keep pressing forward.

Considering his options, he decided he should exercise to clear his head and get some adrenaline going. He ran for forty-five minutes, returned to the motel and showered, before spending half an hour working through his Kung Fu sequences. He was blindingly fast when he needed to be, but for him the enjoyment came from the flow and grace of the execution; the speed was a byproduct of intent coupled with proficiency. He performed his strikes and his isometric upper body exercises with his shirt off, and noted his muscle tone hadn't suffered over the years.

Exercise concluded, he lay on the bed, staring at the ceiling, thinking about Peter and how unfair it all was. It was doing him no good at all.

He walked down to the restaurant and called Stan from the pay phone, using the calling card.

Stan was to the point. "I need you to get four, color, one-and-a-half by two-inch passport photos to me as soon as possible tomorrow. I need to overnight them to my contact. You'll be receiving a spanking new passport from Romania within a week. Cost is $65,000. It's being issued by their passport agency as a favor to their consul general here, who's one of my golfing buddies. You'll be using your middle name as your last name on the passport, so get used to being addressed as Mr. Cross. Steven Cross," Stan said.

Stan had come through for him. Romania, huh?

Stan continued. "I first looked at having you adopted by an El Salvadoran family, and applying for a passport under their flag in order to visit the dying patriarch of the clan, but figured you might have some problems given that many folks speak Spanish, and as far as I recall, yours is limited to high school vocabulary and ordering margaritas. Plus that would have been $50,000 and no EU access. So I pulled some strings and got the Romanians to find you irresistible."

"I always wanted to go to Romania," Steven said.

"Don't. Unless you speak fluent Romanian, you really don't want to be answering a lot of questions." Stan's sense of humor had taken a little vacation.

"Something else has come up you need to know about, Stan."

Steven told him about Peter's murder, and the Anguilla angle. The possible organized crime aspect. The article about the CIA and the brokerage connection, high net worth clients, possible foreknowledge of 9/11 and using it to turn a profit.

He sensed that Stan was unnerved. He was an attorney, not a black ops commando, and there were limits to what he could handle.

Stan succinctly cut to the chase. "People are being murdered for looking into Griffen, and helping you with the site? And you think it's possible the CIA is somehow involved?"

"That's the way it looks right now. There's so much new information coming at me it's getting complicated to figure out. Thank goodness I'm dead for the time being."

"Do you believe there's any danger to me? I had my friend call HS, but he hasn't heard back. Probably because they believe you're dead, so why continue with an investigation on a dead man..." Stan was thinking out loud.

"I think you're safe. They got to Peter through my laptop. I've never sent you any e-mails. There's no connection, other than our past involvement, and that's untraceable." Steven reassured him. All his past work with Stan had gone through a California licensed affiliate firm, and Stan's name wasn't on any of the paperwork.

"Homeland Security can't be involved in the killings. That's too way out. But if you're right about an organized crime element, then you may have bigger problems than the government."

"That occurred to me."

"What do you plan to do next? I'll have the credit card for you in the next couple of days, and the passport in about a week, assuming you get me the photos early tomorrow," Stan reminded him.

"I'm not sure. You'll be the first person to know when something dawns on me."

Steven hadn't quite figured what came next.

CHAPTER 2

Halfway across the country, Spyder pushed back from the computer desk, pinching the bridge of his nose to dispel the residual tension. This was ugly, and getting worse. Setting up a debunking site against the likes of Griffen meant Bowman would need to be extremely careful, and require a lot of coaching. If he was up against professionals he didn't stand much of a chance, although he was a quick learner and did have the military background…which was something.

He rolled over to his small kitchen; sparse, simple, meticulously clean. His powerful arms effortlessly drove the wheels on either side of his chair, a tribute to forty-five minutes of morning weights and isometric exercise, every day of the year. The notion of being an invalid or a burden had driven him to construct an existence where he was wholly self-sufficient, able to fend for himself in every way, with his upper body compensating for the wasted lower appendages that served as a harsh reminder of how quickly things could go wrong in the field.

It had been a while since Spyder had been out of 'the world'; the inside term for clandestine operations used by those in the business. His last gig as an operative had ended poorly, with him narrowly escaping termination at the hands of some angry arms dealers in Nigeria. Eighteen years without any significant wounds, and then, bam, the walls fall in. The wrong local contact had leaked the wrong info in the wrong bar, and unbeknownst to him, alarm bells had gone off and a decision had been made to be safe rather than sorry.

It wasn't as though he hadn't considered the very real danger element of the job. Hell, that had been a big draw for him. When he wasn't doing deep cover, he went stir crazy; normal life being a tedious imitation of his covert existence.

He'd been like that since his teens; an adrenaline junky and a loner. In the quiet periods he would wonder if the job had been made for him, or he'd been made for the job. In the end it was all the same. Spyder did things nobody else wanted to do, in places nobody wanted to go, with the handy excuse for virtually any behavior that he was doing it for his country. It had started out of college, when he'd been recruited by a 'talent scout' tipped off by one of his professors. He'd never even considered saying no.

Of course there'd been sacrifices, but nothing he wasn't prepared for. No woman in her right mind wanted to be with a guy who disappeared for six months at a time with no explanation or warning, so he never had any great stabilizing force to keep him grounded. His parents had long since passed away, so he was the ideal, no-strings-attached asset; smart, savvy, clinically efficient, possessed of a photographic memory, and with zero encumbrances.

Some would think being an agent had taken a huge toll on his personal life, but that had been a trade-off he'd long been comfortable with, and worth the price paid. Then again, he'd never envisioned himself taking two slugs in the back as his car raced away from a blown meeting in the jungle. The embassy had gotten him out on a private plane in the dead of night, a staff doctor having stabilized his shock and temporarily stemmed the blood loss. Three operations had failed to restore his mobility, even though they'd employed the latest techniques. Those were the breaks. Sometimes your number was just up. At least he was alive, albeit a casualty of a silent war nobody knew or cared about.

Now his existence was limited to his condo, his consulting work for several large corporate espionage companies, and cursory interplay with his fellow man via his screen and keyboard. He'd come to a compromise with the planet, taking a generous retirement package that allowed him the freedom to exist as he liked; which happened to be alone, save for an old parrot named Rusty, and surrounded by bookcases filled with arcane tomes on obscure topics like encryption, financial fraud, forensics and cryptography. His housekeeper came in once a week, his groceries were delivered twice a week. He kept things basic.

It worked for him.

Spyder had enjoyed his involvement in the Group, finding the intellectual titillation a welcome diversion from mundane vocational chores involving corporate surveillance, background checks, and white collar larceny. It was hokey, but they were a sort of extended family; a support group of sorts for what he recognized was his stint as an obsessive-compulsive shut-in.

This Bowman's drama had blown his carefully crafted veneer of disinterested control apart. He was back in the world, even if it was only from the sidelines this time around. But most importantly, the game was afoot, and he felt his mind darting automatically down a checklist of survival tactics, his breath quickening in anticipation of the thrill of the chase to come.

He could keep Bowman ahead of whatever was heading his way. Shit, he'd been one of the best. The least he could do was to steer Bowman clear of rookie mistakes that could cost him any thin advantage he might still have.

He opened his fridge, and reaching for a soda, realized his hand was shaking almost imperceptibly. But the tremor was there.

Spyder closed the door, cracked the pull tab, and took a deep breath.

For the first time in four years he felt energized, in play again. Vital.

CHAPTER 3

7:30 p.m.. Long day, but time was wasting. There were a lot of things that needed doing, and Steven's appearance remained a problem. Once they figured out he wasn't dead, he had to assume they'd put the full court press on locating him. He would have to use the slender lead he had to maximum advantage.

Time for a haircut. He drove down PCH into Solano beach, where the atmosphere was considerably more animated and less genteel than Carlsbad. Tattoo parlors, surf shops and counter-culture apparel stores abounded. The area had the ambiance of an MTV video, with hosts of wannabe gangsta suburban kids with elaborate piercings and full sleeve tattoos skateboarding down the sidewalks.

Jockeying for somewhere to leave the little Mazda truck, he spotted an opening on the street adjacent to a group of questionable looking retail stores. Fortuitously, he parked in front of a hair salon; *Ripped Curl*, which featured a tribal art icon of a breaking wave being surfed by a dreadlocked stick figure wielding scissors. Steven figured that was probably as good as any. He went in. A cacophony of angry-sounding rock music blared from speakers mounted in each corner of the small reception area, and a flat screen TV on the wall featured footage of motorcycles doing aerial gymnastics. A knockout receptionist with a pierced nose looked up from her college textbook.

"Hi."

Steven smiled into her deep, green eyes. "Hi."

"Can I help you with something?" Tongue pierced, too.

"Yes," Steven said. "I wanted to get a haircut, maybe some color."

"You want a trim or something radical?" she asked.

"Radical. I'm sick of this look."

"Whatever. I know the feeling. Let me see if Ricky's still here." She got up and walked into the back of the salon. Steven noted how her baby-blue miniskirt barely covered her perfectly sculpted buttocks.

Eight percent body fat. Six-inch high black foam flip-flops. Very tanned, very long, very smooth legs – going all the way up to the top. A thong. A tattoo of barbed wire around one ankle, no doubt symbolizing the extraordinarily oppressive life she'd been forced to lead by her dictatorially repressive parents in her brief sojourn on the planet.

She returned with a tall man with ebony-cum-purple hair wearing all black. Thumb rings. Eyebrow ring.

Ricky, no doubt – he went on to quasi sing-song, in effeminate tones: "Well, hello. I'm Ricky; call me Rico, like *rico suave*. Melanie says you want to get funky, no?" Ricky clearly got funky early and often. Ah well, as young Melanie said – whatever…

"I want to go short, and maybe go darker."

Ricky clapped his hands in approval. "You come on back, then, and I'll hook you up. Mel, girl, could you rinse him while I clean up my station?"

"Whatever."

They walked to the back of the salon, where 'Mel' washed his hair in an absentminded way. She was probably high as a kite on something. Smelled good, though; like vanilla, the ocean, and puppies. He noted her baby doll T-shirt was unconstrained by any bra or other old-fashioned contrivance. Mel was a modern girl. And it was a little cold. Brrrr. Smoking hot Mel being wasted here… *Let me take you away from all this…I have a wildly economical and practical mini-truck. A room with orange shag carpet and daily maid service. Run away with me…*

Ricky, on the other hand, was all about hair. "Okay, handsome, how short is short? You have thick hair, so we don't have any problems there. Maybe a surfer buzz? That might be kind of rad."

Steven resisted uttering a token 'whatever'.

Barely.

"Maybe a half an inch long – surfer cut's fine. Also go dark…" Steven supposed he didn't much care what Ricky did. With his hair. Within reason.

"Dark brown?"

"Yeah."

"I would have said bleach it if you really want to do something fun. Or maybe dye it black. But if it's dark brown you want, you got it." Ricky studied his face for a few moments. "So why the big change? That's a pretty different look." Ricky was somewhat chatty.

"Time for things to change, is all." Steven was not somewhat chatty.

Ricky took the hint and worked in flamboyant silence. The cut took only a few minutes, the color almost an hour. The end result looked back at him from the mirror. He almost didn't recognize himself. He resembled a mid-thirties surf punk. Except the goatee growing in made him look a little older, or rather harder.

"Ricky, you're a genius. How much do I owe you?"

"$30 for the cut, $70 for the dye, hundred even. Pay Mel on the way out." Ricky was obviously interested in getting out of there. It was after nine p.m.. Places to go.

At the front of the shop, Steven gave Melanie $130.

"Thirty's for Ricky."

"Yeah. I got that." Charming Melanie. A people person.

She cocked her head and studied his new persona. "You look good. Ricky did a great job. It's a cool look for you."

Surprise, surprise. Fair Melanie was a young lady of many layers, apparently. Or buzzed out of her mind on Dilaudid. Either way, he'd take the compliment. It was always nice to be flirted with by a scantily clad hottie half your age.

"Thanks. See you around." He left the store. Were he ten years younger, he'd probably have been stupid enough to find out more about young Mel, maybe take her out for a drink. She looked like she could teach him a trick or three. But he had other things he needed to attend to. Couldn't be spending his time chasing the local surf ghetto chicks, now, could he? Still, that thong...

He got into his little Mazda truck, inspected himself in the rear view mirror, and laughed out loud for the first time in a week.

CHAPTER 4

The next morning, Steven's first chore was to get the passport photos, which he did after checking the market. Thirty minutes later, and thirty dollars lighter, he had them – so he made a call and arranged to meet Stan at a fast food restaurant down the street from Stan's house.

Steven arrived first and sat in one of the booths facing the door. Stan got there a few minutes later. He looked around the place, eyes passing over Steven and looking elsewhere, and then returning to him slowly, narrowing...

"Steven?"

"Call me Vlad," Steven joked.

"That's an amazing transformation. Really unbelievable. Oh, I've got a present for you." Stan handed him a box. The latest model Blackberry. "I hooked it up to a service provider using the company account. All the bells and whistles."

"That'll come in handy," Steven said. "Appreciate it."

Stan shrugged. "No worries." He paused, studying Steven carefully. "I just can't get over the new you. What a transformation."

"That's the whole idea. Here are the photos, color. Four of them, as requested." Steven handed him the small envelope.

They discussed the events of the prior day, and after several cups of coffee both were fidgety and anxious to leave. There wasn't a lot left to discuss that hadn't already been covered.

Next checklist item was the watch.

He called his contact in LA and described the piece. They agreed on a price of $34,000 if it came as described. Cash wasn't a problem. He'd go to Los Angeles tomorrow and do the transaction.

Then he made the call he'd been dreading. Penny answered the phone with a dull monotone; she sounded like her soul had been torn out.

"Hi, Penny, it's *Rich Guy*."

"Ste...how...how are you? Is everything okay?" she inquired.

"Good as can be expected. How are you holding up?"

"It's hard. It still hasn't dawned on me this is real. I always thought I'd outlive Peter, but not this way." Her voice cracked. "Last night was really bad."

Steven swallowed. "I can imagine. I remember when Mom died. Last night...I didn't have a very good night either, Penny." He debated telling her about his suspicion about Peter's death being related to him, but decided against it for now. She was already going through enough. They talked for a few minutes, but she was obviously still in shock.

"I'll call you again later on today, okay?" Steven said. "Make sure you're hanging in there. Take care of yourself."

"You too, honey."

CHAPTER 5

New York stood stifling in the brooding mood of June. Sporadic thunderstorms did little to dispel the hanging muggy humidity that sequestered the sweating city. Ensconced in his offices, Griffen was leaning back with his feet up on his desk, talking to someone on the phone. Trading was almost over for the day and he didn't have any active campaigns on the agenda.

Griffen terminated the call, and his e-mail popped up. He read the latest messages and stopped dead. He swore; typed in a web address, and swore again. He picked up the phone and called Glen.

"What the hell is going on? The site's back up." Griffen wasn't happy. His photo was also posted there in all its glory.

"Let me look into it," Glen said. "I hadn't realized it was down."

That's right. Glen didn't know about the servers being taken out, or any of the rest of it. He just knew the topic had stopped being an issue. He also knew enough not to ask any questions.

Griffen grunted. "Could you see if you can find out where it's located and who's operating it again?"

"I'll get back to you when I know more."

Griffen's next call was to Sergei. The receptionist was cordial, making sure he was put through quickly.

"Nicholas, my friend. What a pleasant surprise. I trust everything is well with you." Sergei, good humored, always happy to hear from his old friend, Nicholas Griffen.

"I'm good. But I was better when I thought my problem had gone away. Do you have any update?" Griffen had to be careful here. He didn't want to know too much.

"I have no idea what you're talking about."

"You may want to look at the web, see if there's anything of interest there. Perhaps we can have a drink later today or tomorrow," Griffen proposed.

"I will take your suggestion to heart. I'll get my girl to call if I have time to take a drink or two…yes?" Sergei came over equally cagey.

"That sounds fine, Sergei. Just fine. *Dosvidanya.*"

కొ•ఈ

Steven had tracked down Patricia Cavierti in New Jersey, the ex-wife of Jim Cavierti, via the web – with a little help from the Group. Took all of two hours. He dialed the number. A woman's voice answered.

"Mrs. Cavierti?"

"Who is this?" she asked cautiously.

"This is Andy Tern, from Galvin, Tern and Brinkley, LLP. I've been asked to look into the untimely death of your husband, Jim Cavierti," Steven said. "I just wanted to ask a few questions, if I could."

"Look, I don't know what or who you are, but I don't talk about Jim's passing on. So you're wasting your time," she said, sounding like she was about to hang up.

Steven softened his approach. "Mrs. Cavierti, I appreciate what a terrible tragedy it was for you to lose your husband, but I just need to ask one or two questions."

"Need? Fuck you and your need. Is that clear enough for you?" She hung up.

Well, that could have played out better. The problem with fishing is that sometimes it was hard to lure the fish up to the boat. He redialed.

"Hello?" Her tone didn't sound too auspicious.

"Mrs. Cavierti? I'm so sorry I have to keep disturbing you," he began anew.

"I don't discuss Jim with anyone." She was going to hang up.

"We have information that Jim's death may have not been an accident," Steven declared. Maybe that would capture her interest.

It did. "Who did you say this was again?"

"Andy Tern. We're looking into Jim's accident on behalf of one of our clients, who believes that Jim might have been murdered," Steven tried again.

"Sherlock fucking Holmes, huh? Well I told you, I don't talk to anyone about Jim." Her voice had developed a definite whine, and Steven realized that she'd been drinking – she had a little slur going on.

"Mrs. Cavierti, don't you want to help us get to the bottom of Jim's death?"

"Ha!" she cried. "That's rich. That shit-rat was banging every stripper between here and Atlantic City – and I want to help an investigation? Here, let me help you out. Go fuck yourself." She hung up again.

In New Jersey, Patricia Cavierti glared at the phone for a minute, and then dialed a number that never received inbound calls. "Someone just called and they're looking into Jimmy's accident. Just thought you should know. Yes. Andy Tern, attorney. You're welcome."

❧

After running a few housekeeping errands to pick up necessities such as deodorant and toothpaste, Steven returned to his motel room, and again his new image mocked him as he walked past the mirror that framed the hallway entrance. He looked nothing like he remembered. If someone had been given his description or a photograph they could have stood next to him in an elevator and never known he was the same person. That gave him considerable comfort as he pondered his next move.

He calculated how long he could hang out in a fleabag motel in the middle of Carlsbad before he went bug-fuck crazy. Not very long. Steven needed to do something to get to the bottom of whatever was being perpetrated – to take action. Being stuck in a twelve by fourteen room was not doing a lot to improve his perspective. But at least he was still alive. That was more than he could say for Todd, or Peter.

Shit, he'd spaced on calling Penny. He quickly dialed the number.

"Hey Penny. How did the day go? Doing any better?" Steven asked.

"I stood in front of his office door for must have been an hour, and couldn't stop crying. He was so determined to keep working – had such pride in his skill. And now he's gone. It just breaks my heart," she said. Her voice sounded flat. Medicated. "I found a file that had your name on it, on a Post-it. It looked like the last thing he was working on. Do you want me to send it to you?"

Holy shit. Maybe it had to do with his death. "Penny, I'm going to give you the address of an attorney who'll hold the file for me. He's a good man." He gave her Stan's office address.

"Okay. I'll overnight it to him for Monday delivery. Peter would have wanted you to have it, if your name was on it."

"How are you holding up?" He knew he'd already asked that, but wanted more reassurance.

"As well as can be expected. Some friends are coming over tonight to keep me company, and the doctor gave me some horse pills to help me through this. I'll live. I just want to get through the service. That's the next thing." She was fading as she spoke.

"Penny, I'll come out there as soon as I can. You and Peter, well, you were like parents to me…are. As soon as I get this mess cleared up I'll be there – and I'll tell you everything that happened."

I killed your husband with my hubris and carelessness. That conversation could probably wait awhile.

"I know you will. I'm going to go to the shipping place right now before I forget. These stupid pills knock me out a little. Goodbye, mister *Rich*…goodbye, and know my prayers are with you, whatever happens."

"And mine with you," Steven promised softly as he hung up the phone.

He considered what a frail construct a life was. Not the physical form, which was certainly that, but rather the accumulations and relationships people collected as they moved through the process of living. Then came the day when the bits of carbon and salt and water lost the spark of energy animating them, and all that remained were the memories in the minds of those left behind – and a few meager possessions.

Peter had been a large man, a full-of-enthusiasm, vibrant tower of a man. And now what was left of him? A house in Florida, some papers, clothes, and the people he'd affected during his existence. The world kept turning, not even pausing for an instant as he departed the planet.

Party over, just like that.

CHAPTER 6

The next morning, Steven went down to the usual Starbucks and logged on for his ritual Allied stock check. No trading.

God, of course not. It was Saturday. Duh.

He switched to his Group, where he chatted with Pogo about how to enable IP masking while on his Blackberry. Gordo suggested he create a new e-mail account for any ongoing correspondence because he had something amusing to send him once he was registered. Steven took a few minutes out from the chat and went to Hotmail to create a new Avalons_dad e-mail. Within a few minutes of posting this new e-mail address to the Group he had mail. He opened the message to find an article from yesterday's *Orange County Register* describing the fire on Serendipity, which ended with the sobering news that the owner was killed in the blaze. The word was official. He felt happy about this small reward, which promised to end the trail of pursuit – hopefully. Clean slates and all. He wondered how many people ever got the opportunity to completely reinvent themselves: who they were going to be; where – and how – they were going to live; what they would do; and even what their name was. It seemed like a completely liberating experience, and yet it seemed daunting; a blank canvas required far more effort than an almost completed work. It begged the question: what did Steven want to be when he grew up?

Ya got me there, he mused. Right now he'd settle for being alive.

He disconnected, then finished his drink in preparation for the trip to Beverly Hills. He had a solid two hours or more each direction, so might as well hit it.

The little Mazda hummed its way along on the freeway; the A/C worked well enough to dispel the worst of the heat, so the roads were no more unpleasant in the truck than in the Porsche – which is to say terrible.

Steven was relieved to be able to conclude his business with the watch merchant in Beverly Hills without too much drama – after haggling he got $30,500 for the Patek. Less than he'd hoped for, but he was hardly in a position to dictate terms. And even if the regrettable interaction had been strained, his cash position had radically improved, at least.

He threw the duffel in the front seat, started the engine and pulled onto the highway, narrowly avoiding a collision with a Maybach piloted by an Asian woman wearing a sweat suit, and with a cell phone stuck to her ear. You had to love L.A. He left the Rodeo Drive area and drove west towards Melrose and UCLA. After parking in a back street, Steven sought out an eyeglass store where he scanned the diverse selection; trying on a number of pairs of frames until he found some that altered his appearance significantly. Tortoiseshell Euro-style unisex glasses he thought looked suspiciously like reading glasses available at the drug store for $8, but with a green hue across the top of the brown frames. Of course, these had clear non-prescription lenses, so they were more practical for his purposes. And only $195. A bargain, really – and garish enough to overshadow the face behind them; so they suited his purpose perfectly.

He took them up to the girl at the counter. "I'll take these," Steven said.

The girl nodded. "Okay, do you have your prescription?"

"No prescription. I just want the frames with the lenses as is." Steven got a weird look from her. "It's for a play I'm in," he added, inflating his chest for effect.

"I see." It all made sense. Another actor.

After a stop and go trek down the 405 freeway he was back in Carlsbad by 5:00. He sat in the motel, intending to relax but within a few minutes felt he was going stir crazy, so he drove to a small dojo he'd seen on PCH, and after a short negotiation twenty dollars bought him the room for an hour.

He worked through the physical mantra of positions and strikes, then executed his kicks, blocks and jabs – mutating from Karate to Kung Fu to Jeet Kwon Do with increasing rapidity and astonishing fluidity. He finished off by winding down with a series of stretches. The owner of the facility, suitably impressed, bowed to Steven as he paid for the hour. Steven returned the bow respectfully.

No matter where in the world you went, there was a universal appreciation for the skills he'd cultivated, and the nearest dojo was always where those who understood could be found. Kindreds of sorts. A brotherhood of skill. He was comfortable in and loved that world. It was honest and uncomplicated. He could use a little more of that at the moment.

His years of early martial arts training had served him well in the military. The Marines had tried to convince him to stay in after his four-year stint was up. He'd been brutally effective on several seek-and-destroy missions in the Gulf, notably when his team had been ambushed. Things had gotten ugly and degenerated to hand-to-hand fighting in a small village near the Kuwaiti border; where he'd proved devastatingly proficient. But somewhere during the process Steven discovered he detested killing, so he'd politely declined the offer. He kept his practice to sparring and working out for the love of the art rather than for the practical applications of the skills he'd perfected.

Steven finished up his day at, surprise, Starbucks, armed with his laptop. Nothing much to report, all quiet on the boards. He decided to send an e-mail to Peter's buddy in Canada.

[Cliff. I'm a very close friend and associate of Peter Valentine. He gave me your info and advised that I contact you. I don't know if you've heard, but Peter was killed several nights ago in a hit-and-run accident. I'm picking up the pieces and continuing the investigation he was pursuing into the activities of Nicholas Griffen. Please contact me at your convenience with a telephone number and the best time to reach you so we can discuss how best to proceed. Steven Cross]

He figured he might as well start using the new moniker. That was his name now. Steven Cross. Dr. Steven Cross. All things considered, he actually liked the sound of it. That was one of the few positives to arise from his situation so far.

CHAPTER 7

After a quiet Sunday, Monday arrived quickly. When he checked his e-mail, he had a message from Spyder:

[Bowman – I thought about this over the weekend. You need to get out of the country pronto. It's just a matter of time till they ID the boat guy and discover that wasn't you. Use your window of time intelligently. Get across the border ASAP. All hell will break loose once you're found out as being alive. HS will be back on the trail. Now's your time. Spyder]

Steven had been thinking much the same thing. But he couldn't really leave and go anywhere until he had his new passport.

[I agree. Have to wait till new papers done. End of week.]

Gordo popped online with a message:

[Any idea where you'll be going? – Gordo]

Steven didn't really have a clue.

[Beats me. Probably Mexico first, then it's a wild card.]

Spyder fired back at him:

[My advice is walk across the border. Don't drive, Bowman. Tijuana airport's international, and you can also get to central Mexico from there. To really disappear from everyone's screens, I recommend Central America or Cuba. Cuba's better due to no U.S. diplomatic relations. But it has lousy infrastructure and sketchy internet. Frigging commies. Spyder]

Steven considered the advice.

[I'll keep you all posted on what the plans are as soon as I know something.]

He logged off as Bowman and called Stan, who confirmed that a package had arrived. They arranged to rendezvous in twenty minutes at the original café they'd met at before, across from the big hotel. Steven lugged his bag and laptop to the truck and made his way to meet Stan.

Stan recognized him straight off this time, and after shaking hands and exchanging pleasantries he handed Steven a manila envelope and slipped him a platinum credit card in the name of Prosperous Moon Trading Corporation, with Steven Cross stamped on it.

"I'd start practicing an illegible signature for Steven Cross," Stan advised.

"Steven Cross. I like it. I feel awed and honored to be so trusted by Prosperous Moon Trading," Steven declared.

"The card has a fifty grand limit on it and the bills will automatically be paid monthly. I would still use cash as often as possible for any travel just to be safe. But now you can withdraw money at any ATM in the world – and the card's in the company name, so you won't show up on a computer." Stan had thought of everything, and then some. "Try to keep your expenditures to under fifty grand per month, would you?"

"You ask a lot. How am I supposed to live in the lavish manner I've become accustomed to at the Best Western Carlsbad on less than a fifty thousand a month?" Steven inquired innocently.

Stan peered at Steven over his spectacles before making the obvious decision to ignore his jabs. "The passport should be here Thursday. It's being sent over by diplomatic pouch to the consulate in LA and then couriered to me that afternoon, if we're lucky," he explained. "Your motel is paid through Friday. Let me know if you want to extend it longer; it's not a problem. Any ideas on what you'll do next?"

"I'll let you know. I'm still working on it. Anything from Homeland?" Steven inquired.

"They called my friend back on Friday – said they were investigating you in a matter of national security. My friend pushed back and demanded to know what matter, and they indicated you were being sought in connection with possible funding of terrorist-related entities. 'Possible funding?' my friend asked. They wouldn't say anything else, and my friend pointed out you'd been reported as killed in the paper; true as far as he's aware." Stan looked at Steven. "Sounds like someone framed you with data we won't be allowed to see. That's part of the problem with this. They can accuse you of anything they want and justify their behavior with the whole 'national security' thing."

"So the net is my hundred fifty thousand's gone for the duration?"

"Once they figure out you weren't on the boat – and they will, Steven, you can count on that – we should expect a full court press to take you into custody for questioning. You're being lumped into the same category as a terrorist financier. It's an incredible abuse of the system, but one in today's political climate that's all too common. The money's the least of your problems," Stan advised him.

"I don't expect anyone to miss Todd until his rent comes due in another couple of weeks, so there's not a big risk of me coming back to life for now," Steven reasoned. "In the meantime, I'm going to look through this package and figure out my next move. I'll stay in touch, and I'll call before Thursday so I can coordinate getting the passport. I appreciate everything you're doing for me, Stan." Steven owed Stan big time. Huge time. They both knew as much. And Steven wouldn't forget it. Ever.

Stan looked at him carefully. "Steven, if your theory about the CIA being involved is correct, they're probably the ones who got Homeland Security to pull you in on a pretense. These are big dogs. Now, I'm not saying I buy your idea, but I did want to say if you're right, you might want to consider the scope of what you're up against."

"I get it, Stan, however it's a little late for regrets."

"I agree. But I still don't completely understand why they'd be in the mix."

"I've been thinking about that. Maybe with the number of ex-bankers in Washington, someone figured out that with Wall Street they had the perfect black box to generate income for their ops; you know, we'll look the other way if you're manipulating ABC Corp – as long as some of the profits stick to us. That's the likely explanation, and it fits with why there's no regulation or any attempts to stop manipulation when it happens."

"That would require a lot of folks colluding, Steven."

"Not necessarily. The SEC never goes after large industry participants, so it's not like they're chomping at the bit; just look at their track record with Madoff. Or look at all the obvious fraud in the mortgage derivatives meltdown – where not one of the obvious thieves in that crooked little dance has even been charged. Hell, Stan – they don't even have the ability to prosecute. They're limited to civil suits, and they hardly even do those, except to small fry who are too small to matter. So really we're only talking about co-opting a few key people at the top; and who's going to buck that sort of trend from on high? Are you telling me you can't see that as realistic, with the kind of money we're talking?"

Stan nodded. "I guess after TARP and the way the banks screwed the taxpayer nothing would surprise me…I suppose anything's possible, but you'd figure there are safeguards against that."

"Think about it. The SEC is a revolving door between million dollar jobs on Wall Street and putting in grunt time going after small timers. You really think anyone there is going to stick their neck out and risk going after a potential future employer? Besides, haven't you noticed that even with all the obvious fraud in the 2008 meltdown, nobody went to jail? If you were a kid in South Central and you'd sold a few grams of crack to an undercover cop, you'd be looking at hard time. But if you're a Wall Street criminal who's set up the system for a meltdown, and then made billions plunging the country into economic purgatory, you get a wing of a hospital named after you. Face it, Stan, big crime pays big."

Stan took off his spectacles and shook his head. "This just keeps getting worse the more I learn."

"Welcome to my world."

Steven drove back to the motel, and once in his room he pulled the tab across the top of the package Stan had given him. He examined the contents.

Another envelope.

He extracted it and opened it. Inside were Xeroxed copies of FBI files, including several photos.

He started at the beginning. A photo of Jim Cavierti came first. Not a great-looking guy. Weak chin. Bags under his eyes. The image looked like an enlarged passport photo. Next came his CV: Born James Augustus Cavierti, 1960, in Tom's River, New Jersey. Educated at Columbia University in New York. Business Degree. Worked at Goldman Sachs out of school. Became a founding partner at Griffen Ventures in 1983. Spoke fluent Italian and Spanish.

Next, a photo of Patricia Cavierti, who looked like a solid 'Ten' in the shot. What a bombshell. Then came Jim's financial breakdown, with an estimated net worth at time of death of $25-plus million. Not bad. And that was after-tax money. Apparently Wall Street wasn't a terrible place for a kid from NJ to wind up. $4.4 million house, four cars, second homes in Sicily and Connecticut.

As the afternoon wore on, he waded deeper into Cavierti's history. The family had suspected mob ties via the father, who had a rap sheet for assault, trafficking in stolen goods and weapons possession while on parole. Young Jim had apparently decided not to follow in his twisted footsteps.

Towards the end of the documents was testimony from a government informant, code-named Dash. Steven's interest became aroused at this. Dash raised a lot of doubt about the funding sources for Griffen Ventures' initial rounds. He alleged that Jim had strong ties with the Gambino and Genovese mob, and that much of Jim's success was as a result of financial support and laundering for those groups – in addition to a number of other questionable sources. Part of the testimony was redacted; blacked out. Steven wondered what could have been so sensitive to make an internal FBI file redacted. An ominous turn, to say the least.

At the end of the deposition, Dash indicated the newer dirty money was being hidden offshore, with many Caribbean islands the preferred gateways for laundering – hence the connection. He stated Cavierti had offshore private accounts worth many more millions of illicit dollars – Cavierti had initiated a laundering facility for arms traders out of the Middle East as a side business, by way of Switzerland and then ultimately through Anguilla.

Then more blacked-out areas.

A few company names suspected of being involved with Cavierti were listed. Apparently the FBI had been building a case against Cavierti with the objective of going after him within the year – until Cavierti met his untimely end…

After reviewing the documents again it seemed like all arrows pointed to Anguilla for answers. So he had a destination at last. All he needed now was a plan.

Easier said than done, he supposed; the plan thing.

Steven spent half an hour practicing his new signature. Not bad. Looked like a squashed bug. It would do – after all, he was a PhD. He signed the back of the Visa card. He was in business.

Now he just needed to figure out exactly what business he was in.

CHAPTER 8

"When you tryin' to catch a rat, you need to getchou a rat trap," said the voice outside the curtained window of Steven's room. "One a those little mouse traps ain't never gonna do tha trick. No, what you need is a rat trap!"

Steven listened to the maintenance men as they continued past his door, still discussing the challenges of pest control in the hospitality industry. He was about to head over for yet another hotel breakfast, but he stopped dead as the two men walked by – now debating baiting techniques.

Of course the older man was right.

To catch a rat, you needed a rat trap.

Steven grabbed his gear and made his way to the motel restaurant. He'd actually started looking forward to the pancakes.

Stockholm syndrome, no doubt.

He picked up his cell phone and dialed the international number in Anguilla Peter had provided for him.

"Good morning, Larkin and Reese."

"Good morning. I'm trying to reach Alfred Reese," Steven said.

"Certainly, sir, and who may I say is calling for him?" The receptionist had an island lilt to her voice.

"An associate of Peter Valentine. He's expecting a call from me."

After a few moments pause a deep British-accented voice came on the line.

"This is Alfred Reese."

"Mr. Reese, thanks for taking my call. I'm a close friend of Peter Valentine. He told me he'd spoken to you and you could probably help us? My name's Steven," he said, hoping they could leave it on a first name basis for now.

"Yes, I recall the discussion. Peter comes strongly recommended, and he speaks highly of you. He intimated there are certain sensitive matters for which you need assistance." The deep voice gave nothing away. Alfred had managed to say much while saying very little.

"Correct. It will require expertise in a number of areas, such as banking, company formation, and so on." Steven could also play the discreet game.

"As I indicated to Peter, I've top-drawer resources in all of those areas. I can certainly get the ball rolling for you via correspondence – however, I think for ultimate discretion there's no substitute for conducting one's business in person, if you follow my reasoning." Alfred Reese already reminded Steven of Stan Caldwell. He wondered if they taught obtuse communication in law school.

"I don't disagree. Perhaps you can e-mail me an engagement letter so we have a formal relationship, and then I'll get you more information and plan a visit." Steven had learned the value of attorney-client privilege.

"Excellent. What's your e-mail address?" Alfred asked.

Steven gave him his new Hotmail account.

"Send me the agreement, and I'll sign it and fax it back to you," Steven instructed.

"Very well, Steven. I should probably advise you my ordinary fee schedule is circa three hundred and fifty U.S. dollars per hour, but for the nature of assistance Peter and I discussed, I invoice on a project basis. Is that acceptable?" Alfred wanted to make sure he had a client who wouldn't choke when he got the bill.

"You can rest assured we're comfortable paying on a project basis, and also amenable to paying a premium for superior results." Steven figured that should address the money question.

"I suspect, then, we'll hit it off famously, Steven. I only deliver superior results." Nice comeback, Alfred.

"I assumed as much."

"Keep an eye on your inbox," Alfred said. "I look forward to hearing from you."

Steven got a good vibe from Alfred. He seemed polished, conservative, and expensive.

He'd learned paying top dollar wasn't a bad idea when you were looking for professional help of a serious sort. You don't want the cheapest heart surgeon, you want the best.

To catch a rat you need to getchou a rat trap.

Steven paid his bill and went to his 'office', as he now considered Starbucks to be. He ordered the usual and settled into his corner. The website was now up to 16,800 hits. He checked his new e-mail account and retrieved the document from Alfred. Switching over to his Group, he posted a greeting:

[Hey gang, it's Bowman. Who knows anything about Anguilla?]

A few minutes later a response popped up:

[Little island next to St. Martin. Small population. One or two main roads. It's hurricane season right now. What else do you want to know? Spyder]

Steven wanted to know as much as possible.

[If you were going to do some offshore banking, why would you pick Anguilla? What's there? – Bowman]

Response from Spyder:

[Barclays, Scotiabank and CaribeWest. But I'd probably do most of my business in St. Martin. Way bigger, much more developed, not far. Can't think of many reasons to choose Anguilla. Didn't I read on some questionable website that a certain investment fund had its corporate charter in Anguilla? Spyder]

Steven fired back:

[I thought I read that, too. Always had a hankering to visit. What a coincidence. Any travel tips? – Bowman]

[I'll e-mail you some thoughts later. Spyder]

He spent time surfing the web, researching flight schedules and hotels. Checking Hotmail, he saw a message from the same anonymous re-mailer Spyder used last time.

[First off, I still think you should plan on going through Cuba to get off the US flight log systems. I'd catch a flight from Tijuana to Mexico City or Cancun, then a flight over to Havana. Do a layover for a few days, then to St. Martin, and take a private plane to Anguilla. The more you avoid commercial flights, the better off you'll be. Pay for the Tijuana flight in cash. If you're going to carry over ten grand, change some money into Euros or Canadian dollars, and use a money belt. If you can, buy some gold Maple Leafs too – they'll look like a roll of quarters on an X-ray machine. Carry-on bags only. Buy what you need as you go, and travel light. Hope this helps. Keep me abreast of your adventures. I'll assist however I can.

I'm also digging at the government connection, formulating a theory I'll share with you when I have more meat on the bones. You won't be reassured, if I'm even close to correct on this. – Spyder]

Wow. More to worry about, but a lot of good info. This guy really knew far too much about going covert to be a civilian. He'd never have thought about Cuba or Cancun as a gateway, or using private planes to get around the Caribbean. Or carrying Euros. He checked and found a flight on one of the Mexican airlines from Tijuana to Havana on Friday evening, arriving in Havana Saturday afternoon after a long layover in Mexico City. Perfect. Six hundred fifty bucks. A bargain. Apparently he could get a Visa for Havana at the Mexico City airport seeing as he was Romanian; as an American, it would have been longer and more complicated.

He'd hang out in Havana for a day or two and then catch an island hopper over to St. Martin, then a ferry or plane to Anguilla. Kind of amazing what a little cash and a non-U.S. citizenship could achieve.

He disconnected and packed his laptop and went in hunt of someplace with a copy machine. There was one up the hill. He printed out the Alfred document and signed it with his new signature. Steven had the clerk fax it back before shredding it. Satisfied, he went out to his car and placed another call to the right honorable Mr. Reese.

"Good day, Larkin and Reese." Same lilting island voice. Almost a musical quality to it. Not unpleasant.

"Hello again. This is Steven calling for Mr. Reese."

"Yes, sir. One moment, and I'll see if he's available." She put him on hold.

Alfred came on the line. "I've just received your fax. What can I do for my newest client?"

"I'll be coming to the island Monday," Steven said, "if all goes well. I could use some help in finding a discreet location to stay for several days where I won't have to bother with a lot of paperwork; more of a cash-and-carry place, if possible. Can that be arranged?"

"Of course. I'm acquainted with some of the better resorts here and can easily arrange a room for you on our business account. Rest assured, you won't be troubled with petty demands – identification and such like – I realize how tiring travel can be." Alfred was definitely his man for the job.

"I'll also need a cell phone for my stay. The rest we can discuss when I arrive." Steven didn't want to let too much info get out until he was there and had met Alfred in person.

"Consider it done. I can meet you at the airport or ferry when you arrive, and drive you to the hotel. Just give me sufficient notice. I'll look forward to meeting you on Monday."

"And I'll look forward to seeing the island. I understand it's beautiful," Steven said.

"We tend to like it. Let me know if there's anything else I can do for you in the interim." Alfred signed off.

So the ball was in play. Now all he needed was his passport and he was good to go. He debated doing a currency exchange, but decided to get fifteen or twenty gold Maple Leafs instead. The Maples would be quickly convertible into cash anywhere in the world, and he rather liked the idea of having something besides paper money to barter with. He'd done some research on the web and figured he could easily walk through airport security anywhere in the world but the United States with thirty or forty grand in hundred dollar bills in his pockets without triggering any alarms, so he wasn't particularly worried about carrying cash. But sometimes gold had more cache value, and considering he didn't know where he was going to wind up or what he'd need, it couldn't hurt.

CHAPTER 9

Griffen sat with Sergei in the Russian Tea Room on 57th Street. Sergei was treated like a rock star there, and he basked in the glow of attention the staff lavished upon him. They had one of the private rooms off the main four dining rooms, used by visiting dignitaries and similar VIPs.

"I have no information that would lead me to believe your original problem wasn't solved," Sergei said casually as he sipped his pepper-flavored vodka.

"Have you noticed the website's back up?" Griffen said. "That creates substantial difficulty for me."

"Ahh. That is a different and more nagging problem this time around. The level of sophistication of the operators is considerably greater. We have been unable to locate the server yet. We continue to investigate." Sergei looked at Griffen. "At the end of the day, we handled the root cause. This appears to be a different person or group that has picked up the baton and is tormenting you. I'm not sure you can effectively silence this now it has been out for a while. Too many are familiar with the story."

Griffen frowned. "I can hardly allow my network to be exposed or the organization of my funds broken down and analyzed – much less speculations as to the size and purpose of the offshore entity. That creates problems for all of us." Griffen wanted to make sure Sergei understood there was risk in this for everyone.

A critical mistake on his part.

Sergei reclined a little, and sighed. "Let me explain something to you, my friend. I hire people to perform tasks for me. For example, my driver is in charge of driving my car. If he loses control of the car while driving, it is he who has the problem, not I. And if I am harmed because of his error, he is likely to lose his position of trust and responsibility and face harsh consequences."

He gazed, unblinking his steel-grey eyes as he spelled out his subtle parable: "Now, I love my driver like a son, and would do *anything* to help him with difficulties that are within my ability to impact. If he has a financial problem I can help. If someone would do him harm, I can help. But if he has a gambling problem and bets his house and his other property, and then steals something and has legal problems, my ability to intervene is hampered. I cannot help then."

They sipped their drinks while nibbling at the expansive plateful of expensive appetizers spread out before them.

"Sergei, I didn't mean to imply–"

"It is not a matter of implication. I want to help you with your situation, and will do everything I can. But...just to be clear...it is I who helps *you* with *your* problem, not with *our* problem, *nyet*?"

Sergei was radiating his *it's all just good, clean fun* smile. It was what lay behind the smile that made Griffen shudder at his faux pas.

"Of course, Sergei. I completely understand. And I do appreciate everything you've done." Griffen was backpedaling hard.

"I have been looking at the website," Sergei said, "and the speculations about the level of your commitment in Allied are disturbing." Sergei paused. "Do I have anything to be disturbed about?"

"No. It's not an issue. Your investment is mostly in the offshore fund, which I assure you is in good shape." Griffen failed to mention that he'd shifted much of his position over to the foreign fund at the end of June, making his domestic fund look much stronger for the half-year report to the investors.

As of today, with some of his other bad bets, the domestic fund was only down 15 percent, but the offshore fund was theoretically bankrupt if they had to sell the Allied stock in a freefall – Griffen used a lot of leverage offshore, which could exponentially increase profit, but could also wipe him out if there was a substantial unexpected move. Which would never happen. He just needed that fucking site to be eliminated, and then it would be back to business as usual.

Griffen continued to assure him: "It's never been better. Just look at the new report on the domestic fund – only down fifteen percent in a year where my peers are down thirty. You have nothing to worry about."

Sergei smiled again, a happy man by nature. "I never doubted it for a minute, my friend. We will continue trying to help with your little bump on the road, yes?" He tossed back the last of his vodka. "*Za vashe zdorovye!*"

Griffen left the restaurant, feeling sick. He'd seen the report on the sailboat explosion and was satisfied the original troublemaker was dead. It was his bad luck somebody else had decided to run the website – perhaps even one of his competitors. But he was going to make his luck change soon.

He just needed the stock to increase in price by another forty or so percent, and speculation to increase so he could get out of his long position and build a healthy short position – then the site would almost be helping him. Knock the stock down eighty to ninety percent once he was a few hundred million bucks short, especially with put options that skyrocketed in value even with only minor price moves downward, and he'd make up all his losses and come out smelling like roses.

That would bring the funds back up to the billion dollar mark and erase what had up until now been a disastrous year, making it just a bad memory...

The website complicated the plan because he couldn't control the timing of the damaging revelations – nor the content – and this was foremost a timing game. He remained hopeful, though; it was just a matter of days until Sergei or Glen would locate the new server location, and then they could have it taken out, perhaps hacked irreparably or infected with some sort of lethal virus.

As always, he'd think of something.

CHAPTER 10

By Wednesday, Steven had settled into a morning rhythm that involved running and breakfast, and then time at his favorite coffee-franchise-cum-office.

He had everything in place now for his departure, which was only 48 hours away, tops, then Steven would be safely over the border and on to a new life. He'd toyed with the idea of going back to his house to retrieve his important papers and put them into a safe deposit box, but dismissed it as foolish under the circumstances.

It was another morning at the coffee shop to communicate with the world, and then hopefully Thursday he'd get his passport and be able to vanish. He checked all his usual sites, noticing he had a response from the Canadian agent working the brokerage scandal. He read the e-mail.

[Hello Steven. I'm sorry to hear Peter was killed. It's a tragedy. He explained your issue to me in our last conversation, and I think I may be able to help. Feel free to call me. Best, Cliff.]

Followed by a phone number. Steven saved the e-mail and dialed the number.

"Cliff Tomlin."

"Hello, Cliff. This is Steven, Peter Valentine's friend. I just got your e-mail."

"Yes, hello, Steven. I'm sorry to hear about the accident."

Steven figured he might as well tell him up front what was going on. "Well, Cliff, thanks for that, but I don't think it *was* an accident. We've had a number of alarming things happen since we started our investigation into Griffen, and Peter was meeting a source who was going to provide some incriminating information when he was killed. It doesn't look good."

"I'll take your word for it. How can I assist you?" Cliff asked.

"If you see anything in Griffen's account that looks suspicious, like high volume of buys or sells of Allied stock, please notify me. Allied is the company we're investigating his role in."

"That's a considerable breach of confidentiality laws, and could cause serious problems for me if it ever leaked I'd shared any info with you. But I owed Peter huge, so I'll trust you to be discreet. I guess what I'm saying is, I shouldn't tell you anything, but given the circumstances, fair enough. I'll pass your area of interest on to our mole. Expect an e-mail if there's anything unusual. Sorry again about Peter. He helped me out of a nasty jam years ago – basically saved my life...and my career. Make no mistake, you're asking for a lot, so hopefully this will settle the debt." Cliff seemed like a decent enough sort, and he sounded genuinely saddened by Peter's death.

"Thank you, Cliff. Anything we discuss will remain absolutely confidential, you have my word. It's for my eyes only."

CHAPTER 11

Thursday, he received a message from Spyder:

[Cut the tags out of your clothes if you're going to be traveling under a non-USA passport (a guess) and discard your shaving materials and hygiene products. Buy more in Mexico. The devil's in the details. Don't assume no one's paying attention – assume everyone has you under a microscope and you'll do OK. Good luck. – Spyder]

He'd never really considered those kinds of things, but realized Spyder was right. He needed to eliminate as much as he could that identified him in any way – and he also had to work up a plausible cover story.

Okay...he was Steven Cross, on a Romanian passport. How did that come about? Born in Bucharest, parents moved to Canada when he was young; very young, hence the inability to speak a word of Romanian. They insisted he learn English so he would assimilate, and never spoke Romanian at home.

Sounded good so far.

What was *his* story though? Independently wealthy, he'd inherited his money after working in the family import business. Okay. Why was he abroad? Had a wild hair up his ass to travel for a year or two. Got his brand new passport and hit the road. Was thinking about writing a book and wanted to look at locales. He didn't think he needed much more than that.

He called Stan, who confirmed the passport had arrived in Los Angeles and should be there no later than 4:00. One hour away. That gave him just enough time to visit the cleaners to pick up his order and stop by at the drugstore to get scissors. He filled the hour by completing these tasks and sitting in his truck, patiently removing all the clothes tags; a job longer and harder than he would have thought possible.

At 4:01 he called Stan again. They agreed to meet at a Mexican restaurant by the beach at 5:30, so back to the motel he went, clothes in tow. At 5:30 he rolled into the restaurant parking area. It was early, but on a Thursday night the margarita party crowd was already getting started with happy hour. A throng of red-faced fat guys woo-hooed enthusiastically on the bar area patio, radiating the tiresome drunken belligerence of the privileged and habitually ill-behaved.

Stan wheeled into the parking area immediately after Steven, so he waited as Stan got out of the car, envelope in his hand. They went inside together, choosing to sit at the back, away from the frat party atmosphere. They declined margaritas but acquiesced to a couple of *Pacificos*. Stan handed Steven the envelope.

The waitress deposited their beers and threw a basket of chips in front of them with studied indifference. Two beers. She knew the type. Big spenders.

"So planning on making your way out into the world soon?" Stan asked.

"I'm going to do everything I can to bring Griffen down, Stan. He's hurt me, killed my friends and destroyed my life. And he's getting away with it, so far. Nobody else seems like they're going to stop him, so that's my new project." Steven took a sip of his beer. Icy cold.

"I'm not going to try to tell you what to do," Stan said. "But you have enough money to live pretty much wherever you want in comfort for the rest of your life."

"I'd never be able to live with myself if I didn't do this, Stan. I had money before he decided to take me out. I could have chosen to live elsewhere if I'd wanted. I didn't. I wanted to live here, right where I was, just as I was. He's made that impossible. I want him to pay for that, as well as for Peter and Todd." Steven took another pull on the beer.

"I'm not saying don't do it. I guess I'm just trying to say you may be walking into machine-gun fire, and you don't have to. That's all. There are other ways to live a good life."

"Peter doesn't have that option any more, does he?" Steven asked.

They both fell silent for a few minutes. There wasn't a lot left to say, and neither was in the mood for idle banter. When they were through with the beers Steven opened the envelope and looked at the passport. Steven Cross at your service. He pulled out a pen and did his best squashed bug where Stan had affixed a little sticky arrow saying, 'Sign here.'

Stan peered over his spectacles – Steven was going to miss that... "It's the genuine article, so don't lose it. Stay in touch via telephone, Steven – landlines if possible. I don't trust e-mail at all, and I don't trust cell phones much more."

He stood up, reached out and shook Steven's hand. "I don't want to know where you're going or where you are at any given time. Having said that, if you're in trouble, call."

"I appreciate all the help, Stan. You're a good friend." He smiled. "We aren't going to a funeral, why so glum eh? I'll stay in touch." Steven hoped he was right about the funeral part.

Stan departed to the restroom and Steven exited to the car park to wait for him in his truck. When Stan walked out to the parking area, Steven handed him the Jim Cavierti file through the window.

"Put this someplace very safe. See you around, Stan."

He put the Mazda in gear and pulled away, the image of Stan standing with the envelope in hand in the parking lot a stark reminder of how much his life had changed in just a few short days.

The next morning Steven carefully packed his new duffel and laptop, ensuring no American disposable products contaminated his toiletry kit. The money belt he'd bought cinched his midsection, but it wasn't too bad. You couldn't see it with his baggy button-up shirt on. He made a mental note to stop at a mall in San Diego and buy four or five more loose button-up shirts for comfortable concealment of the belt while traveling.

He went into in the motel restaurant for the last time and got his usual. He ate slowly, enjoying the chatter on the boards while he surfed on his Blackberry. When he was done with breakfast, he left the waitress a twenty dollar tip. For old times' sake.

He didn't need to check out since Stan had paid for everything in advance, so he stowed his gear in the little Mazda and pointed it south. Once in San Diego, he stopped at a mall near the Gaslamp quarter, bought shirts, cutting the tags out at the store, explaining how sensitive his skin was to the chafing nature of the labels.

The cashier couldn't have been more vacant if she'd tried. Nobody cared. Good.

His flight didn't leave Tijuana until 7:50 p.m. but anticipation had set him itching to get out of the country. Steven wove through the trundling freeway traffic and took the last exit before the border, and after circling the decrepit area pulled onto a street about two blocks from the crossing, in one of the seediest neighborhoods he'd ever been in. He stopped the truck, placed his temporary cell phone under the rear tire, and drove over it a couple of times. Smashed flat. He parked the car fifty yards closer to the border and left it, open, with the keys in the ignition. Things would take care of themselves for the trusty Mazda, he was sure.

After satisfying himself that he hadn't forgotten anything, he wheeled his duffel and laptop bag toward the crossing point without looking back.

CHAPTER 12

Getting into Mexico couldn't have been easier. After crossing through some turnstiles, Steven walked past several bored customs agents and a handful of teenage soldiers, and *presto*, he was in the land of mariachis.

He navigated through the congested and filthy area near the crossing, avoiding the beggars and hundreds of vendors with their ceramic Tweety birds and praying Jesuses and similar treasures. Steven followed the foot traffic, and made his way towards the central metropolitan area and spotted a large *Super Farmacia*, where he bought shampoo, soap, deodorant, disposable razors, toothpaste. All *hecho en Mexico*, with the directions and labels in Spanish. He stuffed the plastic bag into the duffel as the pharmacy security guard watched him with measured disinterest.

Back on the street, he'd had about enough of downtown Tijuana within two minutes. Rounding a corner, he spotted a row of cabs sitting at the curb in front of a bar; he got into the one at the head of the line and said, "*El Aeoropuerto, por favor.*" Apparently the driver understood, because soon they were speeding down narrow, dirty streets at triple the speed limit, the driver cheerfully ignoring the stop signs as they flew by.

Steven noted the engine and brake warning lights were both illuminated, and that passengers were untroubled by old-fashioned concerns like seat belts; there were none. The small statue of Jesus on the dashboard did little to comfort him as they narrowly escaped T-boning a delivery van amidst much honking and fist shaking.

He hoped the Mexican blanket, in service as his ad hoc seat cover, only smelled like it had recently been on a sick burro, and wondered how easily lice could attach themselves to him.

The roads were teeming with filth and the odor of raw sewage wafted into the cab window. The hills housed poverty on an epic scale and the area near the border fence was crawling with inhabitants in lean-tos awaiting nightfall for their shot at breaching the fence. He supposed Calcutta made this look like Club Med, but it was still a shocker to see it up close and personal only a couple of miles from a country where you could buy food twenty-four hours a day and where sixty-one percent of the population was fat or obese.

The cab rattled on until they eventually got to the airport, which was surprisingly well-policed and spotlessly clean. He paid the driver in dollars, found the airline counter and purchased a ticket for *La Havana*, also paying in dollars. *Si Senor, con mucho gusto.* The attendant told him in passable English that he could get his visa for Cuba at the airport in DF – *Distrito Federal*, as Mexico City was referred to by the locals.

He exhausted the departure area's shops for stimulating pastimes, ate a questionable burrito at one of the little restaurants in the departure area, and finally boarded the flight to Mexico City with relief. Takeoff was punctual and uneventful. Steven watched through the airplane window as the lights of San Diego receded beneath the tail of the plane, Point Loma still faintly visible even as the sunset's glow dimmed into the encroaching nightfall.

Mexico City Airport at 1:30 in the morning was quiet. He had earplugs, and managed to doze intermittently until things picked up at around 7 a.m.. Fully awake, Steven wandered the huge terminal and people-watched, grabbing breakfast at one of the numerous restaurants populating the departure area. He was somewhat surprised at how clean the entire airport was – he'd been given to viewing Mexico as a filthy, dangerous place where you took your life into your hands when you crossed the border. Instead, he found a first world quality airport with every possible amenity and comfort; there were even numerous American brands at the turn of every corner – Krispy Kreme, 7/11, and American restaurant franchises of every imaginable variety. Again, his flight was on schedule, and he ascended out of the blanket of smog that surrounded Mexico City with little regret at having missed taking in the town itself. This was the most populated city in the world, and easily one of the most dangerous, as well as one of the most polluted. Pass on anything outside of the airport, thank you.

As they approached Cuba, he was struck by the size of the island. He wasn't sure what he'd expected, but he was still surprised by the sheer length of it. They touched down, and he realized, with a jab of adrenalin, that this was going to be the first real test of his new passport – nobody but the ticket agent had looked at it in TJ.

He disembarked, and dutifully stood in the queue for customs. The inspector gave his visa and passport a cursory glance, stamped it and waved him through. That was it. Nothing to it. He'd been anticipating some sort of questioning or at least more scrutiny, but apparently Cuba wasn't worried about being invaded by Romania just yet.

Once through, he found an information booth and asked the woman at the desk if she spoke English.

"A leetle," she explained, holding her index finger and thumb slightly apart in the universal gesture of small.

"What's the best hotel in Havana?" he asked.

"Oh, The NH Park Central and the Melia are berry popular, but I like the Santa Isabel."

"How much will a taxi cost?" Steven inquired.

"About twenty dollars." The dollar was officially unwelcome, but still universally accepted.

"*Gracias.*"

Steven exited the terminal and dutifully stood in a queue for one of the authorized taxis – only select cars were allowed to accommodate foreigners. He asked for the Hotel Santa Isabel, and the surprisingly modern automobile pulled smoothly away. Based on his assumptions about Cuba, his expectation was for a ride in a 1950's Mercury – instead, he got a 2010 Mitsubishi sedan.

After a half-hour trip the cab stopped alongside a three-story building that occupied an entire block a few hundred yards from the waterfront. It appeared to be an old colonial mansion converted into a hotel. After paying the driver in dollars, which he seemed more than happy to receive, Steven carried his bags into the front entrance.

Steven approached the front desk and communicated in broken Spanish that he'd like a room for two nights (*posible un camisa por dos noches?*), to which one of the gentlemen behind the reception area responded in perfect English, informing him that, of course, they could accommodate him. They requested his passport and informed him that the cost would be $140 per night, which he also paid in cash. He'd taken to carrying $600 in a small wallet he'd gotten while at the luggage store; so that he wouldn't be pulling out a wad of hundreds every time he needed to pay for something.

No one seemed the least bit surprised that a Romanian was communicating with them in perfect American English and paying in dollars. It was a world steeped in mystery – and who had the time to wonder over every wrinkle?

The room turned out to be a large, older-styled mini-suite that looked exactly like what it in fact was: a converted series of rooms in what had at one time been a private residence of massive proportions. The air hung stifling when he first walked in, but the A/C reluctantly eased the temperature to a reasonable level within a few minutes, and after hanging up his few shirts and washing his face and hands, he fell into bed and drifted off to sleep, the noise of traffic from the *Malecon* muted by the heavy velvet drapes.

CHAPTER 13

When Steven came to, it was late afternoon. He looked at his watch and calculated he'd been down for three hours. He experimented with the shower, which spurted forth a meager stream of water barely sufficient to get the travel grime off and resuscitate him enough to venture out into the town. Still, he was grateful for it, as his initial expectations of Cuba had been minimal, and his surroundings were actually elegant, if a bit worn in places.

It was easily 85 percent humidity and about 90+ degrees outside, so he donned shorts and one of his new black button-up short sleeve shirts. Before leaving, he locked his valuables and money belt in the room safe and descended the stairs to the lobby.

The streets clamored boisterous and noisy, with music emanating from doorways and windows, competing with the roar of old engines sedulously making their way down the battered boulevards. There were fewer vehicles than he'd imagined, which he suspected was a function of the general poverty of the island – confirmed, to a point, by the crumbling state of most of the buildings. Havana was a city in decay. At one time obviously grand; even by European city standards, but generations of inattention had reduced most buildings to near ruin.

He was propositioned every 30 yards by young ladies looking to make a little cash, further reinforcing the seedy feeling of the place. Through all this he smelled a dizzying combination of cigar smoke and cooking odors, reminding him how famished he was. As he crossed the street at block number four he spotted one of the restaurants the hotel clerk had recommended. He entered and was quickly shown to a table by the window.

There were few other patrons, no doubt due to the early hour, which again was fine by him. He scanned the menu and ordered a bottle of water and a *Bucanero* beer, finally opting for the specialty of the house; *palomilla* served with black beans and rice.

The beer was medium-dark bodied, very strong and extremely cold. The steak barely edible. Still, after the meal he felt like a new man, or at least a slightly less used one.

As he paid his bill, Steven noted that, while not unreasonable, it was about four times more expensive than what the locals likely would have paid – Cuba had a two-tier system which commanded much higher prices from non-citizens. He couldn't really complain, as the locals clearly had little or no money.

Steven left the shade of the restaurant and returned to the heat and humidity, which slammed him like a burst from a blast furnace.

He wandered down the streets to the *Malecon*, the boulevard that ran along the waterfront, entertained by the live musicians in every other doorway. Near the central area he came upon a fair-sized crowd gathered around a pair of young men who were boxing; obviously for show, judging by the hat sitting next to the chalked-out 'ring' – it contained a few dollars and coins. He watched with interest as they parried and swatted at each other, pouring sweat from their exertion as they landed blows in determined silence.

The crowd cheered their respective favorites, and the two lads showed no signs of being even close to calling it a draw as the crowd egged them on.

He felt a tug at his back pocket and spun around to see a thin, ferret-faced local edging away from him through the noisy gathering. He'd forgotten to stick his wallet in his front pocket when he'd left the restaurant, and an enterprising thief had spotted the bulge and correctly surmised that there was money to be had, free for the taking.

Almost.

As Steven moved towards the man, he turned and broke into a run. Steven gave chase as he ran through the side street off the main boulevard and into the less traveled residential tenement area of town.

It really was no contest, as Steven was accustomed to running for miles every morning and was in peak condition. The thief probably hadn't eaten a full meal for days.

After a few minutes he rounded a corner, and the man was leaning against a wall in a dead-end *cul de sac*, catching his breath, accompanied now by a larger man who held an old claw hammer in his hand. Steven took in the situation as the smaller guy pulled out a knife and held it in front of him. The way he gripped it told Steven that he knew how to use it. This was quickly escalating into a deadly situation.

Steven figured he'd give it a go anyway, and addressed them in his broken Spanish.

"Déme mi carpeta y no le lastimaré." (Give me back my wallet and I won't hurt you).

The two men looked at each other and laughed, genuine merriment evident. Who did he think he was? Anglo in girl glasses wanted his wallet back and he'd let them go? That was clearly the Cuban equivalent of a knee-slapper. The bigger one responded.

"Salga, cono, o le mataré." (Get lost, pussy, or you're dead).

Hmmm. That went well, he thought.

It looked like he'd have to do this the hard way. He slowly walked down the alley towards them as they spread out, keeping the weasel with the knife on his left as he approached the bigger assailant, who was now swinging the hammer over his head with his right hand with his left extended forward. Weasel guy crouched down low with both hands in front of him, moving the knife slowly in a circle, still somewhat winded. The bigger man would move first; you could see in his eyes he felt confident, while weasel guy was a tad confused as to why this was turning into an actual fight. The little guy was clearly the brighter of the two.

Time compressed and slowed as Steven entered the state of complete awareness and readiness that he'd experienced countless times before, while in combat in the Gulf and in sparring bouts. He watched, almost detached, as the larger thief moved towards him as though in slow motion, swinging the hammer at his head, and his peripheral senses registered the weasel lunging a few moments later.

Both were right handed, he noted.

Steven leaned back a few degrees and let the hammer swing in front of his face, missing by several inches, and simultaneously kicked the larger man's kneecap, tearing the ligaments and crushing the cartilage, effectively crippling him. He pivoted to dodge the blade but was a few nanoseconds too late, and it sliced the side of his abdomen midway up his ribcage. The thrust was intended to skewer him, but instead glanced off a rib. Steven slammed his cupped hands against each side of the weasel's head, rupturing his eardrums.

Less than eight seconds and it was over. Both assailants lay in the filthy alley, finished, and Steven had only executed two simple moves. To a spectator it would have looked like a rapid kick and then an attempt to catch the smaller man as he fell – not much motion or wasted energy. His heart rate had never increased nor his breathing strained, and the odd sense of time compression lifted, events beginning to morph into real time again.

The big man lay moaning and holding his brutalized knee, and the weasel curled in a fetal position cradling his head, blood trickling out of his ears. The knife had fallen harmlessly away and rested by the wall. Steven bent down and pulled his wallet out of the weasel's shirt pocket, then walked over and ripped a piece of the bigger man's shirt off, pressing it against the cut in his left side to staunch the flow of blood. He whispered to the man.

"*Consiga a un doctor, él está lastimado gravemente.*" (Get him to a doctor, he's hurt pretty badly).

Then he turned and walked out of the alley, retracing his steps to the hotel. He was a little surprised that the knife had gotten him, and attributed it to the effects of the beer. Slowed him down just a hair, which unfortunately translated into a three-inch cut that would require some attention. It was bleeding pretty heavily so he kept pressure applied, allowing the man's shirt to absorb the worst of it. Hurt like a bitch. Served him right for getting careless with the wallet. If you were going to put up a sign saying, 'Idiot here, take advantage' you were bound to get some takers. He hoped the big man would be able to get the weasel to a clinic. The pain from two popped eardrums was excruciating, and there was significant danger of infection.

As he entered the hotel and walked up the stairs to his room he got an alarmed look from the girl at the reception desk. Although the black shirt hid the blood because it just looked wet and slick, there an obvious tear in it – and then there was the blood on his hands.

He sat down at the vanity and removed his shirt to inspect the extent of the stinging wound. Still bleeding, although slower. You could see rib; superficial gash, but deep enough to require attention. He considered using the sewing kit to stitch it up, or perhaps go attempt to find a store that might actually have some superglue – but figured using a doctor would be best, if available. He called down to the concierge.

"*Buenas tardes.*"

"Hello, do you speak English?" Steven asked.

"Yes, of course. How may I help you?"

"I need a doctor to come to the hotel. I cut myself pretty badly on a fence I fell against, and need someone to look at it."

"Eh, I will make some calls. Will you be all right for the time being? Can you wait a few minutes?"

"Yes, but it is painful. I'd appreciate it if you would hurry."

"Naturally, sir. I will call back in just a minute or two. We have a doctor we use for emergencies. I will call now."

"*Gracias.*" Steven hung up.

He wished that there was an ice machine on the floor so he could numb the cut while waiting for the doctor, but this was no Best Western Carlsbad. Few places were. He was out of luck.

The phone rang. The concierge informed him El Doctor was on his way and should be there in ten minutes or so.

Half an hour later, a knock at the door. Steven opened it to find a small, bespectacled man carrying an ancient medical bag.

He introduced himself; "I'm Doctor Juan Carlos Guitierrez. I understand there has been an accident?" His English was passable.

"Yes, an unfortunate encounter with a fence," Steven explained.

"Well, let's see what we have here." The doctor pulled up a chair and sat down on it. He beckoned Steven to stand in front of him. He examined the wound, which was now just seeping a little blood.

"Hmmm. You are fortunate that this, er, fence, sliced cleanly and evenly, missing any organs." He looked at Steven when he said 'fence' with an unmistakable skepticism. He'd seen enough knife fight outcomes to appreciate the type of fence that Steven had fallen against. Still, a man was entitled to his discretion, and who knew, it was a dangerous city and this could have been a matter of the heart. They oftentimes were. Best to focus on the future, not dwell on the past.

"I will need to clean the wound and stitch, and you will require a tetanus shot as well as *antibiotico*, I think, to avoid infection. Are you *alergico*?"

"Excuse me?" Steven didn't understand the last bit.

"*Alergico*, do you have bad responses to any medications?

"Oh, allergic. No, not that I know of."

"*Bueno.* We begin. I will give you something for the pain, I think. Yes? Local only." The doctor extracted a syringe, filled it from a small vial, and injected fluid into the areas around the cut. Steven immediately felt the pain seeping away. The doctor then squirted some into the wound, and the whole area numbed.

"Now we clean."

He swabbed the wound with antiseptic wash and deftly stitched it up. He used sixteen sutures by the time he was done, spacing them fairly far apart. He put a loose dressing on it and left two more bandages with Steven, along with a small tube of ointment.

"This will hurt. I'm sorry, there is nothing else for it," the doctor explained as he gave Steven the tetanus shot. He was right, it hurt almost worse than the 'fence' wound.

"And now for the antibiotic, and you are good as new, I believe, no?" He injected it into the large muscle of the gluteus maximus. The butt. Ouch again.

"Is that it, are we finished?" Steven asked. "How much do I owe you?"

"Money? Ah, let's see. For the stitches, pain medicine, antibiotic, tetanus shot, $80. The medicines are very expensive because of the embargo. I am sorry it is so much."

It was a bargain. In the U.S. a house call and sundry ministrations would have been five times that amount – easily. Steven gave him $100 cash.

"I appreciate the help. It's been a difficult day for me, problems with a girlfriend and then this." Steven needed to ensure that he wouldn't run afoul of any reporting, and wanted to offer a plausible possibility for what the doctor had seen.

"*No problema, Senor.* Ladies can be very unpredictable, no, especially when it is so, eh, hot, *mucho calor.* I have some small experience." El Doctor was a worldly man who understood things.

He looked at Steven. "I would stay away from any more fences for the time being. Put on ointment every eight hours, and have the stitches removed in five days. If you are still in Habana, I would be able to assist; or you can cut them with small scissors and pull them out yourself. Avoid lifting heavy things or placing undue strain on the injury for several weeks. Have the hotel call if there are problems." He placed two packets of aspirin on the table by the door. "I'm afraid there is likely to be some pain, no? Here is aspirin for you. Stronger medications are harder to get."

Steven thanked him again and showed him to the door. He let the doctor out, then lay on the bed. Quite a first day in Havana. Different than a Saturday evening in Newport Beach, that was for sure. It was hard to complain that life was uneventful.

He dozed for a bit, then got up, donned another shirt and went down to the hotel bar. The local anesthesia was wearing off and the pain was starting in. He ordered a Mojito.

When in Rome.

Pretty damned good Mojito, he'd give them that. With nothing else to do to pass the time, he wound up having four before calling it a night. Back in his room, he washed down a couple of aspirin and spent an uncomfortable night tossing and turning.

CHAPTER 14

Sunday he awoke to pain.

His arm, his ass, his side, his head.

The rum in the Mojitos had exacted their inevitable penalty, and the wound both throbbed and burned at the same time. He showered carefully, avoiding soaking the bandage and afterwards changed the dressing – relieved to see some dried blood and clear fluid, but no obvious infection. Good old penicillin had apparently done its job. He choked down some aspirin and went downstairs to the hotel restaurant, where he ordered breakfast. Beans and rice, fried plantains. Very strong, very hot coffee.

Todo bien.

Steven spent much of the day wandering slowly around the city. He ambled across the narrow channel and explored the length of the original Spanish fort that had defended the city for centuries. The new dressing seemed to be holding up and the journey thus far had distracted the pain, so he wandered along the waterfront boulevard, which ran for mile upon mile. Unbelievably, Havana had a fully developed Chinatown. Who knew? He was continually surprised by the level of decay of the structures and the strong, good-natured spirit of the people. He moved through the milling throngs of European and South American tourists, past several elaborate churches, and found himself in front of the famous Hemingway bar, *La Bodeguita del Medio*, on a small nondescript street. Steven was unimpressed. Once away from the waterfront, the heat became oppressive, so he returned to the *Malecon*; packed out with locals because the residents sought out the sea breeze to temper the oppressive heat. After enjoying a cold beer at a temporary bar set up on the seafront main artery, he made his way to Revolution Square, which he thought looked a very Soviet era. Depressingly so. Huge murals featuring Che Guevara and Fidel Castro abounded, and the vibe emanating from the whole city suggested the revolution had taken place a few months earlier – as opposed to over 50 years before.

Steven called it a day on the touristy meandering by four in the afternoon, and after stopping at a dilapidated drugstore to buy some more bandages and a bottle of aspirin, he returned to the hotel and took a *siesta*. When he awoke, he changed his dressing again, which now had very little blood on it at all. Progress of a sort was being made. He ate dinner at a private home he was directed to by the hotel; the home doubled as a restaurant in what was the embassy area of Havana. The food tasted surprisingly good, and once back at the hotel, Steven risked one more Mojito for strictly medicinal purposes. His flight the next day departed in the morning on *Aireo Caribbeano*, and he wanted to be clear-headed for the trip.

He emptied his glass, went into the lobby and had the receptionist put through a call to Alfred Reese's number. Steven got an answering machine, so he left a message that he would arrive sometime tomorrow afternoon and would call from St. Martin.

The receptionist had his bill ready for him. He took it upstairs and looked it over – nothing unexpected. A quick call to the desk ensured he'd get a wake-up call at 6:15 in the morning. That done, he fell back on the bed, exhausted, and listened to the hum of the air conditioner as it struggled to keep the summer swelter at bay.

CHAPTER 15

Kevin Pasteur was an admitted geek. He looked and acted the part; negligible attention to grooming, pigmentation that proclaimed a life spent indoors, military-issue-looking glasses, an unusual depth of knowledge about the latest video games, atrocious fashion sensibility; he even owned a plastic pocket protector for special occasions.

He reveled in the stereotype, and did his best to fulfill everyone's expectations of what a true geek should look like, act like, and be interested in. That he'd made a fortune in software design made it all the more fun for him; afforded him the luxury of being unapologetic about his odd appearance and quirky manners. He was that most reviled of all nerds, the ultra-successful high priest of technology, master of arcane knowledge everyone used, but few understood.

He'd sold his last two companies to larger entities that had needed the expertise of the teams he'd assembled, and he was currently between projects. He didn't need to work anymore but he bored easily, and when he saw a deficiency in a product or a technology he couldn't help himself. He needed to fix it, or improve it. That's just what he did. It had paid well.

He was also a member of the Group.

Kevin – or 'Pogo', as the Group knew him – was a busy boy today.

He was busy making life truly miserable for anyone attempting to track the webmaster of the Allied site, using a variety of techniques that to him were childishly simple. The opposition was probably tearing their hair out trying to figure out what he was doing and how, which amused him immensely. Good help was so hard to find. He'd watched the sorry flailing of his adversaries, and in his opinion, whoever was on the other end of the pixel stream must be a dolt. He almost felt sorry for them.

Almost.

Once he'd written the program to bounce the IPs all over the planet, on a random basis, every 15 minutes, the ultra-busy work was done. He'd set traps along the way so anyone trying to ID him would have to signal their presence. One of his favorite pastimes was to create messages on the boards that contained a link to something that seemed likely to be a giveaway to the webmaster's identity or location, and then record and analyze the IP addresses of the computers that hit the link. He did it in such a way as to time it for when the stock detractors were especially active, thus ensuring whoever clicked in the first 5 minutes of posting the link was a likely bad guy.

So far he'd compiled a nice library of IDs, some of which terminated in surprising places: three were the addresses of prime brokers on Wall Street, a few were random locations in New Jersey, and a handful were from Brooklyn; what looked to be a boiler room. He'd been able to triangulate the identities by comparing the IPs to those hitting the website at key times, such as immediately after he posted news at an odd hour – when only negative posters were clogging the boards.

Pogo was fleshing out his theory that this was a large-scale operation, being managed by one central group but also using a second and third tier of smaller players to support and add momentum. The data supported his hypothesis, and he felt really pleased he'd nailed it.

He'd also committed to becoming an expert within a week or two on how the brokerage system actually worked. That was far harder than writing a simple script to bounce IDs, as there wasn't any central source that described the minutiae of how the machine that dealt with stock payment and delivery actually functioned.

Fortunately, his friend, Andy, worked on Wall Street with one of the smaller broker/dealers and knew a young lady who worked at Griffen's prime broker – the firm that handled most of his domestic trading. She'd been on the job for six years and loathed most of her duties – and her co-workers even more so. She'd met Andy in a bar in the Village a few months ago and they'd hit it off, had been seeing each other on a regular basis ever since to exchange some casual friskiness. Both were highly intelligent and somewhat ill-suited to their vocations, which served as the basis for their relationship. That, and they both drank a lot of vodka and shared an affinity for sushi.

It wasn't a perfect match, but it was close by NY standards.

Andy insisted on going out with Pogo whenever he hit town, and Pogo made sure he did so within a week of hearing about his buddy's new sort-of soul mate. Pogo insisted Andy bring her along on their nights out, and the resulting discussions were illuminating. Pogo had told Andy he was researching a non-fiction book about the stock market, as the writing bug had bitten him, and there wasn't really any top-to-bottom layman's description of how the markets worked from a behind-the-scenes perspective. That didn't surprise Andy – he knew Pogo as a keen intellect capable of anything; he'd witnessed the two companies Pogo had created, with their string of innovative designs. A book about the market? Why not?

Andy had been more than willing to tell a slew of sordid stories (off the record, of course) and the now-and-then girlfriend had poured forth a font of information. Her knowledge base waxed clinical and dry, but comprehensive. That she hated her gig only made her more willing to tell a sympathetic Pogo all the dirty secrets she knew of. By the time the fourth or fifth Cosmo had gone down the hatch she would launch into ten-minute diatribes about how crooked Wall Street was, or how her colleagues were a bunch of scumbag misogynists, or how the machine chewed up its employees and burned them out.

It was pure gold, and now the challenge shifted to steering the discussions into areas where he needed more visibility, while avoiding drinking so much he couldn't remember the details.

He looked at his watch. Dinner time, and then another booze-fest with Andy and Ms. Angry Drinky-Drink. He was glad he didn't live in New York. What a pressure cooker.

In keeping with his character, he donned his best plaid short-sleeved shirt and oversized jeans, and considered his reflection in the full-length mirror. Thirty-something programmer with too much time spent watching hip-hop videos. A non-threatening pencil-neck you could tell your troubles to. Perfect.

A few more nights of this and he'd know everything he needed. He just hoped his liver could take it.

CHAPTER 16

The trip from Havana to St. Martin was bumpy – a noisy half-full turboprop flight. Nobody seemed interested in making small talk above the drone and vibration of the engines. That suited Steven fine.

When he touched down, his passport was waved through with barely a glance. At least now he had two stamps on it, making it appear increasingly plausible he was a globetrotter out to scout backgrounds for his magnum travel opus. When he cleared customs he called Alfred.

"Good afternoon, Larkin and Reese." Same lilting voice.

"Good afternoon. Is Alfred in? This is Steven."

"Just a moment please, I know he's expecting your call." He could hear her speaking to someone in the background.

Alfred's distinctive voice came on the line.

"Hello, Steven. How are you today?"

"Excellent, Alfred. I'm at the St. Martin airport – I expect to be there within an hour or so. Would it be possible to have someone meet me?" Steven asked.

"Of course. I'll meet you myself. How are you arriving, and where?"

"I'm working on the arrival part," Steven said. "Kind of thinking about taking a boat over. I'll call you once I get there."

"You may want to consider the charter fleet down at the waterfront in Marigot if you don't want to deal with customs. I'm sure there are plenty of fast boats only too happy to make a drop-off, even though it's technically a no-no. I'd suggest the beach over by the Cap Juluca hotel, because that's where I've arranged your billet. I know the management well – 'three wise monkeys', so to speak..." Alfred was a wealth of information.

"Are there patrol boats from customs?"

"Ha! No," Alfred said. "I imagine you'll find the security quite underwhelming around here. I think it's safe to presume we aren't on alert for an imminent invasion or such; just the odd police boat puttering around

Sandy Ground and Island Harbour, nothing on the St. Martin side. I'll look forward to your arrival."

Steven stopped at the gift shop and bought a hat, then took a taxi over to Marigot. Sure enough, there were dozens of boats vying for customers. He surveyed the craft bobbing on the waterfront with their dull and gaudy colors, and liked what he saw in a thirty-two foot power catamaran named *Hey Mon II*. He approached the swarthy-skinned captain, who looked stoned-out on weed – or something, and asked if it would be possible to buzz over to Anguilla.

"Anything is possible if you have the desire and the means," the islander replied, in a French-flavored accent.

"I have both."

"There is a ferry. She departs from just over there. Ten dollars," said the captain, pointing over at the larger dock.

"I was thinking about something more private, maybe just drop me off on a beach."

"Ah...but of course...I can pull this boat onto any beach. Would you like for me to await your return?"

"I think I'd like to just wander around there, so one way would be fine."

"For that, I think maybe a hundred dollars is fair?" The captain was already taking his duffel. "Cash, of course."

"Of course."

"*C'est bon*, then we go now, *non*?" He was down the dock and climbing aboard, extending a hand to Steven.

The engines roared to life, and in moments they were making their way out of the harbor to sea. There were six-to-eight-foot rolling swells, so they kept their speed to around eighteen knots as they bumped and buffeted over each advancing wave.

"She reaches thirty knots...*eeeasily*...on a *tranquille* day. A good boat. *Formidable*. I been out in 16-foot seas and never worried. Catamaran – very stable, of course. You have the hundred? Please." Business was, after all, business.

Steven handed him a C-note. "Do you know the beach by the Cap Juluca hotel? I'd like to get dropped off on the next beach over. I have friends who have a place around there and I want to surprise them."

"I know the area. We will arrive in fifteen minutes more."

167

True to his word, they approached the pink coral strip in about twenty minutes, and the Gallic captain expertly beached the bow onto the light golden sand.

He handed Steven a card with his phone numbers on it. "My name is Jean-Claude. You need a trip back, day or night, call me and I can be here in half an hour. I live just along from my boat. *Bon fortune* with your surprise."

Steven took the card and pocketed it. They shook hands warmly, and Steven thanked him for his help. He hopped off the bow onto the wave moistened sand.

Jean-Claude handed him the duffel and laptop. "*Au revoir*," he said, an easy smile on his sun-weathered face. Reversing the engines, he skillfully pulled off, executing a tight turn as he roared back to St. Martin.

Steven looked around in awe. The sheer beauty all but took his breath away. It felt far cooler and less humid than in Havana. He sauntered up a gentle sandbank to where he presumed a road would be; to be rewarded with a hard-packed dirt path leading down the beach to the hotel. The wheels on his duffel became a lifesaver; he extended the collapsible handle, placed his laptop case on top of it and set off on the half-mile hike to the sun-bleached buildings in the distance.

He noted the island was smallish, with not a lot of structures visible. Why indeed had Griffen chosen Anguilla for his fund's home, Steven wondered. St. Martin had far more infrastructure and was much more convenient, with a relatively large international airport (he'd spotted several Air France 747s) and surely a larger banking system. Well, that's exactly what he was here to find out.

He reached the hotel and was relieved to discover it was as pleasant as any he'd stayed at. Modest in size. Not one of the mega-resort complexes. That was good. He approached the front desk.

The female receptionist looked up at him. "Will you be checking in, sir?"

"Yes, in a few minutes, but I need to use a phone first. Is there somewhere I can make a local call?" Steven asked.

"Of course, sir, right over there on that table. Dial nine."

Steven walked over and called Alfred.

"Good afternoon, Larkin and Reese."

"Alfred, please."

Pause. Muffled noises.

"This is Alfred."

"I'm at the hotel."

"That was fast. I'll be there in twenty minutes. How will I know you?" Alfred asked.

"I'll be in the lobby wearing a red St. Martin baseball cap," Steven said.

"Perfect."

Steven's eyes wandered around the reception area. Really extraordinary. White marble, with an expansive view of the ocean and St. Martin.

A staff member approached him with a tray and offered him a rum punch and a hot towel. Ah...it was infused with anise. Very civilized. *If being an international fugitive panned-out like this all the time, count me in*, he decided.

He absently considered the Moorish architecture and the whitewashed exterior. A few minutes later, a tall, thin man in his sixties approached him.

"Steven, I presume?" he asked in his resonant British accent.

"Alfred. Nice to meet you." Steven stood up and shook Alfred's hand, which was the color of coal. Alfred was one of the blackest men he'd ever seen. His immaculate white linen shirt and trousers served to accentuate the depth of his ebony skin. Tints of grey fringed the short, tight curls on his head, with teeth that sparkled white enough to glow in the dark. He carried an equally slim briefcase.

"I like the place. Seems very quiet. Perfect for my purposes," Steven said.

"Shall we check you in now, or would you rather we sit down and discuss said *purposes* a little before we settle you in?"

"Let's talk." Steven sat down in an oversized, overstuffed leather armchair, while Alfred took a seat facing him. Alfred produced a small notebook and a gold pen from his valise.

Steven leaned forward. "I'm interested in any information I can get on Nicholas Griffen, Griffen Ventures or Heliotrope Holdings. The latter is an investment fund registered in the British Virgin Islands, but chartered in Anguilla, and presumably banking here as well. If I can, I'd like to get information on the names of the investors, as well as the total dollar value of the fund, and its holdings of stock, or options, or short positions. Also, anything you can dig up on its banking relationships." Steven sat back while Alfred rapidly scribbled down the information.

"That's quite a tall order, Steven…a tall order indeed. Every single piece of data you're describing is wholly confidential, and protected by privacy laws and iron-clad bank secrecy statutes."

"So you can't do it?" Steven asked him, leaning back into the ample chair.

"Ha! Only a fool would proclaim the impossible," Alfred said, a smile in his eyes. "Consider my observations as mere thinking aloud. Anything can be executed, achieved or acquired – if a price can be agreed. One of the more lamentable elements of the human condition. It will turn out horribly expensive by the time it's all over, I shouldn't wonder, and will require a little finesse and a generous helping of time. But you've found the right person for the task, if I may be so bold. Let me mull over the best way to proceed and get back to you with an estimate." Alfred looked at Steven, head slightly tilted. "Is there anything else?"

"Actually, there is. I also need any information you can get on a man named Jim Cavierti who died here several years ago," Steven said. More scribbling.

"Spell the last name, please."

He did.

"Is that it?" asked Alfred.

"That's everything I can think of," Steven said, "except for the cell phone."

"Yes, of course. Here you are." Alfred pulled a micro cell phone and charger out of his briefcase. "Let's get you checked in, shall we?" He stood up, confidently approached the reception desk and shook hands with the woman on duty, who picked up a telephone and made a quick call. A tall man wearing a hotel uniform emerged from the back area and greeted Alfred like his long lost brother. They conversed while the man fiddled behind a computer terminal, and then they both walked over to Steven.

"Steven, this is Jenkins, my cousin and the manager of the hotel. He'll attend to your every need. The room will be billed to my business and you'll only have to sign your first name for any requirements that you have. He understands your stay here has to be discreet. Jenkins?"

"Nice to meet you, Steven. Here is your room key, bungalow fourteen, a one bedroom suite. Very private, only one other guest staying in that villa building. You can just sign a D for any hotel charges. What last name should we enter into the register?" Jenkins asked.

Steven almost said 'Griffen'. He bit his impulsive tongue. "Malone. Steve Malone."

Jenkins was inscrutable, not even the hint of a blink in his eyes.

"Very good then, Mr. Malone. And how long can we expect to enjoy your stay with us?"

Alfred answered: "At least a week I should think, maybe two. Do you have sufficient room?"

"For you, of course. The rate is $660 per day, plus tax. I trust that's acceptable?"

"Sounds great," Steven said brightly.

"Very good, sir. I'll be charged with ensuring your stay is a pleasant one, Mr. Malone," Jenkins said. "Give us a few more minutes. Simon, our bell captain, will show you to your accommodation."

So, he was done. Painless. Simon collected the duffel and laptop bag, carefully placing them on a luggage cart. He discreetly disappeared.

Alfred shook his hand and bid his farewell. "I'll call you on the mobile phone when I have a project price calculated, together with an estimated timeline. In the meantime, enjoy the hotel and the hospitality of the island. There are worse places to spend one's time." And with that he was gone.

Simon returned just as Steven finished his rum punch. He escorted him out to a golf cart, his bags already sitting on the back, and they were off down a narrow path.

The room was magnificent, as large as a medium-sized apartment. The terrace overlooked the ocean, St. Martin in the near distance. Small tent gazebos dotted the private pink coral beach, and he could see very few guests. The quiet season – literally.

Steven unpacked, hung his shirts and pants, and locked his watches and cash away in the room safe. He hooked up his laptop to the DSL port provided for anyone foolish enough to spend their time in cyberspace while in paradise, and was pleased to see the browser pop up. He checked on Allied, up a dime. Briefly scanning the boards turned up nothing new, although he noted Pogo was stirring up shit with the website by uploading yet more unflattering information about Griffen's fifteen percent decline in net asset value since the beginning of the year. He supposed Pogo had somehow gotten his hands on one of Griffen's semi-annual reports. Nice. That would piss him off.

He was interrupted by a knock at the door. The maid. He opened it and was greeted by a huge bouquet of fresh flowers and a bottle of champagne in an ice bucket. A gift from the hotel.

She placed the flowers and the bucket on the living room table, and another five dollar tip was dispatched. This was already getting expensive.

Lifestyle choices of the dead fugitive...

Whatever.

He pulled himself away from the web and contemplated his next move. Alfred seemed ultra-competent, so that was taken care of – he'd get the information and the bill, all in Alfred's good time. Steven really couldn't do anything without more info.

CHAPTER 17

It was still gorgeous out, so Steven figured he'd languish in one of the tents and read the book he'd picked up in the St. Martin airport when he'd bought the baseball cap. He quickly shaved (goatee coming along nicely) pulled on his new shorts and re-donned his shirt. On the way out he grabbed the book and room key, hung the 'Do Not Disturb' card on his doorknob, turned, and almost collided with a young woman walking from an adjacent room.

He held up his hands in apology. "I'm sorry. Excuse me. I almost ran you down."

Steven appraised her. Long raven hair, deep suntan, late twenties perhaps, hazel eyes, five-foot-four or so – strikingly beautiful. And wearing a sarong around her waist as a cover-up for her bikini, which was fashioned from a black shiny material; and not much of it either, he noted. She certainly gave the ties a run for their money, filling the little triangles out nicely.

Wedding ring. Oh well.

"No, I'm sorry. I wasn't paying attention." Accent? Not French, maybe Spanish or Italian? "*Scusi.*" Italian, definitely Italian. She smiled as she noticed the book in Steven's hand. "He was a genius, no?"

Steven was speechless. Indeed, most had never even heard of him. David Foster Wallace. He appraised her.

"I'm surprised. Not many people know about him." He'd been equally surprised when he spotted the book in the airport store. Perhaps Wallace was better appreciated in Europe. "He's my favorite author, bar none."

Her gaze lingered, as if assessing him frankly – then she offered her hand. "I'm Antonia. Are you on your way to the beach?"

Steven felt a distinct tingle as he made contact with Antonia's soft, warm hand. "Yeah, I was just getting ready to read a bit. I'm Steven. Pleased to meet you. Are you headed that way?" No harm in asking. There were worse things than spending an afternoon on the beach with an Italian goddess, even if she was married. Innocent relaxation. Purely platonic interest, Steven reminded the little devil that had taken residence on his shoulder...

Antonia nodded. "Yes. I was inside taking a catnap. It's easy to get into the habit in the islands. I thought I'd get a little more sun before the day is over." She hesitated. "Would you like to share a cabana?"

Her English was very good, and incorporated such charming choices of terms.

"Sounds perfect. Lead the way." Wow, were the natives ever friendly around here. Still, harmless adventure in paradise, the ring reminded him. Quite a rock on it as well. Maybe the husband was a ninety-four-year-old who was waiting in the room for his respirator to get fixed. Who knew?

They set a steady gait towards the nearby beach, a light breeze cooling them from the worst of the sun's heat, the trade winds blowing favorably. There was only one 'cabana' near their villa, so there wasn't a lot of struggle over choices. Inside were two sun lounges, padded, with folded white and blue striped towels placed lovingly upon them, and a little table.

"I'm going to stay out of the sun for now," Steven said. "Where would you like to be?" Ever the chivalrous one. Whatever you need. Just ask.

"Eh, right here is good."

He adjusted his lounger until it behaved the way he wanted it to, then kicked off his sandals. She removed her cover-up, and he noted with purely scientific interest she was wearing a G-string. Looked like she worked out, too...

A lot. Like movie star a lot.

They both started speaking at once. Laughed. Tried again simultaneously. Laughed again. He motioned with his hand for her to proceed.

"So what brings you here to Anguilla, Steven? How long is your visit?" Such a delectable accent.

"I'm here for some business, some pleasure," he replied, keeping it vague. "Maybe a week or ten days. And you?"

"Maybe a week. My plans are open-ended for now." She also seemed a little vague.

"Why Anguilla for you?" he asked.

"Eh, my friends and I were in St. Martin at a private home and I got tired of the crowds. I didn't feel like being around a lot of people. You know what I mean? I heard Anguilla was quiet, so I came over yesterday." So she was also a recent arrival. But what about the husband? Probably too soon to ask about that.

"I just got in myself. From St. Martin. I know what you mean about the crowds."

"I saw you get off the boat down the beach. I was sitting on my terrace." She studied him again.

He deflected. "How do you know it was me?"

"Red baseball hat and black shirt? Oh, I don't know, crazy guess, no?" She was sharp, charming accent notwithstanding. He silently prayed she wouldn't ask the question.

It wasn't his lucky day.

"Why a private boat on the beach and not the ferry or a plane?" she asked.

"I wanted to get dropped off close to the hotel, and the boat guy said he could get me almost right up on it. Doesn't everyone do it that way?" Keep it light and fun; nothing suspicious.

"You're a very interesting man, Steven, with David Foster Wallace and clandestine boat trips. A man of mystery." She was teasing, toying with him.

"Yes, I use the book to decode hidden messages planted in the paper regarding the movements of beautiful Italian celebrities."

"And, a, how do you say, silver-tongued charmer as well. Is your name really James Bond?" She laughed. He liked her laugh. A lot. What was going on here? She continued. "A celebrity? Hardly. Just a girl trying to get away from it all and have a little peace and quiet."

"You came to the right place. I understand not a lot goes on here. It certainly seems quiet," Steven observed.

They lay for a while in silence, listening to the rhythmic roll of the surf as the breeze rippled soothingly over them. He took in Antonia. Amazing.

"You're getting pretty dark considering you've only been here for a day," he noted.

"I was in St. Martin for three before coming here, so that helped. And it's my skin. I'm *Italiano*, I get dark quickly. Why don't you come into the sun and get some color?" she asked.

Good idea! urged the little devil on his shoulder. He pulled his 'sofa' next to hers and took off his shirt. *Oops. That was why not.* He'd forgotten. Careless. The knife wound. The stitches. Her eyes got suddenly bigger.

"*Ai*, what happened? That looks terrible. Painful." She ran her deep brown eyes over him in a casual yet methodical manner. Seemed to approve of what she saw.

"Oh, a little accident. Looks way worse than it is. I should probably keep it out of the sun." He put his shirt back on. *What was he thinking?* He wasn't. That was a problem. He didn't have the luxury of being able to turn off his brain right now. He'd have to be more careful.

"What kind of accident?" She was back to staring him directly in his eyes. He felt dishonest when she looked at him, but what could he say? It was disconcerting. He'd never felt that sensation before, like she could just see through to his soul. Maybe she was an Italian witch of some sort. Did they have voodoo in Italy?

"An accident. I fell against a fence. Very sharp edge…should have been more careful. It's really not that bad. Stupid mistake, really." He got the feeling that she wasn't buying a word of it. Fence indeed. "So…you live in Italy? You're a long way from home."

"Yes, in Firenze, Florence. I wanted to get away from the tourists in the summer. They invade the city, take it over like a swarm of ants. *Cosi*, my friends had proposed to come to St. Martin." Her eyes fixed upon the island in the distance as she spoke. She looked back at him. "I have to find something to do with myself for the next two months, until the season is over. This is what I came up with so far."

"Not a bad place to hang out, Antonia."

"Or hide out."

Wham.

What was that all about? Had she figured him out so quickly? This was getting way too weird, and potentially dangerous. Or was she talking about herself? Oh well, in for a dollar…

"Everyone's got something they'd like to hide from," Steven ventured.

"Or someone?" Antonia asked, or maybe stated. Again, too close for comfort. Where was this going?

"Who or what are you hiding from, Antonia?" he asked.

"It's a long story, Steven. Maybe the same things everyone hides from, or wants to hide from." That told him exactly nothing at all.

They stayed silent after that for a good while. It was an easy quiet, a relaxed and mutual agreement to stay away from things that were uncomfortable or unpleasant.

From behind their villa a woman in white floated gracefully down the beach, steadily approaching them with a tray supporting a container and two small bowls.

"Sorbet?" she offered.

You've got to be kidding, he thought to himself. It was the afternoon sorbet call.

Antonia looked up. "Please."

He nodded, got up and pulled the little table over to them. The woman scooped out two perfect spheres of what appeared to be orange sorbet, placing them on the table with two miniature spoons.

"Mango. Enjoy." And then the sorbet fairy slipped away, her image wavering in the morning mirage now rising up from the heat of the sand – gone to bestow her gifts upon other good folks in need of frozen confections, her important work done here.

"I like this place very much," Antonia said. She picked up her spoon and sampled the sorbet, which had frosted the outside of the small metal bowls instantly.

"What's not to like?" he agreed. They ate their treats in silence. Another fifteen minutes went by without any conversation.

"I think it's maybe time to go in," Antonia declared. He nodded agreement. "The sun makes me sleepy," she explained.

He looked at her. "Do you have plans for dinner, Antonia?"

An angel popped up on his other shoulder, wagging a sanctimonious finger: *Hey! What the hell do you think you're doing? She's married, dumbass, MARRIED.* Husband possibly waiting in the room, exhausted after being up all night with her. *Or maybe not,* the little devil countered; given the unmistakable interest she's been projecting, and what, with her being on vacation for months...

Antonia took a long time to respond – seemed to be studying something far off in the distance. Finally she spoke, very quietly, so much so he almost couldn't hear her.

"No, Steven, no plans. I'd like to have dinner with you." He felt ten feet tall. Strong like a bull. And the angel had slunk off somewhere to lick its wounds...

"I'll come knock on your door in a couple of hours, okay?" she asked.

"Perfect," he said. And it was.

They gathered their belongings and traipsed over the hot sand back to the villa...in a comfortable enough silence. Both understood something significant had happened and neither wanted to spoil it with words. He stopped at his door, and she smiled at him before continuing to hers. Neither said anything. Didn't have to.

CHAPTER 18

It had been forever since Antonia had been interested in a man, and that had worked well for her. Uncomplicated, undemanding, and easy to control, emotionally. Antonia felt her day in the sun, romantically, had come and gone, and she was fine with that. She still had an empty hole in her stomach only time could heal, and it had been there so long she'd resigned herself to the notion that it would remain her constant companion. Her friends were worried; thought she was depressed, needed counseling or medication. They were well-intentioned, but wrong.

Her battle wasn't winnable. It was more a matter of survival than victory.

Or so she'd thought, until now.

Meeting this stranger, in an exotic locale, and away from everything she knew, had caused a minor tremor in her defenses. She'd surprised herself when she'd accepted the dinner offer. Normally she would have smiled, thanked him, but firmly indicated she wasn't interested; most men got it the first time around, and she'd become adept at avoiding any entanglements or strained encounters.

For whatever reason, this Steven had struck her as different. And it wouldn't hurt to spend another hour or two to get to the core of what had intrigued her. She was a big girl now, and if Antonia excelled at anything, it was self-control and discipline.

Stripping off her swimsuit, she wandered into the bathroom and turned on the shower, marveling at the expansive size of the area. Her reflection caught her eye, and she leaned towards the oversized mirror, frowning at herself. Whatever are you thinking, Antonia?

Her skin was dark, he'd been right about that, and the sun's attention had been flattering. She wasn't surprised by his interest. As her friend Sylvia had recently remarked, she had the body of a fit teenager and an unconventionally striking face – a quality that derived as much from attitude as bone structure. Ever since she'd hit puberty men had fawned over her, so she'd long grown accustomed to it, to the point where it hardly registered except as an amusing and sometimes tiresome ritual.

She flexed a bicep, noted the definition approvingly; pinched the taut skin of her flat stomach, again, with satisfaction. Still in good shape, if a little sunburned. Her inventory of her physical attributes was dry, matter-of-fact. There was no inherent narcissism. She'd never had that quality, even as a little girl; had always been serious, completely engaged in her pursuits, her appearance an afterthought of little consequence to her.

Her mother had been described by admirers as a classical beauty, and Antonia had been fortunate in her genetic makeup, taking after Mom as she did. She thought about their vacations together – to other beaches and remote islands in the Mediterranean, the Adriatic, off the coast of Africa, and recalled how in her teen years they'd been mistaken for sisters. Melancholy turned to sadness as she drifted deeper into the recesses of her memory…she abruptly realized she'd been standing there for minutes, steeped in inward reflection. It had been years since she'd lost track of time like that, her mind probing corridors long sealed off from the burdens of recollection. Corners best left alone. Why now, and why here?

Troubled, she turned on the sink faucet and splashed some cool water on her face. Come on, Antonia, no point going down the bad road; no sense in creating misery when today's been so delightful.

She wouldn't allow herself to ruin this day in paradise – she more than knew she had that capacity.

But not now. Not today. Just take it hour by hour.

She shut off the tap and opened the glass shower enclosure; hot vapor drifted into the cool room like a fragrant mist. Moving into the shower, the water became soothing, timeless, constant – a welcome interruption of her uneasy thoughts. She leaned back her head and closed her eyes, the warm spray streamed down her body, the tingling of its impact on her skin both revitalizing and relaxing. For a brief moment her universe was condensed into the pleasant sensation of water, as it sluiced away the salt and the oil and the troubling ghosts of unbidden visitors from an unwelcome past; a past that had betrayed her, at the end of it; given the lie to the promise of innocence and hope, leaving her damaged, and with a secret that had almost destroyed her.

CHAPTER 19

As far as Griffen could determine, Glen Vesper wasn't offering anything helpful. His advice to ignore the website was fine, except for the dozen or so calls per day Griffen was getting from troubled investors. Those weren't pleasant to deal with, and he suspected his pat answers weren't having the calming effect they'd had several weeks ago. Too much information in the public domain was bad. They had to shut the site down, one way or another. Permanently.

"Give me something, Glen. Anything. I'm getting killed here. Give me some good news."

"Nothing new to report, Nicholas. Sorry," Glen lamented. "Wish there was."

"Can't we go after the site legally in some way?" Griffen wasn't interested in taking the 'pretend it's not there' route any longer.

"The questions are, where's it domiciled, and who do you go after? So far we keep running into a Latvian server that's mirroring the site from an undisclosed location. Barring government-level systems capabilities, we've got no chance of getting past that. And now my tech people tell me the mirroring looks like it moves around Latvia on a weekly basis. Who even knew Latvia had more than one server?"

"So...dead end," Griffen seethed. He wished death and sickness and pain on the site administrator. Envisioned horrible mangling in threshing machine accidents for the new webmaster. It could all be arranged to order...if only he could get his hands on the saboteur.

"Afraid so." Glen rose, and smoothed out the creases in his expensive and well-tailored slacks. "Wish I had better news."

Griffen had arranged another meeting with Sergei, where he heard much the same thing. Nothing new, no way to penetrate the virtual firewall the mirroring had created.

"Come on, Sergei – don't you have pull in Latvia? Can't you just go down to the server location and see where the original signal's coming from?" Nicholas asked.

"It's not so simple, my friend. We have to wait for someone to make a mistake. So far they haven't. But they will. They will. They always do."

Griffen considered his options. "I trust you'll tell me when they do."

Sergei appraised him. "Of course you will be the first to know. Now don't worry. It is just a matter of time."

⁓⁓

Steven rinsed off and considered his new look in the mirror. He'd become more accustomed to it, but it still gave him a little start when his reflection looked back at him. He threw on some clothes and decided to check the web and his e-mail. Pogo posted that he was now providing random multiple mirrors of the site and moving it around every few days.

He logged off, and was struggling with agonizing choices like sandals or loafers when there came a knock at the door. He opened it, to be greeted by Antonia in a simple cream-colored summer dress. She looked like two million dollars. Make that three. She wore a gold charm bracelet and a pair of diamond earrings. She smelled exotic.

"*Buona sera*," Steven intoned in his best faux Italian manner. He'd investigated how to say 'good evening' online.

"*Buona sera*. Are you going to invite me in?" She smiled at him, throwing several hundred thousand kilowatts of pure charm into the mix.

"Of course. Come in."

She moved easily into the room; looking around it, noting the flowers and the champagne.

"Very nice. You look very handsome, Steven."

Damned if she didn't catch him off guard with that.

She smiled. "I think you are blushing. No, I'm sure of it. Ah…nice view. Just like my room." She had amazing timing, that was for sure.

"And you look absolutely stunning, Antonia. If I seem like I'm at a loss for words, it's because I'm still trying to catch my breath."

She threw back her head and laughed in that delightful way…then cocked an eyebrow. "James Bond again, smooth talking the peasant girls."

"Can I interest you in some champagne? Came with the room and I hate to see it go to waste. You really have to help out. Flush the taste of sorbet out of your mouth." Steven admired the way the dress clung to her curves. Some things didn't require a lot of help. Antonia's wardrobe was one of them.

"Thank you, but I'd rather have a drink at the restaurant. I'm starving."

"So what do you recommend, sandals or shoes?" Leave it up to her. Never a bad strategy.

"Sandals, definitely. You're in the islands. Live a little. Let your hair down, Mr. Bond."

They ambled down the path towards the main building. It was a balmy evening, and they made small talk in easy tones as they walked alongside each other. When they reached *Pimm's*, the hotel's high-end restaurant, they entered the foyer and were seated on the veranda, overlooking the ocean. The lights of St. Martin were already illuminated, twinkling in the distance as the sun slowly dipped into a darkening azure horizon. They perused the menu; both finally opting for the blackened swordfish and a glass of wine.

They watched as the fiery orb's reflection faded into the sea, casting an amber glow over the damp sand of the beach. Neither expected service to be hurried – nor were they disappointed.

They continued their small talk as appetizers and bread were brought to the table.

"So, where are you from, Steven?" Out of the gate, a tough question.

"Originally, or now?" Playing for time.

"Now. Where do you call home?" she asked.

"Nowhere at the moment. I suppose Anguilla is home for the time being. I'm sort of traveling around, looking for a new place to call my permanent home." That was the truth.

"How can that be? You mean you don't live anywhere?" She was toying again. But only partially.

"It's the truth. I decided to travel until I find home. So far I haven't found it. I'll know when I do. I won't want to leave, and one day I'll realize everything I ever wanted is there. Then I'll be home." Melodramatic, but the truth again.

"It sounds very exciting, but also a bit sad. If nowhere is home, then you have none."

"I like to think that wherever I am is home...for now. Does that make sense? Tonight, in Anguilla, having dinner with you, I'm home." And he meant it.

"That's very sweet."

"And what about you...what's your story? I know about Florence, but what brings you to the Caribbean...alone?" Emphasis on alone.

"It's really a long story, Steven. A long and sad story. I'm here to escape the sad story, I suppose. I've spent a lot of my time lately being sad, and I'm trying to remember what it's like to not be."

"I've got nothing but time, Antonia. You don't know me; I'm just some stranger on an island. You can tell me anything – you have nothing to lose. Hell, I don't even know your last name. This is your opportunity. I won't bite you; words are just words. Take a chance." Good Lord, had he actually said that? He'd swear he was intoxicated, although he'd only had a glass of wine. Maybe he was having an allergic reaction to the appetizers?

And yet, again, he meant it. That was the alarming part. The little devil had deserted his shoulder, it seemed...running scared, no doubt.

She looked directly at him; as if into the deepest recesses of his being, and apparently satisfied with what she saw there, began speaking.

"I'm thirty years old, and I've been a widow for the last year and a half. I met and married the best man I'd ever met in my life when I was twenty-two, and I lost him six-and-a-half years later to cancer. Unexpected." She looked into her glass of water. "He was the picture of health, no problems, and on his thirty-fifth birthday he went in for his annual physical. A blood test came back abnormal. Further tests confirmed there was something horribly wrong. It was a rapidly growing form of cancer, and I spent the next five months watching a strong, proud, smart man with the world in his hands shrivel and die." She took a sip of the water before continuing.

"We went to all the top centers – money wasn't even a question, but they couldn't do anything. Nothing. And I've spent the last year and a half sleepwalking through life, wondering why him, out of all the people in the world." She stopped, unable to continue.

"Oh God, Antonia, I'm so sorry; I wish I'd never asked..."

"No, you're right. It was time to say it all out loud. As you said, what do I have to lose? What do any of us have to lose?" She turned her gaze to the darkening shape of St. Martin for a moment or two. "I came to the Caribbean with well-intentioned friends who wanted to take my mind off my misery. The problem is every morning I wake up and look in the mirror, only to see myself without him. And it drives me crazy. So yesterday, after yet another night of listening to all the hopeful advice, I decided to leave and be by myself. I came here. And then today you showed up in a red hat on a boat from who knows where, and for the first time in a year and a half I…I felt my heart beat again."

She flooded him with her soulful gaze. "You remind me of him, although you look and sound nothing alike. I don't know why that is." She averted her eyes again, as if contemplating a riddle. "So that's my story to the man in the restaurant who I don't know and who won't bite me. Now tell me the truth, Steven. What's your story?"

He couldn't stick to his cover. Fuck.

Why did this have to happen now, when his life was in chaos? Why couldn't he have met her at a different point? Answer: Because you don't get what you need when you want it, but rather when you need it.

So now his turn had arrived.

What was it going to be?

"I'm almost ten years older than you, and I've never heard a sadder story in my life than yours. Mine's not hard. I've made some money, never met the woman I wanted to stay with permanently, always been sure things would turn out okay. Recently I've been involved in some situations that changed that certitude. I'm in a conflict with some very powerful, very dangerous men who've taken everything of value in my life from me. I can't say any more, but I'll end with this. People near to me have died just for being my friend." Remorse momentarily stabbed his consciousness as he remembered Peter and Todd. What the hell was he doing? Had he said too much? Did it matter?

"They haven't taken everything. You're still here." She paused, reflected, continued. "So, we have both lost our way. Strange, is it not?" she suggested.

"The difference is I got myself into this situation, whereas you didn't," he said.

"I got myself into my situation by meeting and marrying who I did. Those were the cards. I would have rather had six-and-a-half years with him than fifty years with someone else. No one knows how long they have together, Steven." He loved her lilt when she pronounced his name.

The waiter appeared with their entrees. Just what the doctor ordered. They enjoyed their meals, focusing on them while unhurriedly digesting the information they'd just shared.

"Your secrets are safe with me, Antonia."

"I know they are. It has helped." She didn't volunteer more. He didn't ask. They ate, and thought about each other.

The busboy arrived and removed their plates.

"I'd like a drink, Steven. In the bar." He could take a hint, and waved for the bill.

They adjourned to the lounge, where she ordered a Sambuca and he a glass of port. They considered their situation as they listened to the ethnic island music. The sensuous reggae beat pulsed in the background, a plaintive voice singing about injustice and unrequited love. Water lapped and lulled along the edge of the shimmering beach as the phosphorescence of the surf created an ever-changing lightshow for their personal enjoyment. Never before had the heavens been illuminated with such a tapestry of stars, each twinkling softly, as if in quiet harmony with the music, and the primal rhythm of the tidal surge. They watched in wonder as two shooting stars suddenly blazed a trail into the deep horizon, as if racing into sweet oblivion. Celestial fireworks. They looked at each other in silent serenity for a few moments, finished their drinks, and walked back to their rooms. He stopped at his door as she continued to hers. "Goodnight, Antonia," he said, a softness had pervaded his voice.

"Donitelli. My last name, Steven. Goodnight to you, too."

CHAPTER 20

The next day Steven woke up late. He decided to risk a run, figuring that he didn't really involve his upper body if he took it slow, so he wasn't endangering the sutures. He first checked in on the stock, to discover they were having a flat day. No obvious manipulation, just the market doing its thing.

He went out onto the path, starting slowly, and found that if he kept to jogging rather than running his side didn't hurt. He jogged the length of the resort and then over a bridge that separated the thin peninsula beyond from the rest of the island. After half an hour he looped back around. Not much of a workout, but better than nothing.

He rinsed off and stepped out onto his terrace, noticing a solitary figure down at the cabanas. He grabbed his wallet, key and cell and walked briskly to the shore.

"Good morning, Antonia."

She turned and treated him to her radiant smile. "Ah...the man of mystery returns to the scene of his latest adventure... It's gorgeous out here. Are you up for some sailing? I saw in the lobby where they'll rent a sailboat to you with a captain for the day." She wore a pink swimsuit with a yellow pinstripe border. Still a G-string, he noted, and she looked better than he remembered, if that was possible.

"I need to grab something to eat on the way out, but a sail sounds great. We won't need a captain, though. I've done a little sailing in my wasted youth," Steven said.

"I should have known Mr. Bond knows how to sail, as well as all sorts of other things, I'm sure. We'll get to your misspent youth in good time." She shielded her eyes with a hand, scanning for a potential harbor. "Let's see if we can find a boat."

God but that accent was something. You put it into a tanned package wearing strips of fabric, and, well, you obviously had Steven's continued interest.

She pulled on her cover-up, grabbed her beach bag and they made their way to the hotel. The concierge made a call, and within a few minutes they had a 35-foot sailing catamaran for the day.

The hotel offered to shuttle them over to the marina. Steven went down to the little beachside restaurant and grabbed a muffin and a banana, and upon his return they were off.

Ten minutes later they were deposited at a small harbor at Sandy Ground, on the opposite side of the island. They sought out the captain of the catamaran, a relaxed islander named Roy, who Steven took aside and chatted with while Antonia skipped down the rickety dock and hopped aboard the boat.

After being assured that Steven had more than fifteen years of sailing experience, Roy had few reservations about letting his pride and joy out of his sight. He gave Steven some indigenous tips on areas with dangerous reefs to steer clear of and advised him on the location of the ignition and the fuel cutoff.

In the short time since they chartered the vessel, Roy had already packed a lunch for two and placed it onboard, so all that was left was to untie the dock lines and set sail. Steven assured him he would have the boat back by four.

They got underway without fanfare. Antonia was delighted as porpoises surrounded the boat, surfing and cavorting and zooming up splashing out of the water immediately in front of them. She stood astride the bow and reached out, almost able to touch the playful animals.

After a few hours of being pushed along by a frisky breeze, Steven lowered the sails and dropped anchor in a secluded bay that afforded a stunning view of St. Martin. Antonia unpacked lunch and they ate contentedly, rocking lazily on the small swells off the beach. Steven asked about her workout regimen.

"You're in amazing shape, Antonia. How do you do it…what's your secret?" he asked.

She laughed. "Now I am the one to be blushing, eh, Steven? I run several times a week on a machine and lift a few weights. I used to be in the ballet, so this kind of exercise is new for me." She munched on some grapes, lazily dangling a pretty toe in the warm seawater.

"The ballet? Well that explains why you're so graceful. How long did you dance?"

"I was a soloist with *Ballet La Scala* in *Milano* until my husband got sick; then I had to attend to him, and I never went back. I lost the urge, I suppose. Sometimes I miss the dance, but most of the time I don't think about any of it. I moved back to Florence after he – after it was..." She stumbled to a halt.

"Is that where you were born, in Florence...are your parents from there?" He wanted to move far away from the topic of dead husbands. These questions seemed fairly benign, couldn't get him into too much trouble.

She frowned. "My parents are both dead. A car accident, seven years ago. We have many such accidents in Italy; everyone drives like they're crazy. I grew up in *Firenze* and always loved the city's vibrancy. *Milano* is industrial. There is no real charm, no feeling of the history. Once I stopped dancing there was no reason to stay, so back home," she explained.

"What do you do now...how do you occupy your time?" He tried again, hoping this time he wouldn't dig up any more death and mayhem in the response.

"I own a magazine about travel, an international publication my husband started. You maybe heard of it; *Destination Paradise*? I don't run it day-to-day – there's a huge staff – but I'm the big shareholder, and sometimes I edit or write a story. It's as demanding as I wish it to be, and operates itself," she said.

"I was right, you're a celebrity! I knew you had to be famous," Steven teased. Okay, maybe not famous, but still, ballerina and media mogul qualified as more than a shop girl.

She giggled. "Hardly a celebrity. Much of the magazine is run out of New York. I had nothing to do with it until...recently."

"Any brothers or sisters?" Steven asked.

She acted as though she hadn't heard the question. Steven let it go. He didn't understand the shift in her mood, but could sense the whole conversation had made her uncomfortable, and he didn't want to compound the effect. There was a lot going on in her head, that much was clear.

They finished their lunch, washed down with cold beer. She watched him walk around the deck, checking the lines in preparation for pulling up the anchor. She playfully tossed a grape at his head and he sensed its approach, spun and caught it. Popped it into his mouth with a grin.

"Wow! Superman. Eyes in the back of your head?"

He shrugged and smiled. Went back to attending the lines.

"And what about you, Steven? I see by your hands you're no stranger to heavy work, perhaps something outside? Are you a gardener, or perhaps a ditch digger?" she suggested mischievously, back to emitting her sweet sense of fun.

"I do martial arts – have since I was a boy. The training builds certain areas up more than others; the arms and hands, the feet. No rocks or ditches."

"So you are Bruce Lee? I thought he was shorter, and more Chinese. What they can do with the cinema, no?"

A chirping sound emanated from his bag. He walked back to it, poked around inside, and fished out the cell phone Alfred had given him.

Alfred's distinctive voice greeted him. "Steven…how are you…enjoying the island's charms and hospitality?"

"More than you know, Alfred," Steven told him as he gazed at Antonia sunning herself on the bow.

"I have an estimate of the project scope and cost. Figure somewhere between seventy-five and a hundred thousand dollars. I should begin to get information in a few days, and we should have everything within a week or so. Is that acceptable?"

"It's in the range I expected," Steven answered.

"Then we can proceed? I'll provide wire instructions for a progress payment at close of play next week. Fair enough?" Alfred asked.

"Very fair. Call me when you have something. And thanks again for setting up the hotel and the phone and all."

"My pleasure. Enjoy your week."

Steven stuck the phone in his pocket, then pulled up the anchor and raised the sails, cranking the winch. The sea had gotten rougher as the day had worn on, with longer swells and higher gusts of wind. They were actually moving at what Steven guessed to be around eighteen to twenty knots when they rounded Windward Point and made their way back down the other side of the island. It gave a sensation of flying.

He noticed Antonia was enjoying the spray and the speed immensely, standing, hands on hips, towards the bow with her long hair blowing around her, unencumbered by the cover-up. Just a few square inches of thin fabric to shield her from the elements. As God intended it.

They maneuvered back into the dock, and Steven's watch confirmed it was only 3:45. All good. He threw the dock lines to Roy, who'd walked out to meet the boat.

"How was it?" he asked.

"Beautiful," Steven responded. Antonia smiled at both of them and nodded her head in agreement.

Steven helped Roy secure the vessel before calling the hotel. They would send a car right over.

The skipper strolled along with them until they reached the top of the docks.

"You picked a good day for it. Tomorrow will be rougher. An advisory came through that a tropical depression four hundred miles southeast of here has developed into a full-blown hurricane. Might pass close to the island, might miss it entirely, but won't be much fun on the water either way," he reported.

Steven agreed. "I noticed the swell was getting bigger. So that's a storm swell? The wind picked up pretty good on the ride back downhill."

"A hurricane?" Antonia asked. "Isn't that dangerous...when is it supposed to get here?"

"We won't know more until later," Roy explained. "There's nothing to be alarmed about yet. Four hundred miles is a long ways away. And these storms can change direction hourly, lose and gain energy quickly, so there's no telling if we'll even see it."

"How often is the island hit by hurricanes?" Steven asked.

"We see warnings maybe six to ten times a year, and get little ones or medium ones passing close by maybe twice. Every seven to ten years we get a pretty big one." Roy seemed sufficiently blasé about the prospects. *Hurricane, shmuricane.*

Antonia wasn't convinced. "So there's no danger?"

He regarded her. "Little lady, there's always some danger to everything, you know? But I don't think this is worth worrying about. Have a nice trip, enjoy the sun today, ask at the hotel tonight and see if they have an update. It turned from a tropical storm to a hurricane pretty fast, and it might fade back into a storm just as fast, so there's no point in getting worried just yet. Besides. A little wind and rain never hurt anybody."

The hotel van arrived. They thanked Roy again, and Steven gave him a generous tip. Antonia was subdued on the return to the hotel.

"And you, Steven. Do you think there's anything to worry about?" she asked. He was conscious of her sitting closer to him than on the ride out. He liked that. She smelled good; like sun and wet hair and beautiful girl. Good combo.

"I think Roy's right. Let's wait and see what happens. I'm here for the duration anyway. I've never been through a hurricane, so maybe it'll be interesting."

"Doesn't anything scare you, Steven?" She asked the question bluntly. Out of nowhere, as was her style. Maybe it was an Italian thing. Or just an Antonia thing.

"Sure, Antonia. Lots of things. But I have to prioritize what I focus on, and a storm doesn't really move the needle much."

They got to the hotel, and walked slowly back to their villa.

"Would you be interested in dinner tonight, Antonia?" he asked.

"I'd enjoy that very much, Steven. And thank you for a wonderful day. I loved the dolphins and the ocean. I've never experienced anything like that before." She suddenly clapped her hands in joy. "I feel very happy, and lucky. Shall we meet at around seven again?"

Steven felt his heart flutter once more. He was falling pretty hard, pretty fast – and deeper than he realized possible until now. Maybe that vacation romance thing. All he knew was he'd never wanted to be with anyone as much as he wanted Antonia; and that was something that did scare him. He couldn't afford complications, and didn't want to expose any more innocents to his bloody battles. If you don't have anyone you care about, they can only really hurt you. And he was a fast-moving target these days.

None of which he said.

CHAPTER 21

The knock at the door came at seven. Antonia stood framed in the doorway, wearing a shimmering silver sleeveless top and a pair of jeans. Stunning personified. Truth was she could have been wearing a potato sack and the result would have been the same.

"*Entre, mademoiselle,*" he said.

Antonia giggled. "I didn't realize you spoke French."

"You just heard most of my capability," he admitted. "I just don't know how to say enter in Italian."

"*Entrato,*" she told him.

"Well, *entrato, per favore.*"

"Very nice." She came in. "I love what you've done with the place since yesterday."

"Yes, well, I'm talented that way. I'd offer you some champagne, but I already cleared a place in the mini-bar, and I do so hate disorganization..."

"You are a very strange and charming man, Steven. I haven't quite made up my mind about you. The James Bond thing scares me a little, but not so much any more. I hope you picked out a nice place for dinner. I'm starving again."

"I thought that we could try the hotel's other restaurant. Where did you eat the first night you were here?" he asked.

"I ordered room service. It was very good. But the company wasn't so interesting."

Was that a compliment?

"Well, my Italian friend, you're a captive audience tonight. Name your pleasure, and I'll do my best to entertain you, as long as we don't scare the other diners or break any island taboos. Sky's the limit."

"Perhaps the story of Steven will be the theme, no? You look very handsome again tonight. Sailing agrees with you. Shall we go?" Bam. Pow. Right hook, left jab. Tell me your deal, and I think you're hot, too; now where's the salad?

They definitely built them differently in Italy.

"But of course, *cherie*," he said in his best faux-French accent. They breezed along the same path to the main building. The wind was a little stiffer, but still not unpleasant.

The restaurant was Moroccan-themed, incongruous for the island, but strangely fitting. They ordered entrees and a bottle of wine, and sat back to admire the view.

"So, Steven, tell me your story. No games, please. I find you charming, but elusive in your answers. I can't figure out if that's to protect me, or you. But I want to understand the man I'm having dinner with, and have spent the better part of two days with." She studied him. "Where are you from?"

This was the moment of truth. Did he launch into his cover story about Canada? He was torn. He took a long time to answer the question. She seemed to sense his inner struggle. Dammit. *Dammit dammit dammit.*

"I'm from California, Antonia. Although if anyone else asked me I'd have an elaborate answer worked out about my home in Vancouver and my childhood there. What else would you like to know?" He figured he'd just tell the truth, because he didn't want to lie. Stupid. But he wouldn't lie to her.

Sucker.

"Are you wanted by the police…a criminal?" Good questions.

"No, I'm not a criminal, and no, the police aren't looking for me. Everyone in the world except you and an attorney thinks I'm dead; killed when my boat blew up. A supposed accident, although I know it wasn't," he explained.

"Why would anyone be trying to kill you, Steven? You mentioned powerful men. Why you? What did you do to offend them?" she asked.

He paused again. Thought about it.

And then he told her everything. It took a while. All through dinner; the wine; dessert. The bill.

"I was right. You're an amazing man. And I know why you remind me of my husband. He too was braver than anyone else I'd ever met. That quality…it's unmistakable. It shows." She disappeared inward for a minute, into her private world. Then she turned and smiled at him. "Perhaps a nightcap? I hear the band in the bar playing." She didn't wait to hear his answer; got up and moved smoothly towards the doors. What could he do but follow?

They sat at a small, intimate corner table on the veranda. She ordered a Sambuca again, he tried the bar special for the evening, a Bahama Mama. Red, sweet, tropical. They watched the band play steel drum reggae. She reached out and took his hand; felt it as though studying it for imperfections.

"Your skin is so hard along the sides. From martial arts?" she asked.

"Yes, twenty-five years of karate and kung fu will do that. I'm sure your feet had calluses all over them when you were dancing. Same thing," he explained.

He felt an electric current pulse between them as she held his hand. Could have powered a small town off it.

"*Buon*, shall we dance?" She not so much asked if he would, as confirmed now was a good time. *The* time.

Steven wasn't a terrific dancer, but after a bottle of white Bordeaux and a Bahama Mama, he figured he could probably levitate, given a decent headwind.

"You have to ask?" And then suddenly they were dancing, slowly, to the pulsing island groove. She fit like a magic glove, and he found himself spinning her around and almost feeling competent with the dancing thing.

They were the only two in the bar, the only two on the floor, and they could have been the only two in the world. They danced together like it mattered, like they only had tonight. When they finally moved back to their table and sat down, Steven took a sip of water the waiter had thoughtfully placed on the table, and looked at Antonia. Her eyes were brimming, and she had two small tears making their way down her cheeks. She made no attempt to brush them away; Steven reached over and wiped away the salty tracks with the gentle side of his thumbs. Nothing was said. There was nothing to say.

He excused himself and went to the restroom, taking the opportunity to cool off and rinse his face with cold water. When he returned, Antonia was gone. He signed the check, and walked outside. She was waiting there.

"I'm sorry. I need to go to sleep. It's been a long day," she said. He understood. This was way too heavy, way too fast. There was tremendous power, an incredible surge of connection between them, and they were both uncomfortable with it. Now was not a good time. This was serious. They knew it.

"Come on. I think I remember the way home." He took her hand, and they walked back to Villa #14 as the wind whistled through the shivering trees lining the path.

When they reached their building, he unlocked his room. She was still holding his hand. He took her other hand and kissed her forehead.

"Goodnight, sweet Antonia. Thank you for another wonderful evening."

She looked up at him, her eyes again moist. She said nothing, but turned and walked to her room. When she was at her door, Steven called out.

"It's Cross. Steven Cross."

She stopped as she was opening the door. Spoke very softly. "Goodnight, Steven Cross."

And then she was gone.

Back in his room, Steven called the front desk and asked for a nine o'clock wake-up call. He inquired about the weather situation. The clerk reported the hurricane was moving slowly, and maybe surely, in their direction – at around seventeen miles per hour; and was expected to land, if land it did, late tomorrow night. That was still a huge if, though, because hurricanes moved unpredictably. They weren't suggesting an evacuation or any drastic measures quite yet; storms like this could turn and miss the island by a hundred miles – in fact they usually did. There was nothing to do but wait to see what nature conjured up for them.

They would all know more by morning.

And with that thought, Steven took off his clothes and fell asleep, the sound of the surf echoing shell-like in his ears as visions of sugarplum fairies danced in his head.

CHAPTER 22

Antonia lay awake staring at the ceiling, her head spinning from the day's events. She felt like she was still on the boat, the bed gently rocking, the sensory illusion made more realistic by the increasing sound of the wind and waves outside her patio.

She was torn. The mystery surrounding Steven reminded her so much of her brother.

Daniello had been like a dream sibling, defending her from the occasional threat posed by the neighborhood kids, and always available to offer a serious answer to any question she asked. Unlike grownups, he'd treated her as an equal, an adult, never talking down to her or dismissing her concerns as trivial or beneath him. He'd been her protector, her knight-errant, and could do no wrong.

That fateful summer, just a few weeks before her ninth birthday, something had shifted in his demeanor and the way he behaved. Always pensive, his disposition took an unusual turn for the moody, and she saw less and less of him as the season wore on. Her parents were often away for the weekend, leaving her in the charge of their maid and her husband – who handled the gardening and any light domestic work. Dani came and went as he liked, the restrictions of authority having been largely ignored by him for the last year. For what was the point in trying to rein in the natural rebellion of a young man's journey to independence, as long as he wasn't hurting anyone?

Ever since he'd bought his motorbike he'd changed; subtly at first, and then more obviously. Daniello had taken to hanging with an older crowd, many of whom were university students; not a big worry to their parents, as his grades were impressive, and he was planning to attend that Autumn. Antonia noted the difference in his personality, though, and couldn't understand why he became increasingly distant; ignoring her, preoccupied, and smelling of cigarettes and alcohol whenever he came home, usually later and later each night.

And then one night he hadn't come home at all.

The morning had been dismal, she remembered, cloudbursts intermittently hammering the roof of their large country villa throughout the night. It had woken her, and she'd risen from her bed to get some milk, padding downstairs barefoot, silent as a wraith. Her parents had flown to Switzerland for a long weekend, so the house was silent except for the drumming of the rain; the housekeeper lived in quarters by the garage.

She noticed the door to her brother's room ajar, and on the way back up had peeped in, finding only an empty bed. This was a first; it was early in the morning, and he'd never been out all night before. Antonia hoped he was safe, considering the rain and the dangers of the Italian roads.

In the few remaining hours of early morning she drifted in and out of sleep, hoping to hear his engine and the spray of crunching gravel on the driveway beneath her window.

As an ugly grey mid-morning pervaded through the curtains, she heard the housekeeper and her husband loading up their little Fiat for an early trip into town; a weekly ritual involving much squeezing of vegetables and negotiating over eggs and the like. Normally she would have joined them, but she'd been complaining of a cold for the last few days, so they'd decided to let her sleep in. Shortly after they pulled away, her brother's bike had raced up to the house, a cacophony of revving engine and sputtering exhaust. Any ideas about sleep were over; she was wide awake. The downstairs door slammed, and she heard him run up the stairs. That was unusual. He never ran – and was always conscientious about being quiet.

When she opened her bedroom door, instead of a sheepish and tired Dani, she was shocked to find a face that looked like it had been in an accident; bloodied, a cut over his right eye, swelling and bruising distorting his jaw.

"Dani, are you okay…what happened? Where were you all night…was there an accident? Oh my…you're cut up! Dani…"

He had a wild look in his eyes, and she remembered the pungent odor of wet leather, and of something sickly sweet, like pipe tobacco, only stronger.

He frowned at her. "What are you doing here? You're supposed to be in town."

"I…I had a cough, Dani. Are you all right? I think you need a doctor."

"No. I'm... I have to leave. Tell Mamma I'll call, but I have to go south. I made a bad mistake, and I need to go somewhere nobody knows me. I need to grab some stuff, and then I'll be gone awhile."

"But your face..."

He grabbed her by the shoulders, staring down into her eyes. "Antonia, I don't have time. I thought the house would be empty. I only have a few minutes. I need to be out of here. There are some...scary people looking for me, and I don't have time to explain..." He let her go and began pacing like a tiger, his mental torment plain to see.

She was terrified. Dani wasn't afraid of anything, and he was acting like he'd seen a ghost. What was happening?

"Dani..."

He brushed past her. "Get out of my way. I'll call when I can; now leave me alone so I can finish..." As Dani began stuffing random clothes into a bag, she caught a glimpse of a lockbox. He'd pulled it out of the bottom of his closet, where she could see a hole left from a loose board.

Antonia burst into tears. Whatever this was it was bad, and frightening, and her idol was a bloody mess, and was screaming at her, and she couldn't take it. Dani moved to her, in the doorway, and got down on his knees to hug her.

"Angel, I'm sorry, don't cry...it isn't your fault. I messed up, and I have to leave so I can figure out a way to make it better. Don't cry. It'll be okay. Tell Mama I'll call, and don't worry. It'll all be okay..." Dani didn't sound very convincing, but she loved him so much she almost believed it would be okay.

"Please don't leave me alone, Dani. I'm scared. I...this...I don't understand what's happening..."

"I have to go. I'll call soon." He got up, grabbed his bag, and ran down the stairs. She thought about following him, but her legs felt like they were paralyzed. Her whole body was shutting down; it was all she could do to make it back into her bedroom. She registered the front door slamming shut, and then the sputtering of Dani's bike as he tried to coax the engine back to life. It coughed each time he kick-started it, burbled for a second, and then died. She would often wonder if it was the drizzle that had conspired to foul his chances with the motor, or if he'd been so frazzled he'd flooded it.

Suddenly, the gravel drive was filled with other engine noise; at least one car and a couple of Vespa motor-scooters. She peered over the sill and watched her brother grab his bag and sprint for the far end of the drive, hoping to make it to the field that surrounded their house. He almost did, but one of the assailants swung a bat and clipped his arm, sending him sprawling face-first into the gravel. She stifled a scream.

A young, swarthy man she'd never seen before got out of the little car and walked over to Dani, wielding something menacingly. The others joined him, forming a ragged circle around her brother. She couldn't make out what they were saying, but then the young man kicked Dani in the face. The baseball bat thudded again, and then again, and through the drizzle she could see red smeared across the pale wood. She didn't know what to do, couldn't scream, couldn't move. They were killing Dani, in front of her, and she couldn't stop them; there were no grownups around to do anything.

Dizzy, she watched as her brother struggled up onto his hands and knees, shakily, obviously badly hurt and disoriented. One of the men grabbed his hair, and the dark-skinned man moved quickly, swinging a tire iron he'd been dangling by his side. It caught Dani on the temple with a thick wet thud, audible even through the heavy leaded glass of the century-old window. Dani collapsed in a heap. One of the others grabbed his bag and began rummaging through it. Apparently satisfied, they were preparing to leave when the second motorcycle driver pointed towards the house, straight at her vantage point. They all looked up, seeming uncertain as to what to do next; then the car driver barked something, and they approached the house.

Antonia was too frightened to breathe, much less cry. She knew they'd probably seen her in the window, and that if they wanted to get in, they would. She heard the front door rattle, and then heard glass break downstairs. Grabbing her stuffed bunny, she ran into her parent's room, racing for their large closet. Maybe they'd think the house was empty, and that whatever they'd thought they'd seen was a trick of the rain and the light.

She looked at the shelves lining one wall, peered up at a little panel, and made her decision as she heard cautious footsteps creaking on the stairs. She was up in a few seconds, and pushing at the door, stirring cobwebs, moving it grudgingly on its ancient hinges. Crying silently to herself, she climbed into the darkness, and carefully lowered the old boarded hatch back into place. There was almost no light, with water dripping here and there, making the dank, ominous space even more frightening. She moved silently through the collection of ancient chests and moldy boxes, and settled into the farthest corner, behind an old tarp that covered a hodgepodge of wooden crates.

She heard the men beneath her, arguing, and barely kept from screaming when something crawled across her bare leg. Eyes closed, teeth clenched, she didn't dare smack it for fear of the noise it would cause, so she just stayed as quiet as she could – hoping it would all soon end.

Light slanted into the darkness, as someone pushed up the attic door and poked his head in, looking around.

Antonia, trembling in the far corner, remained still as she could, other than the involuntary shudders in her stomach and jaw.

Seconds passed.

Something squealed in alarm as the intruder pushed the door higher, preparing to enter the space. A rat ran across the floor in front of the assailant from one pile of boxes to a wet lump of debris. The man recoiled in nervous disgust and dropped the hatch, his footsteps moving out of the bedroom area and back down the stairs.

Antonia didn't take any chances. Paralyzed with fear, she remained curled up in a fetal position as the noise from the intruders receded, and ultimately became silent.

That was how the constables found her, two hours later.

Bitten nine times by spiders; twice by rats.

She'd never made a sound.

Her parents rarely mentioned Dani after the police concluded their investigation. He'd suffered massive brain damage from the blow to his skull, and after weeks of lying in intensive care, he'd hemorrhaged uncontrollably while in a coma, dying alone in the middle of the night. Without any further information, there wasn't enough evidence to solve the case; his killers had left no clues. Some broken glass, a few muddy footprints in the house, but nothing that ever led to an explanation of why a young man's life had been extinguished on a rainy summer morning.

Nobody had seen anything from the neighboring homes, and nobody came forward to advance a story. Drugs were hypothesized, local gang involvement, revolutionary terrorist cells around the university, jealous attacks by angry boyfriends; all were floated, and ultimately, none explained anything.

A part of her parents died that morning, as did a piece of Antonia. The family tried to put the grisly attack and Dani's death behind them, but it changed everything; there was always the time before that day, and the time after. It seemed so long ago now, at least twenty years, but every now and then the shadows came to visit, and the dream would come, unannounced.

She hated the rat dream.

She hated that it had returned once again, complicating everything further.

Antonia knew tonight would be a long night; a night when sleeping pills and dozing with the lights on was an unwelcome but necessary ritual. She resigned herself to yet another encounter with her demons, and decided whatever happened, she wouldn't let the past interfere with her present anymore. She wasn't nine, and the bites had long ago healed over.

She hoped she could make good on that commitment.

CHAPTER 23

The following morning Steven was startled awake by the requested call, and he vaguely wondered why he'd taken to sleeping so late. Then he remembered; the time change. Nine in the morning here was six in the morning California time. He got up and surveyed the scene outside. A few clouds drifted and billowed in the sky, but nothing ominous. Stiff breeze, though. Small whitecaps on the crests of the water.

He called down to the front desk, ordered breakfast and asked about the hurricane, to be informed it was still moving slowly in their general direction and had been upgraded to a category three overnight. Some guests were leaving early so if it continued to approach, he'd be moved to another suite; the only real issue they anticipated, if it hit, was some flooding on the lower floors. The hotel had seen far worse than a category three and was still standing as testimony.

The web was functioning fine, so Steven checked the stock and the boards. Down yesterday by forty cents, up today by thirty.

He had an e-mail from an unknown address. Opened it. It was Stan Caldwell. The e-mail contained instructions for getting a PGP key and for communicating with encryption. He opened another window and followed the instructions, generating his key. He replied to Stan with an encrypted e-mail as a test, and after a few minutes, he received an encrypted e-mail back. He unscrambled it, and read:

[Greetings. How goes the war? Nothing new here. Been scanning the news every day to find out if you're alive, but so far no go. Hope this message finds you well. Remember, I don't want to know where you are. Stan.]

He typed a response:

[Couldn't be better. Should have a ton of info on Griffen within a week. Life continues to be interesting. I'll need a wire transfer sent next week to an offshore attorney; between $75 and $100 thousand. I'll get you instructions soon. Take care. Dead Guy]

He opened his other e-mail, from Spyder, with trepidation.

[So here's the theory, Bowman; and remember I warned you wouldn't like it. I believe the government is using some trading entities, Griffen's among them, to fund covert operations in areas that can't be officially sanctioned. I believe the rot goes all the way to the top of the intelligence agency. I'm pulling in some favors from some buddies who can confirm this, and should know if I'm right within a short while. If I am, you're up against way more than you thought.

Oh, and just to further ruin your day, I'm waiting for some dynamite on Allied's vaccine secret sauce. If that turns out to be as bad as I think, you'll be able to blow them wide open – it's worse than if you discovered they were shipping light beer to hospitals instead of vaccine. But I need to be sure before I say anything. If I'm correct, this is far bigger than anything we suspected. Watch your back. Spyder]

If the U.S. was allowing market manipulation because it was generating cash from the process then there were no barriers to crime in the markets; and further, the government was allowing innocent companies and investors to lose everything so they could make a buck. Spyder was right; it stank to high heaven.

He now understood how Griffen could feel invulnerable – unafraid of any consequences. He had the cops on the payroll, literally. So what was Steven, or more to the point, 'Bowman' to do if it were all true?

Lost in thought, he heard a knock on the door. Breakfast. Steven realized he was famished. He opened the door to find Antonia holding a tray with his meal on it; breathtaking as usual, in a cotton cover-up. His concerns vaporized instantly.

"You ordered room service, sir?" she said, holding back a smile.

"Wow. That's quite a menu they provide. I'm really glad I ordered the Continental and not the American." He took the tray from her. "Come in. How did you manage...?"

Antonia tapped her temple with a finger. "I saw the maid with the tray and slipped her a tip. She seemed good with that. How did you sleep?"

"Like a log. The untroubled rest of the innocent."

"I don't know about the innocent part, but I'm glad you're well rested." She considered him, stroking her chin. "That goatee makes you look like the devil. Have you always had it?"

"It's all part of my evil disguise as a pirate of the Caribbean. Arrrr. Arrrrrr." He fashioned a hook with one of his hands and squinted in what he imagined was a pirate-y fashion. It wasn't.

She clapped her hands together, threw back her head and laughed. That laugh. He was done for. But the wedding ring hadn't come off; dead husband was still leading in that race. Part of him hated his knee-jerk observation.

"Your roots are starting to grow in lighter. You look like a pop star. What did you look like before you became James Bond?"

"I have lighter hair, wear it a little longer, no goatee. Boring," he explained.

"It probably looked good," she said, studying his cut. She folded her arms and adopted a mock-frown. "So what's on the agenda today, Pirate Boy?"

"I hadn't really thought about it," he admitted. "I talked to the front desk and they said the hurricane was still small, could easily miss us entirely and just rain tonight. Anything strike your fancy for the day? Tomorrow could be stormy."

"I heard there was a place where you could swim with dolphins. Now I'd like to do that. After yesterday's boat ride, I want to touch one – swim with them," she bubbled, having obviously planned the suggestion.

"Sounds like a plan," he said. "You want coffee?"

"Please. Just black."

They spent the next half hour bantering back and forth, and agreed to meet at the front desk in ten minutes or so; she had to change into a swimsuit. He didn't offer to help – he could break a nail or something.

He called Alfred to let him know the wire was set for Monday, and that all he needed was the instructions and amount. Alfred updated him on his progress, informing Steven he'd gotten several names of investors in the offshore fund and would have the rest by day's end. Steven jotted them down. Santa Maria De Ignacius Charity, out of Panama. Terrasol Investment Advisors, from Argentina.

Nothing rang any bells.

Alfred asked him about the hurricane; wanted to know if he'd stay on the island if it looked like it was going to hit. Alfred also told him he was looking into the Jim Cavierti matter, but hadn't uncovered much so far. Steven suggested finding out where Jim had stayed as a starting point. They agreed to talk again later that day or the following day, as and when Alfred accrued more information.

He went back online and contacted the Group.

[Hey, guys, it's Bowman here. Would you find out everything you can about these two entities: Santa Maria De Ignacius Charity in Panama, and Terrasol Investment Advisors in Argentina. They're connected with the Griffen Fund, supposedly significant investors.]

He decided not to make the clandestine connection public for the moment, so he signed off, already late for the front desk.

There she stood…waiting in the lobby for him, chatting with the desk clerk.

Her voice was filled with glee. "They said they'd take us to the dolphin park. It's over where the boat was. They also told me the hurricane is still two hundred miles away – maybe moving north of us, but we won't know for a while longer if there's any chance of it coming here. So for today, everything's good," Antonia concluded. "And look! here's the van to take us. *Buon, andiamo.*"

As they drove to the dolphin park, the driver handed Steven a card with the hotel phone number on it, telling him to call when they wanted a pick-up. They found the entrance to the main building and were informed they'd just missed the 11:30 session and the next available time was 1:30. A hundred twenty-five bucks for one person to swim; *perhaps the dolphins were made out of platinum or laid golden eggs?*

They took a stroll to the outdoor café and enjoyed a well prepared, leisurely lunch. Antonia was chatty, though seemed a little nervous about the hurricane. She had more questions for him.

"So, what do you do after you have all the information you came for…what's next? Where do you go?" she asked.

"I don't honestly know, Antonia. I'll know once I have all the input. What I do know is I'm going to take this Griffen character down. He's not going to get away with ruining my life and killing my friends, among other people. I'm going to put a stop to that." He thought about it. "Now that you mention it, I really don't have the faintest idea what's next."

She nodded. "You and I, then, are alike that way. You don't know what comes next, and neither do I. I don't know what I'm going to do once I leave here; I called my friends and apologized last night, told them not to bother waiting around for me, that I was on an adventure." She took a bite of her sandwich. "It does feel like an adventure, Steven."

"I figure I'm here for at least another week. I don't really have a time horizon past that. Week by week. That's what I've been left with," Steven mused out loud.

"You don't have to make your life about these people. It seems like you have a pretty nice hand of cards. You can do anything you want," she observed.

"Except go home. Except talk to my friend ever again, or pet my dog," he said.

She folded her arms, frowned. "I hope you understand that once you get what you're after there's a whole life ahead of you. It's not just about these men. And like your friend, you don't know how much time you have on this world." She paused. "There is an after, Steven." Antonia looked at him again. He couldn't tell what she was thinking but it bothered him all the same.

"Part of me is afraid to even think about the *after* stuff," he finally conceded. "I'll settle for making it through next week."

After lunch they stood and gazed out at the ocean. Their ocean, of late. The swell was larger than yesterday, the waves rolling the horizon in an almost biblical manner. All was silent aside from the whistle of the wind as it rustled through the surrounding structures.

They made their way back to the main building, where one of the dolphin trainers escorted them into the dolphin area. Steven decided to stay out of the water, leaving Antonia to enjoy her experience with the animals minus any distractions. Soon she was frolicking and splashing and gliding with the velvet-smooth torpedoes of mischief. The animals seemed good-natured, and Antonia had completely surrendered to this watery heaven, kissing the female and being pulled around by the larger male, as the smaller adolescent jumped and flipped around the periphery.

When it was over, Antonia didn't want to leave.

"Oh, Steven, they're so cute. I love, love, love them," she declared. "They're the most gentle creatures. I wish I could stay here forever."

"How about you go one more round at 3:30 – my treat?" Seemed like an sure-fire way to make her happy – therefore worth every cent.

"Ah…you know the way to a woman's heart, Steven. Thank you. I accept your gallant offer." She hugged him gleefully, a damp impression of her sensuous body etching into his shirt – which he minded not one iota. She held him at arm's length, looking into his beaming face. "Quite a gentleman for a secret agent pirate, no? If only you were rich and good looking." She smiled her fifty thousand watt best at him, then turned and dashed back to the building, with a hop and a skip, to let the staff know she was coming for one more turn. He walked back slowly, on air for most of the way. A warmth had flooded into him. He'd taken her words as compliment, not speculation.

Brooding clouds set about darkening the horizon as they returned to the hotel. According to the desk, the hurricane was now a hundred and twenty-five miles out, and it looked like they might get the edge of it. Jenkins was on duty and offered them both upstairs suites in a different villa – sometimes the lower rooms flooded if the storm turned and hit full force. Wind speeds were reported at a hundred twenty miles per hour, meaning there was danger of a storm surge propelling water all the way up the beach.

"What about my pool. Do I lose my pool?" Antonia asked.

Steven stared at her. "Your pool?"

"Yes, my pool. My room has a swimming pool in it."

"You're kidding," Steven said. And he thought his room was lavish? She had a private swimming pool? Wow. He thought about her swimming naked; not a bad visual. Not bad at all. He wondered if she needed a lifeguard.

"No, sir, she isn't joking. Our larger suites are available with private pools, but alas, not in the building we will be moving you to. I apologize, Mrs. Donitelli. Perhaps we can find a way to make it up to you? Some dinners, or maybe complimentary spa days?" Jenkins, always the diplomat, always searching for ways to keep the guests happy.

"It's not so important," she answered truthfully.

Jenkins smiled warmly, entranced by the easygoing charm of her nature. "I'll give you some time to collect your belongings. Just call down and we'll send up a bellman to take your things to the new suites. Thank you for being so understanding."

They hurried to their rooms to prepare for the move. Steven took the opportunity to check in with Alfred, who told him he'd found out where Jim Cavierti had spent his last days; a private super-lux villa on the other side of the island – it came with a staff of ten and rented by the week for fifteen thousand dollars; twenty in high season. Hedges House. Steven wrote it down. Alfred needlessly cautioned him that the internet and phone service could be interrupted by a significant storm – welcome to the islands – and went on to assure him they tended to get things in order pretty quickly afterwards. They agreed to touch base tomorrow.

Steven placed a call to the desk, and Simon quickly arrived at his door, armed with a luggage cart. They transferred him to a villa closer to the main building, Villa #9. His new quarters were identical to his old quarters, which is to say opulent and large. There was another bottle of champagne on ice, more flowers. He called and asked to be put through to Mrs. Donitelli.

"Hello?"

"Please don't think this an obscene phone call. It's just that the prospect of another night in your company has me overcome with anticipation. Forgive the heavy breathing and tell me – is there anything in particular you'd like to request on this wonderful, tempestuous evening?" he asked.

"How about dinner at last night's restaurant again? I think it will be too windy at the other one, no?"

"That's exactly what I was going to suggest," he said. That, and some completely unmentionable lascivious misbehavior. "Eight o'clock work for you?"

"Is good. I still need to get unpacked and shower. Poor little me – I miss my pool. How am I going to occupy my time?" She had a marvelous sense of humor. Even in a second language.

"Okay. I'm in Villa number nine, room nine-o-four," he said.

"I'm in number nine-o-five. Next door again. Serendipity wouldn't you say?"

"That was the name of my boat; Serendipity. I'll see you in a little while. *Ciao*, Antonia."

"*Ciao*."

CHAPTER 24

Steven checked online, and found he had another message from Spyder:

[I put the names through some sources. Should know more in 24 hours. I hear there's a big storm in the Caribbean. Hope you aren't in it. Spyder]

Steven checked the weather sites, and saw the satellite of the storm and the simulations of the path of the hurricane. If it stayed on course, it would just brush the island; maybe some rain and a few hours of heavy wind. Probably hit very late tonight. He realized he hadn't yet checked whether Allied had closed up or down. Incredible how quickly your priorities change when you're hiding from killers on a tropical island with an Italian supermodel, and about to be flattened by a hurricane. Maybe he'd just needed a little excitement in his life. He'd certainly taken the long way around to getting some.

Allied had closed essentially unchanged. He surmised Griffen was doing everything within reason to keep the price up until the website was taken down for good, and then there would be another slew of analyst upgrades and glowing recommendations. Nicholas really was the only turd in his punchbowl – the pump phase of a manipulation required unbridled exuberance, and any hint of doubt could derail it.

Steven needed more information, a lot more, before he could construct a solid case against Griffen and Allied. Speculations and skepticism on his site were one thing, but he needed to dig up buried bodies, dirty deeds, hard evidence. Right now, all he had were suggestions of impropriety. He hoped his hundred thousand bucks would buy enough to hang the bastard, or at least galvanize the hangman into building the gallows and testing the rope; maybe sending the black hood out to the dry cleaner.

Antonia knocked his door at seven forty-five, visibly concerned about the approaching storm. He did everything he could to calm her fears, pointing out that the hotel and island had withstood far worse. She was no less agitated.

At the restaurant, they ordered, and when the meal arrived made small talk as they ate, but Steven sensed she was uneasy about something. He asked her directly what was troubling her. The storm? The new room? His shirt?

"I'm just confused, is all," she confessed. "I've enjoyed my last few days so much, I'm starting to feel alive, after a long period of sleepwalking through life. I never thought I'd feel that way ever again, not after what happened." She crinkled her brow. "I suppose I'm just trying to figure out...it's just hard, is all..."

"I've enjoyed my time on Anguilla immeasurably, Antonia, all because I met you. I'm sorry it's complicated your life, or mine, but I'm not sorry about anything else. Sometimes life isn't simple," he observed. It was true.

"No, sometimes it isn't. *Campai*," she toasted, clinking her glass against his.

"I don't know, Antonia, what happens tomorrow, or the next day, or the next – but I do know meeting you changed something important for me. Right now that's all I need to know," he concluded.

She considered his eyes, the seriousness in his face. "You're full of surprises, Steven. The water runs deep on your side of the table. I just need some time." She took a sip of wine. "You weren't supposed to be here, Steven. I was only looking for a few days away from the crowds."

"I've got nothing but time, my friend. In case you haven't noticed, I'm not going anywhere."

"Eh, and so, we have some wine, and wait for the storms to pass, clear skies to come, no?"

"To clear skies," he said, offering his glass up in tribute.

They finished their meal and retreated into the bar. No live band tonight. The island was hunkering down for hard weather, with just the solitary bartender on storm-watch duty. The night's drink special was 'The Hurricane'. That was funny. He ordered one, and Antonia had her usual Sambuca. They contemplated the rising wind and churning seas in silence, alone with their thoughts. She reached out and held his hand. Electricity crackled between their once lost souls.

And that's how they spent the next hour, holding hands and watching the sea protest the flailing it was enduring from the mounting wind. Steven estimated it was blowing a good thirty knots. They needed to get back to their rooms soon or the journey would be unpleasant. He signed the chit, and the clerk gave them a ride back in the golf cart.

"Looks like it's going to be a good one, huh?" the clerk offered, shouting over the wind.

"Seems that way to me. Any news on the path of the storm?" Steven asked.

"Now they say it's coming straight at us, but that's changed twice already. Nobody knows at this point but the good Lord, and he's not telling. Have a safe night." The clerk dropped them off in front of their villa, quickly spinning the rocking golf cart around for his return trip to the hotel.

They ran up the stairs, and stood in his doorway. She looked up at him, suddenly grabbed onto him, and hugged him very tightly. He hugged her back. They stood that way for a long time.

"Tell me that it's all going to be fine. Everything will be all right. Tell me that, Steven Cross."

"It will. Everything will be all right. You'll see. You have nothing to worry about, Antonia Donitelli."

"Thank you. I needed to hear you say it. Goodnight, Steven." She stood on her tiptoes and kissed him, gently, on the lips, taking her time with the kiss as he held her. She was trembling when he let go. And the tears were back again. Complicated girl. A lot going on behind those hazel eyes.

"It really will be okay, Antonia."

"I know it will. Goodnight." And then she was off, battling the gusts assaulting her door a dozen yards away.

The inclement weather increased steadily and within the hour a hammering downpour let loose on the island. The staff had stocked the room with candles in case they lost power, preparing for the worst. The storm shutters were closed against the angry lashing of horizontal rain, and the wind had taken up a low, eerie wailing as it forced its way through the complaining rafters. Steven eventually drifted off into uneasy sleep state, again dreaming of Antonia, long brown hair blowing in the wind as the porpoises caressed her feet.

A pounding woke him. The shutters? No. He looked at the clock: 2:30 in the morning. It sounded as though the room was in the middle of a wind tunnel. The pounding was coming from the front door. Evacuation? He pulled on a pair of shorts, padded to the door, cautiously opened it, and was almost knocked off his feet as Antonia burst through the door and kissed him – kissed him hungrily, her desire ravenous and palpable. He kicked the door closed as she clung tight to his stirring body, locked onto his face, devouring every bit of his mouth she could get. He grabbed her hair, tugging it gently while pressing her to him as she moaned with increasing urgency.

He was astonished by the ferocity of her passion; as deep as the fury of the storm. She was chaos epitomized, the dam of her libido burst open wide, with a fire of passion blazing out of control.

They couldn't get enough. He pressed her against the wall as they consumed each other. His hand moved down the back of her summer dress, grabbed her buttock, and then slid greedily along her slick opening. She pushed his shorts down and grabbed him, stroked him, never disengaging her mouth from his. He picked her up and she wrapped her legs around his hips, guiding him into her. Their utter need for connection was elemental and brutal and total, accompanied by the howling of the wind, the crashing of the surf and the hammering of the rain; the wailing of the hurricane's wrath melded into their cries of passion and lust and release.

They made love five times that night. Every fantasy he'd ever had, every want, every need, she matched with an intensity and desire that was relentless. She couldn't get enough of him, couldn't be wanton enough to satisfy her hunger; the craving and desire that implicitly drove her. When they finally drifted off to sleep, scents intermingled and wrapped around each other, exhausted, it was finally dawn; albeit a dark and rainy dawn, cast in grey from the turbulent clouds overhead.

The storm had passed by the island and they'd been spared the worst of it. The wind had eased to a moan from the night's strident shriek. The swollen raindrops fell heavily from the sky, and they slept, deeply, she cradled in his arms.

CHAPTER 25

They awoke at midday. The tail of the storm lingered overhead, the rain still slanting down on the roof of the villa. When Steven's eyes opened, Antonia was leaning on her elbow, looking at him. He took in her face and her eyes, hair wild and unruly from last night's adventures. He surely must be the luckiest man in the world.

She spoke first. "Not too bad…for an old guy," she summarized, smiling that smile at him.

"I'm sorry, I don't remember anything from last night; must have been drunk. What are you doing here?" he asked, straight-faced.

"Don't you remember? You collapsed in the lobby. Everyone thought you'd had a heart attack or something. I came back to help them get your diaper off. The staff insisted I stay," she replied.

"Oh. Dammit. I do that sometimes; it's the heroin. I hope the other guests weren't disturbed." Wasn't this fun. "I swear, one day soon I'll quit. It's just so hard."

They stared at each other for a few beats of time. Both began laughing simultaneously. Good laughter. Comfortable laughter.

"Good morning, *Signore* Cross, will you be requiring anything more today? A nice breakfast, or maybe a full day of calisthenics in bed?" she asked.

"If they could invent a way to do both, now that would sell like VWs." He studied her. "You're phenomenal. I can't get enough of you."

"So maybe breakfast can wait…" She smiled, and her head slid beneath the sheet. They made love three more times, dozing dreamily between each bout.

When they awoke it was dark out. The clock next to them was blinking, so at some point they'd lost power. Steven got up and tried the lights. The hallway lit up. Good sign. He walked into the bathroom and tried the shower. It got hot. Also a good sign. He climbed in and began the cleansing process, and then the glass door opened and he was joined by a guest. Cleansing got sidetracked temporarily. Eventually they made it out, and he opened up a package that he'd gotten at the hotel gift shop. It was a small nail clipper. He started snipping at the sutures.

"*Ai*, don't. Go lay down. I'll do that. Do you have, eh, pincers?" she asked, standing there very tanned and very naked with a white towel wrapped around her head. If Steven died tonight, he'd be okay with that. Not a bad way to go.

"Tweezers? Right behind you. Same plastic bag as the nail clippers."

They went into the bedroom, and he lay on his right side as she snipped away at the stitches. She started pulling them out. He felt his skin pulling, but no real pain. Good sign.

"I think I caught part of your intestine. Sorry, *caro*," she quipped. He ignored it. She was done in a few minutes. "There, *finito*."

They went back into the bathroom, and he studied his scar. Then he got distracted and studied her. Much more interesting subject matter. The back of the G-string had left a small T-shaped tan line, and he could see that she was really very tanned compared to her natural color. He turned to her and kissed her hungrily.

"You're pretty tanned," he murmured, between kisses.

"You get that way from lying in the sun, I hear," she said.

He held her. They gazed into each other's eyes. He looked down.

"You took off your wedding ring."

"It's back in my room, in the safe. I don't need it anymore," she said. "That time is over."

"You're beautiful."

"So are you. I wonder how we can get something to eat. Do you think the restaurants are open?" she asked.

"I'll call and see." Steven dried off, and made for the living room to call the front desk. He was informed the restaurants were all closed, but limited room service was available. He asked them to bring up whatever they could find to make a meal for two very hungry guests. The staff happily agreed to put something together and have it up within a half hour. He was told most of the lower rooms had flooded, and maid service had been suspended until the following day so the local staff could put their lives back together and attend to their homes and families. Fresh towels were available in the lobby.

Steven turned, and contemplated Antonia emerging from the bathroom.

"I don't want you to think that I sleep with every hot Italian supermodel celebrity publisher I come across. I have my standards. What kind of pirate do you think I am?" he asked.

"Be quiet and just look pretty, okay? No is necessary all the noise," she said mischievously.

The food was delivered accordingly, a collection of fruit, grilled meats, and chicken and rice. No meal had ever been as appreciated as this one was. They devoured the entire plate – and then made sweet love all over again.

He woke to find that Friday had arrived. His watch said 8:00 a.m.. Antonia lay sleeping on the bed, so he tried his laptop, happy to find the internet was working. He checked his e-mail; there were several messages. The first was an encrypted e-mail:

[Just send me the wire instructions and the amount and it shall be done. Take care. Stan]

Next, from Spyder:

[Santa Maria De Ignacio in Panama raised a red flag with the DEA. It's a shell used for laundering Ecuadorian narco-trafficking money. They build a few low-budget schools in Latin America to maintain pretense, but it's well known in security circles as big drug money. A hit on that one. Nothing on the Argentine company yet. And still working on my other theory. Spyder]

Wow. So our good friend Griffen had dope dealers as one of his significant offshore fund investors. Nice to have solid confirmation he was dirty. He wondered how to go about proving it. That might take some creativity. And it was the offshore fund, not the domestic one, so not as damaging as he'd like. Still, a good start nonetheless.

Next, a posting from Pogo:

[They've stepped up their hunt for the site. I'm moving the mirroring every 24 hours now. Driving them bat-shit. This is fun. Anything you want uploaded? Let me know. Pogo]

He responded:

[Not for now. Just keep jabbing them with a sharp stick. I'll keep in touch. Bowman]

He heard the sound of Antonia stirring, so logged off and returned to the bedroom. She was sitting up, looking at him.

"Been on the computer?"

"Yeah. Turns out my Wall Street friend has an investor that's also one of the world's largest cocaine producers," he told her.

"Steven, this scares me to hear. I have plans for you," she said.

"Do they involve me naked?" he asked, hopefully.

"*Ai*, with the talking. Pretty face, and then you spoil it with the talking. I figure I can clean you up, you keep quiet, maybe I show you off a little. I bet you clean up pretty good," she teased.

He walked over to her, sat down on the bed, took her hands.

"You are an amazing woman, Antonia. Thank God I found you," he said.

"I feel the same way...I am an amazing woman."

He swatted at her playfully.

Then she became serious. "No, sorry. You are everything I ever hoped for. I didn't know if I was going to come to you the other night, or try to leave the island." Her mind returned there for a moment. "I think we can both thank the hurricane for much, Steven. For forcing me to choose. For making me choose to rejoin the living."

"Hurricane Antonia," he announced.

"Do you understand what I'm saying, Steven?" she persisted.

"I do." No joking now.

They kissed. She pulled away.

"My face is getting very hurt, *caro*. I need a break. The goatee has to go. The sooner the better."

"Who said anything about needing to kiss?" he replied. It was his turn to slip under the covers.

They finally made it to breakfast at eleven.

The hotel was steadily recovering its poise. They'd lost about half their beach to the storm, carried away by the heavy seas. The waiter told them it would be back within a week or two; nature's washing machine on rinse. They ordered, and Steven turned on his cell phone. No service. The infrastructure was a little slow in catching up.

They ate voraciously and happily, exchanging mutual admiration over the food-laden table. Steven asked her what she wanted to do with her day. She cocked an eyebrow.

"Maybe we lie in the sun a little, you can read, and then a nap?" she said. Sounded good to him.

"A fine plan, my little hurricane."

CHAPTER 26

Saturday, Steven was awakened by the jarring ring of the hotel phone. It was Alfred.

"Sorry, Steven, but cellular service is still out and there's no other way to reach you. I'm calling from a public box, by the way. I've got two more names. Imperial Equipment Corporation in Zurich, and Adriatic Trading out of Moscow. He really does have an eclectic mix of investors, doesn't he?"

"Considering that the Panamanian one is a front for the Ecuadorian cocaine cartel, I'd say so," Steven observed.

"Really?" Alfred said. "That might land him in hot water – even in the more forgiving jurisdictions, such as Barbados. I didn't realize we were dealing with groups incorporating such obvious liabilities."

"I'd be very careful every step of this inquiry you're doing, Alfred. Bad things have already happened. I'm not sure they won't continue to happen." Steven wanted Alfred to understand he was dealing with dangerous people – the Ecuadorian deal was unmistakably malevolent.

"Point taken. I tried sending you the wire instructions, but I'm having a spot of difficulty with the internet since the storm. I'll try again today," Alfred advised him.

"My attorney on the other end confirmed it's good to go, so whenever you send me the instructions I can execute."

"Very well then. Have a marvelous weekend, why don't you…things should be back to normal soon enough. Try to make the most your current situation."

Steven smiled to himself. "I'll do my best, Alfred – that's a promise."

Antonia had gotten into the shower by the time he was off the phone. He joined her under the streaming water, and she was happy to receive him. He absently hoped there was a good supply of hot water available. Showers took a long time in room 904 of late.

Once their morning routine was completed, Steven told Antonia he needed a few hours by himself to check on some leads. She wanted to accompany him, but he was adamant.

"I've already lost too much by underestimating the danger involved. I won't risk you. It's not an option, Antonia. I hope you understand." He wasn't going to give on this new policy of his.

"It's your game, so I guess you can make the rules," she decided matter-of-factly. "I'll stay here. I can read your David Foster Wallace book." And just like that, it was settled.

At the hotel, Steven asked Jenkins what the most discreet way to get around the island would be, absent an ID being presented. Jenkins recommended taxis, or hiring a car and driver. Steven opted for cabs, but asked for a lift over to Sandy Ground; he'd start there, even though the boat explosion had occurred outside of Island Harbor. Maybe Roy had some ideas as to who owned the boat that had exploded. It wasn't that big an island, and all the skippers probably knew each other.

The hotel van dropped him off at Roy's, and he made his way down to the dock. It was gone – wiped away by the hurricane, with just a few drunken pilings left sticking out of the water. But the hardy little catamaran was floating offshore about thirty yards; anchored, with no damage. Roy was sitting and drinking coffee at a bench outside the little café, which was undergoing major roof repairs.

Roy greeted him. "Hey, Mon, how's it going? You made it through the storm… still here, huh?"

"Yeah. I see the dock didn't make it. How did the boat survive?" Steven asked.

"It was pretty hairy. I took her off the beach, put out three storm anchors, and rode it out. Had to use the engines to keep from pulling the anchors up for a few hours there. Big seas, I tell you that; confused, coming from all around. Wet, too. It was a long night." Roy was pretty salty. Steven could envision the tumultuous scene and he wouldn't have done it for any amount of money.

"You're a braver man than I, Roy. Hey, do you remember a couple of years ago a boat ran aground on the reef outside of Island Harbor and exploded?" Steven asked.

"You know, I do remember hear tell of something like that. Big explosion. I wasn't there, though. Don't know much about it."

Steven dangled the question. "Any idea whose boat it was?"

"Now that you mention it, I don't know. Maybe it was the guy's boat?" Roy speculated.

"I don't think so. He was here as a tourist for a week – from the States. It just seems strange that a large speedboat could be in these waters and not be a local boat. I mean, how would you get a Scarab over here as a tourist?" Steven was thinking out loud.

"Could be it came over on a big yacht as a tender? Or from St. Martin? I don't know, wish I could help you. You might want to go down to Island Harbor and ask. I don't know whose boat it was, though." Roy seemed pretty open, so Steven had no reason to doubt his word. That made it weird. Small island, not many boats, so whose was it?

Steven walked back up to the road and called a cab, which he took to Island Harbor, on the far end of the island. He walked around the waterfront talking to the captains and some of the local vendors. Most remembered the explosion, but no one had any idea who owned the boat. One skipper in particular had interesting thoughts on the topic, though:

"I remember at the time, this big boom happened and then a bunch of black smoke and all – but not much debris. I thought it was strange. If big Scarab goes kapow, you think you'd find bits of her everywhere. Still, the sea's an odd mistress. She keeps her secrets to herself."

So everyone remembered the explosion, but no one saw the boat actually run aground, and little debris was found. The skippers suggested it was probably a St. Martin boat, rented for the day. Wasn't a local, that was for sure.

He next stopped at the newspaper's offices. The owner was there, but he was evasive, and actively unfriendly towards the end of the discussion. Steven couldn't understand why the guy was so annoyed at someone expressing interest in a piece of news he'd covered several years earlier; it made no sense.

Steven had lunch at a resort that overlooked the harbor, and asked the waitress about Hedges House; she pointed to a collection of villas on the hill down the cove from where they were located, and said it was one of those. He figured he could do that tomorrow. He wanted to check on the St. Martin boat angle first. He finished his meal and caught a cab back to Cap Juluca.

Antonia was seated on the terrace reading his book.

"Isn't that a little dense for you?" he said.

"I read it slowly. Some of the words I don't understand but the overall I do." She closed the book and jumped up to embrace him with a shower of kisses. "How was your spy work?"

"Okay I suppose. Roy lost his dock, but saved his boat. What's weird is that nobody knows anything about the boat that exploded. I need to make a phone call to St. Martin and check on some things." He really was puzzled.

"I'm starving to death, wasting away waiting for *Double-O-Seven* to get back. Feed me, you bad selfish man," she demanded.

"You have but to ask."

They strolled down to the restaurant, and she had lunch while he nursed a beer. The girl could eat. Loved her seafood.

Steven completely forgot about the phone call to St. Martin until it was almost dark. He dug Jean-Claude's card out of his wallet.

"*Allo.*"

"Jean-Claude, this is your friend you dropped off on the beach the other day. Do you remember?"

"*Ah, bien sur*, Anguilla, *non*? Were your friends surprised?"

"Very. Listen, I wanted to ask, do you remember a boat explosion here a few years ago? Tourist was killed?"

"I remember something. Not much. Why?"

"I'm trying to figure out whose boat it was, whether it was a rental from St. Martin. Could you ask around for me?" Steven asked.

"*Oui*, I can, but I don't think you will have luck. I know all of the boats here, and she wasn't one of the fleet. Still, could have been a private boat.

I'll check and see what I can find out. Do you have a phone number?" Jean-Claude asked.

Steven told him he didn't, but would call again tomorrow evening.

"*Bon*. Do you need me to come get you soon?"

"Keep the boat full of gas. Probably next week."

Sunday morning he was awakened by a sultry Italian making passionate overtures, and he made a mental note that he hadn't had this intense a sex drive since he was sixteen. They couldn't get enough of each other, and there was a lot of lost time to make up for. Afterwards, he concluded that he was the lucky beneficiary of her almost-two-year dry spell, and then he was forced to focus his attention in other areas, and so chased away the unchaste thoughts.

Rested and somewhat guilty over having put his exercise routine on hold, he floated the idea of a morning run to Antonia. She was receptive, pointing out he must have already burned up twenty calories from his lovemaking efforts this week.

They ran over the bridge and up the main road, avoiding the infrequent scooters that served as the primary method of transport for the locals. Antonia kept up easily, which didn't surprise Steven given her age, body, and other demonstrated endurance capabilities. She could easily match him. Youth is wasted on the young.

When they returned, they showered and ate brunch. Steven again had to invest a few hours into his project, and Antonia settled into the chair on the terrace to continue reading his book.

He had the van take him to the main inland town, an area called The Valley, and took a look around. Not much there. After a brief reconnaissance, he caught a cab to the resort near Hedges House, walking up to the sun-bleached villa on foot. It was a breathtaking view, and the grounds were immaculately groomed. He guessed the house was eleven thousand square feet if it was an inch.

Approaching the main entrance, he was greeted by a young woman sweeping the front porch area. They exchanged pleasantries, and he explained he was doing research into the boat accident from a few years ago, and so was interested in talking to anyone who remembered it or had been working there.

"That's before my time, but Miss Talya was here, I think. Let me go see if she's available. Who shall I say is calling for her?"

"Marvin Simpson," Steven said. "Thanks a million."

The girl was gone for a good ten minutes. She returned accompanied by a large woman with an officious air pervading her stature.

"I'm Miss Talya, Mr. Simpson. Jessie here tells me you are interested in a boat accident? Jessie, run along now, there's cleaning to be done, girl." Miss Talya was three hundred pounds of island matron.

"I was trying to find someone who remembers the group that was here, and could specifically tell me anything about the boat that blew up," he explained.

"Mr. Simpson," she oozed, "we don't discuss our guests as a matter of policy, you see? I'm sorry I can't help you. I'm sure you understand."

"Of course I understand. I am willing to pay for a little recollection, though. Not about your guests' behavior, more just who was here and where the boat came from." He showed her the corner of a hundred dollar bill. "Was Mr. Cavierti here with his wife…or anyone else?"

She glared at him. "I told you, we don't talk about our guests. I don't know nothing 'bout no boat," she declared emphatically, losing her matronly accent.

"So it wasn't the villa's boat?" He figured he'd try for that, at least.

"We got no boats, and I can't tell you about something I don't know about, now can I? You best be going." She recovered her matronly persona. "There's nothing for you here, Mr. Simpson. I trust you can find your way back the way you came?" And with that she turned and strode back into the house.

Huh. So not the villa's boat, and it wasn't an island rental. That was a loose end. Where did the boat come from? And judging by her reaction when he'd mentioned Mrs. Cavierti, he guessed old Jim boy hadn't been here with her. Now all he needed to figure out was who *was* here, where the boat came from, and what it all meant in the larger scheme of things. Nothing to it.

Steven walked down the winding drive and back to Island Harbor. He stopped along the way, asking any locals he encountered if anyone remembered the group that had been at Hedges House when the horrible accident happened. He got exactly nowhere. Most were friendly, but a few were unpleasant, and didn't seem interested in talking about the incident.

Oh well, he supposed that was just typical small town-cum-island isolationism. After a few fruitless hours of this, he retraced his steps and caught a cab back to the resort; higher up the beach than their hotel – he wanted to get Antonia a sun visor for their exercise runs and it seemed like the kind of location to sell them. He bought the best one he could find, and jogged back along the beach to the Cap Juluca.

When he got to the room, he presented Antonia with his gift; to her obvious delight. She'd taken a nap and felt well rested, which she demonstrated in an unmistakable way for Steven; they spent most of the approaching evening in bed, and as an afterthought arranged for a late dinner.

Just before they walked out the door, Steven remembered to call Jean-Claude, who confirmed it was definitely not a St. Martin boat.

Now that was a real logical problem from the standpoint of the official accounts. You had a boat exploding off the reef, killing a high-visibility tourist in the process, and yet there was no trace of any boats missing on the island, and none from St. Martin, either. And a 32-foot Scarab speedboat wasn't the sort of boat a visiting yacht might have as a tender – and even if one did, it would have to have been a mega-yacht, which meant you'd think there would be someone on the island who remembered the story – it wasn't as if boats exploded off the coast every month.

No part of this added up, and Steven's nose for rat was detecting a strong, pungent odor. Those who should have known something were reacting to his gentle enquiries as though he was trying to sell pedophilia snapshots, and he had the distinct impression that anyone with any knowledge was circling the wagons. Which made Steven curious. Why all the melodrama? What was being hidden?

So now he had a genuine mystery on his hands.

The case of the disappearing boat.

Book Three ~ Checkmate

A position in which a player's king is in imminent danger of capture – where the player has no legal move to make without being captured by the opponent's next move (i.e. cannot move out of check). A player whose king is checkmated loses the game.

CHAPTER 1

Steven had been asking questions all over Anguilla about the mysterious motor boat explosion that killed Nicholas Griffen's partner several years before, and reactions had varied from puzzlement, to polite disinterest, to overt hostility. He wasn't sure what to make of the stonewalling, but the curious reactions convinced him that the explosion somehow tied into the larger battle he was waging against Griffen.

Anguilla had largely recovered from the recent hurricane and life had returned to normal. As with most things on an island in the Caribbean, the local attitude of 'no worries, be happy' seemed a formidable response to any obstacles nature threw at them.

A phone rang in one of the local homes in The Valley; a residence more grandiose than most in the well-feathered neighborhood. It was answered by an authoritative voice.

"Yes?"

"I thought you ought to know," the matron began, "a man came by Hedges House today, looking into the Cavierti thing, and asking questions about the boat."

"Who is this man…any idea?" the voice inquired.

"A Marvin Simpson. He said he's investigating the incident."

"Any idea where he's staying or how long he's here for?"

"I told you all I know. I'm concerned about this. What's going on?"

"Don't be, Miss Talya – everything will be fine. Thanks for calling."

The authoritative voice belonged to a dignified black man who now stood pensively in his study reflecting on the events from a few years back. He thought about the call, then walked to his desk, looked up a number in his address book, and dialed. No answer; he'd have to try tomorrow. Why now, after over three years, was someone snooping around? He was worried. Which an unusual state of affairs for the Chief of the Anguillan Police Department.

❧❦

On Monday morning Antonia slept late, giving Steven enough time to get some work done. He checked his e-mail; the wire transfer instructions from Alfred had arrived. He forwarded them on, encrypted, to Stan, then noticed a message from Spyder, who was still working on Argentina, but had gotten a hit on the Swiss company:

[Swiss firm is a conduit for middle-eastern arms money. Probable trade with sanctioned countries and Jihad groups, blacklisted technology and devices, missiles, bio agents, nuke technology. Selling bad things to people who shouldn't have them. Spyder]

Further evidence the game he was in had a deadly element; he really would be in mortal danger if he exposed them. A shiver of apprehension ran up his spine.

Spyder was checking on Adriatic Trading as well, but no bingos yet.

Antonia stirred from her slumber; yawned lazily whilst stretching then called to him: "Steven…come to bed."

He logged off and went to join her in the bedroom. "Don't you understand I'm more than just a piece of meat? I have thoughts and ideas. I have feelings, too," he complained.

"Of course you do, *caro*. Now, can you lick right here?" she suggested, offering very specific guidance.

How could he refuse?

They headed out for another run in the late morning, deciding to spend the day on what remained of the beach. He noted he was still very interested in the way Antonia looked in her G-string, even after having spent almost a week with her rolling around naked. That bode well for the future.

Which stopped him in his tracks.

The future.

He'd started to imagine a future with Antonia in it, where he wasn't battling financial predators and dodging bullets. But that future was a dangerous place to explore, because he needed to stay focused on the matter at hand in order to have any future at all. He now had no illusions this wasn't a potentially terminal threat, and by stirring the pot and going after Griffen he'd affixed a bull's-eye firmly to his chest.

"I'm glad you stayed, Antonia," he said as they walked onto the warm pink sand.

"I think in the end, I had no choice. You're my destiny, Steven. I just have this feeling. I hope that doesn't scare you," she said. He wondered again if she were psychic. Reading his mind again. The power of G-string-related paranormal occurrences in Italy was well documented somewhere, he was sure.

"I feel the same way, Antonia," he said. "I just don't want you to be in danger or get hurt."

"The only thing that would hurt me now would be losing you, Steven. Everything else is unimportant."

The day wore on in a pleasant and sunny manner. The sorbet fairy dutifully made her rounds, ensuring they were suitably refreshed before shimmering off with her frosty delights.

His cell rang. It was Alfred.

"I have some interesting information regarding the banks' perspective on the offshore fund. They're deeply troubled, because they feel the margin exposure they have leaves them with insufficient collateral to protect them in the event of a catastrophe."

"How can that be?" Steven asked.

"I have a good contact at the primary broker the fund uses, and according to him they have allowed Griffen's offshore fund incredibly high leverage – on the order of ten to one. As Allied decreased in value over the last month the value of the collateral declined precipitously as a percentage of the portfolio. Simply put, the Allied position is upside-down, and if anything went wrong with the stock and it started dropping significantly, there would be risk of forced liquidation of not only the assets of the fund, but also a decent chunk of the bank's net asset value...largely due to the leverage."

"Wow. So Griffen got in over his head, and now the banks are at risk as well. I wonder what his plan is to get out with his skin?" Steven mused.

"I couldn't possibly speculate – not my area of expertise. But to summarize, you have some extremely worried people at CaribeWest bank, and a documented multi-million-share position in Allied that's underwater and vastly over-leveraged. I can document the investors and the position. The banking concerns, however, are obviously oral and must remain that way."

Steven shook his head in disbelief. The sort of leverage Alfred had described is part of what had taken down a lot of the U.S. banking system — he couldn't believe anyone was still allowing that kind of reckless risk-taking in today's economic environment. He supposed greed never changed, though. To get and keep a fund like Griffen's as a client, with hundreds of millions in assets, many small brokers or banks would break every rule ever conceived so they could make their next bonus.

Now the trick for Steven was to get all of the information into the right hands.

CHAPTER 2

The chief of the Anguilla police, Robert Townsend, had checked with all the hotels first thing in the morning for Marvin Simpson, with no success. Ditto for customs records. There simply was no such person on the island, at least officially.

He dialed the number he'd tried the night before. Griffen answered.

"Talk."

"Mr. Griffen, this is Robert Townsend, from Anguilla."

"Yes, Robert. How nice to hear from you. I heard you had a little storm recently. All safe, I trust?" Griffen could pretend to care with the best of them.

"No permanent harm, thanks. I'm afraid this isn't a social call. I've been notified that a man's been probing around, conducting an investigation into your partner's boat accident. He's been asking some difficult questions. Are you aware of an investigation, or know who this might be?" Townsend asked.

"No. But I can't think of anything positive that would arise from the results of an investigation," Griffen observed, "and so anyone investigating it should be considered hostile."

"So how would you handle it?"

"If it was me, I'd be concerned about the incidence of violent robberies on some of the islands after natural disasters. When people lose everything, they can get desperate; they're likely to do things they otherwise wouldn't. Sometimes these things get out of hand, go astray. You'd know more about that than I would," Griffen suggested.

"Too true. There are always elements that will prey on opportunistic targets."

"Keep me in the loop if anything comes up. I hope I've been able to help," Griffen. said

"Helpful as always, Mr. Griffen. I'll keep in contact."

❧❧

"Chief, the guy asking all the questions about the boat is at Ripples. Looks like he's on his way in for dinner. White, goatee, dark blue button-up shirt, tan pants, short hair. I was driving by and saw him standing there, waiting for someone." It was the newspaper owner, his voice distinctive enough not to require identification.

"We'll keep our eye on him," Townsend replied. "Thanks for calling."

He dialed another number.

"Bobby, get a couple friends and head over to Ripples," the chief instructed, giving him Steven's description and a contract price.

"Whoa. How bad you want him roughed up?" Bobby asked. That was a lot of money for this sort of an errand.

"I don't want him talking to anyone any more. Ever."

"That's cold, boss. But for that kind of cash, will do."

❧❧

Antonia emerged from the shuttle with a glow of radiance. She wore a very short black dress that accentuated her shapely, tanned legs, and carried a small black purse with a long gold chain strap. The purse chain matched the gold highlights in her high-heeled sandals and earrings. Casually elegant. The Italians sure knew how to dress. Among other things…

Every head turned as they walked into the restaurant. *Get used to it*, Steven told himself. The curse of accompanying Italian bombshells around town; he supposed he could steel himself for a lifetime of that. Rough duty, but someone had to do it.

They ordered the grouper, and conch soup to start. She had a glass of sparkling white, but he passed; his stomach had been getting that knot in it for the last day or two, and he wanted to be sharp at all times.

They savored their meal, and discussed how long they wanted to remain on the island. Antonia favored another week, and then maybe try St. Barts; she'd heard good things about it and wouldn't mind a little French cuisine and style. Steven was open for anything, and said as much. He had no plans. Whatever she wanted was fine by him.

"How long do you think it will take for you to be done with your investigation?" she asked.

"I don't know, but I'm getting closer. This new information I got on the list of investors goes a long way to building a case for prosecuting Griffen, if not his domestic fund. I really just need to understand who all the players are – and then I can mount a good offense."

"So a month, maybe?" Antonia obviously wanted a definitive.

"I hope so, honey. I want this to be in the past. I'm going as fast as I can," he answered honestly.

"*Buon*, then maybe you can grow your hair and stop the bad dye job…and I can introduce you to my family," she concluded.

Those were words that would have ordinarily sounded a full-scale alarm for Steven, but strangely he felt nothing but contentment at the idea. Maybe she'd slipped date rape drugs into his soda.

"I'd like that, Antonia. I really would."

❧◦☙

Griffen was settling in to watch the news when his cell phone rang. He looked at the number, but didn't recognize it. He hit return call, and a heavily accented voice answered, "*Da?*"

"This is Griffen. Someone called?"

He heard some fumbling with the phone. Sergei's voice came on the line.

"How are you?" Sergei asked. "Everything is good?"

Griffen's heartbeat spiked by twenty beats per minute. Why was Sergei calling at night and at home; to check on his wellbeing?

"Couldn't be better. To what do I owe the pleasure of your call?" Griffen asked cautiously.

"Interesting information from California. I thought you should hear it here first. Apparently the webmaster we all thought had the terrible tragedy befall him is still with us. It was another unfortunate. A boat cleaner. Tragic luck," Sergei said.

Griffen's blood chilled momentarily. He collected his thoughts. What now?

"The poor man. I trust you'll let me know if our friend resurfaces? I can't wait to congratulate him on his good fortune."

"I will. I hope you will do the same if you hear from him." Sergei disconnected.

Could the man in Anguilla be Steven Archer? Was that possible? He dialed an island number. The chief picked up.

"Were you able to attend to the problem you called about?" Griffen asked.

"It's being handled as we speak."

"This may be a gentleman who's made my life very difficult lately. Name's Steven Archer. Please call and let me know how things turn out."

"Will do. I'm sure we will be able to identify the remains," the chief said.

"The islands can be a dangerous place."

"Indeed they can. Goodnight."

CHAPTER 3

The island breeze washing over Anguilla after the hurricane was fresh and invigorating, smelling of the ocean, and subtly scented with the ubiquitous tropical flowers that had somehow survived the storm. Even after the devastating few days the island had just endured, most of the shops and restaurants were open for business.

Steven's vague uneasiness during dinner hadn't abated, and while he didn't want to upset Antonia by seeing ghosts around every tree, he was also in a heightened state of alert. The instinct that had served him so well was telling him that all was not right, and he'd long ago learned to trust it. He didn't know what triggered it – whether it was a change in the energy of those nearby, or a sensation of being scrutinized, or some indefinable sixth sense – but Steven was feeling on edge, and he didn't dismiss that easily.

Antonia took Steven's arm possessively as they left the restaurant and strolled down the narrow, deserted streets towards Sandy Ground's main drag – if you could call it that – to grab a taxi.

Steven sensed someone walking behind them, approaching at a faster than normal pace. He also spotted a figure standing up near the next corner; lurking in the shadows. Make that two figures. The scenario quickly took on an ominous flavor – couple out alone, nobody around, and suddenly the dark street had a crowd. From force of habit, Steven automatically began slowing his respiration and controlling his adrenal response. He pulled Antonia tighter and whispered in her ear.

"There may be some trouble here. Don't get involved. If it's a robbery, give me your purse and stay behind me at all times. Trust me." Antonia looked at him, alarmed, but didn't give anything away. She reached into her purse and extracted something; probably her wallet.

Things happened fast after that.

The two figures stepped out of the darkness. Islanders. Rough looking. They were both holding ominous-looking pieces of iron pipe. Steven pushed Antonia behind him, against the wall. The man who'd been following them joined his two associates. No pipe, but a long screwdriver, likely sharpened. This didn't look like an ordinary robbery to Steven.

"Hey, now, look at what we have here. Good-looking pair of lovebird visitors. Do you have a few dollars for some poor islanders to help them get by?" the taller of the three asked.

"Sure, just don't hurt us. You can have whatever you want."

"Well, now, that's mighty friendly of you. I see your little lady is dressed for a good time. Maybe we can show her one once we're done with you?" the taller man continued.

"Don't hurt her, please. We're just tourists," Steven pleaded.

The one with the screwdriver was amped on something. "Just gimme your money, you piece of shit."

The taller of the pipe-brandishing men took a step forward. "Hand it over."

"I'll do what you want…honey, give me your purse."

Antonia handed him the purse with one hand, Steven keeping between her and the group as much as possible.

Steven took the little bag, then looked around alarmed, knees buckling, arm reaching to the side seeking some sort of support. He staggered a few steps forward then grabbed at his chest and throat, making choking sounds, and rolled his eyes up into the back of his head.

"Oh God…ack…my…ack…" He fell forward and hit the ground. The assailants seemed momentarily rattled, which was just enough time for Steven to pivot using his hand and shoulder, and kick the legs out from under the closest man. He went down hard, striking his head with an audible thump on the asphalt, and Steven completed the job by driving a kick straight into his groin.

One down. But it was going to be tougher from here on out.

The tall man lurched towards Steven, but his height was a disadvantage while Steven lay on the ground. Steven knew he'd have to lean forward and bend at the knees to aim a blow with the pipe, which is precisely what the islander did. Steven arrested the whistling descent of the pipe with the chain from Antonia's purse – gripped in both hands – and used the man's own momentum to pull him over then catapult him into the air with a flex of his leg. The man went head-first into the road, trying to break his fall with one hand while the other still instinctively clutched the pipe – which Steven wrenched free as the man struck the pavement. Steven swiveled, rose up on one knee, and delivered a rapid pipe blow to the man's leg. He heard bone crack. The man screamed.

The third man screamed at the same time. He'd dropped the screwdriver and was clawing frantically at his face.

"Are you all right, Steven?" Antonia gasped.

"Yeah. What about you…what happened to him?"

"Pepper spray." She held up the small canister, hands shaking from shock and fear.

Steven stood up, dusted himself off, and swiftly kicked the screwdriver assailant in the solar plexus to put him out for a few minutes. He walked over to his first victim, and saw blood trickling from the back of his head. He bent over him and took a quick pulse. Very weak. Might be a goner. Steven stood up and approached the tall thug, who was cradling his fractured tibia and moaning like a baby.

He squeezed a nerve meridian at the base of the attacker's neck. The man screamed. Many of his teeth were broken or missing from the fall, and his neck was quite possibly fractured as well. Steven crouched down beside him and spoke softly.

"Who sent you?"

"No one. We just…wanted some money."

The nerve meridian got another, longer squeeze. More screaming.

"One more try, then I'll break your other leg and you'll spend the rest of your life on crutches. Who sent you?"

"I…the police chief…Townsend…don't hurt me anymore…please…"

Why was the police chief participating in attempted murder?

"Do you know who I am?"

"Argh!…no, mon…we was just told you was at the restaurant…someone saw you there…you been asking too many questions…"

Questions? So the police chief must have had something to do with the boat explosion, and he was willing to kill to protect his secret. *Must be some secret.*

"Okay, last one for you. Were you supposed to rob us, or kill us?" Steven's tone was conversational, with no obvious malice.

"It's not…you…you weren't supposed to make it…"

"I appreciate your honesty," Steven said. He rabbit-punched the man in the same nerve meridian, causing him to instantly lose consciousness.

Antonia had turned away from the scene. She didn't want to watch what was happening. Steven didn't blame her.

Suddenly, the attacker who'd gotten the pepper spray in the face lunged at Steven's back with the screwdriver. Steven heard him, sensed his approach. He shot his right leg backwards, supporting himself with his left arm and knee, catching the islander full in the throat. The assailant dropped the screwdriver and collapsed with a sickening thud. Steven stood up, kicked the screwdriver out of reach, and leaned over him; he wasn't going to make it. Crushed larynx. *Damned fool; he should have stayed down. With his eyes messed up like that, he didn't have a chance.* There was nothing he could do about it now.

Steven stood, and walked to Antonia.

"Let's go. We need to move. Now."

She stared at him, lost in some other world, a vacant yet horrified look on her face as she slowly registered the bodies strewn about the little road. A low, indistinct moan came from her throat, and Steven had to catch her as she fell into his arms.

Steven supported her trembling body as they began walking down the hill. Antonia's steps became steadier as they increased their pace. He dialed the hotel on his cell phone. Jenkins picked up.

"Can you get the shuttle to us at Sandy Ground dockside?"

"Absolutely. We'll be there in ten minutes."

"Thank you, Jenkins." Steven hung up.

He turned to Antonia and held her close. She was still shaking badly and her face was deathly pale. Shock?

"These guys were playing for real, Antonia. They would have killed us. That's what they were supposed to do," he said.

"I know, Steven. It was just so...brutal. I...Oh God...I..."

"It was. I'm sorry you had to see it." That was an understatement.

Antonia made a visible effort to pull herself together. She gathered her resources and started processing again. "What do we do now?"

"You have to behave normally, as though everything's perfect." He paused, thinking it through. "I think we go back to the hotel, I call Alfred and let him know what happened, then I check out and leave. I'll go to the resort down the beach, and then walk back along the surf-line and join you in your room; then we'll figure out what to do next. They obviously don't know what name I'm using or where I am, or they would have opted to take me out at the hotel, so it's probably safe 'til tomorrow. By that time, it'll be too late to track me." It wasn't a bad plan.

If the chief of police had his name or hotel he would have arranged for him to be ambushed on the way to the room, where it would have been a sure thing. So they only had a description. He figured they'd start looking for him tomorrow morning at the earliest – the assailants weren't going to be providing a lot of information to anyone any time soon. Two of the three attackers were unlikely to ever speak again, and the third wouldn't be in any shape to converse for at least a day, given the last nerve strike. He would be pretty messed up for a good while.

The shuttle arrived a few minutes later and picked them up and they traveled back to the hotel in silence. When they got to their room, Steven called Alfred and reported what had happened. Alfred said he would call Jenkins and have him check Steven out as of yesterday morning, and remove his firm from the billing ledger. Alfred promised to call back once he'd talked to Jenkins, and recommended Steven get off the island pronto. Distance seemed like a very good idea. They agreed Alfred would call again soon, and terminated the discussion.

Steven explained the situation to Antonia.

"So what are you going to do?" she asked.

"I'll see about waking up very early, and catching a boat on the beach. The same one I took here."

She gazed emptily into the distance and made a small movement of her head, as though some inner dispute had been resolved.

"I want to go with you, Steven." No hesitation. Clear, measured. And with a distinctly adamant tone.

He considered her statement. She would be in danger any time she was close to him as long as this was in play, which made the possibility of their staying together impossible in his mind. He explained that to her.

"I know," she replied. "But I can stay in the same town, and you can still visit, eh? And it would be convenient to book a hotel under the magazine's name, no? What you secret agents would call a good cover?"

Steven shook his head, dismissing the idea. She looked him in the eyes and nodded, silently imploring him to reconsider.

Shit. Steven hated to admit it, but she was right. He had many more options if she was with him — at least with him at arm's length. And anyone hunting for him would expect a single man, not a couple, so there was a natural misdirection in there being two when his hunters were only expecting one.

He considered the assailants he'd left in the street. Even if they managed to deliver a coherent report on the attack, all they could know was that he'd picked up a date for the evening — not an uncommon event in lush tropical vacation hideaways. He weighted the pros and cons, and decided that as long as he kept moving and avoided arousing suspicion, as he had with his questions on the island, there was virtually no real risk attached.

But the danger element didn't sit well with him. Enough people had been hurt by being associated with him. He was extremely reluctant to take that chance with Antonia. Steven regarded her pretty but resolute face. He could tell she'd already made up her mind, and was busy calculating how long it would take to wear him down and convince him of the merits of her decision. He already knew her well enough to understand she'd be intractable on this, so he finally capitulated, recognizing that resistance was futile.

He sighed. "Okay, here's the deal, then. I'll catch a boat off the beach, and we can meet up in St. Martin later. Didn't you say your friends had a villa there?"

"Yes. I'll call them first thing." Her face brightened. "I can take the ferry over tomorrow."

He looked at her and smiled. "Well, you get your wish, my friend," he said. She looked at him quizzically. "You'll see me without a goatee sooner rather than later."

His cell rang again. Alfred told him to go to the front desk and pay in cash. At once. Pack up and leave. He told Alfred his plan, who was okay with it as long as Steven was gone by morning.

Steven fished out Jean-Claude's contact card and dialed the number on it.

"*Allo.*"

"Jean-Claude? It's the beach guy from Anguilla. I need a pick-up tomorrow morning on the same beach, about six or thereabouts? I have an early flight."

"*Bon*, no problem." Jean-Claude paused, calculating. "Early morning pick-up is hundred and fifty dollars. Is okay?"

"That's fine. See you at six a.m. on the beach."

Steven went online for one last time and looked at his e-mail. There was a message from Stan:

[*OC Register* reported this evening that you're not dead — the police finally figured out it was the boat washer. You're famous again.]

Great. When it rains... He disconnected, packed his gear, gave Antonia his laptop, and made his way to the front desk. Jenkins had sent the night man off to run an errand, so it was just the two of them. He paid his tab and Jenkins thanked him, handing him a receipt with yesterday's date on it; made out to Steven Malone. He told Jenkins he'd arranged for a pick-up on the main road, and thanked him for all the hospitality.

Steven walked up the drive, and once out of sight of the main hotel, he circled around and headed down the beach to Villa #9. Antonia was waiting for him, apparently fully recovered from the incident and the shock of being so close to such sudden brutality. She threw her arms around him and kissed him like he'd been absent for a month. When they finally disconnected, he pulled his hygiene kit from his duffel and held it up.

"Shaving time," he declared.

He went into the bathroom and shaved the goatee. It came off easier than he'd thought it would. He had a slight tan line, but that would blend in after an hour in the sun.

Steven came out of the bathroom. Antonia cocked her head to one side, and then to the other. She squinted at him. Crinkled her nose.

"Hmmmmm. Hmmmmmmmmm. Can you put it back on?"

He grabbed her, threw her onto the bed, and kissed her again. She seemed amenable. More than. It was a long night.

At five a.m. the bedside alarm went off. Steven got up, meditated, and prepared to leave. He woke Antonia and assured her he'd meet her that afternoon, and wrote his cell phone number on the a sheet of paper with the hotel's logo embossed across the top. He folded it carefully, and handed it to Antonia.

"I'll see you in a few hours. Buy a black baseball hat and wear it on the ferry. That way, if for some reason I lose my cell, I'll see the hat from a distance." He was wearing his red St. Martin hat.

"Steven, I'm worried about you. I hope you know what you're doing," she said.

"Everything will be fine, honey. We'll be together in just a few hours. Try to get over on the three o'clock ferry. That'll give me some time to take care of a few loose ends," he said.

"Goodbye, my pirate prince."

"Goodbye, Antonia." Steven glanced at his watch; he'd be hard-pressed to get to the beach in time. He slipped out the door to greet the dawn, leaving the most beautiful and passionate woman he could ever imagine for the cold uncertainty of the future. *What an asshole*, he concluded. Why couldn't he just drop this now? Homicidal islanders and Peter's face immediately dominated his consciousness, and he remembered why that wasn't an option.

He jogged along the beach, and rounding the point, saw a boat approaching. Jean-Claude was on time and ready to go. Handing him the duffel and laptop, he hopped aboard, and after a quick reverse maneuver they were skimming along towards St. Martin at every bit of the thirty knots the skipper had boasted about. They'd be there in fifteen minutes at this speed. Steven handed Jean-Claude the $150 and looked over the flat, placid waters.

"Where's the best cup of coffee on St. Martin?"

❧

The phone rang and rang in Griffen's office at 7:15 as he walked through the doorway. He grabbed it.

"Mr. Griffen?

"Yes."

"It's Townsend. I'm afraid I have bad news. The men that were chartered with handling the issue we discussed met with some resistance."

"What the hell does that mean?" Griffen snapped. "Speak English."

"One of them is dead, one's in a coma, and the third is also hospitalized in critical condition. He hasn't regained consciousness."

"You picked the wrong guys, obviously."

"Obviously."

"Let me make a call. I have a friend who may be interested in helping. I'll call you back." Griffen called Sergei, and relayed the information.

Sergei was intrigued.

"He took down three men? That's impressive. Perhaps his military background was more extensive than his records indicate. Hmm. Anguilla, correct? I'll see about getting some assistance there today. Let me have your associate's number. I shall call him directly. Let him know to expect me." Sergei jotted down the number and hung up.

Griffen called Townsend back, and told him a friend who 'specialized in handling complicated situations' would be in touch within the hour.

Griffen had never been genuinely worried in twenty-plus years on Wall Street. Now he understood how it felt to be unsure of the ultimate outcome of a situation he was involved in.

He didn't like it one bit.

CHAPTER 4

When he got off at the dock in St. Martin, Steven pulled out his Blackberry and activated it, checking for a reception. Bingo. The signal came in nice and clear, so he could communicate online. That was a plus.

He explored the quiet streets until he found the small café Jean-Claude had recommended, ordered coffee and a croissant, and mulled over his next move in the dangerous game that was unfolding. Getting out of the Caribbean seemed like a prudent step now he realized the head of Anguilla's police force was corrupt enough to condone murder in order to shut him up. Besides which, his mission there was essentially accomplished since Alfred now had the goods on the investors.

The two wild cards were the company in Moscow and the company in Argentina. He needed to understand their roles in the fund makeup if he were to build a complete case. That they were dirty was a given; but he didn't understand in what manner they were dirty, and that was a piece of information he needed to nail down.

Argentina was a lot closer than Moscow, he figured; so maybe going to South America wouldn't be a bad call. He could hire a private investigator and find out what the deal was in Buenos Aires. Maybe Spyder or the rest of the gang would have some bright ideas.

He checked online, and immediately identified one big problem. All the flights from St. Martin to anywhere but France went into the U.S. system; which he certainly had to avoid, especially now he was alive and presumably actively being sought by Homeland Security. He doubted they'd be scanning the globe for him, but avoiding American soil and an American test of his new passport and identity seemed prudent.

He could fly to Paris, and then back-track to Argentina, but that meant twenty-two hours in the air. Tough one. He'd have to figure that out. Also, he needed to get a lead on a sharp Argentine PI who could work quickly, and with discretion. That would likely be another significant hurdle. He knew the country was still in turmoil from the constant disruption of its chronically unstable government, but beyond that, he really had no idea how to proceed.

Then there was the mystery of the boat and the partner. Was the partner taken out – killed by Griffen or some other player associated with him? Was the whole thing a cover-up? That's the way it was apparently playing out at this point. It was the only explanation that made any sense, given the heavy-handed tactics they were using to prevent any serious investigation from occurring. People didn't usually kill unless there was a lot at stake – that seemed elemental. But what was being covered up? It seemed that there were more questions now than ever. Every time he peeled a layer off the onion, more presented themselves. He had the uncomfortable sensation that he was missing a critical chunk of information.

Steven sipped at his coffee and watched as the town groggily came to life, pedestrians reluctantly emerging from their homes and dawdling their way to work. Island living was clearly slower paced than on the mainland, and nobody seemed in any particular hurry to get anywhere.

His thoughts turned to Antonia. How could he keep her out of harm's way? He knew she wanted to stay proximate to him, and he'd given his word, but was that really smart? It was selfish from his standpoint to bring her into this. Of course, it was selfish from her standpoint to want to be near him. The whole thing was one big ball of self-interest. He supposed that's what made the world go 'round.

Steven found it difficult to accurately assess his feelings for her. How much of his attraction to her could be attributed to being in an exotic place, away from the humdrum rules that bound their lives, and how much was real? He didn't think it was a simple holiday infatuation, but with all that had happened in just a few short days, how could he be sure what he was feeling? She was an astounding woman, unlike anyone he'd ever met; strong and smart, incredibly passionate, possessed of a diabolical sense of humor, and completely in sync with his rhythms. So how was he going to deal with this little unplanned hitch in his grand plan? She was flesh and blood, and if he slipped up she could become another casualty. He had enough blood on his hands at this point. The last thing he wanted was to endanger Antonia.

The problem remained that she wasn't all that interested in having Steven make her decisions for her. That complicated matters.

All he could do was keep her away from any further fallout. She was a big girl, who seemed as headstrong as she was beautiful. And she wanted to help.

Just like Peter — who'd been killed for his effort.

Helping.

Him.

Steven finally decided he'd have to make the best of the situation with Antonia. She was an adult, and besides being stubborn as a mule, was highly intelligent. He'd been honest with her, and she was dead set on accompanying him, so he would have to concentrate on keeping her safe to the best of his abilities, and be extremely careful in his investigations from this point on. No more do-it-yourself interviewing. He'd hire private investigators to do the footwork, and stay in the background, out of harm's way. That was safest for them both.

After paying for breakfast he traversed the breezy waterfront, familiarizing himself so as to be acquainted with the layout later in the day. Satisfied he was oriented and understood the basics of the town's geography, he made his way through the huddled streets until he came upon a hair salon. A young girl was just opening it up. He went in and communicated that he wanted to get his hair colored.

"*Bon, quelle couleur?* What color?" she asked.

"*Noir.* Black," Steven told her.

The rest of the transaction went smoothly. Forty-five minutes later he had black hair; sort of a Joey Ramon post-punk artist look. Very Romanian, he thought absently.

Next up, he went in search of one of the information booths situated around the town, to see about air charter companies. The woman there was not very helpful, exuding a 'you are nothing, leave me alone' attitude. Very French, and not exactly consistent with someone hired to give out information. What a strange island. So it was back to the waterfront and the small café, and back on the web; there were several air charter companies in the surrounding islands.

He jotted down a few phone numbers and looked for the nearest major airport that had regular flights to Buenos Aires. Hmmm. Caracas, Venezuela. About six hundred or so nautical miles, as the crow flies; or the small plane flies, in this case. Looking at the schedules, he learned that Aerolineas Argentinas had daily direct flights from Caracas to Buenos Aires.

He called the charter companies. Caribe Air Specialists, had a turbo-prop Cessna 414A II that would take about three hours to fly to Venezuela. They were willing to take the charter for $6,000, or $5,400 cash. He booked it for the following morning, then made reservations online for the flight to Buenos Aires.

Everything was falling neatly into place.

Next, he checked availability for St. Martin hotels, just in case Antonia couldn't get in touch with her friends. Plenty of availability, so that wouldn't be a problem. He called the Cap Juluca.

"Mrs. Donitelli's room, please. Number nine-o-five."

"Certainly, sir. One moment."

Ring. Ring.

"*Hallo?*" Antonia answered.

"*Buon giorno, cara,*" he replied.

"Steven! Oh my God. I'm so happy to hear your voice. How is everything?" She sounded excited.

"It's all good. You can come over on the ferry whenever you want. I'm done with my stuff," he said. "I miss you already."

"Me too. I'll leave right now."

"Call me when you get to the ferry terminal. Were you able to get hold of your friends?" he asked.

"No, I think they may have left already."

"No problem. We'll get a hotel once you're here. Oh, and we'll be going for a little trip tomorrow."

"Where are we going?" she asked.

"It's a surprise. Just hurry up and get over here."

"Okay. *Ciao*, pirate boy."

"*Ciao*, Antonia."

As Antonia was paying the hotel bill a policeman came up to the desk and asked to speak to the manager. Jenkins appeared, and she overheard the officer asking if there was a man staying there who had a goatee and short hair, about 6'1", using the name Marvin Simpson or Steven Archer. Jenkins went through the motions of looking through the computer, and said that no, no such person was checked in. Jenkins asked why the police were looking for him, and the reply was: "To assist with our inquiries into an assault."

Jenkins promised to keep a sharp lookout.

The shuttle delivered her to Blowing Point, where she purchased a ticket on the ferry and called Steven, briefly letting him know she was on her way. She held off on telling him about the encounter at the hotel, deciding that such information was better imparted in person. She was worried that the police, in their search for Steven, were characterizing him as the perpetrator of an assault; and was further troubled they'd apparently had a very accurate description of him. Antonia noticed a policeman watching the passengers waiting for the ferry, no doubt scanning for Steven. His plan to get off the island discreetly, first thing, had proved prescient. She hoped his luck held.

As she sat lost in her ruminations, the boat arrived. Only a few people disembarked; several workers, a couple of locals carrying shopping bags, and a group of somewhat bewildered-looking tourists.

She collected her belongings and noted a police car parked by the little reservation area. Two rugged-looking men with carry-on bags were escorted off the ferry by an officer and waved past customs. They looked very tough, like mercenaries, and she heard them talking to the policeman, answering the inevitable questions about their trip. Russian accents, heavy on the consonants.

A chill went up her spine in the ninety-degree heat.

She noted one had a pronounced scar across his nose, where it looked like something sharp had struck it, breaking it in the process. Both were well-muscled, sporting crew-cuts and with a military bearing and carriage. And both emanated a sense of danger and menace.

Then they were past her, climbing into the car, and she was boarding the boat for St. Martin.

CHAPTER 5

The trip across to St. Martin was shorter than she expected. Twenty minutes and Antonia was standing on the dock at Marigot. She carried her bags through customs and up to the street (thank God they were on wheels) and looked around, spotting Steven's red hat thirty yards away; he was busy studying the passengers disembarking from the boat after she had, making sure she hadn't been followed. It both frightened and reassured her that he was on top of things – being cautious. She figured when he was satisfied, he'd make the first move towards her. She looked back at the boat to watch the last of her shipmates making their way up the dock; looked back around, and his hat was gone.

She felt his arms encircle her from behind.

"Hmmmmm. Welcome to St. Martin, beautiful."

"It's nice to be here, handsome."

She turned to face him, laughing in surprise at the black hair and wrap-around sunglasses. He was holding his cap in his hand. She kissed him.

"I didn't recognize you. Now you really look like a pop star. What's next, a Mohawk?" she teased.

"Depends on how my boy band audition goes," he answered.

She told him about the police looking for him, the cop at the terminal, and the suspicious-looking Russians getting off the ferry. That jolted him.

"Sounds like they're bringing in pro talent since the amateurs didn't get the job done. I'm not surprised they know my name; word travels fast. Thankfully, I'm no longer a U.S. citizen, and they don't have any information about my new passport," he explained.

"So what nationality are you? Swahili? Serbo-Croatian? Vanuatuan?"

"I'm a nobleman from Bucharest. Vampire country."

"Romanian?" she asked.

"Yup."

"I always wondered what a hot gypsy would be like. Heard good things. Now I see the reputation is deserved," she mused.

"Is it my dye job that gets you the hottest?"

"No, it's the five identical button-up shirts that drive me wild. I must have you now. Take off your pants."

"I have news as well. I hope you've always had a deep and abiding dream of visiting South America. Tomorrow you'll get your big chance," he said.

"Oh, Steven. Rio? Carnival? Copacabana?" she asked excitedly.

"Uh, not exactly. How does Buenos Aires sound? The Paris of South America?"

She paused. "I've actually heard marvelous things about Argentina. Big Italian population, mostly from Genoa in the Twenties and Thirties. Good food and wine. When do we leave?" she asked.

"Tomorrow morning, first thing," he explained. "I chartered a small plane to get us to Caracas, and then we'll catch a jet to Buenos Aires."

"It sounds wonderful. Is there a bed around here?" she inquired.

Steven laughed. "Don't you think of anything else?"

"I suppose we don't really need a bed. We have to be practical. An international secret agent and pop star like you, always on the run, must be endlessly inventive, no?"

Steven had seen a billboard for Les Printemps, a resort hotel located about five miles from the port area, which had availability when he'd checked online. They took a taxi, and Steven walked the grounds while Antonia checked in. She came out to him once she was done – they were in room forty-four. They'd agreed to stay separate so he wouldn't be on record as having been at the hotel.

Once they were safely ensconced in the room, he checked on Allied while Antonia got settled in, and saw it was slowly dropping day by day. Knowing what he did about Griffen's position, that had to be hurting. He again wondered what Griffen had up his sleeve, and how he could short circuit it. He tapped a message to the Group.

[It's Bowman. Can anyone find some other companies that have been pumped and dumped by Griffen, and put together a profile of how the manipulations occur? I'm trying to figure out what the next move will be.]

He then went to Hotmail and sent Spyder another message:

[On the move again tomorrow. Off to Argentina to check out Terrasol. Any suggestions for a PI or how to go about looking into things?]

He logged off and considered what he knew. Griffen's offshore fund was verifiably involved with dirty money, probably laundering, at the very least. It was also underwater and precariously over-extended on the Allied position. The bankers were worried. The missing pieces consisted of who the other investors were, and what Griffen's next step was on Allied's share price.

From his side, he needed to make all the information public with one big, credible splash, and stay alive in the process. He was almost done with part A, and would have to consider how to achieve part B.

❧

Sergei got a call from his field director, Sasha, who had disappointing news from the islands; there was no trace of the mysterious Marvin Simpson. He'd never passed through customs, never stayed at a hotel, and the police had been unable to deliver any leads. It was possible he was staying in a private residence; it was also possible he was already five hundred miles away. Anything was possible.

Sergei advised Sasha to keep the team in place since they were already there. He'd flown them to St. Martin on one of the company jets, a Citation Ten, so they could get just about anywhere quickly if and when the mystery man surfaced. And surface he would. Sergei was sure of it.

He considered that Griffen might have finally bitten off more than he could chew, because so far this one man had disrupted much of Griffen's plan for Allied, and was now proving to be a formidable adversary. He hadn't run and hidden; he'd instead gone on the offensive and begun probing for Griffen's weak spots. And he'd taken down three armed men on the island with seeming ease. Even if they were amateur thugs, that was impressive. This was not a good man to be up against, Sergei mused.

Sergei hoped Griffen knew what he was doing with the financial end of things. The website told a compelling tale of a manipulation now gone badly wrong, and where there was smoke there was often fire. He'd have to monitor this closely. He decided against calling Griffen with the latest; he was doing his friend and colleague a favor by not signing up for hourly reporting to him.

It would be interesting to see what this Steven Archer's next move would be.

❧❦

Steven and Antonia spent the evening over a slow dinner at the hotel's restaurant, where they discussed travel plans. Antonia wasn't a huge fan of small prop planes, and truthfully, Steven wasn't crazy about them either; but if it got them off the island and to Caracas quickly, so be it. He'd booked business class seats for the seven-hour flight from Venezuela to Buenos Aires, and planned to throw his jet ticket from Caracas on his company credit card and reimburse Antonia for her costs in cash. He didn't want any record of her connected to him, even on an anonymous credit card. He was starting to get the hang of the whole paranoia thing. Griffen had made that easy enough for him.

The next morning they were up at 6:30, and at the airport by 8:00. They approached their pilot, who took the $5,400 cash from Steven and confirmed the flight was expected to be smooth. The plane seemed sturdy and could fly up to thirty thousand feet, although their flight plan would have them cruising at twenty-six thousand feet most of the way. Once their luggage was stowed they were soon bumping down the runway and onward to Caracas. Antonia fell asleep within an hour, and so Steven spent the trip gazing through the window at the spectacular views of the islands, set in an ultramarine ocean, as the engines droned their monotone lullaby.

CHAPTER 6

Robert Townsend got the call right after he'd settled into his seat with his first cup of coffee of the day, relaxing with his feet up on his desk. It was an islander. He wouldn't identify himself, but he wanted to know if there was any kind of reward for information on the white man with the goatee, Marvin Simpson.

"I suppose we'd be willing to pay for information," Townsend told him, "depending on how good it is, of course." He'd just bill Griffen for whatever he had to part with. That's how the game was played.

"It's good all right. I want ten thousand dollars. I can give you everything you need to trace him. Everything."

"It's a deal. As long as the information's as good as you say it is."

"I'll meet you at headquarters in an hour. The information is rock solid." Simon hung up, and smiled to himself. They were safely off the island for a full day, so why not make a few dollars selling his knowledge? He could tell them about Antonia Donitelli, had copied her hotel phone records, and could give them some other tidbits about the man.

Money was money. And it was hard to come by on an island. A fellow had to be practical to prosper in such a harsh environment, after all.

⊱⋆⊰

When the little plane arrived in Caracas, their first hurdles were to clear customs and get to the commercial terminal, which was in a different part of the airport than the charters. It took a while, but their flight didn't depart until nine p.m., so they had time. Stiff from the trip, they walked around the large departure area, the movement giving them a liberated feeling, as did the anonymity of being in a crowd. They chose a reasonable-looking café near the entrance, where they ate a relaxed lunch before deciding to go clothes shopping for Steven; who didn't have much apparel other than two pairs of long pants and his shirts. The weather in Argentina called for an average high in the fifties, and lows around freezing. The seasons were reversed in the Southern Hemisphere, so they were headed to Buenos Aires in the dead of the Argentine winter. Clothes designed for the tropics wouldn't cut it.

They ventured into town, stopping at the store recommended by the information booth attendant at the airport. Even though the selection of goods left something to be desired, within half an hour Steven had a serviceable heavy jacket, a blue blazer, and a couple of long-sleeved thermal shirts.

Antonia took a little longer to satisfy. She'd packed for summer and also needed clothes, but didn't really like much of what she saw. She had several pairs of jeans with her, so she limited herself to an overcoat and two sweater tops.

She was pensive as they rode back in the cab. The reality of the situation was weighing on her mind. On a whim, she'd flown to South America with a man she'd only known a few days, who was involved in a dangerous conflict that was starkly immediate and real; and this man was being hunted by some seriously nasty characters who would clearly stop at nothing to take him down.

She glanced at his profile. Strong cheekbones, the kind of non-traditional handsome she would have described as 'interesting', and with an energy about him that was both troubling and seductive. Her intellect told her this was a bad idea, but her emotions needed her with him. That was a conflict she was unfamiliar with, having numbed herself to any real feelings since her husband died, instead focusing on neutral matters such as running the magazine.

Antonia was overwhelmed by their powerful attraction for each other – how natural their interactions seemed, how easy they were together. Whatever this was, it warranted more time.

She thought about it. She had resources, and once she knew more, could probably help him. It wasn't clear how at the moment, but she was confident she'd figure out a way. Right now the best thing she could do was get rested and think about all the players and the pieces that Steven had described. Maybe he'd missed something. Two heads were usually better than one, even if he imagined he could battle the whole world by himself.

They'd be careful. At least for the moment, things seemed safe; they'd slipped away from the islands free and clear. There was no trail to follow, no tracks to give them away; that was a positive. And considering they were traveling to the other side of the planet, she sensed they would lose whatever problems were pursuing them...at least for a while.

For now, a while would have to do.

They spent the rest of the afternoon in the airport business lounge. As if by mutual agreement they avoided any discussion of the drama and violence on the island, preferring to keep to more pleasant territory. As the day wound down, Steven used one of the lounge computers to check online, and saw that Spyder had responded to his query. He suggested staying at a place called the Alvear Palace Hotel, in the Recoleta district in the city center, wherever that was. He wrote it down and returned to Antonia, who was surveying the crackers and peanuts provided by the airline with something short of enthusiasm.

Restless, they wandered around the terminal to kill the remainder of their wait, ate an unremarkable dinner at the airport restaurant, and then boarded their plane for the trip to Argentina.

They dozed all the way to Buenos Aires.

CHAPTER 7

Ministro Pistarini airport was a good hour drive from downtown, located in a rural area far on the outskirts of Buenos Aires. When the plane's wheels screeched down on the tarmac it had just turned 6 a.m.; barely light out. By the time they got through customs it was 7:00. They made tracks to the cab line and asked the driver to take them to the hotel. Steven figured that in the dead of the Argentine winter, in the middle of an economic downturn, it wouldn't be that hard to get a room; even absent a reservation.

The sky had a grey, sullen air – discharging a constant drizzle on roads slick with oil and water and sundry bits of debris.

The city was a huge, urban sprawl spanning many miles. Quintessentially Latin-looking high-rise apartments cluttered the horizon; stained concrete towers with dilapidated balconies stretching skyward; ugly and tawdry and smacking of financial hardship. The outer reaches were not an attractive place, with the ever-present shanty towns giving way to slightly less prosaic tenement-level housing in the shadows of the city; progressively improving in quality towards the center of Buenos Aires proper.

Once downtown, the surroundings transformed into those of a European capital, with huge boulevards, monumental French-style architectural masterpieces, and block after block of stone edifices and super-modern high-rise glass buildings.

The hotel was situated a few blocks from the massive La Recoleta Cemetery, where Eva Peron was buried; a moneyed area, with Chanel and Gucci stores strategically positioned amongst high-end jewelry stores and banks. Their cab pulled up to the 19th century building, and they found themselves descended upon by a uniformed doorman with an oversized umbrella, who whisked them up the stairs into a lavish, old-style marble lobby replete with stunning chandeliers, tapestries and oils, and all the usual grandiosity that places catering to the ultra-wealthy convey.

Antonia approached the desk and in Spanish requested a room. After much discussion and bowing and scraping, a suite was provided. They were shown to their quarters by a crisply dressed bellman. When the hotel doors opened at their floor, there was a butler standing proudly in the elevator lobby area. Every floor had one.

Once they were comfortably ensconced in their digs, Steven asked how come they were able to get upgraded and why they'd been treated so well.

"Simple. I showed them my card. When you're the publisher of one of the world's leading travel magazines, hotels tend to notice," she said, smiling.

They were both exhausted after sleeping only fitfully on the long plane journey, so they decided to nap for a few hours. They showered and crawled into bed, exchanging soft, warm kisses as they snuggled together. Both were out within minutes.

They awoke in the hour before noon, and after a quick, refreshing session in the shower they prepared to explore the town; Antonia, as always, was feeling famished. Steven wanted to acquaint himself with the geography of the area. He checked his e-mail on the Blackberry, which to his surprise worked flawlessly in Buenos Aires. Gordo had e-mailed him with the name of a reputable investigator. Steven wrote the name, address and phone number down.

He still had the Anguilla micro-cell he'd gotten from Alfred, but it was dead. Another one for the garbage. He made a mental note to pick up a disposable phone first thing.

They descended into the lobby, where the hotel valet loaned them umbrellas before they exited; it wasn't so much raining as misting, but they were thankful to have them nonetheless. Wandering around the little neighborhood, hand in hand, they came across a cell phone store just around the corner from the hotel; and so within minutes, with Antonia's help, he had a new, untraceable phone.

Antonia grabbed a few *empanadas* – little meat-filled pastries – from a small restaurant across the street from the famous cemetery located only a few blocks from the hotel. They decided to explore it, having not much else to do with their time.

They spent the remains of the morning wandering around the labyrinthine grounds of the huge graveyard. In Buenos Aires the custom was to build small buildings for the tombs – you descended the stairs of many of them into shadowy underground chambers, where the coffins lay beneath a scant veneer of dust. Others housed ornate stone caskets hewn from the same rock from which the buildings were constructed. It reminded him of the cemeteries in the Garden District in New Orleans.

They were in the far end of the walled cemetery, which easily covered six square city blocks, when Steven noticed a sketchy-looking character shadowing them a few aisles down. He also noted they were in a section of the cemetery with no other people around. He started to get an alarmed feeling. He whispered to Antonia.

"Don't turn around, but I think we're being followed. Let's start picking up the pace. I think we're being set up for a mugging."

Her eyes grew large and she nodded imperceptibly. They began to increase their gait, making a bee-line for the entrance, where there were guards in attendance.

"Do you think it's the people who are after you...how could they have found us?" she wondered, as they moved quickly down the narrow pathway.

"No. I think it's gypsies, or some local thieves. I didn't see any weapon – and the one I got a good look at seems pretty low-end. I don't think we have a lot to worry about, but why tempt fate?"

Steven didn't want to have another altercation while Antonia was around. She'd already been exposed to enough violence.

"It was probably dumb to wander this far into the grounds without noticing that the crowds were gone," he admitted.

The Thursday morning streets had been empty, with most of the natives at work or in school, and there were few tourists in Buenos Aires in the middle of winter. It was just plain stupid of him.

He saw another figure shadowing them on a parallel path a few rows down on the opposite side – they were flanked on both sides. When they reached the next tomb, Steven stopped her with his arm, and they turned and moved up between the tombs to where the second man had been. They peeked around the corner to observe him further along his path – about twenty yards, looking down a different row in the direction that they'd just come.

So he was right about being followed. His grip on the umbrella tightened instinctively.

They crossed the path quickly and ran up three more tomb aisles and then cautiously resumed their approach to the main entrance. The closer they got, the less likely a problem would occur. They peered down each row of tombs before crossing and moving.

Nothing.

Another row.

Nothing.

They wheeled wide around another corner towards where the entrance should be; and there was the first man, about thirty feet away, in a tattered and filthy multi-colored sweater, looking around with a puzzled expression.

They spotted each other at the same time. Steven and Antonia ran down the path towards the guard area, and almost collided with one of the security officers rounding a corner. Antonia explained in rapid-fire Spanish what had transpired, and the guard quietly radioed on his walky-talky, calling for backup.

Crisis averted, they made their way the rest of the distance to the main gate and departed the grounds. What should have been a mild diversion had developed into an unsettling promenade, and a reminder that they weren't in Kansas anymore.

They kept on moving, away from the cemetery area towards the Park Hyatt, where the concierge had waxed lyrical about a number of fabulous restaurants huddled beneath an overpass. On the way past, Steven stopped at their hotel to check on the safety of the area; the hotel receptionist told them that the streets were generally safe for a couple, but that it was unwise for a single female to wander them. Reassured that they were likely fine as long as they stayed on the main arteries, they approached the overpass area, and sure enough, there stood an array of eight different dining establishments built under what resembled an elongated tunnel, with one of the big boulevards running overhead.

Antonia's heart was set on the Argentine steak restaurant, insisting their first meal had to be beef, beef, and more beef. Argentina was renowned for its beef, and Steven had no beef whatsoever about her selection – so beef it would be. They ordered and discussed the battle plan while they waited for the steaks to be seared to their liking.

"I need to interview a private investigator, and do some research on this Terrasol company. If I'm lucky, we'll know what's going on within a few days, and we'll be able to figure out where we go next on our adventure," Steven told her.

"I can help you," Antonia reasoned. "My Spanish is good, whereas yours is abysmal. Let me come along…"

"It's true. And while I appreciate the offer, as we saw in Anguilla there's some real danger involved, and I won't have you exposed, honey."

Steven wasn't going to endanger her. He had no idea what lay ahead in Buenos Aires, but he had no intention of letting Antonia be anywhere near when he was 'working'.

"I suppose eating dinner with you is too risky, then, because that's what we were doing when we were attacked," she observed through narrowed, hazel eyes.

Ouch.

"Look, you're now the most important thing in my life, and if these animals think they can get to me by hurting or using you, they will. I won't take that risk. I need to keep you away from anything I'm doing here, Antonia. Sorry."

He was determined not to let her convince him otherwise.

She considered him for a long time. "That's sweet. Maybe you are more than just a sex toy after all." She took a sip of water, then her eyes brightened. "If I can't play super spy with you, then I'll go shopping. I've heard Buenos Aires has amazing shopping. Maybe I can even find you some reasonable clothes," she suggested.

Their steaks arrived, big and bad and tender as could be – every bit as wonderful as Argentina's reputation promised. They ate ravenously, making noises of approval as they gourmandized together.

Steven waved a forkful of the succulent, marbled beef. "Let's see if there's someone who can escort you from the hotel to the shopping areas, while I deal with the detective. I thought I heard you complaining that you needed more clothes."

"Oh, *caro*, that's a wonderful idea. Two sweaters won't last me very long. And perhaps I can even find you something that doesn't look like hand-me-downs!"

They finished their platters and took a leisurely stroll back to the hotel. Antonia arranged for a shopping guide while Steven called the number Gordo had given him.

"*Buenos dias. Ferreira Investigationes.*"

Steven asked to speak with Mr. Ferreira: "*Buenos dias. Es posible hablar con Senor Ferreira?*"

"*Si. Momento.*"

"*Hola,*" a male voice greeted.

"*Hola,* do you speak English?" Steven asked.

"Yes. May I be of help?"

"I'm looking for a private detective to investigate a company in Buenos Aires. Is that something you can do?"

"Yes, we specialize in corporate investigations. Would you like to come in and discuss the matter, *Senor...*?" Ferreira asked.

"Cassidy. Sure. Would today be a good day?"

"*Si,* of course. Do you know where my offices are located?"

"Yes, I can find them," Steven said. "I'll be there in an hour."

"*Bueno.* Until then, *Senor* Cassidy."

Antonia was in an animated discussion with a woman from the hotel concierge staff. As Steven walked over, Antonia introduced her as the shopping director.

He introduced himself. "Nice to meet you. I'm Matthew."

Antonia glanced at him, didn't miss a beat. "Isabella is going to show me where I can buy anything I can think of. She's Italian!" she exclaimed, eyes bright as diamonds.

"How wonderful. Antonia, can I interrupt for a second?" he asked.

"Of course. Isabella, just a *momentito,* okay?"

They walked a few feet away while Isabella studied the walls.

"Sorry about the Matthew thing, but we can't be too careful. We should have discussed this earlier. As long as we're here in the hotel, I'll be Matthew, okay?"

"Okay, *Double-O-Seven,* Matthew it is. Should we speak in code, too? *The red lion sees the white bird flying overhead?*" she asked, deadpan.

"I know it seems dumb, but I just want to make sure you're safe. Will you please do this for me?"

She softened. "Oh, *caro,* I was playing. Of course I will. Hmmm. Will you still be Matthew when I'm..." and she whispered in his ear. "Why, Matthew, I think you're blushing! Do you have a fever? Maybe it's a cold, eh?"

And she spun around to go shopping with her newly-discovered relative. She blew him a kiss. "*Ciao,* Matthew!"

Shortly after they left the hotel, Antonia stopped and asked her new guide-friend if there was a phone from which she could make an international call. There was a long distance service bureau a block away. So they made their way to the glass-fronted building.

Antonia excused herself once she was inside.

"I'll only be a few minutes. I just need to take care of some loose ends back home," she explained.

"No problem. I completely understand."

Antonia retired to one of the booths. Once inside, she opened her little purse, withdrew an address book and placed it on the shelf under the phone, carefully considering her next move. Steven had explained more of the detail of what he was doing, and how he hoped to get out of this mess, but she wasn't convinced he'd thought it through. He needed help. Of course, she'd never come right out and say it, but that didn't mean she couldn't take some steps, make some calls, and see if she could nudge fate into a more compliant direction. She was the owner of a well-respected publication, and that world, especially the New York literary and publishing world, was small.

She had a burgeoning idea of sorts; vague and amorphous, but the outline of a tandem effort that could help had crystallized in her mind as they'd spent more time together. The trick would be in executing it so she didn't introduce any more complications into his life or give away any information, or put them in any danger. This would be delicate; something she preferred to do on her own.

She hoped it was the right thing.

One commitment she'd made to herself after the fight on the island was never again to be passive and let events carry her along. This wasn't Italy, and she wasn't a child anymore – and there was no way in hell she was going to just stand by in silent horror as the world came crashing down on a loved one; with evil men ruling the day yet again. Antonia needed to do something, but something subtle, leaving the brunt of the heavy lifting and chest pounding to Steven. If she could improve his chances of ending this, could help in unseen ways by making surgically precise moves, she was going to pull out all the stops she could get her hands on.

She dialed the first number.

CHAPTER 8

Steven's taxi stopped in front of a severe, four-story office building of concrete three miles from the hotel. Steven paid the driver, and ducked under the building's awning to dodge the afternoon drizzle. Consulting the directory, he found the entire third floor was held by Ferreira Investigations. He proceeded upstairs and introduced himself to the receptionist; a stunning twenty-ish Latin beauty wearing a skintight top and pants that looked like they'd been airbrushed on.

Argentina. So far, a great country.

He was escorted to a large office in the back, where a medium-sized balding man with a mustache rose from behind an obviously expensive desk to greet him.

"*Senor* Cassidy. Nice to meet you." They shook hands.

"*Senor* Ferreira. A pleasure."

"Please, call me Domingo. Or Dom."

"Ahh, Domingo. Then please call me John."

Steven was going to have to start writing all his names down. Matthew. John Cassidy.

Yikes. This was getting complicated.

"Well, then, John. What brings you to my humble firm?"

"Domingo, I have a laboratory equipment export company I've been approached by a local group to partner with. I want them checked out, thoroughly."

Steven had decided that unless he had attorney-client privilege he wasn't going to tell a straight story, no matter how highly recommended the PI.

"Of course, that is what we do. A full investigation, including photos of the principals and a full company background check is three thousand dollars."

That was interesting. Photos. "Why do you take photos?"

"Ah, well, in Argentina, sometimes the people representing themselves to be, shall we say, in business, turn out to not be connected with the company they are claiming to be with. We've found it helpful to take pictures of all the senior officials to verify who you are talking to is who you should be."

Domingo knew his business.

"Sounds like a good idea."

"Yes, and now we have very high definition camera phones it is easy to capture people unaware."

"I'd like to sign you up. The company is Terrasol Investments, and they're here in Buenos Aires," Steven told him.

Domingo wrote down the name. "Good. We will begin immediately. I will require $500 as a retainer, and the balance before we turn over the dossier we assemble."

Domingo and Steven shook hands.

"Should I give you the cash, or your receptionist?" he asked.

Domingo chuckled. "Perhaps it would be better to give me the cash. She might get the wrong idea, and then you'd be in real trouble…"

Steven counted out $500 and handed it to Domingo.

"Do you have a number where I can reach you?" Domingo asked.

"Not yet," Steven said, "but I can call you tomorrow to find out what you've been able to unearth. I'm staying with friends, and plan to get a cell phone in the next day or two."

"*Bueno*, then we speak tomorrow. *Gracias*, John."

"*De nada*, Domingo."

Steven was online when Antonia came breezing back into the hotel room. She had several large bags of clothing; most for herself, but there were a few items he noted were masculine.

"*Caro*, here are some socks and some underwear. You needed some more. And a pair of grey wool dress slacks, so we can go out someplace besides fast food. And a dress shirt, and, wow, look at this, a tie!" she enthused. It all looked very expensive.

Steven smiled. "I don't think I've worn a tie since my mom's funeral, Antonia. But for you, I'll make the ultimate sacrifice; just don't ask for it every day."

She modeled her purchases for him. By the time she was done, she was standing in the middle of a pile of clothes, naked except for her thong underwear. She studied the clothes, and then Steven.

"Put your tie on, *caro*, just your tie, and come here. I'm beginning to think you aren't interested in me any more," she complained.

He complied as instructed. Naked guy with tie and dyed black hair.

"You want the glasses too?" he asked.

"Surprise me. But hurry up…"

Come early evening, he checked back in to see what the stock had done. Closed above $31. It seemed to be fighting tooth and nail to stay above $30. He saw a marked increase in discussions about manipulation and questionable management integrity on the message boards – so obviously the website was still live and getting plenty of attention.

Steven needed to break all of his findings on the site, at the very least, but it would be far better if he could get wider coverage.

He navigated to the Group. Gordo and Spyder and Pogo had been researching companies that had been similarly manipulated by Griffen in the past, and they'd come up with four in the last several years. All had the same pattern associated with them according to Gordo:

[Here's what they typically do. Goes a little something like this:

1 - Griffen works with one of his pet investment banks and takes a company public, or appears on their filings as a major investor

2 - Company receives a year or two of insanely positive press and analyst coverage

3 - Stock increases in price 500-1000%

4 - After churning for a few months at its highs, stock plummets 95+% and press turns negative

5 - Presumably, Griffen is short and makes fortune down, as he did as the stock rose

6 - Stock languishes as near worthless from that point on.

Seems like that's the MO. I'd be on the lookout for items 4-6 next. Gordo]

Pogo had chimed in on the thread as well:

[I can document the occurrences for the other companies so it's all verifiable. Do you want me to put it on the site when I'm done? Pogo]

Steven thought about that.

[No, let's hold off. I have some pretty damaging documentation coming my way, and I think the way forward with this is to find a kindred spirit to break it all. If we do this right, it will bury his ass good and deep]

Next, he checked in with Stan; sent him an encrypted e-mail:

[Any further word on the bank accounts or from your attorney friend on the situation, now that I'm alive?]

He decided to call it a day and logged off. Antonia was snoozing face down on top of the covers, naked as a lovebird. He meditated in the suite's living room before gently waking her by tickling her ear with the tip of his new tie.

They tried another one of the restaurants under the bridge for dinner, this time a big Italian place. It was empty, even at 10:00 at night. Apparently, in Argentina, as in Spain, it was not unusual to eat dinner at midnight or 1:00 a.m. before spending the hours until dawn at a nightclub. No wonder the productivity of these countries was low. The meal was amazing, though, with Antonia declaring it the best Italian food she'd had outside of Italy, and better than most she'd had there.

They had an after-dinner Sambuca, and she was in a kind of heaven, speaking Italian to the staff, reminiscing about the old country, commiserating about the weather. It was a nice end to a long twenty-four hours.

CHAPTER 9

The next day he called Domingo for a progress report.

"Domingo, it's John. Did you find anything out yet?"

Domingo sounded disturbed. "I don't think you should do business with these men, John. I'm going to return your $500. I'm not interested in investigating."

"Wait a minute, Domingo. What happened?" Steven asked. "What did you find out and why are you so uninterested in pursuing this?"

"Terrasol is a company that is owned by the Wolfsatz," Domingo explained. "They are a German gang that has been here for fifty years. Ex-Nazis, I think, and they're responsible for much of the drug trade and slavery in the country."

"What do you mean, slavery?"

"They abduct very young girls from the provinces and from Brazil and sell them to brothels here and abroad; children, really, only eleven and twelve years old. And the drug business is in Buenos Aires – heroin and cocaine in the barrios. This is bad news, John. Walk away from this."

"Where is Terrasol headquartered? Would you be willing to take pictures of the people coming in and out for a few days so we can document who's involved?" Steven asked.

"I..." He paused. "No. I will not be involved in this anymore. This is dangerous for one's health, no? Come by and I'll give you back your money." Domingo sounded scared. And something else. He couldn't quite place it.

"Keep the $500, my friend," Steven said. "Thanks for doing the research."

"Ah, no, is okay. Where can I send it? I can meet you," Domingo offered.

That was strange. Why was Domingo so eager to give him his money back? It had to be because he wanted to find out his location. His arm hair bristled.

"I'm at a private residence over by the *Teatro Colon*. Seriously, you can keep the cash. It's yours." Steven wanted to discover if his instincts were correct. If they were, Dom wouldn't take no for an answer. He would want to get Steven over to his office or find out where he was.

"John, I cannot take money for something I did not do. I drive by the *Teatro* every day on the way home. It is no problem to drop by. What is your address there? I'll stop by this afternoon when it's convenient for you."

Bingo. Something was definitely going on here. Steven paged furiously through his little street map of the area around Teatro Colon. He looked at one of the building numbers. *Calle* Bolivar. 1145 Bolivar.

"I'll be at 1145 Bolivar, number two, today at around 3:00. It's in the district a few blocks from the *Teatro*. Just knock at the front door or press the buzzer. My friends left town for the weekend so I'll answer the door. Number two. I appreciate it, Domingo." He hung up.

He told Antonia his suspicions. She was furious.

"What a pig. He's worse than an insect, selling you out. What are you going to do?" Her outburst didn't last long, but you could see the flash of anger in her eyes.

"I'm going to go have a cup of coffee or hang out on the corner on *Calle* Bolivar, wherever that is, and see who shows up. Should be interesting," Steven concluded.

"I'll go with you. They won't be looking for a couple. We can get you a raincoat and a different hat, and have coffee together. A lone man might look suspicious."

She was right. He hated to involve her, but she was right.

They headed in the direction of the *Teatro* district, acquiring a black overcoat and a fedora-style rain hat for Steven along the route. Antonia thought he looked like Humphrey Bogart or a spy in a Le Carre novel.

"You know how to whistle, don't you?" he asked.

His Bogey left a lot to be desired, but she seemed delighted by the attempt.

After a couple of wrong turns they found the street. 1145 Bolivar was a multi-story stone apartment building, so he'd been lucky there. Across the street and on the corner stood one of the thousands of small coffee shops that dotted Buenos Aires.

Once inside, they took a seat, ordered coffee, and waited. It was 2:40. At 3:05 a car pulled up, and four men got out while the car double-parked in front of the building. Two of the men went up to the door and looked for a buzzer, while the other two positioned themselves by the side exit gate.

Steven paid the bill, and he and Antonia disappeared around the corner as the echo of rapping on the apartment door followed them down the street. He got on his PDA as they returned to the hotel and tapped out an e-mail to the Group.

[First PI compromised. Need reliable second one in BA. Also, anyone ever hear of a group in BA called Wolfsatz (phonetic)?]

Antonia was seething with indignation over the episode, which he supposed was her substitute for fear. Once they arrived at the hotel, they returned to their room and discussed what to do next. Steven wanted to get more information on the Wolfsatz, and was delighted with the idea of a group of Nazis, who'd come over after the war to set up a criminal enterprise, being tied to the Griffen offshore fund. Talk about a pejorative spin. How did you explain that to your legitimate investors? Drug Cartels, Arms Dealers, Nazis. Nice bunch.

He checked his PDA, and there was another message from Spyder in his Hotmail inbox. It was the name and phone number of a PI in Buenos Aires. Spyder said he was dependable, a one-man shop – and used to handling sensitive matters. Steven called him.

"*Servicios Alliente*," a woman's voice announced.

"*Buenos tardes. Diego Alliente, por favor*," Steven replied.

A few moments, and then a man's voice.

"*Sí?*"

"*Diego? Habla Ingles?*" Steven asked.

"Yes. How may I help you?"

"My name is John Cassidy, and I need to have some photographs taken of some men that work for a company I'm considering doing business with. I need to be sure they are who they say they are. They may be criminal or dangerous, though; I have an unpleasant feeling about them. Is this something you can do?" Steven asked.

"Of course. It will cost you $600 per day, minimum two days; half in advance. I handle all of the photography myself," Diego explained.

Diego would start first thing Monday. Whenever he got something, he'd e-mail the photos to Steven. The retainer could be dropped through the mail slot at Diego's office over the weekend. It was all very efficient, which increased Steven's confidence in the new PI's ability to perform.

Steven wrote out Terrasol's name and address, put six hundred dollars into an envelope with the note, and wrote Diego's name on it; he'd drop it off tomorrow, on Saturday. He logged into Hotmail and created another one-time e-mail address, and then wrote that on the note.

You had to love the Internet.

CHAPTER 10

Griffen received the call from Anguilla around mid-day. Townsend had gotten the hotel phone records for a young lady Steven Archer had apparently initiated a relationship with; an Italian, Antonia something-or-other. Townsend promised to fax the information to him with the details; there were calls to St. Martin, and three to Italy. They'd gotten her passport number from the hotel, and ran a preliminary search on her through Interpol, which turned up no criminal record. Townsend told him that according to his source, one of the employees at the hotel, they'd been inseparable the entire time they'd spent there, and it was likely they were traveling together.

The Anguillan police chief's advice was find Antonia, and you'd find Steven. Not bad counsel.

Griffen instructed him to fax the details over, and considered his next step. Sergei meant well, but if they were dealing with an Italian traveling on an Italian passport, he leaned towards getting his Italian 'investors' involved. He'd have to feel Sergei out and evaluate his attitude on the idea. He'd been getting mixed signals during the last few discussions, and he needed someone who was going to take care of his issue quickly and definitively; which so far, for all his efforts, Sergei hadn't been able to do.

Griffen certainly had no intention of revealing to his agency investor the depth of the problem he had. He knew they were just as likely to handle it by pulling their money and 'dealing' with him as they were to help him. So there was no appeal from that source; he'd already used up his capital with them by requesting a little assistance early on, with the Homeland Security play. No, the last thing he needed was for them to view him as a liability, bungling around with Russian organized crime figures.

Maybe it was time for some professionals from the old country.

They spent the weekend mostly in the hotel room, except for the odd sortie to restaurants and Steven's errand with the PI. On Saturday night they attended a tango show – at Antonia's urging. She insisted that once they had more time they would return and take tango lessons. She'd never seen anything like it; neither had he. There was an intrinsic grace and fluidity to the movements; a dignity, if you will. As he watched the performance it dawned on him how much he'd missed while cocooned within his little neighborhood in California. There was a whole world out there he'd never imagined.

On Sunday, Antonia had booked a spa session for herself, so he was left to his own devices for half the day. In the hotel, he visited the surprisingly well outfitted gym and ran on the treadmill for an hour, and then, since he was the only one in the room, worked on his form and strikes for another hour. He'd missed the activity after sitting on stuffy planes and hanging out in hotel rooms, and he made a mental note to start running again as soon as was practical. He went back upstairs and sluiced himself off in the shower before browsing the web via his PDA. He'd gotten an e-mail from Spyder on the Germans.

[Wolfsatz are regional players in the white slavery/prostitution trade and the drug and arms business in BA. They've been around since the Forties and started off as a moneymaking enterprise by ex-Nazis. I'm forwarding some classified documents I came across from one of my sources at an intelligence agency. Don't ask how. Hope it helps. They're extremely violent. Don't F with them. Spyder]

There was an attachment, two pages of scanned documentation on the Wolfsatz; the information wasn't up to date because whoever had compiled it had apparently lost interest when the original leadership died off, to be replaced by the next generation. The document was thorough, listing fourteen different companies they controlled, including one named Tierra Sol. So that's why the initial data scan didn't pick it up. Terrasol. Tierra Sol. A simple spelling glitch.

He sent back an e-mail:

[Thanks. Can you get similar proof on Ecuador and Swiss Co's? Verbal won't work. I need docs.]

Now he had documented proof that one of the four major investors in the offshore fund was playing with dirty money, and oral statements that the Panamanian and Swiss companies were bad. If Spyder could get docs on the other two, that left the Russian trading company. He was starting to like his odds a lot better, and Griffen's a whole lot less.

He told Antonia what he'd discovered and about the documentation on the Germans, and she was cautiously optimistic; the Argentina chapter seemed about over, but now that he'd gotten what he'd come for the obvious question was where did he want to go next? He was thinking maybe Moscow, which Antonia felt was a terrible idea. She had friends who'd been there recently, and the whole city was controlled by warring segments of the Russian mob, making for a dangerous and brutal environment to encounter under even the best of circumstances; sort of a Chicago in the Twenties with Slavic accents.

That gave Steven an idea. He pulled up his Hotmail and sent a query off to his Canadian secret service contact, Cliff Tomlin, asking him to run Adriatic Trading through their computers to see if it got any hits. He figured there was no harm in asking.

Antonia sidled up to him. "*Caro*, why not Italy? I can show you around. You can ravish me regularly. We can eat too much and drink good wine, and I know every inch of it. Why not?" Antonia had been thinking long and hard about their next destination.

Italy? Why not indeed? He needed someplace quiet he could lay low and put the whole case together; someplace safe, far away from any bad guys. Italy sounded as good as anywhere, and Antonia knew the lay of the land. You couldn't get much farther from Newport and Argentina, which seemed suitably prudent at this point.

They talked about Italy for hours, and Steven, who'd never been, soon found himself warming to the idea. It sounded like there were far worse places to hide out, and far worse people to hide out with than Antonia; so perhaps Italy was good. That could make things easy; her whole power and contact base was there, and he didn't know what he'd need, or to expect, over the next few weeks.

The problem with being on the run, he was finding, was that the little things became difficult, a production. Trying to remember what name you just gave someone, for starters; or being prepared to flee on a minute's notice for another thing.

So Italy.

CHAPTER 11

Late afternoon on Monday, Steven called Diego to see how things had gone.

"Oh, fine," he said casually, "although there wasn't much traffic in and out. I got pictures of six different men and two women; one group of three men, a couple, and three different individuals. I already scanned them and e-mailed them to you a half hour ago; sorry about the resolution, it's pretty low. I'll be back there tomorrow again. Would you like to stop by and pay the second half tomorrow about this time, and pick up the photos?"

Diego was completely professional; a good recommendation, obviously.

"That would be great. Let me take a look at the pictures. Thanks for the good work."

"No problem, *Senor. Adios.*"

He went down to the business center, and logged onto a computer; the Blackberry wasn't the right device to view photos with any level of detail. He pulled the message up, and noted it contained a zip file. He opened the attachment and unzipped it, then examined the photos; they were blurry from the poor input resolution, but good enough so he could make out the faces.

The couple was first. A J-Lo look-alike accompanying a young Don Juan type in a tailored suit. Next were two different men, both in casual clothing, both obviously Aryan. The next was a middle-aged woman with a perennial frown etched into her face. Last were three men in casual clothes, obviously deep in discussion. All were shot framed by the door of the building. He took one more quick look and started closing the photo windows, and then froze.

The three men.

The one in the center looked familiar. He couldn't place it; maybe a celebrity? Someone he'd seen at the hotel? Then it hit him. Holy shit.

He closed the windows and made sure the Hotmail message was saved before forwarding it on to Spyder and Stan Caldwell for safekeeping. He did the same with the intelligence document on the Wolfsatz after encrypting it; Stan could act as a backup for him in terms of data accumulation.

Steven sat in the chair for a few minutes, thinking the whole thing through, wondering what it all meant. Then the light bulb went off. He felt like jumping up and screaming Eureka. Instead, he thanked the attendant at the desk for use of the computer, and returned to the room.

Steven reported to Antonia what he'd seen on the screen downstairs. She was also completely surprised, at a loss for any response.

"Jim Cavierti? I thought he was dead? Killed, no? On the boat? Are you sure it's him?" Antonia didn't get it.

"It's him."

"But why the explosion, why fake his death?"

"I don't know."

But I have a few ideas, Steven thought, and they all pointed to a leak at the FBI. The only question was why.

CHAPTER 12

Tuesday, Steven and Antonia perused the flights to Italy. There was a direct flight that night on Aerolineas Argentinas, departing at 11:30 p.m. to Rome. They booked two seats in first class, side by side. They'd stay in Rome overnight, and then go spend some time at a family apartment in a small town named Todi for a week or so while they figured out what to do next. She was excited, chattering brightly about all the places she wanted to visit with him; Venice, Chianti, Umbria, Portofino, Cinque Terra, Siena. Just the names of the towns and regions sounded exotic as they rolled off her native tongue.

He had a good feeling about this; felt like he was finally moving towards something good, a positive in his life. All the issues he'd faced so far were receding in his mental picture of himself, to be replaced by a vision of the two of them together, happy and fulfilled.

Steven stuffed his duffel, which was at the bursting point with the addition of the raincoat and other items, and prepared for checkout. The plan was to pack, leave their bags with the bell captain, and go to the Italian restaurant one last time; purely in the interests of comparison, as he was about to go eat the real thing. Afterwards they would swing by Diego's and drop off the remaining cash, then head out to the airport before Buenos Aires' rush hour got started.

He logged onto his PDA, and went to his e-mail, where he saw the Canadian had responded quickly to his request. The message was short and to the point:

[Adriatic is known to us. One of several Russian Mafiya companies active in North America and EU. Murder for hire, drugs, extortion, arms, you name it. Hope this helps you. If Peter was involved in investigating them, I can understand why he might have been killed. Regards, Cliff T]

Bingo. The final connection. Griffen had the Russian mob as one of his key investors. South American Coke Producers, Nazi slavers, Middle Eastern arms merchants, and the Russian mob. No one too dirty or too evil to launder money for; bring it on, it's all green. Steven fired off a response:

[Is there any way at all I could get some sort of document that would corroborate the Adriatic info? Not for publication. Promise.]

He was left with a lot of questions. How had Griffen gotten Homeland Security to come after him? How had Cavierti known about the FBI indictment? Who'd killed Peter and Todd? And who'd butchered Avalon? Why Allied, specifically? Why was Cavierti in Buenos Aires consorting with Nazis? And most importantly, how could he bring Griffen down and expose Allied as a scam? He suspected he might never know the answers to many of his questions, but he'd need to figure out the last one or his entire crusade would have been in vain.

He guessed the Wolfsatz's desire to have a little chat with anyone investigating them was not necessarily Griffen-connected, but rather standard operating procedure; he'd left no tracks on that, so he was safe from repercussions.

The Anguillan police chief was probably trying to protect Cavierti as well as his own ass for having perpetrated a massive fraud to deceive the FBI. Who knew whether it was even a boat that had blown up? It could have been a dinghy packed with an incendiary device – which would simulate a boat explosion; that would explain the lack of flotsam and the absence of any local boat.

Antonia called from the bedroom and interrupted his ruminations.

"Honey, I'm almost done. Can you come help me with this stupid zipper? I can't get the thing closed." She was battling with her massively overstuffed bag, and the bag was clearly winning. He stepped in to help, and between the two of them they were able to temporarily defeat the resistant fastening. He kissed her. She kissed back.

"I love you, Antonia Donitelli."

She stared at him as though a snake had bitten her – sending her into shock. Her lower lip quivered, just once at first, and then almost uncontrollably, and her eyes brimmed with tears. She threw her arms around him and sobbed into his shoulder. He held her. For a long time.

"I love you too, Steven whatever-your-name-is-today. I do. Completely." She was both laughing and crying simultaneously. "You've made me so happy. I love you so much. Oh God, Steven..." and then she resumed crying, the laughter part over. She kissed his lips, his nose, his cheeks, and soon they were wrestling their way out of their clothes, their urgency stoked again. *Good that we're not on a schedule*, was the last thought he had before all thoughts abandoned him and it was just her and lips and skin and hair and...

As they sipped their coffee, Steven called Diego to see if he could stop by a few hours early to drop off the cash. The phone rang without being answered. Probably out to lunch. He was getting that queasy feeling in his stomach again; but it could be the pasta and the wine. Still, he felt uneasy. He'd try to call again before they took a cab to the airport.

They whiled away another half hour at the restaurant before paying their bill and making tracks. Antonia could sense something was wrong. She asked him what was going on.

"I'm probably just being overly cautious, and the receptionist is out to lunch. I'll call again at the hotel," he explained.

His nerves were raw from the last three weeks, but they were almost in the home stretch; he could see light at the end of the tunnel.

"So you think...what? What are you agitated about, eh? This man doesn't even know your name, correct?"

Antonia was right.

"I'll call again. If no one answers, I want you to take a separate car to the airport and I'll meet you there, okay?"

"But Steven..."

"No buts, Antonia. I've learned to trust my gut on this stuff. Just do as I ask...please?"

"I hope they answer the phone."

She wasn't happy. He didn't blame her. He hoped they answered the phone, too.

They returned to the hotel and claimed their bags from the bell desk. Steven called Diego again – still no answer. Considering it was now 4:00, lunchtime should have been over; but then again, in Argentina things did kind of run late. Part of him said to just leave town and forget about the PI, but another part argued that he needed hard copy photos, not grainy scans.

His need for the photos won out. He handed Antonia his bags, asking her to please wait for him in the airport lobby area by the ticket counter. She was far from happy about the situation, but agreed grudgingly.

"You watch out, *Double-O-Seven*, you're not made of steel. Be careful, please, eh? I have some people I need to bring you home to meet."

"No worries. I'm just going to drop off the money and be out of there. I'll see you in an hour or so."

CHAPTER 13

They went their separate ways; she off to the airport, and he to Diego's. The rain beat down on the procession of traffic, making for slower going down the boulevards. When they pulled up to Diego's building, he had the cab driver wait, and went to the front door and tried it. Open. He pulled out his cell and dialed the number; he listened to the phone ringing upstairs.

No answer.

His unease grew.

He paid the taxi driver, ambled down to the end of the block and slipped around to the back of the building. Nothing obviously wrong, no shadowy figures holding walkie-talkies. He returned to the main street and stood in the doorway of one of the adjacent buildings for ten minutes or so. There was no suspicious traffic, no black cars pulling up.

Perhaps he was being paranoid again.

Diego maybe didn't have the most responsive receptionist; that didn't mean every door held danger and menace. Snap out of it, he told himself. Stop getting spooked; just give Diego the cash, get the photo, and go to the airport.

Easy.

Let's not make this more difficult than necessary.

He returned to Diego's building, opened the front door, and slowly walked up the stairs. He tried the door to the office, suite 200; the knob turned. He pushed it open. Medium sized office, no one in the front area, no evidence of anything wrong, unless you considered a receptionist absent from the front desk sinister.

Bathroom break? A little afternoon delight? An errand?

He called out.

"Diego? Are you there?"

Nothing.

He contemplated turning around and leaving, but he needed those photos if he was going to hang Griffen with Cavierti. Thumbnails could be tampered with. He hated that he needed to see this through, but he did; he'd come too far...

Steven walked towards the back of the suite, past the reception area to what he presumed was Diego's office, and was stopped by the smell; a cloying and familiar odor. He'd smelled that before.

He pushed open Diego's door, and retched at the horror before him. Diego had taken his last photograph. He was tied, naked, to his chair – the extent of his torture grossly apparent by the cigarette burns on his arms and chest and groin. Cause of death was disembowelment. A young girl he assumed to be Diego's receptionist lay discarded on the floor, throat cut, naked, likely raped.

The stink in the small space threatened to overpower Steven's senses.

He darted to the window, slid it up, and took in some long, deep breaths of air. Was this the Wolfsatz sending the message, 'Don't fuck with us?'. But why then the torture...what were they after?

His description, of course.

Any info Diego might have had relating to his identity or how he could be located. They couldn't have been too happy he hadn't known anything.

Steven scanned the carnage, mind racing.

The photo. He needed the Cavierti photo.

He rooted around the office, finding nothing but an empty file folder lying next to the body of the receptionist. Out of the corner of his eye he spotted an old scanner on the floor, next to the credenza; it was worth a shot, he supposed. He bent down and pushed the ancient eject button; a photo exited the document slot. *Cavierti.* At least he'd caught a little luck. He carefully slipped the black-and-white into an envelope, and after taking a last hurried look at the unfortunate couple on the floor, returned to the window for another gulp of fresh air.

A creak emanated from the front office.

He stiffened. There was no way that was good. If this was the same group that had paid his fake apartment a visit, they'd have the downstairs sealed off, no doubt from the inside this time, so that was a no go. He looked outside and considered the fire escape; it was up or nothing. He rolled up the photo and stuck it in his inside jacket pocket, and uttering a silent oath, climbed out through the window, carefully shutting it behind him.

Though a good foil for noise, the pelting of rain made everything slippery; but at least he had on his rubber-soled shoes. He ascended quickly, stealthily as he could, ears strained for any movement below.

He made it to the top floor just as he heard a noise emanate from Diego's office. Steven glanced down; an unfriendly face glared up at him from Diego's window.

Partially obscured by a pistol barrel pointed at Steven's head.

He kicked in the window he was facing and dived, elbows up, through the jagged frame, rolling on the floor as he regained his bearings – shedding shards of glass and droplets of water. He staggered into a headlong, upright position and tore past the bewildered office staff yelling, "*Policia. Llame los policia!*"

He pushed open the office door and heard unmistakable echoes of footfalls urgently ascending the stairs below. He rapidly surveyed the area, spotted a likely doorway and lunged through it, springing up the short flight of steps to yet another door; he burst through to find himself on the wet rooftop, surrounded by piles of rubbish, pipe, and planks. Wheeling around, he slammed the door shut and jammed a short, thick plank against the doorknob, wedging it against the surface of the roof – then ran and grabbed a dead TV set and shoved it against the base of the makeshift prop. That might slow them down a little.

He spent a few valuable seconds racing around the perimeter of the roof, hurriedly looking for options.

Crap.

He hated heights.

But he hated being shot, tortured and disemboweled even more.

He let out a primeval shout of defiance as he sprinted and leapt across the void to the next building, slipping on the slick but abrasive roof when he landed, slamming onto his back.

Damage assessment: momentarily winded; a spike of pain through the spine and into his legs; it hurt, but he hadn't broken anything. Good.

A series of gunshots blew whistling through the barricaded door at Diego's building, signaling that he needed to keep moving if he wanted to survive. He rolled onto hands and knees, struggled upright and gingerly approached the edge of the roof.

The next building was a story lower.

This just got better and better.

He summoned another primeval scream, and racing as hard as he could, threw himself out into space, arms and legs milling to gain precious inches.

Time slowed until he hit the roof hard, knocking the air from his lungs. He registered that he was still conscious – but was he okay?

A flash of pain stabbed his ankle. Ligaments, not a fracture, he knew from harsh experience.

Fuck.

He was way too old for this.

He groaned his way onto his feet and tried the rooftop service door. No luck. Locked. Hurriedly scanning the area for another escape route, he limped to the far corner of the building, thankfully discovering a fire escape. He cautiously lowered himself down the side of the eroded edifice while clinging to the metal roof gutter, ignoring the sensation of skin tearing into the jagged steel handhold. Nostrils flared, Steven summoned up a stable grip on the unfaithful surface of the decrepit steps.

The thumping of footfalls sounded from the roof above. If he was still on the fire escape by the time they made it to the edge, he'd be dead meat.

Preparing himself for more pain, he loosened his grip to increase the rate of descent, leaving a thin trail of blood on the rails as he lost his footing and slid faster still. He dropped the final story onto the sidewalk of the little alley and rolled to mitigate the momentum from the fall.

His ankle shrieked in protest over the new pain in his knee.

Tough shit.

Live with it, pussy.

He raced down the wet, narrow space, trying every door.

Locked. Locked. Locked.

Open.

Thank God.

Steven ducked inside the room, quickly bolting the door behind him.

Another office building.

He took a few deep breaths of mind-clearing air and padded to the front of the building to get a fix as to what street he was now on.

Big boulevard.

Eyes alert, he stepped into the mix and hailed a cab – a plentiful commodity in Buenos Aires. A taxi pulled smartly to the curb almost instantly.

Steven collapsed into the back seat in a state of relief.

"*Aeoropuerto, por favor.*"

The driver nodded and leaned over to activate the meter.

The rear passenger window shattered and the front of the driver's head blew onto the dashboard and windshield, spattering Steven with a mist of warm blood. He kicked open the opposite door and rolled onto the pavement, to be almost flattened by the blaring, glaring oncoming traffic. He sprang into a crouch and dodged between the cars, which in Buenos Aires fashion were moving at roughly double any sensible speed. He sped off, up and over his pain barrier as he zigged, then zagged across the eight lane road.

He felt a tug at his new jacket and heard a ricochet a few feet in front of him; looked down and saw a bullet hole smoking in his jacket. No hit.

He picked up his speed.

His ankle radiated pure agony.

Another ricochet, further away and behind him. Honking and squealing brakes, a collision in back of him. More honking.

His consciousness narrowed and his focus became laser-like as he poured on the steam. One more ricochet even further behind, the accuracy diminishing with distance as he hurried to the other side of the boulevard, the claxon of sirens approaching. He kept low, dodging between the trees that occupied the island in the middle of the thoroughfare. He saw an opening in the oncoming flow of cars and propelled himself across the other eight lanes.

Near miss.

Another.

Amid the blare of the angry horns he kept running, as hard and as fast as he'd ever run before.

Three blocks up he entered a small one-way alley with no signs of further pursuit.

Steven slowed to regroup and calculate where to go next; the optimal choice would be a hotel with a taxi stand. He jogged one more block and got lucky. Checking the street to confirm he wasn't being followed, he jumped into the first available cab and told the driver to floor the gas all the way to the airport if he wanted a healthy tip; he was late for his plane. The car roared from the curb as Steven shivered in the back seat, soaked to the skin.

He slowed his breathing, deliberately forcing his heart rate back under control. It appeared that he'd made a clean getaway, if you could call a gunfire-fueled chase clean. Physically, he hadn't been so lucky, but he recognized that it could have been far worse. His ankle was swelling and he'd left chunks of his hands on the roof, but he was alive; that was more than he could say for Diego and his secretary. And now, also some poor taxi driver, no doubt with a family and life he cherished and took for granted.

It was hazardous option, being around Steven – *if you were given the choice*. People were getting killed. He put his head back and closed his eyes as the adrenaline drained from his system, leaving him exhausted and shaken.

Antonia stood waiting for him, arms folded, at the ticketing area.

"Steven! You're soaked. What happened?" She took in his clothes, his filthy grey pants, the hole in his coat, the bleeding hands, the thinly disguised limp. With a knowing but worried look she turned and opened his duffel, pulling out a pair of khaki pants and one of his long-sleeved pullover shirts.

She pointed at the men's room sign, lips tight but firm in their resolve, he noticed.

"I'll tell you later," he said, and went to clean up.

CHAPTER 14

Griffen's private line buzzed. He was getting ready to visit his place in the Hamptons for the weekend; summer in the city was sticky and hot, and he enjoyed the country, if you could call the Hamptons the country. He picked up.

"Someone's causing trouble in Buenos Aires," the caller told him. "Hired two different PIs. Our friends almost got him. Sounds a little bit like your boy, but a different look; maybe hair dye."

"Fuck. What is it with this guy? All right, thanks for the heads up," Griffen said.

He rang Sergei and let him know their mystery man might have made his way to Buenos Aires. Sergei was noncommittal. That wasn't good, but then again, Sergei probably had much bigger concerns than some thorn in Griffen's side.

Sergei asked to be kept informed.

The conversation hadn't played out as Nicholas had hoped; he sensed a growing impatience with the situation from the Russian. Perhaps he'd do better to lay low with Sergei for a while.

He riffled through his contacts and selected the number of his original investors in the fund; one of the Italian groups involved in a variety of businesses, not all of which were one hundred percent legal. The Italians had a lot of contacts, old contacts established over generations, and they had a lot more pull than the Russians, who were relatively new at the game. He made a call and explained the situation; gave all the details he had, and indicated he needed assistance in solving his problem.

The Italian agreed that the key to locating Steven was finding Antonia, and pointed out that anything could be accomplished with adequate planning and funding; that a hundred thousand dollars would handle it, and to consider the matter as good as concluded once money changed hands. Griffen assured him he'd be back in touch within twenty-four hours to arrange a wire.

Griffen felt his spirits lifting already – things were looking up.

෯෯

Steven returned from the restroom looking better. He rooted around in his bag, pulled out his hygiene kit and kissed Antonia.

"I've got to give myself a haircut," he said. "They saw me, so they'll be looking for a man with dyed black hair; I'm afraid it's head shaving time. I hope you still love me as bald guy."

He went back into the restroom and entered a stall, using the sideburn clipper on his electric razor to trim all but a fine stubble of hair. When he was finished, he inspected the result in the little kit's mirror. Not as bad as it could have been; enough sun had tanned his scalp so that he didn't look like a chemo patient. He was actually pretty funny-looking, wearing a toilet seat protector around his neck to keep the hair off his shirt. After removing the impromptu cape he exited the stall, inspecting himself in the larger mirrors as he donned his glasses. He looked like some Euro-trash lounge lizard. Pump up the jam, call me DJ Phunky-Phresh.

It would have to do for now.

He approached Antonia, who doubled over with laughter.

"Oh my God. You look like you're in U-2, or designing clothes in Milan. That's incredible; embarrassing but amazing. No one will recognize you, truly, *caro*," she said, giggling the entire time.

"Thank goodness for baseball hats."

"I still want you, you big bald Romanian love-god. Let me feel it." She rubbed his head. "Ooh, it feels so strange. What name shall we call you now? Sven? Lars? Gunther?"

She was enjoying this a little too much, he mused; then again, why not?

"Let's get me checked in," he said, "and then I'll tell you what happened in town."

As they walked through the large terminal, Steven limping from the trauma his leg had endured, he told her about Diego and the receptionist, leaving out the more gruesome details. Then he related the chase – the cab driver. She looked at his hands, and put her finger through the hole in his jacket.

"A bullet? They came very close, Steven. Very close."

He removed the jacket, soaked as it was, and switched to the blazer he'd bought in Caracas. The jacket went into the garbage, along with the trashed trousers and sodden shirt he'd been wearing, and his cell phone. Suddenly his duffel had more room.

They entered the first class lounge and relaxed, safe for the moment.

Their flight didn't depart for a few more hours, so he checked the web. Stan had replied that there was nothing new on Homeland Security, and the police were treating the boat explosion as an accident. Whoever had done the job had been good enough to fool the local cops. Stan presumed the HS investigation into Steven was ongoing.

Steven asked him to scan the original file photo of Jim Cavierti and the two-page FBI summary and e-mail it to him; he wanted to start assembling the case.

Spyder had gotten back to him and disclosed he was working on obtaining some documentation on the Ecuador cartel/Panama company and the Swiss arms group from the DEA and several intelligence agencies. Stay tuned.

Steven logged off and gingerly held Antonia's hand, cautious of the cuts on his. Argentina had turned out to be a near-terminal destination but he'd accomplished what he'd set out to do, albeit with a trail of bodies in his wake.

Lost in thought, they waited for the plane that would take them to *Italia*. He hoped the worst was over. For both their sakes.

CHAPTER 15

Rome was chaotic, a nonstop symphony of utter pandemonium. Antonia took the lead now they were on her turf, and in short order she'd arranged for transportation to the Westin Excelsior, a turn-of-the-century building near the Spanish Steps.

The taxi drivers in Rome made the Argentines seem like they were on Quaaludes and Steven could have sworn they were going to die in a fiery blaze at least five times on the way to the hotel.

Antonia didn't appear to notice.

They were both out of it after the grueling thirteen-hour flight, and their stay in Rome was going to be limited to one night. Then they were on the road; the plan was to rent a car and drive to Todi, which Antonia said would be quiet by Italian standards. Not many tourists were likely to be there, compared to the rest of Italy.

The hotel's façade was spectacular, and after only a few minutes at the front desk they were shown to their room. Steven unpacked while Antonia made arrangements for a car rental. It didn't take long, and she transitioned to unpacking along with Steven.

They agreed to eat at the hotel and get some desperately needed sleep; the flight over had been turbulence-ridden almost the entire way, so they'd only gotten rest in fits and starts. Following a lackluster room service dinner they barely made it out of their clothes before they were deeply asleep.

At ten a.m. the alarm sounded, prompting them to pack their belongings and go in search of a cellular shop. Even on a Sunday, and with many stores closed, they'd purchased a phone for Steven within forty-five minutes and were ready to go.

Their errand in Rome concluded, they grabbed coffee and discussed the route they'd take to get to Todi; which was in Umbria, about ninety miles north of Rome. She figured the trip would take two hours. Her travel plan sounded good to him.

The coffee was unlike anything Steven had ever tasted; black, incredibly strong, and flavorful. So far, he liked Italy.

When they returned to the hotel and checked out, their car was waiting outside of the lobby area – a diesel Nissan quasi mini-van/SUV. Not exactly a Ferrari, but with plentiful space for all their luggage, and it came with a map.

They grabbed some rolls and fruit, and were on their way.

Antonia drove, which was just as well, as he wouldn't have had the requisite foolhardiness to conquer the bustling Roman traffic, whereas she seemed almost bored with it. Once they'd crossed the city perimeter the freeway opened up and the going got far easier. They flew through the countryside in a diesel-fueled blur. As they approached Umbria, he was intrigued by the number of castles peppering the landscape; every hill had the remains of a fortress on it, and many were the basis, the centerpiece, of small towns built around them. Not much had changed in hundreds and hundreds of years – most of the buildings were many centuries old, yet still being lived in and used exactly as they had been for generations.

When they arrived in Todi, several things struck Steven. First, the roads were paved with ninth and tenth century cobblestone, and all of five feet wide, which barely accommodated the width of their modest little car. Second, the entire place was a hill town built within ancient fortifying walls. As they negotiated the rising, winding streets, it was like being transported back eight hundred years; same buildings, same ramparts, same streets. Eventually they pulled up to a three-story building off the main square and Antonia wedged the car up onto the sidewalk.

"We're here," she announced cheerfully.

He squeezed out of his door and looked around. It was the 12th century. He almost expected a man in armor to walk around the corner, or a horse-drawn carriage to pull up. Antonia stood on her tiptoes, stretching to find the expected house key in a dank crevice. Successful, she creaked open the ancient door and Steven followed her up the steps with the luggage. He heard her give a squeal at the top of the stairs; a happy squeal.

"Uncle Dante! What are you doing here? I thought you were in Chianti!" Antonia exclaimed in Italian. She rushed to embrace a rotund, grey-haired man standing in the living room.

"I thought I'd stop in and make sure you got here okay, girl." Dante looked over at Steven, and switched to English. "You going to introduce me?" Dante's English was as good as Antonia's.

"Oh, of course. This is Steven. The one I told you about. Steven, this is my Uncle Dante; this is his place," she said.

"Nice to meet you, Dante," Steven said, putting the bags down and shaking Dante's hand.

"Likewise. Antonia's told me a lot about you. I understand you're having a little trouble. Let me know if I can help; I know a lot of people." Dante looked at Steven with an expression that implied he indeed knew all sorts of people.

"I appreciate that. Hopefully, I won't have to take you up on it," Steven said. Old Uncle Dante promised to have a trick or two up his sleeve. Just a feeling, but Steven had learned to trust his gut, and his gut said don't fuck with the old Italian uncle.

Dante smiled at him. "Hey, all you gotta do is ask, no?" He turned his attention to Antonia.

"Antonia, you're more beautiful than ever. I don't see how you do it. This is one lucky guy, this Steven, a lucky guy indeed," Dante said, looking at Steven to confirm he'd gotten the message.

"Oh, Uncle Dante. I think we both got lucky." Antonia was beaming.

"Well, now I see you got here safely, I'll get out of your hair, head back out to the country house. You call me if you need anything, eh? Anything at all. Nice to meet you, Steven. Take care of her, she's very precious to me. You two enjoy yourselves. The time goes by quickly, you know?"

And with that, Uncle Dante descended the stairs, waving at them over his head. The front door closed, leaving them alone in the house. Steven took in his surroundings, and was surprised by the interior; it could have been right out of the pages of Architectural Digest. Hardwood floors, stainless steel appliances, ultra-modern furniture, 50 inch LCD TV.

"My uncle gutted it two years ago and renovated it. Everything's new. It's been in the family forever," she explained.

"I'm impressed." He truly was. He'd pictured them sitting by the fireplace in a stone chamber as they'd pulled up the hill, and this was more like some posh post-modern hotel.

"You can use his computer. It's all the latest and the fastest everything. He's a nut about that."

He inspected the terminal area, and indeed everything was current technology.

"Where's your uncle staying while we use his place?" he asked.

"He's got a villa in Chianti where he spends four or five months a year. He also has a big place in Sicily where he winters," she explained.

"Is he retired?" Steven wondered what her uncle did. Villas, apartments…he'd done pretty well for himself.

"Mmm, sort of. He's a businessman, is involved in many different enterprises," she said. She didn't seem to want to go into more detail, and he didn't push it. Steven suspected Dante was well connected in a lot of different ways. Italian, wealthy, knew a lot of people – people who could maybe help if you were in trouble. Two plus two…

They unpacked, and while she was hanging her clothes he gave Uncle Dante's computer a whirl and got online. He downloaded his proxy mask, and checked on e-mails. One was from Spyder, with two attachments:

[Ask and ye shall receive. I'm enclosing a three-page dossier on the Ecuador Cartel's known fronts, courtesy of the DEA. Much of it redacted, but with Santa Maria in Panama clearly identified. And another intel document, one page, on the Swiss group. There's a lot more on them, and the whole file is over thirty pages, but this should be enough to hang them. Hope you're enjoying your travels. Spyder]

Hallelujah. Now he had the documents for three of the four. He sent Alfred a reminder e-mail that he needed the hard copy list of investors from the bank and the brokerage statement showing the large short position.

Stan Caldwell had scanned the photo and the FBI file and sent them to Steven, so he downloaded those. Steven saw that Gordo had also finally sent the summary he'd asked for. He opened the first message:

[I have the whole thing laid out. It's easily documented, but took some bandwidth. I'll send it to you zipped in a few minutes. Pretty astounding they've gotten away with this crap.

And I was able to get some intel on Allied's flagship product from a little bird at the FDA, and it's a mind blower. I included a brief summary, but the short version is it's a vegetable oil that's harmless if ingested orally, but has a 100% auto-immune damage likelihood in mammals if injected – and these clowns want to use it to increase supplies of rarer vaccines.

Some of the large Pharma companies have products like it, all of which are basically poison, and many of which are banned in their current forms in the U.S. – although recently, the big companies tried to backdoor it into the U.S. during the whole swine flu hysteria. I never really understood why such an innocuous flu got such massive media attention, like it was the new black plague. Apparently that was all about money. Even if the shit destroys your immune system, they have the patents on it, and what's a country filled with misery and increased health care costs if a few big Pharmas can make a few more billion a year from their toxic soup?

As an example of how deadly this crap is, one was used as an adjuvant to stretch the supply of the Anthrax vaccine given to many Gulf War soldiers – there's your simple, obvious answer to the 'Gulf War Syndrome' of chronic, incurable auto-immune dysfunction. The science has been around since the 1930s, which was before medicine knew much about the immune system. Short version is that it's a killer and should never be used in humans for any reason, much less to increase vaccine supplies.

Think I'll short a bunch of Allied in anticipation of a change in their fortunes. Gordo]

He opened the second message and then the attachment, and unzipped the contents. Gordo had been amazingly detailed. Like he'd promised, it was all laid out, unmistakably. Griffen and Allied were sunk. Now Steven just had to strategize how best to hang him.

All he needed to put it to bed was the Canadian document on the Russians, assuming one was forthcoming. He was getting close to end game.

When he refreshed the screen, he saw a response from Cliff in Canada, and it had an attachment. He read the message:

[This can never be published. It's an internal document; not secret, but still, not for public viewing. Please use it judiciously. Hope it does the trick. C]

He opened the attachment, the first page of a Canadian government report on the activities of the newly developed Russian Mafiya players and their various known fronts. Most were blacked out, but Adriatic Trading was not. It left nothing to the imagination.

Cliff had removed any information that could lead back to him, had sanitized his end so his role in obtaining the document was effectively masked. Steven understood he'd gone far above and beyond the call of duty, and that his debt to Peter was getting paid off rapidly. Cliff was an honorable man.

Now he had everything.

He sent an e-mail off to Stan Caldwell about Cavierti:

[Cavierti's alive, saw him in Argentina, have the pictures to prove it. My theories as to why he faked his death are:

1) He found out from a leak at the FBI he was going to be indicted and had to disappear in a way that would shut down any further investigation.

2) He discovered Griffen had found out from a leak at the FBI he was going to be indicted, and that Griffen was planning to have him eliminated, so Cavierti beat him to the punch.

He's now either acting as a conduit between Griffen and the Wolfsatz, or is working with them unbeknownst to Griffen, helping them build out their business, perhaps with his New Jersey mob connections. Either way, it looks ugly for our man Griffen.]

Antonia had come into the little study and stood watching him. He told her how he'd completed constructing the case, how this was the final stretch. She smiled, sharing his victory, but there was a hint of something else. He couldn't place it.

She walked over to him and put her arms around his shoulders.

"So everything drops into place, no? Now, are you ready to see the town?"

"You bet. Although I have a feeling I'm already looking at the most precious treasure that Italy has to offer," Steven reasoned.

"Enough. I'm already sleeping with you. No need to charm your way into my underwear," she admonished, but the compliment had set her eyes sparkling. "Come, let's walk around."

CHAPTER 16

Dante sat in his car outside of the walled city, speaking in rapid Italian to a black-haired man in his fifties, who nervously rubbed his pock-marked face. The discussion didn't take long. The man watched as Dante's Mercedes disappeared around the bend, and then he turned and walked through the gates into Todi; just another non-descript Italian in a black leather jacket, carrying a medium-sized travel bag.

⇛⇝

Dante's townhouse stood thirty yards off the main square; where a beautiful old church occupied the place of prominence at the far end of the *Piazza*, which also accommodated some small coffee shops and bookstores. Lining both sides of the narrow streets, many of which really were no more than paved footpaths, were small restaurants and cafes, and every type of store imaginable.

Summer tourists ambled around here and there, but the hill town didn't have an aura of being crowded or overwhelmed.

Steven and Antonia spent the afternoon exploring; wandering the small alleys and side streets off the main arteries. Many of the building doors were from the Middle Ages; five and six and seven hundred years old, their original coarse key slots evident alongside the retrofitted newer locks. The street cobblestones were grooved from centuries of wooden wheels grinding into them, their passage still palpably evident from the erosion. Steven could imagine rats scuttling down these same arteries during the black plague, and the wooden carts for the fallen making their slow procession, as the cries of 'bring out your dead' echoed around the walls.

His internal eye saw prosperous merchants decked out in their finest velvet and plumes in the sixteenth and seventeenth centuries, riding atop their steeds, as peasants carrying bundles of vegetables or firewood hurried to get out of their way. It was a place redolent of the past, and more than anywhere he'd ever been he was conscious of the ghosts of generations gone by still inhabiting the city's walls.

Evening was spent at Antonia's favorite restaurant, a small *trattoria* at the base of the town, whose owner greeted her as though she was his long lost daughter. Antonia seemed to have that effect on people. As they ate, he reflected upon how close he'd come, several times, to a fatal termination of his crusade, and he was grateful they'd been fortunate enough to escape unharmed. He just hoped they were insulated enough now, in this little nowhere hill town, so the demons chasing him would lose the scent.

It seemed inadequate, but that hope was the best he could muster.

The next morning Steven arose early and suggested they go for a run. Antonia reluctantly agreed. Soon they were sprinting down the narrow streets and out through the walled town ramparts to the winding road below. The business of life in Italy was just getting underway, with horses pulling plows in the fields and old women carrying baskets on their heads, exactly as their predecessors had for the last millennium.

It was wildly incongruent to see a new Porsche with Swiss plates stopped at an intersection waiting for a flock of sheep to cross the road, but that was a scene they passed as they made their way around the bleached stone walls.

Steven was getting a feel for the country's history, and his own relative insignificance in the scheme of things. Undoubtedly, every person who'd lived in Todi had nurtured dreams and hopes and passions and fears they believed were uniquely important and distinct, and they'd all lived their lives out to whatever end was destined, rich or poor, young or old, beautiful or ugly, tragic or happy. Yet what really endured were the walls and the earth. He was experiencing how it was hard to take yourself too seriously in Italy.

It had all been done before.

Antonia explained the region's past to him, with tales of many other walled cities throughout the area, each one with its own character and charm. She described the feuding families and the long-standing rivalries that spanned centuries; one town she wanted him to see was San Gimignano, a walled city in Tuscany where there were dozens and dozens of towers constructed by the wealthy town aristocracy of the eleventh and twelfth centuries. Some were magnificently built, each vying with the other for the title of tallest or most extravagant; the vanity and excess of the past still standing long after the petty competitions were over, their sponsors and builders deceased for many centuries.

He was captivated by Antonia, and equally captivated by the country they were running through, as she told tale after tale. She was a purebred, and he was again struck by the strange and improbable confluence of events that had resulted in their meeting, much less falling in love. It was an odd world.

They ate a peasant lunch outside the town walls, and by the time they returned to the house it was morning in the U.S.. Steven rinsed off and requested a couple of hours to finish up some odds and ends on the computer and finalize his case against Griffen.

She hugged him, before breezing upstairs to make some phone calls.

As the day wound down, the sun slowly dipped into the Umbrian hillside.

"Honey, where do you want to eat tonight?" Steven asked. Food played a central role in Italy, which fit with his temperament; a guy's gotta eat.

"What about Albierto's?" Antonia called from the bathroom.

"Again? Isn't that the fifth time in the last few days?" Steven was just giving her a hard time. He loved the little place, and the owner treated them like royalty.

"Do you know anywhere else that has pesto like theirs? Come on, my treat, eh? You can buy the Sambuca afterwards."

She made a compelling case.

They took their time getting ready, and enjoyed the early evening stroll to the little *trattoria*, looking for all appearances like newlyweds completely engrossed in each other's company.

A figure trailed them at a distance, blending into the small groups of tourists still lingering from the afternoon's sightseeing; stopping occasionally at the odd shop, pretending to look in the windows. He watched Steven and Antonia enter the restaurant, and situated himself at a café on the small side street adjacent to the entrance, keeping an eye on it. He shook a package of Gitanes, lit his thirty-second cigarette of the day, pulled out a newspaper and ordered an espresso. He didn't have the air of a pleasant man. Nor a patient one.

But it wouldn't be much longer now. He inhaled the acrid smoke from the black tobacco, sat back, and waited.

After dinner, Steven and Antonia strolled hand-in-hand up the dark, winding street. The hike wasn't unpleasant; it had become a ritual for them to walk the town after dinner before stopping in for a nightcap at the café on the square.

Seventy yards behind them a figure ambled slowly, the only noteworthy feature of his otherwise nondescript appearance his long overcoat. Though it had drizzled a little that morning, the rest of the day had been sunny, lending the coat an air of eccentricity.

The man in the overcoat dropped his cigarette butt on the street, leaving it smoldering as he followed them. A light breeze carried the wisps of smoke back down the hill.

Steven was excited at the imminent prospect of putting this whole episode behind him. He felt vindicated, but it was a bittersweet victory; he couldn't help but think of all the people who'd lost their lives during the unfolding of the complicated affair. Antonia sensed his melancholic mood, and silently hoped to herself that time would heal his wounds.

And they had the rest of their lives to enjoy each other's company and create a compelling future together.

The man watched the happy couple meandering up the cobblestone street, and smiled to himself, his tobacco-stained teeth making for an unpleasant visual. This was going to be too easy. He flipped off the safety on the silenced Beretta pistol he clutched in his right-hand pocket. They were now the only ones on the road. No moon, little illumination.

This was his chance.

He carefully extracted the pistol from the long coat and picked up his pace. Sixty yards. Fifty yards. Forty yards. He was getting close to his kill zone, padding silently on crepe soles. Twenty yards with a silencer was the maximum distance for reasonable accuracy. Thirty yards. He closed the distance and steadied his gun hand against a pillar; Steven's head fell dead in his sights. He squeezed off a shot.

Antonia tripped on the cobblestones, her heel catching in one of the fissures in the ancient road. Steven caught her, stooping forward quickly in the process. He heard a ricochet off the stone ahead of him, and simultaneously felt a burning in his shoulder; he'd been shot. He'd heard that sound before, in Buenos Aires, so he didn't need the searing pain from his scapula to alert him bullets were flying.

Fuck.

He pulled Antonia up and pressed them both against the wall, using an abutment to shield them from any fire, looking up and down the narrow winding street as he probed the back of his shoulder. The wound was superficial, a graze. He'd been lucky. It was very dark, and the occasional overhead bulb would do little to help him see their assailant. But that could work both ways; the million-dollar question was where had the shot come from?

He whispered to Antonia: "Don't say a word...someone's shooting at us. Take off your shoes and be ready to run."

She looked panicked. He didn't blame her; he was no match for a gun. Their only hope lay in speed, surprise and darkness. She stepped out of her heels.

"You're hit," she whispered, taking in his bloodied shoulder blade.

He heard a rustle from down the street, just a few yards from where she'd stumbled. The gunman was approaching.

"When I say run, do it...as fast as you can," Steven instructed.

She nodded.

He tensed. "Now!"

Steven grabbed her, and they bolted fifteen feet to the next small lane on their right – more a passageway than a road – and ducked around the corner. Pitch black, no lights. That was good.

Then the distinctive barking of a silencer. A ricochet. And another.

Antonia let out an abrupt cry, and went sprawling down into a heap just as they'd made it into the alleyway. She clutched the side of her abdomen, blood seeping through her fingers, tears of anguish streaking her face, pain and shock etched in her expression. She looked up at him and shook her head.

"Leave...me. It's you...they're...after."

Steven picked her up, wincing at her groans of pain, and staggered over to the shadows of a doorway; an ancient arch built in the eleventh century. He put his finger over his lips, signaling silence.

She was breathing heavily, hoarsely.

Muffled footsteps approached at a run from the other street. The gunman. Steven pressed himself against the doorway, confirming Antonia was out of sight.

The footsteps stopped at the corner and the gunman peered around, squinting down the small lane. He scanned further up the larger street they'd been on, cocked his head, listening – then made his choice. He came running down their alley.

As the gunman came level, Steven spun in a crouch, sweeping the gunman's legs from underneath him, noting with satisfaction that the killer had pitched heavily onto the cobbles.

But he hadn't let go of the gun. This was no amateur, like the Islanders; he was a pro. Steven had to move quickly.

He jumped on the gunman.

More scorching pain as a bullet seared through his right leg. He had to get the gun away. He struck his assailant in the face, delivering a series of brutal blows, and then his head exploded and his vision blurred. The gunman had smashed him in the temple with the butt of the pistol.

Steven was momentarily dazed, borderline blacking out, incapacitated. The man pushed Steven off him, and stood up, still gripping the weapon, slowly raising it to finish the job.

"*Arrivederci, alito della merda,*" he said, wiping blood from his eyes.

Antonia screamed from the alleyway.

"Noooo!"

As he prepared to squeeze the trigger the gunman registered a noise behind him, and was startled when his legs gave out, simultaneous with a spike of pain in his lower back. *What the hell?* He collapsed onto the cold cobblestones, face first, the pistol clattering harmlessly into the gutter.

The black-haired man extracted the ice pick from the gunman's spine and leaned over his paralyzed body. He carefully pushed the spike through the man's ear and into his brain. The gunman's legs twitched spasmodically, stiffened, then lay still.

He looked around, satisfying himself that no one was in the area besides Steven and Antonia; nobody had seen or heard anything. He scooped up the gun and quickly pulled the dead assassin into a doorway, leaning him into a drunken sitting position. There wasn't much blood; ice picks weren't messy. The body looked like a reveler taking a nap, not an unheard-of occurrence in Italy in the evening. It only had to look convincing for a short while. He'd swing by with his car in a few minutes and retrieve the corpse. He moved over to the doorway where Antonia was lying, and spoke to her in Italian.

"Where are you hit?"

"In...in my...lower stomach, the side," she moaned. She looked around, and switched to English. "Steven...Steven...are you...are you all right?"

The man pulled her hand away from the wound and took a quick look. She was bleeding heavily.

Dark blood.

He quickly put her hand back to stem the flow, took off his black leather jacket and put it over her shoulders. He turned to Steven, who was struggling to his feet, and addressed him in halting English.

"You. Okay...walk?"

Steven touched his swollen upper leg where the second bullet had penetrated. It had missed bone, passing through the outer muscle. He was losing blood, but not enough to be terminal any time soon.

"Yeah. *Si.*"

"You help she. I come car *pronto.* Go *ospedale.*" The man was struggling with the language, but his message was clear.

Steven nodded, and staggered over to where Antonia lay. The ice-pick-man vaulted around the corner and ran down the hill. Steven collapsed next to her, and took her hand. Her skin was pallid and cold. She looked very scared.

"He's going to get a car. We'll get to a hospital and they'll have you fixed up in no time," he promised. She tried to smile, and then he saw her eyes go out of focus and her hand drop from her abdomen. His heart let out a whimper.

"Antonia. ANTONIA!" He shook her shoulders.

"Antonia, don't fade on me. Stay with me. I love you, Antonia. More than anything. Don't leave me now." Steven's voice trembled with horror and anxiety and grief. She was silent, her breathing shallow, blood soaking her side. He heard a motor working its way up the hill.

"Antonia, hold on. Help is coming. Just hold on." He lifted her from the doorway, cradling her body. She weighed so little. His leg shrieked bolts of agony, and his shoulder was on fire, but he didn't care. He'd eat the pain as just dessert for his recklessness.

"Please hold on, Antonia, please, don't die, don't die..." He rocked her, whispering her name as a mantra until the car finally came around the corner. She stirred, her eyes fluttering open momentarily, and looked at his beaten-up face, streaked with tears. "I...love you...*caro*..." she murmured, and then she was gone again.

"I love you too..." he said, nuzzling her with his bloodied nose. "Just stay with me a little longer."

Their mystery protector jumped out of the car and threw open the back door of the Audi sedan. Steven carefully placed her in the back seat and then crawled in with her, holding her upper body while applying pressure to the wound. The door slammed shut, and he registered the trunk opening, and the man dragging the corpse over and stuffing it into the back. Finished, the man hurried back to the driver's side and slipped behind the wheel, tossing a towel to Steven.

The car lurched into gear and screeched away.

As they careened down the serpentine streets towards the gates of the city, the driver pressed a button on his cell phone and spoke in rapid Italian:

"*Allo.*"

"Dante, it's Santo. We had a visitor here. I was able to take care of it, but it got messy – they're both hurt," the man said into the phone, his voice almost a whisper.

"How bad?" Dante asked.

"She took a bullet in the side of her stomach, and the man's hit in his leg and arm. It all happened before I could do anything," Santo lamented.

"It's a good thing you stuck around. Are you certain there was only one visitor?" Dante sounded cold, efficient.

"Yes. I spotted him this afternoon, tailing them, but I wasn't certain. He moved so fast, it was over in less than a minute." Santo wanted Dante to understand he'd done his best.

"I'm sure you did everything you could. Do you need anything?" Dante asked.

"No, I have it under control. He's not bad – Antonia is...but I think she'll live. I'm taking them to the hospital by Perugia. We should be there in ten minutes or so." He paused while he made the turn out of the gates of Todi, flooring it once they were on the larger road.

"Dante, I know this shooter. Once I was up close I recognized him. He's from Palermo, one of the Gambrizi group." Santo knew many of his peers in the Italian syndicates. It was a small world.

"That's interesting. I'll have to give Giovanni a call in Palermo and clarify the situation. Take care of the cleanup and call me from the hospital. I don't want anything else to happen to them while they are on my watch, *capiche*?" Dante sounded nothing like the good-natured elderly patriarch who had welcomed the couple to Todi. That façade was gone, replaced by a serious and menacing demeanor, a man who was accustomed to giving orders and having them followed. And he was furious.

"*Capiche*. I'm sorry, I was just thirty seconds too late." Santo hesitated. "Dante, I can't stay around the hospital and answer questions. It's probably best if I leave once they're inside."

There was silence on the line, then: "You got it. Just ensure they make it safely."

Nodding, Santo disconnected and concentrated on his driving.

Santo was a sociopath, having killed his first man when he was twelve, using an ice pick, which became his instrument of choice. His mother had been accosted by the man daily while she went about her duties as a maid, and one day something had snapped in Santo's head, and he'd had enough of the bully grabbing at her. Santo killed him the next morning, as the man relieved himself at the urinal in the restroom of the hotel where she'd worked, then had gone to school – there was a big soccer match he was supposed to play in during lunch and he didn't want to miss it.

Twenty years later he'd lost count of how many he'd helped into the afterlife. It didn't really matter.

It was just a number.

Fifteen minutes later they pulled up to the emergency entrance of the modern hospital at the base of Perugia. Steven jumped out cradling Antonia, while Santo darted to the emergency room, yelling in Italian to get a doctor, there'd been a shooting, a horrible accident.

The staff descended upon Antonia, who was quickly placed on a gurney. They immediately hooked her up to an IV and cut her dress away, before wheeling her through double doors into the main hospital. A nurse told Steven in broken English they would both be taken to surgery, and asked him to lay on a gurney too. He complied, and the nurse took the scissors to his pants.

The shift supervisor was speaking with Santo in the lobby area. She asked Santo what had happened, and he told her that he'd been driving by, and apparently the two of them had been the victims of a robbery gone horribly wrong. He was just a good Samaritan.

The supervisor notified the police, and Santo was asked to wait there so they could take his statement. He agreed, of course, no problem, glad to help – he'd be right outside, having a cigarette; the whole experience had unnerved him, he was sure she understood.

Santo walked outside, lit a cigarette, and returned to his now blood-soaked car. He called Dante to let him know he was going to dispose of the corpse somewhere in the countryside, somewhere it would never be found, and then he was going on a trip. Dante agreed it was a good time of year for him to take some time for himself; the job would be his when he returned.

Santo started the car, and pulled off into the night.

CHAPTER 17

Steven was in and out of surgery quickly. The bullet that grazed his shoulder had left a quarter inch groove, requiring only cleaning and bandaging; the wound to his leg was a straightforward swab-and-stitch procedure. The bone was unaffected, and no arteries had been hit; just primarily trauma to the muscle and skin.

Half an hour after going into the room, he was wheeled out. They'd never even put him under, just used local anesthesia – at his request. A CT scan of his skull came back with no excessive irregularities; he had a mild concussion from the pistol-whipping, nothing more. His temple got five stitches and his IV got some morphine, making him drowsy and killing the lion's share of the pain. He wouldn't be running anytime soon, but he'd live.

Steven was resting comfortably in a temporary room, awaiting the outcome of Antonia's operation, when the police came to ask for his account of what had happened. One of them spoke marginal English, and half-heartedly questioned him. Steven made up a slurred story about a bungled robbery attempt, stating he didn't remember much, concussion and all. The police seemed satisfied and left him to his recovery.

Several hours later, one of the nurses woke Steven from an uneasy slumber and put him into a wheelchair, IV and all, and rolled him to another room. Antonia lay on a bed, hooked up to various monitoring devices, IV flowing; pale, but alive. The surgeon who'd operated on her entered shortly thereafter, and spoke with Steven in good English.

"She's lost a lot of blood, and we had to work for several hours to get her internal injuries mended. Fortunately the bullet didn't bounce around, and we only had to fix the intestines along its path. With the blood loss she's very lucky to be alive. Another twenty minutes and I'm not sure she would have made it." The doctor looked beat. Dark circles under his eyes. Five o'clock shadow. It had been a long and grueling night.

"But she'll live, right…she'll be fine?" Steven demanded.

"It's too soon to say, but she's in remarkable physical shape and has a strong heart. I'd describe her condition as guarded, but improving by the minute."

"Thank you for saving her, Doctor. Thank you so much." A flood of relief had begun to course through him, even as he looked down at her pallid face. "She'll make it. She's a survivor."

Dante called Giovanni at 10:00 a.m. the next day. His inside man at the hospital had given him the full report – Antonia would live, but was still in critical condition. She was stable now, and the prognosis was good, but it had been close.

"Giovanni, how are you? Long time since we spoke, no?" Dante was dead serious today, none of the usual jocularity and playfulness to his tone.

"Dante, to what can I attribute this delightful surprise?" Giovanni became suspicious, and somewhat alarmed.

"Well, I was hoping you could help me out. One of your capos was in Todi, and apparently shot my niece and her friend. Do you know anything about this?" Dante inquired.

"I know absolutely nothing about this. He must have lost his mind. Are you sure that it was one of my men?" Giovanni lied, not unexpectedly. Holy shit. What had gone wrong?

"I believe so, but we could be mistaken. My niece is very precious to me, Giovanni, like a daughter, really. She's had such tragedy in her life, and now this. It's inexcusable." Dante was icy calm, and Giovanni knew from past experience that Dante speaking in this iceberg manner was not at all good. It meant that he was enraged; and when Dante was enraged, he was deeply enraged – striking out, in a calculated and ultimately devastating way.

"Dante…I have no knowledge about whatever he was doing. I swear, I'd never do anything to harm you or your family. You know that." Giovanni didn't like where this could quickly lead, and wanted to put an end to it here. He didn't carry the weight to take on Dante. He would be squashed like a bug if he tried.

"Giovanni, perhaps this was a huge mistake, and perhaps the target was not Antonia. Her new love has had some difficulty with some characters in America, and it could be that he was the goal." Dante wasn't a fool. He'd figure it out.

"You should know something now, Giovanni. She is like my daughter, and he has brought her back to life, which makes him like my son. Anyone that moves against him moves against me, and anyone who would harm my children will incur my full and immediate wrath, and I will not only hold them responsible, but their wives and children responsible as well. Wouldn't you do the same thing if someone went after your young ones?"

Dante was ready, almost spoiling to go to war, to destroy without remorse. He'd done it before. Giovanni knew he was serious, and that his reply would be the most important words he'd ever spoken.

"Of course, Dante. I would scorch the earth. I had no idea that anyone from my organization was involved with anything like this. You have my word. As a gesture of contrition that one of my men was involved in this, unbeknown to me, please, let me pay for any medical costs, and let me offer any restitution you feel is appropriate." Giovanni had gotten the message, and wanted out of this. He got it. He didn't want a war with Dante, or to find one of his sons decapitated or overdosed. He'd do whatever it took to stop this here and now.

"I knew you'd understand, Giovanni. If you hear of anyone that might have accepted a contract on my niece's friend, would you share with them the relationship that he now enjoys? Again, he is like my son, and I will treat anyone wishing him ill accordingly."

"Dante, I can't imagine that anyone would be foolhardy enough to risk angering you. Please accept my complete and full apology if one of mine was stupidly involved in anything. I can guarantee that your family will have not only your ample protection, but mine as well, from now on." Giovanni felt a gush of momentary relief that he wasn't being told they were at war.

"I think maybe you should think about making a contribution to Antonia's recovery. I'm thinking fifty thousand U.S.. She'll be in the hospital for some time."

Naturally, Dante wanted to kill some people, but had considered the issue, and decided that what he really wanted to achieve was an end to any attempts against Antonia and Steven – forever. So he'd make Giovanni pay, and hold him directly responsible for their safety.

"I'll send you the money today, Dante. Again, if this idiot was involved in anything, it couldn't have been against Antonia, and would only have involved her new friend. I'll spread the word of his family status." Giovanni genuinely wanted Dante to know Antonia wasn't supposed to have been hurt. The money was nothing, a formality. He understood that he was now on the hook for their safety, and would relay the message accordingly.

"Please do. And say hello to your wife and children, Giovanni, wish them my best, eh? So many troubling incidences occurring, it should make us appreciate those we love."

Dante hung up.

Giovanni thought it through. He'd sent his best man, with specific instructions to avoid any harm to Antonia, and the whole thing had blown up in his face. He was lucky that Dante hadn't had his whole family taken out as retribution. Very lucky, and he knew it. Dante was one of the most powerful of the syndicate heads, and it was only due to his desire to keep from starting a full-scale war that Giovanni's family was still allowed to flourish.

A series of calls volleyed across the Atlantic. The New Jersey family was informed of the immediate cancellation of the contract by Palermo, and the reason why. New Jersey consulted with their leadership, and it was determined that the contract couldn't be fulfilled, that attempting to do so wasn't worth the delicate balance of relationships that were being put on the line in the old country. Dante had powerful contacts with the New York organization, and they couldn't risk a rift there over one lousy contract.

They would never have accepted a sanction against a member of an Italian syndicate's family – that was way off-limits, and by invoking his protection, Dante had made Steven bulletproof. Literally. The decision to cease and desist permanently was communicated back to Palermo.

The leadership decided that they would return the hundred thousand dollar fee to the client. Some things weren't worth rocking the boat over, and when they got calls from the old country advising a contract was dishonorable it was time to move on to something new. They'd tried, but things hadn't gone according to plan. A shame, but what could you do?

Sometimes things just worked out that way.

CHAPTER 18

The staff gave Steven a sleeping agent, knocking him out cold for a solid six hours, dozing in the room next to Antonia. When he came to, his body felt weak and stiff – his wound protesting like someone had poured battery acid on it. The nurse assured him that was good while she gave him a stinging shot to prevent infection. He felt groggy from the painkillers and sleeping pills and sore from the fight, but was anxious to see how Antonia had fared.

He wheeled himself into Antonia's room, relieved to see she'd regained some color overnight, looking stronger and healthier. The doctors told him she was doing amazingly well – if she continued to strengthen she could be released before the end of the week. They wanted to keep her under observation to make sure the surgery hadn't introduced any complications; she needed to be truly mended before being discharged, but the prognosis was positive.

Uncle Dante had insisted they spend their recovery time at his villa near Florence, where Antonia could be attended to by a private nurse and a proper staff, safe from any further unpleasantness. That was fine by Steven, especially since it was obvious their location in Todi was blown.

Antonia opened her eyes when she sensed his presence by the bed. She looked alert, but drugged.

"How are you feeling?" Steven asked.

"Like a truck ran over me. How about you?"

"Same truck hit me, but not as badly. I'll live. A little bump on the head and a few stitches; I've had worse."

She smiled. And then got serious.

"It's not over, is it?"

"It won't be over until I take Griffen down, or he takes me down; sorry, my angel, but that's the way it looks. It's gone too far. This attack proves it. We'll never be safe until he's out of the picture and behind bars, robbed of his influence and his money."

"Oh, Steven. Why can't we just walk away?"

"He's got too much on the line. I have to finish this – leave him nothing left to play for; I'd hoped we were far enough from his reach here, but apparently there's no such thing. I'm sorry I got you into this, Antonia..."

"*Caro, buon*, then I think I have a way for you to get this story out in a dramatic way. I put out feelers a while ago, and I'm sure I can help make something happen. Let me talk to some people. I do own a New York-based magazine, you know." She considered it. "I bet my senior staff know some big-game reporters in New York who'd be interested."

Made sense. If she could get someone reputable to break the story in a big, credible paper, that would flatten Griffen. His investors would go nuts and the manipulation of Allied would be short-circuited. Then they'd be safe, as Griffen's energy went into defending himself from criminal charges, rather than trying to silence Steven's site. And think of the rotten apple-carts it would upset with his cartel of criminal cronies. That at least would occupy him for the foreseeable future.

Though it hurt to smile, he did. "It's really big news, honey. This would be a death blow for Griffen – it would shut him down."

"*Buon*, then I will call my friends in New York tomorrow and see if they can get someone interested. Owning a magazine does have some, how you say, perks?" She looked a little sleepy, no doubt from the medications and the lingering effects of the blood loss. "Stay with me, *caro*, while I take a nap. I'm tired. We'll deal with all of this later, okay?"

He kissed her hand. "You just concentrate on getting better. I'm not going anywhere."

The next two days were spent peacefully at the hospital. The staff had moved a second bed into Antonia's room, and supplied Steven with a computer and internet access to keep him amused. Steven spent considerable time agonizing over how to accomplish his objective without bringing about yet more destruction upon himself and those he loved. It had to be handled delicately.

Steven wasn't a starry-eyed idealist, and under no illusions he could stop a concerted scheme facilitated by some of his own government's agencies, so he focused on how he could take down the Griffen network and at least damage the bad guys enough to take some of the joy out of the game. He thought he had a pretty good plan, and now needed to execute it briskly.

Antonia exuded a remarkable resilience; the doctors were quietly amazed by her progress. On the third day she was joking with her doctor, chatting with Steven almost non-stop, and looking very much like she was ready to be out in the wide world.

Today was the day, according to the doctors, so Dante had made arrangements for a car to pick them up and take them to Chianti for an extended vacation and recovery. Neither of them resisted the suggestion; they didn't have a pressing agenda of places to go. Antonia, true to her word, had followed up with New York, to be assured that the prospects of finding a credible journalist to break the story looked promising.

That evening, Antonia got a call on her cell. She spoke in rapid Italian, bubbling with excitement as she got off the phone. She explained her chief editor in New York was close friends with Robert Manson; a legend...one of the top investigative reporters in the world, who'd been key in breaking stories responsible for getting a president impeached and taking down several of the largest companies in North America after uncovering fraud. The best news was that he'd agreed to meet Steven in Paris at Charles De Gaulle airport on Friday to hear him out. Manson was arriving to interview the French President, and would take an hour to meet Steven.

Antonia's connections had afforded Steven access he could never have hoped for, and he now had a shot at blowing the Griffen scheme wide open with the most credible artillery he could imagine. For the first time in a long while, he felt like the tide was turning – thanks to Antonia. Antonia...

By now he wasn't surprised, but nonetheless Steven was captivated by the villa's blend of magnificent rustic character with every conceivable modern convenience. It occupied several acres half an hour south of Florence, with a compound of buildings built around a great house that had eight bedrooms and rose three stories above the olive trees and grape vines. It was easily thirty thousand square feet, with a full-time staff of a dozen workers. *Nice little country retreat* – Steven wondered what Dante's main residence was like.

Antonia insisted they go into Florence and get him some reasonable clothes...and have a real hairdresser attend to his appearance before Friday. Not a bad idea, he reflected, considering a sideburn trimmer was never intended as a high society hair-grooming tool. He protested the idea of her leaving her convalescence at the villa so soon after being released, but she assured him she'd be fine with an attendant and a wheelchair. Besides, she was stir crazy already; the villa was almost worse than the hospital. She was ready to claw her way through the walls after only a few days of country solitude.

He relented with a smile; she had that 'Tinkerbell' way about her sometimes, a spirit that needed to radiate.

So off they went. Steven had what remained of his hair cut, with Antonia, presumably, offering the hairdresser directions in staccato bursts of Italian. Antonia was relishing her liberation after being cooped up; seemed more than game for it, and the wheelchair worked out perfectly. Steven had a feeling he and the attendant would be more exhausted than Antonia by the end of the day, traversing the busy shops and streets, searching for clothes that met her approval.

Friday morning they drove to Florence. Steven caught his plane to Paris. He was scheduled to meet Robert Manson in the Air France First Class Lounge at 1:00; Antonia's editor had told Manson to look for a man in his late thirties wearing a red St. Martin baseball hat. The old hat trick came in handy. Steven's flight arrived at 12:30, and he was seated in the lounge by 12:50.

At a little after 1:00 a voice behind him asked: "Steven?"

He rose and turned to greet Robert Manson, who looked tired from his transatlantic flight, though still ready for action. They adjourned to one of the private meeting rooms, and for the next two hours Steven took him through the intricacies of the scheme, offering copies of all the documents along with a binder he'd prepared. Manson asked a lot of questions, and by the point they'd run out of time he'd pretty much absorbed it all.

"That's the whole ball of wax," Steven told him. "He's touting junk biotech companies whose products are garbage or worse – making a fortune from a speculative bubble he creates with his contacts in the media and with the brokerage houses, then makes another fortune when he kills the speculation and the stocks fall through the floor. All the while managing an offshore fund that's laundering cash for the scum of the earth. Oh, and let's not forget his partner faked his death to escape an FBI investigation. But maybe most importantly, the scale of the problem extends to far more than Griffen; our government's sold us down the river, and is using the manipulations to line its pockets. And now you have the file, and all the proof." Steven took a breath. "What do you think?"

Manson framed his comments carefully. "Well, I want to independently verify your background on the companies and his investors, but if it checks out, I think this is a hell of a story – especially the adjutant auto-immune destruction part," Rob observed.

"I agree completely."

"So, yes, this is what we still call news, even in this day and age. What you've described is the systematic robbing of the markets by a career criminal, to benefit some of the biggest known crooks in the free world; and he's getting away with it. It makes you wonder how deep the rot goes…" Manson stood up and shook Steven's hand.

Steven patted his arm for good measure. "I'm just hopeful you can expose this, and put a stop to it…at least in this case."

"I get it, Steven. Really. Give me a week. Now if you'll excuse me, I have to go interview a President."

The flight back to Florence gave Steven time to reflect on whether he'd put his best case to Rob Manson. He replayed his presentation in his mind; went over it for any holes. There weren't any.

Now it was almost over. Everything that he'd worked for – lost so much for – was in someone else's hands. He felt oddly deflated.

Antonia met him at the gate. Even in Italy, where there was no shortage of incredibly stylish and beautiful women, Antonia was a stunner, sparkling even in the dense airport crowd. She'd insisted on standing up to meet him but was resigned to being trundled back to the car in the wheelchair by the silent and discreet attendant – one of Dante's domestic staff. Despite her injury she couldn't contain her excitement and wanted to know all about the meeting.

"Eh, so he will be your knight in shining armor. That's what it sounds like. I think you may have won, Steven," she said.

"We'll see, Antonia. We'll see. But it's looking good from where I'm standing."

The drive back to Chianti was enjoyably quiet, although Steven noted the driver was no less aggressive and reckless than Antonia when it came to negotiating the Italian roads. *Must be something in the water*, he decided. Still, it was good to be back with her. Now, he just hoped his meeting had achieved its purpose.

They'd both know soon enough.

❧

On Sunday afternoon, Steven got a two line e-mail.

[Monday morning *New York Times*. Your info checked out. Left a message to get Griffen's side this AM, no response. Get ready for shit to hit the fan. RM]

CHAPTER 19

The article broke on Monday, front page of the business section. It laid out, in detail, the entire scheme; from the offshore fund and its criminal clients, to the mechanisms used to tout, and then crush, the manipulated companies. Impeccably documented, it was the equivalent of a nuclear blast. Manson was a force to be reckoned with – his special report would inevitably drive law enforcement to investigate the allegations, as well as spur other reporters to pick up the trail and expand coverage. The obvious criminality involved and the roster of clients reading like a rogue's gallery of the world's most despicable miscreants ensured it would be covered by the mainstream media. Lurid stories sold papers, and this was as lurid as it got in the dry world of business journalism.

ॐ

The phones at Griffen Ventures were ringing off the hook at 5:30 a.m.. Griffen got his first call at home from Glen Vesper at 6:02.

"Have you seen the *New York Times*?" Glen began.

"No, I just got out of the shower. What's up?" Griffen asked.

"Go online and read the article by Robert Manson, front page of the business section, and call me back on my cell. It's a disaster." Glen hung up.

Griffen's blood froze. He ran to his computer and logged on, then navigated to the *New York Times* site. He read the article. His vision blurred and his blood pressure spiked through the roof. He realized he was hyperventilating. Griffen read it again. He was sweating, though it was sixty-eight degrees in the house. His hands began to shake uncontrollably. How the fuck had they gotten this stuff? He called Glen back.

"This is bad, Glen."

"How much of it is true…any…all? What documentation could they have on your offshore investors, and how could they have gotten this level of detail?" Glen was trying to figure out what kind of damage control, if any, he could implement.

"I have no idea. Goddamn it. Glen, assuming it's all accurate, what should I do?"

"I don't think I can advise you very well at this point. I would expect an indictment within twenty-four to forty-eight hours, though. Thinking out loud, you have to be around to be served. Just an observation," Glen said.

"Can we sue the paper? Get a retraction?"

"You can sue anyone. That's why I'm asking if it's true. If it isn't, we go in with guns blazing. If you have a who's who of international criminals as your investors, and it can be shown you're engaging in money laundering, racketeering and securities manipulation, you're dead meat, Nicholas. I say that as a friend," Glen stated.

Griffen tried to kick his mind into gear, find a way out. "If, hypothetically, I was out of town for this, could I mount a defense from another locale?"

"I can't counsel you to leave the country. But if you'd theoretically gone on vacation yesterday, I could probably mount a decent defense. The real question is, is there a defense?"

"I'll get back to you on that. I'm not going into the office today, for obvious reasons. I'll be on my cell."

What the hell was he going to do? It would be a matter of minutes before he started to get serious calls from his domestic investors on his cell, alleging breach of fiduciary obligation, or worse yet, fraud. And his offshore investors wouldn't be thrilled they'd been publicly exposed – it put the fund at risk of being frozen if there turned out to be a sustained outcry.

He needed to play out the scenario. If, or rather when, the Attorney General or the FBI or the SEC went after him, it would endanger his domestic accounts, and they would effectively have control over the offshore fund through him – assuming they had him in custody. They could subpoena all the records and prove a pattern of manipulative trading, so that would be a Milken-level prison sentence, at least. Then you had the laundering charges, which would be more like twenty more years if they got serious. Throw in civil suits from damaged shareholders and he'd be worse than dead. That wasn't an option.

His cell rang again. He looked at the number.

Washington.

Fuck. Emil.

"Griffen."

"I just read the paper. This is very serious. We can't be associated with anything criminal. Your involvement with undesirable elements has made you persona non-grata, and I can't do anything to help you. We'll need to extract our funding immediately, no excuses. I have a call in half an hour. I suggest you think about what you're going to do. Again, we cannot afford any embarrassment or exposure on this, and you've overstepped what we can run interference on. I'd suggest you forget you ever heard of me, immediately after you wire our funds to the Turks and Caicos account. The alternative could be unpleasant." As always, Emil's voice was not menacing; actually quite business-like, but the implication was clear.

Griffen was on his own, their protection suddenly gone. That sealed his fate. He'd have to get them their cash back this morning, or risk not seeing tomorrow; they were one group he couldn't screw around with. Their money was in the fund's slush account, so it wasn't a huge problem, but their lack of backing was. Goddamn it. How had it imploded so quickly? Think. Concentrate.

He had to get some breathing room to work this all out. The percentage of his domestic fund comprised his personal money, and would be frozen once an indictment came down, which looked certain at this point; you couldn't have the *New York Times* say you were a crook and not get indicted, not when it was Robert Manson reporting. So it was a question of when.

How long did he have?

His offshore account in Anguilla was worth thirty-five million dollars, but that was pledged as collateral for the offshore fund, and was locked up by the bank. He could kiss that goodbye. That left his Cayman account he brokered through Canada. That was only four million dollars. Not enough to mount a good defense or disappear and live well. He'd have to make four turn into thirty in a hurry if he was going to have any options. He needed more time.

But time had run out.

CHAPTER 20

Steven buzzed and bubbled with sheer elation. He wanted to dance around the room. The bastard had gotten punched right between the eyes. *Enjoy that, you piece of shit.*

He was disappointed the article hadn't had any of the information on the probable intelligence angle, but figured it had gotten killed at the editing stage. If you were going to tell the American public they were being screwed out of their retirements to fund covert operations in bum-fuck, you'd better have irrefutable evidence, not educated guesswork.

Manson hadn't used the Cavierti material, either. Probably because the photos weren't ironclad proof. They could have been doctored, or shot three years ago. Still, he had a back channel to cause some discomfort with the info.

He got online and sent the scanned photos and the FBI dossier to Cliff Tomlin, explaining the circumstances behind Cavierti's faked death, along with his current whereabouts. He figured that would buy Cliff some points with the FBI and would also hurt the Griffen network, presuming Cavierti still worked with Griffen, which seemed most likely.

The market wouldn't open for another two hours, so he chatted with the Group. They were all giving each other cyber high-fives for a job well done; except for Spyder, who was absent from the party.

Steven had Pogo upload the entire *NY Times* article on the site, so it would be available for perusal for more than one day. He also had Pogo create a section on the site devoted to other companies manipulated by Griffen, and uploaded all the data Gordo had assembled. That was eye-opening stuff, all right. No question about there being a systematic manipulation – the patterns were absolutely clear once you understood what you were looking at.

※

"I can't be involved with this, Rick. If he's still around when they indict him, it'll be a given they start peeling the onion on his domestic investors. We can't allow that. I can't be implicated in any way." The man speaking was in his mid-fifties, and carried himself well. He was already at his desk at seven in the morning, alert and in command.

"I agree. I'll speak to our manager, and have him call the gentleman in question and convey our concerns in the strongest possible terms."

"I think a call to the DA, indicating there are dynamics that are more federally-driven on the U.S. accounts should buy us enough time to get them sanitized. He'll play ball; won't want to step on our toes," the older man told him.

"I'll follow up on that. Is there anything else, Mr. Vice President?"

"Not for now, Rick. Keep me apprised of the situation. That will be all."

The older man sat down heavily in the seat behind his desk, the crest of the United States of America adorning the wall behind him.

※

Ten minutes later, at a private investment-banking firm in Washington, a short, bird-like man was pacing in front of his speakerphone.

"Rick, I get it. I had no idea this idiot had half the criminals in the world laundering cash through his offshore fund. I'm pretty sure he kept the U.S. side clean, but at this point, who knows?" The man spoke very quickly, a rapid-fire peppering of words.

"Stewart, you know we have complete faith in you and your ability to make this turn out well. If I may be so bold, might I suggest the best way for this to play would be for him to disappear? Then his second-in-command takes over temporarily, and any investigation is limited to Griffen personally, and his offshore entity."

As the senior aide to the Vice President, Rick handled sensitive issues and problematic situations. He was aware of the Agency's involvement in Griffen's financial structure, but had served as a Chinese wall between the

Vice President's affairs and theirs. He'd actually viewed the Agency's presence as an insurance policy that Griffen would never be scrutinized, and so never troubled the VP with that information. But he hadn't factored in a frontal assault from the press. Now it was damage control time, and he had to contain the fallout to the offshore fund. The domestic end could not be subject to any investigation.

"Easier said than done," Stewart said. "I can be a bird whispering in his ear, but I'm not sure the DA will walk away and leave the domestic accounts out of it." Stewart Pinkerton was a partner in the banking firm, managing a coterie of high-profile investors.

"Be creative, Stewart, there are ways to trade that off. No one wants to hurt innocent people here. I can take care of the local issues, and chat with the DA to compartmentalize the damage to the offshore entity." Rick was a problem solver. When he called, people listened. He'd make some calls.

"Talk's cheap. You don't know Griffen. And what about your guy's friend? The favor? That's still in play."

"I think we have to consider that favor done. Self-preservation is now the imperative. Would it help if we did a conference call and I spelled things out?" Rick was perfectly willing to share his wishes with Griffen in terms he'd understand.

"Perhaps it wouldn't hurt to speak to his attorney. I know of the man; good reputation. Glen Vesper. I'll have a word with him first, and keep you out of it unless there's no other way." Stewart wanted to keep his client happy. The fish didn't get bigger than this one, and it could be disastrous to his reputation and power base if he lost the account. He'd do whatever it took.

"Keep me informed, Stewart. This is receiving the highest levels of visibility. Do I make myself clear?"

"Crystal, Rick. Crystal."

❧

Glen Vesper weighed up the ramifications of the current situation. On the one hand, his friend and client had just had his life destroyed in the press. Even if none of it were true, and Glen had no illusions it wasn't, Griffen would surely be finished running money on the Street. Robert Manson didn't go to press with an article unless he had all the facts; nor would the

Times' attorneys allow one word of it to be printed unless it read like the gospel and was completely documented. The world would assume it was accurate.

On the other hand, he would probably be able to bill between half a million and a million this year to defend Griffen. Too bad the insurance didn't pay in the event of fraud, which they would certainly contend that laundering for drug lords and Nazis amounted to; he couldn't disagree, really. What had the fool been thinking? He supposed Griffen had never really believed any of it would come to light. Which it wouldn't have, until someone had gone to great lengths to dig it up and slot the puzzle pieces together. Glen sensed Steven Archer's presence in the day's activities, but that was no matter at this juncture. What was done was done.

His cell phone rang.

"Glen Vesper."

"Mr. Vesper, this is Stewart Pinkerton, of WJ&P. You've heard of us?"

"Of course. What can I do for you?"

"One of your clients would appear to be in some difficulty as a result of an article in the *Times* this morning, and I thought I could offer some thoughts on the subject, seeing as we're substantial investors in his domestic fund."

"Why call me? Call Griffen. Shortest distance between two points." Glen didn't like this at all.

"I have an inkling that may be delicate. I believe you're counsel to his group, and as such we share attorney-client privilege, given that we are large investors," Stewart reasoned.

"I could argue that, but consider it to be so. Proceed."

"I think I can safely convey that the U.S. structure would be untroubled by any investigations, and the focus would remain on Griffen and the offshore fund, should your man be unavailable for comment." Stewart should have been a politician.

"Are you saying what I think you're saying?" Glen asked.

"Mr. Vesper, if your client was not available, I think we could ensure resources would be deployed in more productive areas than looking for minor white collar criminals outside of U.S. jurisdiction." Stewart was out of ammo after that. But he did need a concession.

"That's a remarkable insight, Stewart. But how do you benefit, or should I perhaps say your clients?" Glen asked.

"It would be very helpful in building the credibility of the domestic fund back if a new, independent manager was brought in, while the current second-in-command – Matt Conway – ran the day-to-day operations. I think it would also be advisable if my firm pulled our investment, effective last year, and was off the ledger, as it were." Stewart had now gotten to the meat of it.

"I can't fault your desire to distance yourself from the current manager's alleged behavior; prudence would dictate that. Do you have any ideas for a new permanent manager?" Glen asked. He understood. They wanted the records wiped.

"I have some ideas, but I'd like to get an agreement in principle first. I'm sure you understand." Stewart had a hole card, but he wasn't going to show it until he had a deal.

"Just to be clear, if my client steps down, effective immediately, in light of all the controversy and these unfair accusations, the domestic fund would remain untouched and there wouldn't be an international manhunt? No extradition, no long arm of the law?" Glen required clarity on this. "And you have the ability to commit to that, given your relationships and clients, if we remove you from this mess?"

"Yes, I think you have the essence of the idea. There would be some saber rattling, but at the end of the day your statement would hold true."

"Can you be reached at this number?" Glen asked.

"Always." Stewart hesitated. "The initiative has a shelf-life, Glen. I wouldn't take a long time considering it."

"Time is money. I'll get back to you."

❧

Griffen's cell chirped at him. It was Glen, who recounted the deal that had been offered, by cutout, from the VP's people. He advised Griffen to take it. Glen pointed out that guaranteed prosecution was a far less attractive choice than an assurance he wouldn't be hounded by the law once he was across a border. Off the record, of course.

Griffen wasn't so sure. He sounded flustered.

Glen told him he had about an hour to consider the deal. In the meantime, he'd work on a statement indicating Griffen would step down as the head of the domestic entity. He also spelled out that he'd require a $500 thousand retainer to defend him, payable today.

Glen told Griffen to strongly consider the deal and call him back.

Griffen would never be able to do business again after that. His career would be over, and he'd be unable to salvage the offshore fund due to the Allied play, now that he was all over the newswire. That would create serious difficulty for him with his 'sensitive' investors – the hundred million apiece they'd invested with him was beer money to Ecuador or Sergei or the Argentines; but he'd be tainted, and they'd hold a grudge.

He'd probably do well to lay low and disappear, come to think of it, for a host of reasons. What a mess.

He was finished. The Street ate its young, and Allied was going to lose most of its value when trading started, meaning his biggest positive – money – would vaporize within a few hours. Hell.

Griffen called Glen back.

"I've considered the options, and for the good of the fund I'll step down..." he started out.

"Let's cut to the chase, Nicholas. You need to get me a check for $500K, or instruct Matt Conway to do so. Then I'd be thinking long vacation if I were you." Glen had a lot to do, and there was no point in playing nice.

"Glen, off the record, how about my assets? The house, the place in the Hamptons? What about my domestic bank account? It has about $1.2 million in it. And my money invested in the domestic fund?" Griffen wanted to understand where he stood in terms of resources.

"Forget about the houses. By the time you could sell those, they'll have been seized. As for the fund, between the IRS and the DA and the other agencies, that's gone." Glen thought about it. "As far as the personal account, you could always pull some cash out once the banks open. Or go down to the diamond district and buy a million dollars' worth of smaller stones with a cashier's check or a wire transfer. They won't have been able to lock up the funds yet. Hypothetically, of course." Glen figured that the whole topic of fraudulent conveyance was a lesser issue if you weren't going to be around to face the charge.

"Of course." Griffen understood. Be in Manhattan in an hour or so, hit the 47th Street wholesalers, and have one of them take a walk with him for a block or two to his bank.

Then hit the road.

"So just to be clear, you are accepting the deal and will have me issue a press release. And will be cutting me the $500 thousand check?" Glen liked clarity.

"That's correct. Looks like I'll be going into the office for a while this morning after all, to write your check and congratulate Matt."

"I'll stop by. Say 9:30?"

"That'll work. See you then."

కఠఠ

Griffen called his car service and told them he wouldn't require the limo today; he'd be driving himself. He packed two suitcases, took a lingering look around the house, then walked to his garage and put the suitcases in the trunk of his black SLS AMG Mercedes.

He started the car and opened the garage door. Then a thought occurred to him, and he got out and went back and opened the house's connecting door to the garage, propping it open with a paint can. He went into his kitchen and turned on all the burners on his Viking range, and then blew out the flames. He sniffed, satisfied he smelled gas.

Griffen trotted back to the car and lowered the garage door. He'd be damned if they'd get their hands on his papers or any of his personal effects. Fuck everyone. The place would blow sky high, just a matter of when. Accidents happened all the time. Hopefully when they rang the bell to serve the warrant.

For the first time that day, he smiled.

CHAPTER 21

Griffen made it into the office at 8:50 a.m., entering the building through the service entrance. Security had barred the reporters waiting in the lobby from getting into the elevators, so he wasn't molested when he got to his floor.

There was a positive hush as he walked through the firm's doors. He didn't have a lot of time so he strode straight to his office and sat down, ignoring the tension and the stares. He flipped open the fund checkbook to cut a five hundred thousand dollar retainer check for Glen.

There were just a few other odds and ends to tie up. Like who was going to run what was left of the fund, and how he could make his exit safely, without attracting undesired attention.

"Matt? Get in here," he yelled.

A minute later Matt came in.

"Nicholas, I'm just, well, I'm stunned. It's...well...what do you want us to do?" Matt Conway asked.

Griffen stared at him. "Congratulations. You are, as of this minute, the new head of Griffen Ventures. There will be a new managing director replacing me soon, but in the meantime, you're the man," Griffen told him.

"I don't know what to say…"

"Sorry it didn't happen under better circumstances – but that's life in the big city. You'll do a great job. For now, if I were you, I'd get out of Allied and sell as many call options as you can find buyers for, the further out the better. Then short the stock all the way down."

"What are you going to do?" Matt asked.

"I'm going to go deal with the offshore situation. I'm still the manager of that fund, so I'll be gone for about a week. Unwinding it will take some finesse with the bankers." That would explain his absence for a little while, which is all he needed.

"Anything you want me to do?"

He handed Matt the envelope with Glen's check in it.

"Give this to Glen and tell him I'll call."

Then Nicholas Griffen left his office for the last time.

He cabbed to West 47th Street and stopped at a jeweler he'd gotten some tennis bracelets from; he ran a wholesale business. High-quality goods; reputable. Griffen explained he needed about a million dollars worth of one to two-carat loose stones, all GIA certified D-E color, VVSI or better. And he needed them within an hour.

The man didn't even blink. Just asked what form payment would be in.

Griffen explained they'd be walking to his bank and getting a cashier's check; just the jeweler, a security guard, and Nicholas. Would that be a problem?

Apparently not.

Forty minutes later they walked into Chase. Griffen asked to see the manager and explained he was making an investment that would require a cashier's check drawn from his personal account. $1 million even. That got the manager's attention. Griffen advised him to check his balance, and also look at his company account if he had a problem, which had $24 million in it.

The manager was back with the cashier's check in ten minutes. The deal was done. The jeweler and he shook hands and went their different ways; Griffen with $1 million of stones in a small velvet bag, and his jeweler with about a $200 thousand profit. Not a bad morning for one of them.

Griffen flagged down a cab and gave him the address of his office garage. His cell sounded off again, this time with Sergei's distinctive ring. He considered not answering it. That idea went nowhere good.

"Good morning, Sergei," Griffen answered, sounding cheerful.

"What is this with the *Times*? Why is Adriatic's name exposed…and what is the damage to our capital in the offshore fund?" No 'how are you, how can we help, are you okay?'.

"Sergei, I told you, we're fine on the fund. We have a high-risk play in place on Allied, but the reward is huge. We do this all the time so it's nothing to be alarmed about." Technically, kind of true. Only there was much to be alarmed about.

"It is unacceptable that Adriatic was exposed in the same sentence with the Ecuador Cartel. I have to–"

"Sergei, listen. I have no control over that. You can thank that Archer prick for it, I suspect – although we'll never know for sure. What I can do now is damage control." Griffen wanted to cut this off before it went any further. A pause. Good. Sergei must be considering his words. Then:

"What do you intend as your next move?"

Griffen took a breath. "I'm going to step down from the domestic fund and go salvage the offshore entity. I have a lot at stake, Sergei; not just your money but most of my money, too. I have to unwind the Allied play and save our capital from the wolves." Yes, that sounded convincing.

Sergei was pacified, at least momentarily.

"Look, Nicholas, I understand there is risk in what you do, and I didn't think we invested in a CD, so I accept risk as part of your strategy. But I do need you to tell me the truth. Can the offshore fund recover?" Sergei asked the question carefully.

Sure, if oil was discovered under Allied headquarters, or the president of the company became Secretary of the Treasury within the next forty-eight hours and could authorize billions in bailouts.

"In my opinion it can, Sergei. It won't be easy, and that's why I'm heading for the islands to deal with the situation personally. I need to put all my energy into fixing this." Which is why I'll be gone for a while, he thought. "I'll need to move the fund to a different jurisdiction and change the charter once this is over to avoid any unpleasantness from U.S.-based investigations. But one thing at a time." Griffen paused for emphasis. "It's my money at stake, too, Sergei."

"I hear what you are saying. For all our sakes, I hope you are successful. Stay in touch and let me know what is happening." Sergei sounded partially convinced. Griffen had bought himself some maneuvering room.

Sergei was not a stupid nor provincial man, for all of his pretended bear-like clumsiness with language and good-natured bombast. He had a feeling he was being lied to, but he couldn't be sure. Griffen was in trouble because his investors' identities had been made public, but that was a different issue than whether or not the offshore fund was in serious financial jeopardy. Griffen had always rebounded before and they'd made lots of money together – so he'd give him the benefit of the doubt.

For the time being.

❧❦

Griffen pressed speed dial on his cell. A number in Canada answered.

"Pendragon Investments."

"Let me speak to a broker," Griffen said.

"This is Doug. What's your account number?"

"792294."

"And the name on the account?"

"Griffen"

"Password?"

Griffen gave it to him.

"Yes, sir, how can I help you?"

"I want to buy three million dollars of September put options on Allied Pharmaceutical. APDT. I like the fifteens, twelves and tens," Griffen instructed.

"That's going to take some time, sir. Right now the stock is volatile. It's trading at twenty-four dollars in the first half hour of trading, down almost twenty percent."

"Do it. I don't care if I have to pay a premium. Get it done, or sell calls to achieve the same net result. Call me back on the cell number you have on record," Griffen said.

He hung up. Traffic wasn't heavy for a Monday. He stopped at another Chase branch and pulled out forty grand in cash, explaining he was buying an antique clock and the seller demanded cash. The teller didn't really seem to care much, just filled out the federally-mandated forms.

He looked at his navigation system, and calculated the time it would take to get to the Canadian border; worst case, a few hours. No real hurry. With the speed the government worked, it would take days to issue an indictment. He had all the time he needed to disappear.

His phone rang; it was the broker from Barbados who handled Heliotrope.

"Nicholas, we have a serious problem. I'm afraid we are under-collateralized for the Heliotrope account, and given the Allied movement today, we're going to have to start selling unless we get a wire transfer of, well, it looks like somewhere in the neighborhood of $28 million." It was the senior partner.

"I think you might want to reconsider that. By the end of the week we'll be seeing it back in the low $30 range. This is a blip." Griffen was bluffing, but it was all he had to keep the price from plummeting out of control until he could get his puts purchased. "If you want to protect the position and raise some cash, sell some puts – Septembers should be good. It'll be like free money once this recovers." The offshore fund was dead meat; why not have them subsidize his personal put buying?

"We go back a long time, Nicholas. Are you sure about this?"

"You know I've got a lot of my personal money in the fund. I'm telling you selling puts in the teens is as good as gold, better even, and this will not be a problem by next week." Griffen played a mean hand of poker.

"Okay. We'll sell $5 million worth of put contracts to help defray some of the expense until this stabilizes. I hope for all our sakes you know what you're doing."

"As you pointed out, I've been doing it a long time." He hung up. It was too bad the brokers and the banks would get hurt, but they'd be fine. They were big boys.

He had other things to concentrate on now. He gunned the gas, enjoying the pulse of power as he pulled onto the freeway.

He'd live to fight another day.

CHAPTER 22

Steven watched the trading. Allied had stabilized at around $11; a catastrophic plunge for the day. Even though it was now public knowledge the stock had been played, it would still take time for many investors to believe the whole thing was a sham and dump their shares. Many would wait for a bounce to sell, which Steven believed was a fool's errand given the article, but that's what made a market. As it was, there was no way the company would recover from the revelations in the article, so a trip to the penny stock 'pink sheets' was a foregone conclusion.

Steven considered the damage the fall must have inflicted on Griffen, and smiled. He checked his e-mail, and saw a message from Stan Caldwell, with an attachment:

[Thought you'd like to see this, if you haven't already. Looks like the end for him. Stan]

Business Wire. 9:30 A.M. Nicholas Griffen, Founder and Manager of Griffen Ventures Investment Group, today announced his resignation as director. "Due to the controversy resulting from the libelous and false statements irresponsibly published in the New York Times, I feel that the group has been unfairly tarnished and will continue to be damaged if I remain the director. Therefore, effective immediately, I am naming Matt Conway as interim manager until an independent individual can take the position full time. It is unfortunate certain segments of the press have chosen to abuse their power in a deliberate attempt to harm our investors. I am confident that the allegations contained in today's article will be proven to be baseless and without merit." Griffen Ventures Investment Group has been a leader in biotechnology investment for over 20 years.

Steven sent it to Pogo to upload onto the site. This was a great day. He'd lived to see his adversary get hung out to dry, and was watching his portfolio increase in value by being correct about the Allied fraud. He felt sorry for those who had been duped into investing in the company, but he'd done everything he could to alert the world that the company was a sham, and the website had sounded the alarm for weeks to everyone who could read. Anyone with even a casual interest in the stock would have had to have done some research on it, and with the site so prominent on the message board discussions, they would have had to simply ignore the facts and stay long anyway.

Financially, Steven had done well by being on the right side of the trade – for once. His short position had more than tripled in value and he'd bought put options as well as sold calls most of the way down; going five times the money on those already. By the time the smoke cleared, he'd have made a lot of money, and while that was hardly compensation for the losses he'd suffered at the hands of Griffen – Peter and Todd's faces came unbidden into his consciousness – it still meant that he was now 'of secure means' and could do pretty much whatever he liked from this point on. Maybe spend more time on his cryptography hobby – the market had occupied much of his time, as had running for his life, but perhaps now he could indulge that vice. Whatever. He'd figure it out.

Steven looked down the hall. He watched Antonia as she sat reading a book in Italian, singing softly to herself, a leg absently swinging off the side of the chair, and realized it was finally over. The whole thing. Just a few loose ends, and he'd be free to move on from this whole sorry episode and live his life; a life with the woman of his dreams.

જ∼⌒

Griffen's cell interrupted his thoughts – he muted the car stereo when he saw the number displayed. It was Canada calling. The broker confirmed his account number and identity, and confirmed that he'd purchased $2.96 million dollars worth of Allied September put contracts. Griffen instructed him to place limit sell orders on the puts when Allied hit $9. Why be greedy? That would net him, by his rough math, $14 million, plus the original $3 million invested, and the $1 million in diamonds and the $1 million remaining in Canada in cash – close enough to $20 million for jazz. He paid no tax on the gains, because the Canadian account was undeclared and treated as a foreign investor from the U.S.'s standpoint, a hundred percent tax-free. $20 wasn't $30 million, but he could still have a nice life.

Griffen terminated the call and hit the mute button on the stereo console. Music flooded the interior of the car.

He hummed along with the CD player and watched the scenery going by, ruminating where he wanted to live in his forced retirement. Costa Rica? Could be too close to the U.S., and a lot of Wall Street players liked to hang out there, so perhaps not such a hot idea. Pity, that, because it was so hospitable and the natives were very, very friendly. Maybe Thailand? Decisions, decisions. He'd stay in Toronto tonight, and hop on a plane tomorrow.

Griffen liked the sound of Thailand. He'd always been an aficionado of all things Asian, and the region had the reputation of being very forgiving of the sorts of entertainments well-heeled Caucasian gentlemen of a certain age favored.

He was sure he'd be able to get a flight to Bangkok out of Toronto, if not direct, then avoiding the U.S. flight system. He had nothing but time once across the border, so he wasn't particularly worried.

Griffen stabbed at the stereo controls and cranked the volume. Def Leppard boomed from the stereo, and he bobbed his head with the beat.

In spite of the adversity thrown his way, in the end, life was good.

≈∙≈

Steven saw the headline when he opened Spyder's e-mail. Wow. A broad smile spread across his face as he read on:

According to the attached *NY Times* article, Griffen had been charged with eleven counts of securities fraud, money laundering, and violation of banking laws. Oddly, the domestic fund wasn't being charged, although the DA indicated he was reserving the right to do so at a later date. It was only the offshore fund and Griffen named in the article – that sort of figured, because all the evidence pointed to the offshore entity as the one used to handle the criminal funds.

Griffen was a wanted man now, and would be on the run for the rest of his natural life. That was somewhat comforting, although it wouldn't bring back any of the dead.

He saw another e-mail from Cliff with an attachment. He opened the message.

[Thought you'd find this interesting. Our man on the inside at the brokerage reported Griffen placed a huge order on Monday morning to buy

ZERO SUM

Allied puts. It would seem he was betting on the stock dropping. Enclosed is the brokerage statement. Note the $9 limit order. Cliff]

So he'd bought a ton of puts the second he figured out the jig was up? Smart, Steven supposed. After all, he'd done the same thing.

Steven opened the attachment and considered the buys; ran the math on his calculator. Griffen made almost $15 million off his play when he sold at $9. The only conclusion was that he'd known it was going to go through the floor, and had decided to profit personally even as his offshore fund crashed and burned, taking the banks and brokers and investors' money with them.

What a piece of shit.

Steven thought about it. What could he do with the information? It was confidential and part of an ongoing investigation, so he couldn't send it to the papers. And given the Canadian origin he wasn't sure what the U.S. authorities could do about it.

Then Steven had a terrible and wonderful idea. An idea so evil it shocked him for a second.

He realized it was truly Karmic. The great circle. What comes around, goes around.

Perfect.

CHAPTER 23

In the offices of Griffen Ventures, an all-hands meeting was underway. A dignified, impeccably dressed and groomed man was addressing the staff.

"Matt here has done a remarkable job during a challenging and volatile period in the firm's history. I'm pleased to be taking over as Managing Director, and appreciate all the hard work you've put in during the recent difficulty. Consider this the beginning of a new era for Griffen Ventures."

The speaker came across as polished and sincere. His name was Samuel Finch – a well-known investment manager recently recruited from Vanguard. His resume read impeccably, and featured an MBA, as well as a six-year stint with the CIA, ostensibly as an international banking expert.

"As my first official duty, I'm changing the name of the fund to Midas Ventures Biotechnology Investments. It's more in keeping with our current goals and identity. Let's hope that it bodes well for our future performance."

After a few more platitudes, the meeting was adjourned. Samuel called Matt into his office.

"I want to sell December calls on Allied today, and short the stock to vapor over the next week. Say $20 million worth." Samuel wanted to make a buck or two off the play.

"Easy enough, sir," Matt remarked.

"Call me Sam. I also want to sell January calls on Prometheus Industries, to the tune of $40 million. I have a feeling they're deeply overvalued here. Let's start shorting them too, but not fast enough to raise suspicions," he instructed Matt.

"Any insights on why you have this strong feeling?" Matt asked him.

"Let's just say I have a hunch it would be a good trade," Samuel said.

He'd actually been told by Rick that Prometheus was going to be the subject of a federal investigation, which would tunnel its share value over the next month. The Prometheus short would put the fund up by at least 25 percent for the year, ensuring that even with all the drama, most investors would keep their investment in the fund. They were, after all, in it for the money.

Everyone was.

❧

In his Buenos Aires condo, Jim Cavierti was packing his bags when he heard his door open. His heart sank. He'd expected to have enough time to get away before they heard the news about Heliotrope; he'd only found out in the last few hours himself.

Griffen had fucked him. Big time.

All it would have taken was one phone call to give Jim a warning that the fund was going to be rendered illiquid, and he could have disappeared within an hour. But after twenty years of partnership and forty-five years of friendship, Griffen hadn't bothered. And now he'd left Jim to explain the situation to the Germans.

Five men walked into his bedroom. It had a magnificent high-rise view of downtown and the river. Truly panoramic.

"Jim, we've just heard that our investment has been rendered worthless," said the shortest of the group. Helmut Weiss was the head of the Wolfsatz, an utterly ruthless man in his seventies whose stock in trade was murder and abuse.

"Helmut, I just found out myself. We've all been screwed by Griffen. I had twenty million in that fund right along with your money," Jim explained, which was true. He still had many millions from his side businesses with the New Jersey mob and the Germans, but he'd also lost a big chunk of cash.

"I understand, Jim. But what am I to do now? I can never really know if or when you had knowledge of your partner's actions. Do you see my predicament?" Helmut had a problem, all right. Which meant Jim had a bigger problem.

Helmut looked around the room; saw the bags half-packed on the bed.

"Going on a trip?" he asked.

Jim knew it was over. He didn't say anything. Didn't have to.

"Boys, why don't you help Jim with his trip? I thought I saw his car waiting downstairs," Helmut said with an awful grin. He turned and walked out of the room.

"No, please, no, listen, Helmut? HELMUT? I DIDN'T KNOW. I SWEAR I DIDN'T KNOW..." he heard the front door close.

He looked at the men.

"Please, don't do this. I can make you all rich. Please. Just listen." Jim was getting frantic. They grabbed him under his arms.

"I have millions. I'll give each of you a million dollars if you let me go. Please. Think about it. A million dollars. Just tell Helmut you killed me, and you'll all be rich. Rich," he pleaded.

The leader of the group walked over to the sliding glass door that sealed them off from the balcony, and pulled it open.

Really a remarkable view.

Thirty-one stories, and you could see the *Teatro Colon*, the Cemetery, the River, the Boulevard of Liberation – literally the whole city laid out like a tapestry before you. It was one of the best addresses in town.

The wind bit cold on the skin. A little drizzly, still. You could smell a tinge of exhaust and hear the noise of traffic from a distance.

"Please...oh, God no...just listen, two million apiece, seriously, two million, where are you ever going to see that kind of money..." One of the goons slammed his fist into Jim's jaw, knocking out most of his teeth and abruptly terminating the negotiation. Brass knuckles. Tears streamed down his alarmed face, mingling with the blood and remnants of teeth leaking out of his ragged mouth. A stain spread at his crotch.

"Ahhh, *Scheise*. Get rid of him," said the leader.

"Nnnnppph...mooo...nooooooo...noooooooooooooo..." moaned James Augustus Cavierti – the very last sounds he ever uttered, as the third man grabbed his feet and they sent him sailing over the balcony, out into the grey Argentine sky and towards the cold and final embrace of the sidewalk below.

CHAPTER 24

"Fore!" The Vice President connected solidly with the ball, his form perfect, and watched as it sailed off into the distance towards the ninth hole. He was an avid golfer, and loved the early Fall for the crispness of the air. It had a certain exhilarating snap to it.

A security detail stood a discreet distance away. His partner in the game today was Dennison Harding, a longtime friend and prominent business personality, the CEO of Camber Funding Group – a fund that specialized in technology and biotech plays. Dennison was a lean, dashing-looking sixty-year-old with a good tan and great teeth, framed by a full head of salt and pepper hair. His demeanor bespoke old money, breeding, panache.

"Great shot, Mr. Vice President," Harding observed.

"Thanks. It was good, wasn't it?"

"Really good, I'd say." They got into their cart and made their way to the next hole.

"I'm sorry things didn't work out for you on that other matter. I did everything I could. Who knew?" said the Vice President.

"Well, it's not the end of the world. I would have liked to have seen the stock go to fifty dollars before I had to pull the plug, but sometimes shit happens," Dennison reasoned. "We still did well on it. A shame, though; it could have been a home run. We were close there for a bit. Really could have worked out spectacularly."

"There was no way of knowing our player would have misjudged his information control so badly. Stewart vouched for him before he was pointed at Allied. That's the problem when you have amateurs in the game. It's impossible to predict the stupidity factor. Oh, well, no good deed shall go unpunished, right?" He smiled at Harding. "Again, apologies all around. I tried," said the VP.

"Stewart's a good man. No hard feelings. Like they say, you win some, you lose some." They got out of the cart, looked carefully at their balls and the line of sight to the ninth hole.

"It's only money. We'll make it up on the next one," Dennison concluded.

They both sighed, weary of the weight the world had placed upon their shoulders.

"I'll bet you five dollars you can't get your shot in two strokes," said the VP.

Dennison took another look at the shot, and broke into a wide grin.

"You're on."

CHAPTER 25

Griffen was enjoying his enforced retirement immensely. He had a huge house overlooking the water in Phuket, Thailand; a retinue of servants to attend to his driving and cooking and cleaning needs; and a regular rotation of very young, very willing girls to keep his body fit and his mind amused. He'd tapped into the local sub-culture, had a virtually limitless supply of narcotic substances available to him, and employed a security team that was loyal, experienced, and first rate. Life was good.

He missed the action of the Street, but he was getting rather used to the international lifestyles of the rich and pampered. And there were few better countries to be rich and pampered in than Thailand; where a man's needs were understood, and with no silly taboos or social mores to keep one from enjoying all life had to offer.

The villa he'd rented on Surin beach was very private, up the coast from Patong Beach. The town and all the action you could handle was only a few minutes away. Most everyone he encountered spoke English, especially in a resort area like Phuket, which had lots of American and Australian visitors; primarily college-age tourists; for Thailand was still inexpensive compared to the rest of the world. The island itself was lush and incredibly verdant, no doubt a function of the torrential rains that irrigated the area all through spring and summer. If you could handle monkeys everywhere and bugs the size of baseballs, it wasn't a bad place at all to pitch your tent.

Griffen had decided to stick around until March or so, and figure out where he'd spend the other half of the year by then. He'd bought his way into a Thai passport, and he was untroubled by the U.S. judicial system's fist-shaking; it was all clearly for show – there had been no serious attempt to track him down. While it was true he could never go back, he was having the time of his life here, so what was he really missing out on? Phuket Island wasn't Manhattan Island, but at the end of the day, who cared? You could get a fourteen-year-old girl for the night for $30, or rent them by the week for $150. The Villa cost him four thousand per month; quite a bargain for such a lavish, palatial hideaway.

If he felt like going out and getting a bit of stimulation, he took in the cockfights; and there were a several kick-boxing venues where he could watch the locals literally kick the crap out of one another.

When he'd left Canada, he'd opened an account in Luxembourg and transferred much of his money there. Once that was done, it had been child's play to open a local account in Thailand and transfer $500K. That was a king's ransom here. You could live very well in Phuket for thirty grand a year, and like royalty for seventy. He'd set it all up as smooth as a Swiss watch, and so far was enjoying himself more than he would have imagined possible. Good food, good sex, good drugs and alcohol... It was uncomplicated.

He'd been untroubled by much of anything for the last ninety days and had easily slipped into the lazy lifestyle.

It was currently 7 a.m., local time. He wondered what had woken him up. He looked over at his latest companion, Lin-Lin, fifteen years old and fast asleep. His head hurt from last night's booze and drugs.

Maybe it was dehydration that had roused him.

No, it was smoke.

He smelled cigar smoke coming from downstairs.

Those lazy fuckers had better not be hanging out in his house, smoking his cigars, instead of patrolling the grounds. He'd hired a top-flight three-man round-the-clock security team to make sure his tranquility remained undisturbed. Thailand was not the safest area in the world if you were wealthy. You were a target, plain and simple. A smart man took precautions.

He was a smart man.

Griffen climbed out of bed and stared through the big bay window. Another spectacular day; clear skies, high eighties to low nineties. How could you beat it? He pulled on a pair of shorts, donned a silk robe and slippers, and walked groggily down the stairs to the great-room.

God, his head was splitting. He needed a Percocet.

When he turned the corner from the stairwell, he saw someone sitting in the large armchair at the far end of the room, in the shadows. Smoking one of his cigars.

That fucker was as good as fired.

"Hello, my friend," the smoker said.

Griffen's heart missed several beats.

"Long time we haven't talked, *nyet?*" Sergei said. Conversational. Nice to see you.

Griffen's powers of speech had deserted him. His eyes flitted around the room in panic. He knew this couldn't be good.

"It took some time to track you down. You didn't leave much to follow – did a pretty good job disappearing. But money always leaves a trail. Always." Sergei blew out a cloud of cigar smoke. "These are good cigars, Nicholas. Cuban, I see. And I noticed your alcohol selection is premium. As I presume your opium and cocaine to be. You have a nice setup here." Sergei cast his eyes over the plush furnishings.

"Sergei, I..."

"Tut, tut. No need for long explanations. Although, maybe it would be fun to hear it. Fun to hear the 'Why Sergei lost a hundred twenty million in my offshore fund' speech. Okay, you have the floor. Speak up."

"Sergei, it...it isn't what you think. I tried to get out of Allied and convince the banks to support the price, but no one wanted to touch it after the article. Even then, I tried to salvage it, turn things around. It was just an impossible situation. I lost thirty-six million. It was a bad deal all around, that's all."

Sergei started clapping. Slowly. Seemed to be enjoying himself.

"Bravo. Really. Very touching. I am impressed, and I'm not an easy man to impress, you know." He got up, walked over to Griffen and lay an arm around his shoulder. "Walk with me. I want you to see something."

They moved to the large dining room, around the corner from the great-room. A cherubic man wearing round wire spectacles stood rinsing something in the sink, humming to himself. Several bowls sat on the bar counter behind him, along with what looked like a toolkit, and some wires. Below the bar sat a bucket, next to a chair.

They continued past him and out onto the patio, and down to the beach. Another man stood on the sand, holding another bucket, throwing food out to the gulls wheeling around the surf line.

"It really is a nice place you have here. I think I would like to have a place like this, too."

Griffen felt overcome by numbness and fear and shock.

"You look pale, my friend. You must have a lot on your mind. Would you like to feed the birds? I find it's very relaxing. Therapeutic, even. Yuri, come over here, let our friend feed the birds while we talk. It was all a big mistake, apparently. He tried everything to save our money. He told me; there wasn't any other option."

Yuri approached with the bucket. Griffen had a very, very bad feeling about this.

"Come, feed the birds, and tell Yuri all about the big mistake," Sergei said sotto voce.

Yuri thrust the bucket into Griffen's arms.

He looked into it, then dropped it; stepped back and retched.

The birds circled overhead, eager to scoop up the contents spilled onto the white sand. Ears, fingers, a penis, some toes, what looked like an eye, but could have been a genital.

"Your security team wasn't prepared for ex-Spetsnaz men. But who could have expected us to drop by?" Sergei sounded reasonable. Looked reasonable. "Nicholas. There's no need for more stories. I was sent a copy of your Canadian brokerage statement; probably by your friend Steven Archer. Who knows? It showed your three million dollar put purchase on Monday morning, right after you told me everything was going to be all right. Also had the sale on it. Almost fifteen million dollars."

Sergei flicked the penis with his toe towards a particularly aggressive brown gull, which grabbed the prize greedily and flew off with it.

Griffen felt faint, dizzy. His head swam. He felt himself blacking out. He tried to speak, but the only sound that came out was a feeble croak.

"Yuri, help Nicholas back up to the house. Vasily should be ready for him." Sergei studied Griffen's pale countenance. "It was always about trust, don't you see? Once we lose trust, then what do we have left?"

Sergei dropped the cigar on the sand. Crushed it with his foot.

"Come, my friend. We have much time to make up for."

CHAPTER 26

The lake rippled gently with a spirit of enchantment as the mountains watching over dipped their lofty reflections deep into the blue of the water. A small sailboat cruised lazily parallel to the shoreline, with no particular destination in mind. The sails were not ones rigged for speed, a leisurely pace rather, bobbing the little boat along as it followed its prow to wherever. A young woman in white shorts and a horizontally striped blue and white top sat in the cockpit of the boat facing a brown haired man, who was lying back controlling the tiller. A picnic basket sat to the side of them. They were enjoying a glass of sparkling wine.

"I'm warming up to Lake Lugano," Steven said. "Although the pace around here is a little too hectic." The lines creaked for a trice as a whiff of breeze puffed them steadily along. The shore barely moved.

"Eh, you are too used to all the drama, no? Spy man and pirate, now you become drama queen once things are *finito*?" Antonia asked.

"Maybe we should buy a dog," he said, apropos of nothing.

"A dog?"

"And figure out where we want to live, for good. I like Florence a lot, but your apartment is noisy and the traffic's too crazy. Maybe something in Campione, or in the country on the outskirts of Florence?"

Steven had long since succumbed to the infectious charm of Italy – so he was fine hanging his hat there. As long as he was with Antonia, he'd be happy. God knows he'd made enough off Allied to live wherever they wanted; not that she had to worry about money.

"I like Campione," she said brightly, "it's very picturesque. But there are also some nice farmhouses and villas south of Florence, maybe twenty minutes or so. We should go house-shopping there, you and I."

She looked more beautiful than ever.

Their passion for each other was still all-encompassing, even after four months. Her brush with death had brought them closer still, if that was possible, and he'd proposed to her one week after her release from the hospital. Dante had been a gracious host; and even though he wasn't particularly clear about how he made his money. He was always soft-spoken and obviously doted on his niece. He and Steven had taken to playing chess every afternoon, accompanied by the inevitable coal-black cups of coffee, and a snifter of cognac. Dante invariably won.

Steven joked with Antonia he suspected that was why Dante let them stay there – he enjoyed beating the pants off Steven, and Steven enjoyed the coffee and aperitifs. It was a satisfying equilibrium.

Now that Steven had put a stop to Griffen's manipulations on Allied, there wasn't much turmoil in their lives, which was a good thing. Of course, he couldn't go back to the U.S. while the Homeland Security issue was still open; although in truth he had very little interest in returning. He felt that chapter of his life was over, and considered himself more a citizen of the world now than of any given country. Stan continued working on bringing the matter to a satisfactory conclusion, but had little confidence that it would be resolved any time soon; so for now, Steven was an exile from the States, albeit a wealthy and happy one.

That didn't really bother him a lot, as there was an entire planet brimming with wonderful places to live; like Italy, for example. He'd been completely content since he'd touched down in Rome, and he had no sense of homesickness or nostalgia for California. It was as though that phase of his life was over, and a new and exciting one was beginning. So be it.

Chianti had been good for their peace of mind; and as time went by, the threat of any further ugliness receded. It became obvious that taking Steven out wasn't a priority for anyone any more. Nothing would be accomplished, and the cast of remaining miscreants in Griffen's drama had bigger fish to fry. The investigation into Griffen had pretty much shut down his network, as all the cockroaches had scuttled away from the light. Wall Street had always been rife with fair-weather friends, but nobody wanted to be near the blast zone when a scandal like Griffen's was exposed. That made Steven's role in the exposure one of minimal interest once the damage was done – and nobody wanted to double down on their liability by trying to get even. Griffen was gone, and that was that.

Steven had changed since the shooting. At first, he'd been restless and uncomfortable; the warrior returned abruptly to peacetime pursuits, still unconsciously watching his rearview mirror for signs of challenge or danger. Gradually, he'd relaxed, and been forced to come to grips with having a future. His priorities had shifted, and his time with Antonia had mellowed any residual fury at a system that had nearly cost them their lives. The anger at the injustice had melted away, replaced by a sense of peace and hope and harmony.

He just didn't care about any of his old concerns anymore. He had what he wanted, had discovered what was important to him, and vowed to make the most of their life together. He'd realized a big part of the reason he'd gotten so involved in the stock conflict in the first place was because he'd been drifting, living without any real passion; comfortable, but incomplete. Collecting watches, a convenient romantic interest, sports car, boat, obsessing about money…it all seemed so remote and trivial now. In a way, he supposed the ordeal had done him a favor, by snapping him out of his complacency and giving him a second chance to really live.

The regrets still came sneaking in at night, but less frequently of late. Peter's death would always haunt him at some level; but overall, he was healing emotionally, albeit more slowly than he had physically. That was okay too. It was important to grieve, to recognize mistakes, to digest, and move forward. It might take time, but time was something he felt like he finally had in good supply.

Once Antonia had recovered, they'd traveled around Italy, enjoying the different flavors and moods that each town and region offered. Days turned into weeks, and weeks into months, and the longer he spent there, the more roots he felt like he was putting down. Steven loved the country areas; Tuscany and the Amalfi coast; Antonia just loved Italy.

The one thing that was clear as they traveled was that they were going to be together for the duration. Their bond had grown increasingly powerful, eclipsing all other concerns or priorities. In each other, they'd found home, and they were there to stay.

It was a lazy, dreamlike time, where anything seemed possible. More out of a sense of guilt at being unproductive than a desire to actually work, Steven had toyed with the idea of getting a vineyard in Chianti and making wine; but he'd discarded that concept once he'd seen the amount of labor that went into growing and harvesting and crushing and fermenting. So he had no plans, no particular agenda, just an all-consuming desire to be with Antonia. They'd been inseparable since she'd left the hospital, and hadn't spent a single day apart since.

"Antonia, I don't care. Campione, south of Florence, wherever. As long as I'm with you, I'm home," he told her.

She looked at him. His hair had grown in quickly, and was about two-and-a-half inches long now. She could imagine him with longer hair. He'd look very dashing.

"I feel the same, *caro*. You are home, and I'm home, too. It feels good," she said, stretching her legs out. She nudged his crotch with her foot. "You want to drop the anchor, maybe fool around?"

With one hand he untied the rope that held the sail and let it fall.

"I thought you'd never ask. What does the captain have to do around here to get a little love?" he complained, standing up to move to the front of the boat.

"*Ai*, with all the talking. Still with the words. Can't you just look pretty and dance for me?" she asked, and pulled off her shirt.

There were worse things to be than a boy toy for an Italian nymphomaniac, he reasoned. Far worse things. She was pulling her shorts off as she went below, looking at him impatiently. *Mama mia*. What a life.

He dropped the anchor into the water, tied it off, and went to greet the sweetness of his destiny.

ABOUT THE AUTHOR

Russell Blake lives full time on the Pacific coast of Mexico. He is the acclaimed author of the thrillers: *Fatal Exchange*, *The Geronimo Breach*, *Zero Sum*, *The Delphi Chronicle* trilogy (*The Manuscript*, *The Tortoise and the Hare*, and *Phoenix Rising*), *King of Swords*, *Night of the Assassin*, *The Voynich Cypher*, *Revenge of the Assassin*, *Return of the Assassin*, *Silver Justice*, *JET*, *JET II – Betrayal*, *JET III – Vengeance* and *JET IV – Reckoning*.

Non-fiction novels include the international bestseller *An Angel With Fur* (animal biography) and *How To Sell A Gazillion eBooks (while drunk, high or incarcerated)* – a joyfully vicious parody of all things writing and self-publishing related.

"Capt." Russell enjoys writing, fishing, playing with his dogs, collecting and sampling tequila, and waging an ongoing battle against world domination by clowns.

Sign up for e-mail updates about new Russell Blake releases

http://russellblake.com/contact/mailing-list

Printed in Great Britain
by Amazon